THE RISING

Elizabeth couldn't deny what she was seeing; there was no way she could be imagining this. The ground covering Caroline's coffin—even under her own feet—was now nothing more than a heaving, churning black tangle, like storm clouds being ripped apart by gale-force winds. Elizabeth resisted a dizzying wave of vertigo as she looked down, imagining she was floating high in the sky. Her awareness was drawn inexorably down, into the black voice below her.

Through the darkness, she could see with near mind-numbing clarity something struggling to emerge from the black maelstrom at her feet. Long, thin, and white, at first it looked like some kind of strange insect or creature, scrambling upward toward her. Her eyes struggled to pierce the pitchy blackness, to focus clearly on what she was seeing, but for long, drawn-out seconds, all she could perceive was a white smear of activity fluttering like helpless birds caught in a storm. And then, in a jolting instant, she saw what it was— two hands, reaching up toward her out of the darkness beneath her feet . . .

/////

"Impressive and chilling. Here's a writer who writes about the dark side of life as if he has lived for centuries on the other side. First-rate fiction!"

—**John Coyne** on *Winter Wake*

DEAD VOICES

Also by Rick Hautala

*Winter Wake**
Moonwalker
Little Brothers
Night Stone
Moonbog
Moondeath

*Published by
WARNER BOOKS

Simone Ireland

DEAD VOICES

RICK HAUTALA

WARNER BOOKS

A Time Warner Company

WARNER BOOKS EDITION

Cover illustration by Richard Newton
Cover design by Don Puckey

Warner Books, Inc.
666 Fifth Avenue
New York, N.Y. 10103

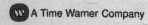 A Time Warner Company

Printed in the United States of America

First Printing: December, 1990

10 9 8 7 6 5 4 3 2 1

ACKNOWLEDGMENTS

I hope this won't start sounding like a list of "thank yous" for an Oscar, but I want to acknowledge the people who have helped me with this book . . .

Detective John Chase of the Westbrook, Maine, Police Department, answered some very unusual questions about police and detective work without batting an eye. His willingness to discuss his work not only helped me, but actually suggested lines of action the story could take.

Mike Kimball, who, along with three to five phone calls a week to urge this book to completion, started the whole thing off by telling me about E.V.P. (electronic voice phenomenon) and those voices from the "violet world."

Bill Barry, who carves a mean-looking walking stick, conjured up the *Autobiography of Benvenuto Cellini* for me, which helped inspire the cemetery scene.

Dave Hinchberger, who runs the *Overlook Connection*, constantly gives me and my writing some major boosts . . . I'm just glad he doesn't pass his phone bills along to me.

My trusted manuscript readers—Chris Fahy, Kathy Glad, and Mike Feeney—who, with their support and brutally honest reactions, make my books much better than I could make them alone.

And Brian Thomsen, my editor at Warner, who makes my manuscripts bleed, is taking my "rough cuts" and turning them into polished stone.

Also, I have to mention the section entitled "How to Raise the Dead" in Jacqueline Simpson's book *Icelandic Folktales and Legends*. Those three pages are perhaps the scariest I have ever read, and if you scout them out yourself, you'll see why!

And finally—as always—I want to thank Bonnie, Aaron, Jesse, and Matti because they not only created the time and space for me to write; they also created the necessary distractions that pulled me away from it from time to time.

CONTENTS

PART ONE

Listen!
The dead are speaking!

There's something quieter than sleep
Within this inner room!
It wears a sprig upon its breast,
And will not tell its name.

—Emily Dickinson

A sick person pining away is one upon
whom an evil spirit has gazed.

—Homer

Prologue

". . . *Another incident, which the reader may find curious, albeit inconclusive, concerns the arrest and subsequent execution of one William DeBarry, a brewer of ale in the village of Dunbane, Scotland. According to the Magistrates Records for that year,* A.D. *1579, DeBarry was apprehended by a group of enraged citizens in the cemetery behind St. Jude's Cathedral. Long reputed to be a wizard and servant of Satan, he apparently was engaged in the disinterment of a corpse, in this case the body of his son, Jonathan, who had died the previous winter. DeBarry was taken to the local magistrates, who acted swiftly and, within a week, tried and convicted him of 'witchcraft, most foul and heinous.' Like many reputed witches and warlocks of that era, he was burned at the stake in the village square.*

Unfortunately, the records of his trial and subsequent execution have not survived in their entirety; but portions have, and from them we can reconstruct the scene.

DeBarry, a widower of some ten years, had been an object of suspicion and mistrust for many years in the village. He had a reputation as a man not to be crossed and, on several occasions, according to the fragmentary trial transcript, had overtly threatened his neighbors with 'curses foul and damnable.' One Harold O'Keefe, another local brewer, testified that, through DeBarry's 'evile Spells and Sorcerie,' his ale had not fermented properly for the past three years, thus destroying his longstanding reputation as a brewer.

When first the populace, carrying torches, prayer books, and crucifixes, entered the graveyard, DeBarry was observed sitting within a crude and unholy design which he had inscribed upon the ground with white powder at the foot of the grave of his deceased son. At five points of a crudely drawn inverted pentagram, the symbol of Satan, black candles burned, dripping, so said several witnesses, wax 'as red and thicke as blud.' Also, within the unholy design were, 'assorted instruments of Evil,' although the chronicle fails to specify exactly what those implements were.

The boy's coffin had been exposed and thrown open. Grave vestments were cast about on the ground where DeBarry sat, cradling the pitiful corpse of his son in his arms and rocking back and forth on his knees. Several participants testified that he was muttering the Lord's Prayer backwards, in Latin. The air was heavy with sulfurous fumes, and several eyewitnesses attested that they heard and saw the shapes of demons and devils, lurking in the shadows on the tombstones of the Christian-dead.

The magistrates hesitated not in convicting DeBarry as an 'Agent of Satan and Servant of the Beast.' Throughout his trial, he spoke little other than the oft-repeated accusation, 'Had you not interrupted me, I would have had him back!'

DeBarry was taken in chains to the town square, where he was burned. His ashes were removed to a sewerage gully on the outskirts of town, where they were spaded under, and the ground sprinkled with salt. Local tradition maintains that, even unto the present Nineteenth Century, the only vegetation that will grow on the spot is a rank weed with small, red flowers, known locally as devils-weed. . . .''

—Quoted from Practicing the Black Arts,
        published by Frederick and Cole, Publishers, 1872.

ONE
Late Night Visitor

1.

Stinging pellets of ice beat like tiny bullets against Elizabeth's face as she raced up the steps to the front door of the darkened house. All around, the night hung as if the storm clouds, heavily laden with snow, were pressing down on her, smothering her. She felt as though she had to fight her way forward, futilely batting her arms against sodden, clinging blankets that slapped her heavily, holding her back. In spite of the inches-thick cushion of snow, her shoes clacked loudly on the wooden steps. Due to her exhaustion, the stairs seemed to telescope outward, multiplying to dozens instead of the seven she had counted from the ground.

Finally, she reached the relative shelter of the doorway. She pressed her weight against the door and fumbled for the doorknob. There was no time for the formality of knocking. She was desperate! She had to get inside the house and out of the storm. Her hands were chilled and didn't want to work as she struggled with the latch.

Was the door locked?

At last, after what seemed like long, sludgy minutes, she heard the tumblers click, and the door swung inward with a heavy, rusty-hinged groan. With an explosive sigh of relief, Elizabeth stumbled into the chilled darkness of the house.

Tendrils of melting snow water ran down her face and neck, and under her coat, making her shiver wildly as she looked around the deserted house. It looked as though no one had lived here for years. The strong aroma of stale air, of dust and decay, reinforced that impression. She could hear the storm outside the house, moaning softly, like the sound of someone in pain.

"Damn!" Elizabeth muttered. Her chattering teeth diced the single word into tiny pieces.

She was slightly surprised that, even with the lights off, she could see the distinct outlines of three closed doors in the entryway, hovering like rectangular slabs of black marble in the gloom. One was to her left, one to her right, and one in front of her. The feeling of confinement, of being trapped in a box, was almost overwhelming. She found the wall switch and madly flicked it several times. Nothing happened. Of course the power was off. Even if someone *was* still living here, the lines were probably down this far out in the country.

Elizabeth knew she couldn't spend the night here in this icebox of a house. Although the place seemed vaguely familiar, she didn't know who—if anyone—lived—or *had* lived—here. Besides, she knew she couldn't stay here long. She had to leave . . . had to get to where she had been going. As she glanced frantically around the dark house, Elizabeth was filled with an almost overwhelming sensation that she had forgotten something . . . something important. If she stayed here, she knew something she was supposed to do wouldn't get done.

Either that, or else something *bad* would happen!

But what was it? she wondered as bone-deep chills wracked her body.

In her panic to flee the broken-down car she had left more than a mile back on the snow-choked highway, what she was supposed to do had entirely slipped her mind. Maybe, she reasoned, it was just that, after struggling through the cold and the darkness, it had simply eluded her. She knew that whatever it was would come back to her as soon as she got warm and dry . . . as soon as she started feeling a bit more secure.

But *why* the hell, if it was so damned important, couldn't she remember what it was? She took a few tentative steps toward the closed door to her right.

Why was she so sure something *bad* would happen if she forgot . . . and what could it be?

. . . Or was there something she *should* forget . . . something bad, something horrible she was *supposed* to forget?

Trembling from both the cold and her own disorienting sense of uneasiness, Elizabeth reached out toward the door on her right. With a little effort, she turned the knob, swung the door open, and, leaning forward, looked into the room. It was much smaller than she had been expecting, and—surprisingly—it was a bedroom, not the living room or dining room she had been expecting to see on the first floor.

Against the far wall, between two lace-curtained windows, was an old four-posted, canopy bed. Beside the bed was a nightstand with a large, shaded lamp. The heavy bedspread draped to the floor, looking a sickly yellow in the gloomy light, and vague lumps of antique furniture—two tall bureaus and a slouched chair—stood along the walls to the left and right. Also on the left, Elizabeth could see a black rectangle that must be the bedroom's closet door. The windows were both open a crack, and snow drifted like gritty powder onto the sill and floor. The storm wind whistled as it stirred the curtains.

Looking up, Elizabeth was unnerved that she couldn't see the bedroom ceiling. The walls simply stretched up and seemingly outward, as though the room had larger dimensions above the floor. The odd angles of the walls were lost in the darkness overhead. For all she knew, they extended all the way up into the storm clouds. Although she couldn't see them, Elizabeth felt heavy clots of black cobwebs wafting like funeral lace in the upper reaches, and the walls seemed almost to drip with darkness, as though they had been splattered with gallons of thick, black paint that was still sliding down to the floor in inky puddles.

As she glanced around the room, not daring to enter, the walls seemed almost to shift position, expanding and contracting like the fretwork of breathing lungs. As they seemed to press in close on her, Elizabeth was startled by the sensation that she was about to be crushed between them, as if between colliding boulders. Aware of the burning ache in her lungs, she pulled back from the room, as though it held a deadly threat.

For several seconds, Elizabeth hesitated in the doorway, not knowing if she should enter and look behind the closet door, or else move into another part of the house. A growing sense of desperation, of imminent danger, was coiling up inside her gut like an overwound spring. It was obvious there was no one in this small room, but that didn't stop her from calling out.

"Hello? . . . Is anyone here?"

Her voice echoed in the vast darkness with an odd reverberation, sounding close and thick. She felt a tingling through her entire body. She wanted to leave, to close the door firmly shut behind her and forget about the unnerving sensation this room gave her, but she couldn't tear her eyes away from the bed and the partially opened windows. Milky light, as powdery as chalk dust, filtered through the lace curtains that wafted in the vagrant breeze. She thought she heard a faint stirring, as though cloth was rubbing against cloth. Hurriedly she pulled back and slammed the door shut.

Back in the entryway, Elizabeth backpedaled until she bumped into something solid. She leaned her back against the closed front door, brutally aware of the chill it gave her as she fought to control her rapid-firing nerves.

At last, when a measure of calm returned, she looked at the closed door to her left, opposite the one she had tried. If that had been the living room on her right, converted into a bedroom, no doubt for an elderly or sick resident, then this door, she reasoned, would open up onto either the dining room or the kitchen. Her feet practically glided over the floor as she went up to the door and gripped the cold brass doorknob.

Her heart gave a tight squeeze in her chest when the door swung open, revealing a room almost identical . . . no, not almost—*absolutely* identical to the one she had just left! The four-posted bed, the furniture, the closed closet door, the windows—everything was exactly the same! With a strangled, gagging sound, she staggered back into the hallway.

What the hell *is* this place? she wondered as she frantically scanned the surrounding darkness. How could I lose my way and end up in the same room?

Outside, the storm beat against the side of the house as hammer-fisted gusts of wind rattled pellets of ice against the windows. Elizabeth was shivering wildly as she approached the third door. A cold draft snaked across the floor, tugging at her feet. Her hand shook violently as she turned the doorknob and pushed the door open.

"No . . . !" she muttered as she stared, horrified, into the same room again. "This can't . . . This can't be *happening*!"

Her mind filled with the sudden, terrible knowledge that even if there were a hundred doors in this hallway, all of them—every damned one of them—would open up into this room!

Choking back a scream, she turned and started to run. Her feet slipped on the floor as though her boots were coated with grease. The entryway seemed to distort, and the door, like a life raft to a drowning person, was incredibly distant until, with the suddenness of a car accident, she slammed into its cold wooden panels. She clawed at the doorknob to turn it and practically ripped the door from its hinges as she opened it, expecting to plunge back into the blizzard. Instead, she found herself standing in the darkened bedroom.

Elizabeth wanted to scream; she wanted to fall onto the floor and sob with the knowledge that, no matter what door she opened, she was being forced to enter that room. And now she was trapped, as she had feared . . . as she had *known* she would be all along!

Her heart leaped into her throat when she saw that *this* time she was not alone in the room. She could see the darkened silhouette of a person, sitting on the edge of the canopied bed. Elizabeth's throat closed off, trapping all sound and air inside her lungs.

In the instant of surprise, Elizabeth raised her hand to her mouth, as if she could force even a small amount of air into her chest. As soon as she let go of the door, it slammed shut behind her, echoing with a hollow *boom*. Entirely against her will, she felt herself pulled into the center of the floor even as the room expanded in a dizzying, black outward rush.

The woman!

It was a woman, sitting silently on the edge of the bed. She hadn't been there before, of that Elizabeth was positive . . . unless that rasping sound of cloth had been her, extricating herself from under the sheets. In the dim room, Elizabeth couldn't distinguish any of her features other than a frizzy nimbus of gray hair, hanging loosely around her head and shoulders. The light from the windows behind her made her hair glow like steely smoke.

"Come on in, Elizabeth," a crackling voice said softly, hissing like a cold wind in the room.

As the woman spoke, the room seemed to brighten slightly. Either that, Elizabeth thought, or else her eyes were adjusting to the darkness.

"What do you . . . ? How do you know my name?" Elizabeth stammered. She could see—or else sense what she couldn't actually see—that this was an old woman. She was dressed in a tatter of filthy rags, the hem of her dress like a tangled spiderweb that melted into the floor. Her shoulders looked slouched and bony thin beneath the bulk of several layers of clothes. The indistinct features of her face looked haggard and cracked.

"I know . . . a lot of things about you," the old crone whispered as she looked down at the floor, apparently in deep thought.

Elizabeth's eyes were also drawn to the floor where, only faintly, she could see . . . something. Oddly, it looked like a large shopping bag, the kind the department stores hand out at Christmas time.

The curtains in the bedroom windows seemingly shifted back and forth to the heavy sigh of ragged breathing, but Elizabeth wasn't at all certain if it was the old woman's or her own.

The whimper in Elizabeth's throat began to build steadily, and she knew that it would become a full-scale scream if this . . . this *vision* didn't go away. This was impossible! her mind shrilled. This can't be happening!

Peering up at Elizabeth, the old woman's face glowed like an eerie gray blotch on the darkness. Her skin was a tangled network of dark wrinkles that deepened as she looked at Elizabeth and smiled. At least half of her front teeth were rotted and missing, but it was her eyes that caught and held Elizabeth's attention; they glowed with a deep, lambent red, like hot coals fanning to life on a hearth.

"Come over here, Elizabeth," the ancient woman said. Her voice was as cracked and rotten as her teeth. It whispered like a sightless moth in the darkness. "Come over here and sit down."

Saying that, she reached down to the floor and raised her shopping bag up level with her glowing eyes. Opening the mouth of the bag wide, she held it out in Elizabeth's direction. The paper crinkled like a blazing fire.

"See what I have . . . ?" the crone said. "See what I've got for *you*?" Her voice had an irritating whine now, like an engine, racing futilely as it rose in intensity.

Elizabeth's mind was swirling as she craned her neck and, against her will, peered into the blackness inside the bag. Without any sense of motion, she found herself being drawn toward the old woman, being pulled inexorably toward the open bag and whatever was inside it.

"No . . . I . . ."

That was all Elizabeth could say; nothing more than a strangled cry as the icy blackness inside the bag drew her helplessly toward it . . . *into* it, as though it wanted to swallow her.

She screamed, and the room, the woman, and the shopping bag she was holding instantly transformed into Elizabeth's own dimly lit bedroom. With one convulsive grunt, Elizabeth found herself sitting up in bed. Her face was bathed with sweat, and both of her hands were pressed hard over her mouth. Her eyes were wide open and staring, horrified, at the black rectangle of her closed bedroom door, its shape a visual echo of the closet doors she had seen in her dream and of the gaping mouth of the old crone's shopping bag.

Slowly lowering her hands, Elizabeth took a deep breath. A jab of pain slid like a knife in under her ribs, but she barely noticed that compared to the sense of dread and horror she still felt from the nightmare. After several shallow, shuddering breaths, she felt her panic increasing, rather than lessening. It quickly spiked to needle-sharp intensity, and another sharp scream threatened to rip out of her mouth. Only with effort could she force her mind to accept fully that it had only been a dream.

Elizabeth reached for the bed-stand light and flipped the switch. Warm, lemon yellow light instantly filled the room, making her eyes sting, but that pain didn't measure up to a tenth of the numbing fright she could still feel coiling like a black snake around her heart. Glancing at the clock by her bedside, she saw that it was almost three o'clock in the morning. The last thing she wanted to do, other than return to that frightening house and its occupant, was to wake up her mother and father. At thirty-eight years old, she told herself, she was much too old to wake up from a nightmare, afraid of the dark.

As her heartbeat slowed down and her breathing seemed deeper, calmer, Elizabeth snapped the bed-stand light off and settled back into bed. In the darkness, she tried to find the courage to smile contentedly to herself and let herself feel cozy and safe in her old bedroom. Just knowing that her mother and father were nearby if she needed them, to tell her things were all right, should have made her feel better; but alone with her thoughts and the disturbing memory of the nightmare, she felt no real security or internal strength.

Maybe, she told herself, she had been silly to expect that coming home would change anything . . . silly because, no matter what she told or didn't tell her parents about what had happened between her and Doug before she showed up this evening on their doorstep, she knew deep inside that she hadn't left many—or *any*—of her problems behind when she left her husband back in New Hampshire.

Wiggling her head deep into the well of the pillow, Elizabeth closed her eyes so tightly that spiraling patterns drifted in front of her eyes. She wished with every fiber of her being that traces of the nightmare she'd just had—or thoughts about how much she should tell her parents she had been through this past year and a half—wouldn't disturb her sleep the rest of the night. For better or worse, in sickness or in health, just like those vows she had taken —and broken—with Doug, here she was, back home again. And no matter *how* many reasons she might have to do it, she vowed she absolutely wouldn't disturb her parents' sleep just because she'd had a nightmare.

2.

The sun was up but hiding behind a thick bank of fog when Elizabeth went outside for an early morning walk. Her father was already at work in the barn, so she avoided heading out that way to see him, if only to clear her own mind before the inevitable intense discussion about what had happened between her and Doug. Last night, when she had arrived at her parents' door so late, she had only hinted at the situation, and she realized that, in the days ahead, both her father and mother, in their own ways, would grill her on the impending divorce she had announced.

Elizabeth's lungs filled with the cool, moist air as she measured a brisk pace down the driveway and turned right, heading up Brook Road toward town. She couldn't possibly tally how many times she had walked down this road to town while growing up here in Bristol Mills, Maine. Unlike most of her friends, she had not been allowed to get a car in high school, so, partly as a defense, she had made a virtue of walking the three miles to downtown, where everyone hung out at what was now the 7-Eleven. Back then, the store had been called Frank's Variety. As an adult, she had maintained walking as her exercise of choice, and even though she had slacked off over the past few years—the last year and a half, especially—now that she was back home, she was determined to become an avid walker, if only for her physical health. Her mental health . . . ? Well, that was something else.

The steady *slap-slap* of her feet on the pavement and the wind blowing into her face did a lot to remove the last vestiges of her nightmare. Although unnerving traces of its frightening memory still lingered, right now she was intent on letting her mind dwell only on more pleasant thoughts—on memories of her childhood, of happier times, and on positive thoughts about her future, such as being able to spend more time getting to know, *really* know, adult to adult, her parents and her two aunts, Junia and Elspeth, who still lived in town across the street from the 7-Eleven. Over the past year and a half she had worked quite intensively with Dr. Gavreau, trying to fit the pieces back into her life. She wasn't going to let bad thoughts—and *certainly* not silly nightmares—ruin the good things she had begun to feel about herself.

But as she walked down Brook Road, sucking the moist morning air into her lungs in greedy gulps, the muffling fog and the chill in the air all worked against her positive thoughts. It didn't take long to realize why; she was less than a half mile from the intersection of Brook Road and the Old County Road, and, looking ahead and to her left through the gray fog that blanketed the road and surrounding woods, she could just barely distinguish the black iron fence that surrounded Oak Grove Cemetery.

"Oh, boy . . ." Elizabeth muttered, as she involuntarily slowed her pace and stared ahead at the twining tendrils of fog. The sun, no stronger than a forty-watt light bulb, was trying with little success to force its way through the mist. She shivered and let her breath out with a long, heavy sigh.

The closer she got to the cemetery, the more Elizabeth could feel her tension mount. It was the same icy tension she had felt last night in her nightmare. Beyond the cemetery fence off to her left, the sloping hill was littered with tombstones. Even the closest ones were no more than vague lumps, looming out of the morning mist. The silent rows of stone vanished behind a gauzy gray curtain at the top of the hill. She couldn't see them, but she knew they were up there.

A chill deeper than the morning air gripped her shoulders and shook her. She remembered how cold she had been in the abandoned house of her nightmare.

"Don't be stupid," she commanded herself as she wove across the road to the opposite side. She wanted to put as much distance as possible between herself and the cemetery, but she was unable to tear her gaze away from the heavy iron grillwork of the head-high fence, or from the slouch-shouldered tombstones. She tried to think only about how the cemetery had made her feel as a child. Sure, it was spooky, and just about every Halloween someone pulled some kind of trick out there; but she and her friends had actually enjoyed playing around up there and pulling a few of their own scary pranks.

"But not anymore . . ." Elizabeth said aloud, feeling the words like hot coals in her throat. "Sure as *shit*, not anymore!"

The cemetery gate was open, and, as Elizabeth walked slowly past it, she couldn't stop her eyes from traveling up the twin-rutted dirt road and over the crest of the hill to where everything dissolved into dimensionless gray. What was she expecting to see? she wondered. Or what horror might be out there, hidden behind that curtain of fog?

The knot in her stomach tightened when, as clearly as if someone had spoken the words beside her, she thought, *It all changes once someone you know—and love—is buried up there!*

Flicking her eyes ahead, Elizabeth could see the octagonal shape of the stop sign at the intersection. She told herself, if she could just force herself to keep going, to get past the cemetery and head into town, everything would be all right. On her way back, she could take another route, maybe cut through old man Bishop's yard, like she had as a kid. Or even if she came back this way, the sun would probably have burned off the fog by then, and she would see that she was just letting her fears and guilt and regret carry her away . . . just like her nightmare had last night.

Elizabeth's sneakers scuffed in the dirt by the roadside as she slowed her pace even more and looked over at the cemetery. Her eyes were transfixed by the eerie view, and her mind filled with a bottomless blackness as she tried to imagine the density of the darkness seen by the people she loved who were buried up there. It was infinitely deeper than the fog or night . . . and she knew *that* darkness would *never* end!

". . . No," she said, no more than a whimper.

She knew she wasn't dreaming this; it was just as real and solid as those mist-shrouded gravestones, just as cold and unyielding as that black iron fence.

All around her, the fog muffled the few morning sounds she could hear—a car, passing by on Route 22 . . . a robin, singing in the woods behind the cemetery. She had the sudden, panicked thought that, even if she screamed for all she was worth, the sound of her voice would fall flat and never carry beyond the radius of what she could see. And whatever horrors the fog hid would be unleashed!

All Elizabeth could focus on were the heavy iron bars of the cemetery fence, and the silent gray gravestones. The density and the claustrophobia pressed in on her mind, and, before she had made a conscious decision, she had wheeled around on one foot and started walking briskly back down the road toward her parents' house. Even before the cemetery was out of sight behind her, she could feel the weight of some unseen presence at her back, closing the distance between them. With her fists knotted into tight balls and her legs pumping madly, she started running as fast as she could down the road. Mist speckled her face with moisture that mingled with cold sweat as she ran . . . ran as if some ghoulish, sheet-draped figure from the cemetery was close at her heels.

3.

Elizabeth's mother, Rebecca, a frail, white-haired woman of nearly sixty years, stood at the stove, surrounded by the sounds and smells of frying bacon and eggs. She glanced over when Elizabeth entered the kitchen and sat down heavily at the table in her accustomed seat. Rebecca's clear blue eyes let show only a small amount of the concern she was feeling.

"So, did you sleep well last night?" she asked casually as she turned back to tend her cooking.

Fresh out of the shower, and feeling much better—as well as a bit foolish for letting her imagination get so hyped up on her walk—Elizabeth simply shrugged and grunted a response that could have been taken as either yes or no.

"Your old bed wasn't too uncomfortable for you, was it?" Rebecca asked.

Elizabeth shrugged again. "It was good enough for me when I was a kid. It's good enough for me now."

Rebecca almost said something about Elizabeth using the double bed in her sister Pam's room, but, remembering that that was where Elizabeth and Doug would sleep when they visited, she let it drop. Instead, she said, "You know, the aunts might have something they're not using. You might want to give them a call. Better yet, why don't you drop over for a visit? They'd be hurt if they found out you were back home and hadn't come right over."

"I was thinking I might swing by there later today or tomorrow," Elizabeth replied. "I just want to get settled, first. They'll understand. How have they both been, anyway?"

"Oh, they're the same as always, I suppose," Rebecca replied. "Older—like the rest of us. I think Elspeth's getting noticeably weaker. She's not on top of things the way she used to be, and she seems to sleep an awful lot of the time. But then, what can you expect at eighty-two? And Junia—well, Junia is Junia. She's still as bright and chipper as the morning, even at her age, but I—"

"What?" Elizabeth asked, when her mother seemed unwilling to continue.

"Well . . . I dunno," Rebecca went on. "I just think she's been getting sort of . . . weird lately. Too wrapped up in all that astrology stuff she reads all the time."

Elizabeth shrugged. "She was always interested in astrology, doing charts for people in the family and all. It's just a harmless pastime."

"Oh, I know," Rebecca said. "It's just that . . . I just think too much of anything like that isn't healthy."

"Well, anyway—I plan to stop by soon," Elizabeth said. "Maybe I will ask them if they have a better mattress."

"I didn't think you slept very well last night," Rebecca said. "I thought I heard you talking in your sleep." After blotting the bacon with a paper towel, she flipped the eggs onto a plate and brought them over to the table and placed them in front of Elizabeth. Just as the plate touched the table, two slices of toast popped up. Rebecca went back to the counter to get them. "This was gonna be your father's, but I can make him some more. There's coffee in the pot and orange juice in the fridge."

"Umm . . . thanks," Elizabeth said, not making a move to get either for herself or to start eating.

While her mother busied herself at the stove, preparing another breakfast, Elizabeth let her gaze drift out the picture window at the expanse of backyard. The sun had, indeed, burned the fog off while she was in the shower. Warm, yellow May sunlight lit up the silvery grass and the thin line of trees that bordered the field, and, in the distance through the trees, she could just catch a glimpse of the Nonesuch River, which was the southern border of the town of Bristol Mills as well as of her parents' property. On the tall maple tree beside the barn, where a grayed and fraying length of rope from Elizabeth's and Pam's childhood swing still hung, the leaf buds swelled as big as ripe, Bing cherries.

Up close to the house, off to the left at an angle, she could see the opened double doorway of the cow barn. Every now and then, the dark silhouette of her father would shift past. She knew that he had most likely already put in two or three hours of work before breakfast, just as he always had. Age wasn't going to slow *him* down, by Jesus! As much as Elizabeth had hated all the hours she had been required to work in that barn when she was growing up—hours she would much rather have been off, playing with her friends—she couldn't help but remember with fondness the barn's shadowed coolness permeated by the sweet smell of cow manure and hay chaff.

"I hope you weren't . . ." her mother started to say, but then she let the rest of her comment drop as her eyes slid uneasily back and forth from the stove to her daughter. "What I mean is . . . well, I wonder if everything's all right?"

Elizabeth wanted to say *Everything's just peachy-keen*, but that wasn't what came out.

"No, I—uh, I just had a bad dream. That's all. Probably I was just burned out after such a long drive."

She wondered how her mother was viewing her. Did she see her for what she really was, a woman of thirty-eight years who was married and had had a daughter? Or did she see her as a ten-year-old girl who had cried out in the night, terrified by some childish nightmare? Straightening her shoulders, she looked squarely at her mother and added, "Of course everything's all right . . . I mean—given the circumstances."

Rebecca cleared her throat and, folding her arms across her chest, rubbed her forearms vigorously with her hands before she continued. "Well . . . Doug called while you were out for your walk this morning."

Instantly, Elizabeth's neck and back felt doused with cold water.

"What did he . . . have to say?" she said, once she was finally able to force the words out.

Rebecca began flipping over the strips of bacon with a fork, as though keeping busy could spare her from going any further with this conversation.

"What did he say?" Elizabeth repeated, more insistently.

"Your father picked up the phone in the barn and talked to him," Rebecca said. Her voice was nervous and hushed. "Doug said he was concerned for you. He said he was worried about your mental health and that he was afraid—"

"Afraid I might do something stupid?"

"No," Rebecca said mildly. "He said he was afraid you were going to follow through on your threat to divorce him."

"*Me* divorce *him*?" Elizabeth shouted. She exploded with laughter as she brought her fist down hard onto the table, making the plate of food and silverware jump. "*I'm* not the one who wants a divorce!"

"That's not what he told your father," Rebecca replied. Turning her back to the stove and the food sizzling there, she came over to the table and placed her hands lovingly on Elizabeth's shoulders. "So tell me, honey," she said, staring intently into her daughter's eyes. "What exactly happened between you and Doug?"

Elizabeth felt her gaze harden as she looked up at her mother. If *this* was how it was going to be, having to defend herself at every turn for what had happened and for what she had—and *hadn't*—done, then coming back home hadn't been such a great idea. Maybe she should have just taken off for someplace else. Biting her lower lip, she found it impossible to maintain eye contact with her mother, so she let her gaze drift back out the window.

"What happened between me and Doug . . . ?" she echoed hollowly as she shook her head. "You know damned right well what happened between me and Doug! We're separated, and *he's* the one who's filed for a divorce because—because of everything that's happened."

Rebecca smiled warmly and tilted her head to one side. "Yes," she said, her voice almost a whisper as her eyes glazed over. "I know *what happened*, if that's what you're talking about. I know, and maybe I can even begin to accept the bare *fact* that Caroline is dead; but you've never told me how you *feel*, Elizabeth . . . how you feel *inside*." She patted her daughter lightly on the chest.

With a shuddering breath, Elizabeth shifted away from her mother, who took a few steps back. Sitting forward with her elbows on the table, Elizabeth pressed her hands over her face and shook her head. "How I feel about my daughter . . . about Caroline dying? How I feel *inside*?" she said, between pain-wracked sobs. Uncovering her face, she looked up at the tormented expression on her mother's face. "I have no *idea* how I feel inside! I suppose that's why I've been seeing a psychiatrist. Don't you think so?"

She saw and appreciated her mother's surprise at this revelation. Reaching into her bathrobe pocket, she pulled out a small, brown prescription bottle and placed it squarely on the table in front of herself before she continued. "And I suppose that's why I'm taking *these*. Because after everything that's happened, after everything I've been through, I'm so . . . so buried under it all that I don't *know* how I feel. I'm not even sure I *can* feel anymore!"

. . . Or even *want* to feel, she added mentally.

With that, the stinging in her eyes intensified, and before she could try to stop them, hot tears were flooding down her cheeks. In an instant, she felt reduced in size until she truly felt as small as the freckle-faced, ten-year-old girl her mother probably saw her as. Thin, weak, and shaking, she again covered her face with her hands, and her shoulders shook as her tears poured out.

Rebecca moved quickly to her side and hugged her tightly. For just a second, Elizabeth resisted; then, looking up, she buried her face into her mother's neck and let the pain out in one long, tortured wail. Within seconds, the collar of Rebecca's dress was saturated with tears.

"There, there," Rebecca said as she gently stroked her daughter's hair, pausing with each stroke to cup the back of her head. "You just let it out. Let it all out. Tears water the soul, you know."

A storm of emotions raged within Elizabeth, and she wished desperately that she could tell all of it to her mother; but she searched her mind and feelings, and found that she didn't have a clue where to start. It was all so tangled and complicated.

"You don't have to talk about anything you don't want to," Rebecca said soothingly as Elizabeth continued to cry into her shoulder. "You're home now, and you know your father and I want you to stay here as long as you want to, until you're back on your feet." For several seconds, they stayed that way, mother and daughter embracing, each feeling comforted just knowing the other was there.

And maybe this is all I need, Elizabeth thought, through the turmoil of her emotions. Or, at least, maybe this is enough.

Suddenly, Rebecca stiffened and pulled back. Looking over her shoulder toward the stove, she hissed with frustration. Gently backing away from Elizabeth, she quick-stepped over to the stove, where curls of thin blue smoke were rising from the frying pan.

"Oww—now I've gone and burned the bacon," Rebecca said as she snatched the frying pan from the stove and then, grabbing a fork, hastily flipped the charred strips of meat onto the counter.

Elizabeth took a napkin from the holder on the table and started wiping her watering eyes; then she roughly blew her nose. The sudden interruption of their embrace left her feeling embarrassed and disoriented. While her mother took care of the kitchen emergency, she just sat there.

"Oh, this bacon's ruined," her mother said with a huff as she held up a shriveled, black piece for Elizabeth's inspection. "I'll have to start over."

Elizabeth shook her head, and, in a voice that sounded frail and watery, said, "That's okay. Dad can have mine. I wasn't really hungry, anyway. Toast will be fine."

Elizabeth got up shakily and went to the refrigerator to pour herself a glass of juice. She sat back down at the table, silently lost in her own thoughts while her mother went to the door and yelled to her husband that it was time to eat. Before long the silence of the house was broken by the sound of heavy feet tromping on the back steps. With a hefty sigh and a solid slamming of the door, Kendall Payne, Elizabeth's father, walked into the kitchen and slung his jacket onto the back of one of the kitchen chairs. He carried with him the strong odor of the barn.

"Mornin', Ma . . . 'n' Liz," he said, gruffly nodding at Elizabeth as he hurriedly washed his hands at the kitchen sink. He reached for the half-full coffee pot on the counter and poured himself a cup. Without adding either cream or sugar, he took a slurping sip before going over to the table and sitting down. He took one bite of his breakfast, then wrinkled his nose and said, "These eggs're cold. Should'a called me in sooner."

As she nibbled on her toast, Elizabeth twisted away from her father, hoping he wouldn't notice her pale, tear-streaked face; but she knew from having grown up with him that, although he said little at times, he never missed much.

"So, Elizabeth," Kendall said, turning to her after taking another bite of eggs followed by a sip of coffee. "What's your plans?"

Leave it to her dad to be so damned blunt and to the point, she thought. After giving her nose another blow into the napkin, she looked at him, not caring how red-rimmed her eyes might be.

"I don't know," she said, her voice hitching slightly. She noticed that her mother was slyly watching their interaction over her shoulder as she busied herself washing the frying pan at the sink. "I told you both last night that I just needed to get away. I was hoping I could stay here awhile . . . until I can start pulling things together."

"I already told you, you can stay with us for as long as you want," her mother said quickly, before Kendall could reply in his slow, measured way. Elizabeth looked at her dad and felt thankful when she didn't see a contradiction in his eyes.

"It's just that, you know, after Caroline . . . and all, and Doug going for a divorce and all, I just felt like my life was . . . was—out of control." She ended with a helpless shrug, painfully conscious that she hadn't been able to say the word *died*.

Caroline had DIED!

Her lower lip began to tremble and—*damn it all!*—she could feel the tears burning in her eyes again. Looking down, her gaze landed and stuck on the bottle of prescription tranquilizers on the table in front of her. She hadn't taken one yet this morning, and although she felt as though she should, she just couldn't do it now—not with her parents watching.

"You could've called 'fore you come," her father said. "Seems kind o'strange, you appearin' on the doorsteps 'round midnight, tellin' us you left your husband 'n' askin' if you can stay here awhile."

"You know what they say about home, Ken; it's where they have to take you in, no matter what," Rebecca said mildly.

A tightness took Elizabeth by the throat, but she forced herself to speak. "Last night . . . Doug and I had one hell of an argument. It wasn't the first, but it was the worst. So I just packed and took off, spur of the moment. It wasn't exactly something I planned or anything."

"So you don't know what you're going t'do?" her father asked.

"I think what Elizabeth should *do*," her mother said, addressing her husband before Elizabeth could speak, "is take as much time

as she wants or needs to decide. Her bedroom's been empty all
these years. We can give it a fresh coat of paint, get some new
furniture, and she can live here as long as she wants."

"No, Ma," Elizabeth said, glancing back and forth between her
parents. "I don't want to be a burden on either of you." Her voice
was still raspy from her recent crying jag, but she forced it to stay
steady.

"You know you won't be a burden!" Rebecca said sharply.
"Will she, Kendall."

Kendall rubbed the side of his face with the flat of his hand.
His stubble of beard made a harsh sandpapery sound. "You ain't
forgot how to milk a cow, have yah?"

"I don't think so," Elizabeth said, chuckling faintly.

"Well then, 'slong's I get a bit of help out to the barn now 'n'
then, I don't spoze you'll be overburdenin' us."

A trace of a smile flickered across Elizabeth's face. She looked
slyly at her father, trying to gauge his true reaction and wishing
he would come right out and say something like, *You know we
love you.* But he just sat in his chair, stone-faced, as he ate his
breakfast while gazing out at the pasture. His eyes looked lost,
unfocused, and if she hadn't known better, she would have thought
he hadn't even been paying close attention to their conversation.

"I'll probably just stay here awhile, though," she said softly.
"Just until things get straightened out between me and Doug. I
don't know. Maybe I'll end up getting a job in town so I can pay
my own way—"

"T'ain't necessary," her father said, his eyes still fastened on
the view outside the kitchen window.

"Maybe not," Elizabeth replied, "but I've got to do something
with my time. You and Ma don't want me moping around the
house all day, now, do you?"

"I'll tell you one thing, though," her father said. For just an
instant, his eyes flickered over to his daughter, but then his lower
jaw tightened. "I've got a good mind to give Doug a call and tell
him a thing or two . . . 'specially after what he said—"

"Kendall," Rebecca said, her voice rising threateningly.

"What did he say?" Elizabeth asked, feeling a sudden, dark
lurch in her stomach.

"Maybe I shouldn't go repeatin' things," her father said gruffly, "but I'll tell you som'thing." His voice lowered with menace. "I never much cared for that man."

"Ken-*dall!*" Rebecca snapped.

He flashed her an angry stare but went on undeterred. "No— I promised your ma years ago I'd never come right out 'n' say it, but, considerin' what's happened lately, I don't see no harm. I always thought you could've done much better than Doug Myers, and I always thought it was wrong for you to drop outta school just so's you could get married. Truth to tell, I always thought it was a mistake when you 'n' Frank Melrose broke up right after high school graduation—"

"Ken-*dall!*" Rebecca said, her voice rising with intensity.

Looking squarely at Elizabeth, he went on. "I told you then I thought it was a mistake. Still do."

Elizabeth's face flushed when she heard voiced something she herself, even years after she'd married Doug, had thought often enough to tickle her with guilt. It was almost funny how her father, who seemed at times so detached from what other people thought and felt, could usually get to the point so quickly once he started to speak his mind. When it came to nailing down what was important, leave it to good ole' dad to do it the quickest and the best.

"No matter what you or anyone else thought at the time," Elizabeth said weakly, "Frank and I had our differences that we just couldn't straighten out. And I loved Doug when I first met him."

"I always thought you were foolish not to finish college. 'N' then to marry a high school history teacher! I worked hard so's I could send both you and your sister to school, you know."

"I know you did, dad," Elizabeth said. "And I appreciate everything you and Mom did for me. But I really did love Doug, and I always intended to go back to school. I just never got a chance to, and then Caroline was born. And things weren't so bad for us. Sure, we struggled, but you can't tell me you and Mom haven't struggled to get by. It's just that Doug—" Her voice broke off for an instant, and she had the flashing fear that she was going to start crying all over again. "He seemed to—to change . . . especially after Caroline died."

There! she thought, feeling a small wave of triumph. *I finally said it!*

"'N' to think that after everything you've been through," Kendall went on, "to think that he blames you for what happened!"

In spite of herself, Elizabeth stiffened. She clenched her hands into fists in her lap, just to keep them from trembling. Her throat closed off before she could say anything.

"He said jus' this mornin' that, far's he's concerned, *you* killed Caroline!"

Her father's words hit her like the full-bore blast of a shotgun. Elizabeth heard her mother's sharp intake of breath, but all she could do was look at her father through a pained haze. She was unable even to breathe.

Placing his fisted hands on the table in front of him, Kendall took a deep breath and made as if to stand up. Even through the astonishment she felt, it cut Elizabeth to the quick to see the flush of anger on her father's face.

"He said that . . . that I—" she stammered, but that was all she could get out. Stunned, she sat there, watching her own anger and pain reflected in her father's face.

Finally, she reached the limit of what she could stand. Pushing herself away from the table, she got up and started toward the living room doorway. A whirlpool of panicked confusion threatened to suck her down. She had been hoping that the waves of grief and guilt she still felt whenever she recalled what had happened to Caroline that night a year and a half ago would stop once she was safely home; but now darkness, cold and numbing, swelled even stronger inside her mind. She reached for the wall to support herself, fearing she was about to black out.

"Are you sure you're feeling all right?" she heard her mother say, sounding as though she were speaking from a great distance.

"Yeah, I—I'm just exhausted from last night and all," Elizabeth replied, even though the backs of her legs felt like rubber and there was a loud *whooshing* in her ears.

"Maybe you should go back to bed," her mother said. "I can call you down for lunch."

"That might not be a bad idea," Elizabeth said, her voice no more than a whisper. She turned and walked quickly through the living room, up the stairs, and down the hall into her old bedroom. With a shuddering sigh, she collapsed face-first onto the bed, feeling the clean pillow press against her face like a cool, rushing tide. She lay there, trembling as though wracked with fever, for what could have been ten minutes or ten hours. Never really drifting off to sleep, her mind filled with distorted echoes and memories of things she had been through and fears of things that she might yet have to face, and she was filled with the hollow fear that absolutely nothing had changed—except possibly for the worse.

And all the while she lay there, her eyes closed and stinging with tears, a hissing voice whispered in her mind . . .

He thinks you killed her! . . . Doug thinks you killed Caroline!

4.

Around four o'clock, after spending most of the afternoon cleaning up and rearranging the furniture in her bedroom, and with her mother outside seeing how Kendall was doing overhauling the tractor, Elizabeth took the opportunity to call Dr. Gavreau, her psychiatrist in Laconia, New Hampshire. After briefly explaining to him that she had left Doug and was back home, she asked him what she should do about her ongoing therapy with him.

"Well, we can continue to work together if you don't mind the commute," Dr. Gavreau said. "It'd be, what—an hour and a half each way?"

Elizabeth grunted agreement.

"Either that," Gavreau continued, "or else you can start working with someone local."

Although she was intimidated by the idea of cutting off her work with Gavreau and starting fresh, Elizabeth was positive she didn't want to go back to Laconia, where she and Doug had lived . . . not for *anything*.

"Do you know anyone around here you could recommend?" she asked.

"As a matter of fact, I do," Dr. Gavreau replied. "Just a few days ago at a conference in Denver I bumped into a colleague of mine, a Dr. Roland Graydon. He lives in . . . South Portland, I believe he said. Have you ever heard of him?"

"Uh, no. The name doesn't ring a bell," Elizabeth replied, wondering how he could expect her to know anyone in an area she hadn't lived in for almost twenty years.

"Years ago he and I went to medical school at Duke together," Dr. Gavreau said. "When he told me he was living in the Portland area, I think I even might have mentioned your name. I knew you were originally from around there . . . Bristol Mills is near South Portland, isn't it?"

"It's the next town over," Elizabeth said.

"Well then, I don't think it would hurt for you to give him a call and set up an appointment to meet him. I'd chance to say you might be able to work quite well with him. His name must be in the phone book."

"Thanks for the lead," Elizabeth said. "I feel kind of funny, though, not working with you any more. I'll follow up on it right away; I promise."

"Don't worry," Dr. Gavreau said. "I won't take it personally. I know these things happen. My bottom-line concern is for you."

"Thank you very much," Elizabeth said, choking up. "I . . . really appreciate what you've done for me." As she was talking with Dr. Gavreau, she took the telephone directory from the counter drawer, looked up Graydon's number, and jotted it down on a piece of paper. As soon as she hung up, she dialed Graydon's number, before she could chicken out. After four rings, she heard an answering machine click on.

"Damn! I hate these things," she muttered, when she heard the tape-recorded message begin to play.

". . . So if you leave your name and phone number, I'll get back to you as soon as possible. Wait for the beep."

Roland Graydon's voice sounded pleasant enough during the brief recorded message. Actually, Elizabeth thought, it had the mellow tone of a late-night FM disk jockey. As she waited for the beep and mentally phrased her message, she felt herself tensing up, wondering what kind of man this Dr. Graydon might turn out to be.

—Beep—

"Uh, hello, Dr. Graydon. This is Elizabeth Myers. Paul Gavreau in Laconia gave me your name and told me to call you to set up an appointment. I've been seeing him for almost a year now, ever since my ten-year-old daughter . . . Well, I guess we can get into all of that later. You can reach me or leave a message at this number any time. We don't have an answering machine, but someone's usually around the house most of the day.'' She repeated her parents' phone number twice, mumbled a quick ''Thank you,'' and then hung up.

She noticed her palms were sweating, and she rubbed them together vigorously as she began pacing back and forth across the kitchen floor. She saw the prescription bottle up on top of the refrigerator where her mother had put it; she considered taking a tranquilizer now but stopped herself, determined not to use the medication unless she absolutely needed it. Instead, she decided to try for another walk around the old neighborhood.

Maybe, she thought, *now that the sun is shining brightly, I might even make it out past the Oak Grove Cemetery.*

TWO
Plot 317

1.

The warm, May night air sliced into the cruiser through its open windows as Frank Melrose and his partner, Brad Norton, drove down Main Street in Bristol Mills. It was still early in their shift, but they had decided to stop by the 7-Eleven for a coffee break—especially after the incident they had just finished checking out.

"I'd say old lady Weatherby is getting to be quite the pain in the ass. Wouldn't you?" Norton asked, glancing over at Frank.

Frank snickered, letting the steering wheel play loosely in his hands. They passed Hardy's Hardware store on the right, and Frank's trained eye scanned the darkened storefront for any sign of trouble. Not that he expected it, but these days, even in a quiet Maine town like Bristol Mills, you could never tell.

"I have to thank you for backing me up, though," he said. "If you hadn't been there, I might've been ripped to shreds by that savage beast."

Norton hissed with frustration. "I don't see how you can be so —so, I don't know, so not pissed off about this! It'd be one thing if there was ever anything to these complaints of hers, but—*shit*! She's getting to be like that kids' story, about the boy who cried wolf. You know the one I mean?"

Frank grunted.

"Well . . . one of these days—or nights, probably, because you and me seem to get most of her calls—she's gonna come up against something that's for real, and we ain't gonna go out there because of . . . of shit like tonight."

"What do you mean, 'shit like tonight?' " Frank replied. "There was *absolutely* a 'wild, rabid dog or wolf' clawing at Mary Weatherby's front door, trying to get at her."

Norton's disapproving hiss got louder.

"Okay, okay," Frank said, "so the rabid wolf turned out to be the neighbor's miniature poodle, who'd gotten off its leash. Still, she was scared out of her mind."

"Who was more scared?" Norton asked sharply. "Old lady Weatherby, or that damned dog?" He cocked his head to one side, considered for a moment, then began to laugh as he recalled the incident. "I mean," he said, his shoulders beginning to shake as the humor of the situation got to him, "did you see the expression on Mary's face? God*damn*! If *I* was that poodle, I would've pissed myself as soon as she peeked out the door at me with that pancake makeup she was wearing."

"You see, Brad. You just gotta look for the humor in these things—and be grateful we don't have a whole bunch of shit to deal with like we'd get in a *real* city," Frank said. He smiled over at his partner, who was almost out of control laughing. When Frank put on his turn signal and slowed for the turn into the 7-Eleven parking lot, Norton glanced over at one of the houses on the opposite side of the street and, cutting his laughter short, slapped his hands together.

"Oh, Christ—that's right. I forgot to tell you," he said. "Did you hear Elizabeth Payne's back in town? Seeing her aunts' house there just reminded me of it."

"You mean Elizabeth *Myers*, don't you?" Frank said. He had felt a cold twisting in his stomach the instant Norton said the name. "Myers is her married name." His hands involuntarily clenched the steering wheel, hard enough so that the heels of his palms began to ache. He swung around in the parking lot and stopped the cruiser up close to the store, where he could look across the street.

"Not any more, from what I heard," Norton said. "If you can trust what Betty was saying."

"And what—exactly—was she saying?" Frank asked. He had never paid much attention to or put any credibility into anything Betty Stevenson said. She worked the counter night shift at the 7-Eleven, and just about everyone in Bristol Mills acknowledged that she had the lowdown on all the town gossip before anyone else. Sometimes, Frank half-suspected she made up some of it just to see sparks fly. It sure seemed as though she knew things about people even before they knew it themselves.

Norton glanced at Frank. "Betty said that . . . well, you know what happened to Elizabeth's daughter and all about a year ago."

Frank nodded and bit down gently on his lower lip. He sure as hell *did* remember; he had been on duty that night and had heard the call for the rescue unit over his police radio. Because the accident hadn't happened in Bristol Mills, he hadn't responded; but he had monitored the radio transmissions and had spoken to the rescue personnel after they returned from the hospital.

"Well, Betty says several people saw Elizabeth out walking this afternoon along Brook Road. And she heard from Gail Allen that Elizabeth's husband is divorcing her. She's come home to her parents—I guess to stay awhile, by the sound of it."

"I—uh, I hadn't heard that," Frank said tightly as he began digging into his hip pocket for his wallet.

"No, no," Norton said, waving his hand in front of Frank's face. He already had his door open and one foot out on the pavement. "I'll buy. You got it last time."

Saying that, Norton got out and walked into the store, returning a few minutes later with two large cups of coffee. Both men silently stirred in the sugar and half-and-half, then ripped out the tabs on the plastic covers so they could sip without spilling while they drove.

"Betty have any more pearls of wisdom?" Frank asked, nodding toward Betty's back, clearly visible through the storefront window. He hoped his voice didn't reveal the true level of interest he felt. Norton simply grunted something Frank took to mean no, so Frank started up the cruiser and pulled out onto Main Street, heading north out of town.

He drove slowly past the aunts' house, his mind almost reeling with the rush of memories. He figured he must have driven past Junia and Elspeth's house at least ten times a day every day of his life; and every time, his mind inevitably turned back to Elizabeth and their high school romance twenty years ago. Once Elizabeth had married Doug, he'd had to give up on the idea that they could ever rekindle what they had lost. Even now, knowing she *might* be divorced, if Betty's gossip proved true, he realized that he and Elizabeth just weren't the same people they had been back then. The past was dead and gone, and he knew he'd be wise to leave it that way.

Still, a faint spark began to warm his chest, and he wondered how he would act and what he would say when he finally saw Elizabeth. In a small town like this, it was inevitable; it was just a question of how much or how little he should actively work toward that first meeting.

"You aren't trying to start a traffic jam or anything at this time of night, are you?" Norton asked with a chuckle.

"Are you criticizing my driving?" Frank snapped. He hadn't realized he was driving as slow as he was, and his partner's laughter irritated him. "You think you can do any better?"

"No, no—I was just . . . never mind," Norton sputtered. He took a slurping sip of coffee and nodded at the road ahead of them. "Just drive. Sorry I said anything."

"Hey! If you don't like the way I drive, why don't you take over for a while?" Frank said angrily, slamming the shift into PARK. He got out of the cruiser and walked over to the passenger's door. Through the open window, he irately waved Norton over to the driver's seat. "Go on! Go on!"

Norton looked up at him, a confused expression on his face, then brightened and said, "Oh, I see. You're all hot under the collar 'cause of what I said about Elizabeth Payne, right?"

"That's *Myers*! Got it?" Frank shouted. "Just get behind the fucking steering wheel, or I'll write you up for insubordination!" He opened the car door and wedged himself onto the seat. Norton had no choice but to move over, while being careful not to spill his coffee. Once he was settled behind the steering wheel, he looked over at Frank and opened his mouth to say something, then thought better of it, shifted the cruiser into gear, and took off down the road. About half a mile past the 7-Eleven, Norton veered left onto Brook Road.

Frank immediately noticed where they were heading and wondered if this was a random choice or if Norton had consciously decided to turn here, knowing that Elizabeth's parents lived about three miles down this road. He told himself not to let it bother him. He stared out the open passenger's window, sipped his coffee, and continued to mull over what he had learned about Elizabeth being back in town and—maybe, just possibly—soon to be divorced. As they were passing Oak Grove Cemetery, he suddenly slapped Norton hard on the arm and shouted, "Pull over! Quick!"

"What?" Norton said as he veered over to the side of the road. "You haven't even finished your coffee. Is your bladder giving out on you already?"

With the cruiser's tires rasping loudly on the dirt shoulder, Frank jabbed his thumb toward the passenger's window. The glow from the headlights illuminated one of the two wrought-iron gates that led into Oak Grove Cemetery, while the rutted dirt road that cut straight between the gravestones and up over the hill was cast deep in shadow.

"What—? What is it?" Norton asked, twisting around in his seat when Frank grabbed the cruiser's spotlight and started swinging it back and forth across the front of the cemetery. The black metal rail of the fence sliced the beam of light, making it strobe wildly. Wavering shadows swept dizzyingly across the tombstones nearest to the road.

Norton didn't have long to wait for an answer. The bright oval of yellow light crept up the hill and fixed on a mound of fresh-turned soil between two headstones right at the crest.

"No one's being buried out here tomorrow that I know of," Frank said suspiciously. "And I don't think Barney'd be digging a grave this time of night. Do you?"

Norton grunted and shook his head tightly as Frank opened his door and stepped out into the warm night. He took a second to adjust his utility belt. The spotlight beam was still trained on the mound of dirt at the top of the hill, drawing his attention.

"Give a call into the station," Frank said over his shoulder to Norton. "Tell 'em we're checking out something suspicious at the cemetery."

"Hey, man, I don't think we need to—"

That was all Norton got to say before Frank swung the spotlight around and shined it full force into his face. Shielding his eyes from the blinding light with one hand, Norton waved his other hand wildly at his partner.

"Jesus Christ, man! You fucking trying to blind me?"

"I said radio in—*now*, Goddammit!" Frank commanded. He clicked off the spotlight and, reaching to his holster, unsnapped his revolver and let his hand wrap comfortably around the grip.

Norton picked up the radio microphone and thumbed the switch. He quickly told the dispatcher back at the station that they were at Oak Grove Cemetery "checking somethin' out," and that they would call for backup if they needed help. He signed off and got out of the cruiser to join Frank, who was waiting just inside the cemetery gate.

Frank shivered as he looked at the night-stained rows of tombstones. The darkness inside the cemetery seemed somehow thicker, deeper than the night on the outside. Only a thin sickle of a moon rode low in the sky, and the stars looked like white powder sprinkled across black velvet. From the wetland down behind the cemetery hill, the loud sound of spring peepers filled the air, sounding like jingle bells. The mound of dirt that had caught Frank's attention was a slouch-shouldered hump, clearly marked against the starry horizon.

"Let's just go have ourselves a look-see," Frank said, taking the flashlight from his utility belt and clicking it on. The grass along the center strip was heavy with dew, and it wet Frank's shoes and the cuffs of his pants as he and Norton started up the dirt road. Norton also held a flashlight, and walked along beside him, unable not to notice that Frank had his hand on his revolver.

"You didn't see anyone, did you?" Norton asked, keeping his voice hushed as he scanned back and forth, trying to pierce the surrounding darkness with his eyes.

"I barely caught a glimpse of that mound of dirt," Frank said. "Looked suspicious to me, is all." He thought his own voice sounded tense, but there was a harsher, more urgent tone in Norton's voice that caught his attention.

They walked about a hundred yards up the road, then came to a stop at the crest of the hill. Everywhere they looked, tombstones stood their silent vigil in the night, some of them catching faint beams of moonlight and reflecting eerie gray and blue light, dew glistening in the neatly trimmed grass between grave sites.

"Ahh, it ain't nothing," Norton said, as they approached the mound of freshly dug earth. "Just Barney's been working and didn't finish up."

"Bullshit!" Frank snapped. "Take a look at this."

He was shining his beam down into the freshly dug hole, and what he and Norton saw illuminated there instantly nauseated both of them. Before Norton could say anything, he was down on his hands and knees in the grass. The violent retching sounds he made filled the night, overpowering the lulling song of the spring peepers.

The hole had obviously been dug within the past hour, if the moist-looking soil was any indication, and Frank knew right away that this most certainly *wasn't* a new grave. Someone had overturned the headstone and had dug the six feet into the earth to expose the top half of the buried coffin. The lid had been smashed in and then torn upward, Frank figured either with a shovel blade or an ax. Jagged spikes of wood stuck straight up like teeth, and the wood of the coffin was dented and gouged, as though whoever had done this had worked fast and furiously. None of that would have sent Norton to his knees vomiting, however, or made Frank's stomach churn as though he had swilled battery acid. It was the condition of the exposed corpse, at least what was left of it, that sickened both of them.

"For Christ's sake," Norton sputtered, once the initial wave of sickness had receded. He stood up shakily, unconsciously wiping his mouth on his sleeve. "Who in the fuck could *do* something like this?" He was unsteady on his feet and had to lean against one of the other tombstones for support while he took several deep breaths. The moist spring air was sour, almost fetid as it filled his lungs.

Meanwhile, the putrid smell that wafted up from the hole in the ground, mixing with the fresh aroma of Norton's vomit, made Frank choke.

The top part of the coffin lid had been ripped open, and the body inside had been dragged up into a sitting position. The corpse—an elderly looking man—was propped against the dirt wall of his grave. His waxy, pale face was splotched with decaying skin, and the thin, gray hair was caked with dirt and hung in clumps of rotting scalp. His lips were peeled back and his mouth gaped open, as if he were railing against this desecration in speechless protest. The corpse's tongue hung out to one side, looking like a huge white slug that had died while crawling from his mouth, and the rotting funeral clothes had been shredded by the vandal's efforts; Frank wondered if this was all normal deterioration of a corpse, or if the person who had opened up the grave had purposely mutilated the body. Fighting waves of nausea, which hadn't been helped by hearing Norton vomit, Frank stared in disbelief at the disturbed corpse.

"For Christ's sake," he muttered. "Will you look at that!"

Still unable to speak, Norton did no more than grunt as he edged his way cautiously to the side of the grave and looked down.

"Look at his left arm," Frank said, his voice wound up tightly. "Whatever sicko did this must have used their shovel or something to cut off its left hand!"

2.

While Frank secured the area, making sure not to disturb the freshly dug earth or mess up any of the footprints around the site, Norton pulled himself together enough to go back to the cruiser and radio in the incident. He asked the dispatcher to call Barney Fraser, the Oak Grove caretaker, and tell him to come right out to the cemetery with a plot plan, if one was readily available. He also requested two detectives from the Criminal Investigation Division and an evidence technician to come out to the scene as soon as possible.

Half an hour later, the investigation was in full swing. The detectives and the evidence technician were busy collecting soil samples, making plaster of Paris casts of the tire and boot prints, and taking photographs of the area from every conceivable angle. The sudden blue flash of the camera constantly lit up the night in harsh relief. One of the detectives kept complaining how he wished the culprit had been kind enough to leave the shovel behind so they could lift some prints. No such luck.

Frank and Norton stood beside the cruiser, which was still parked outside the cemetery gate, and watched the activity at the top of the hill. They had strung the entire perimeter of the cemetery with wide fluorescent-yellow plastic tape that read in black letters: CAUTION —DO NOT ENTER—POLICE ZONE.'' The flashing police lights had brought out a few curious neighbors, but, at least upon first being questioned, no one recalled seeing anything suspicious earlier that evening. Frank wished there was something more he could do, other than just making sure some curious onlooker didn't inadvertently ruin some evidence.

"Did Fraser tell you whose grave this was?'' Norton asked, as he and Frank sipped at the coffee one of the men from C.I.D. had brought them.

"Burial plot 317,'' Frank said evenly. His stomach still felt queasy, and the coffee wasn't helping.

"No, no,'' Norton said, "I mean who was buried there. Who's the guy they . . . dug up and took the hand from?''

Frank shook his head and, fighting to keep his voice steady, said, "He didn't have to. I read the turned-over headstone. It was Jonathan Payne.''

Norton nodded, still wide-eyed with fear.

"Elizabeth Myers's uncle,'' Frank added, speaking softly, as though to himself.

Norton shook his head with total bewilderment. "So that means the grave I was leaning on . . . after I got sick . . . that must've been the grave of Caroline, her daughter.''

Frank nodded but said nothing as he bit down hard on his lower lip. His stomach did another sour flip-flop.

"Coincidence—or what?'' Norton said, after a shuddering sigh.

In the flashing blue light of the cruiser, Norton's face still looked pale and drawn. In over ten years of working together on the Bristol Mills police force, this was the worst Frank had ever seen Norton shaken up. It made the backs of his own legs feel unstrung, especially when he considered the "coincidence,'' as Norton put it, of them finding this right after they had been talking about Elizabeth.

Maybe it was just a coincidence, Frank thought, wishing the acid taste would leave the back of his throat . . . then again, maybe it wasn't.

"I think I'll take a stroll around the perimeter again, just in case we missed anything the first time," Frank said. "You wanna come along or wait here?"

Norton didn't move, seemingly content to stay where he was. He sent Frank off with a wave of his hand. Frank was actually glad Norton had decided not to come along, because what he really wanted to do was just be off by himself, to try to absorb some of the thoughts he had to deal with.

He walked off to the left of the cemetery, staying on the outside of the iron fence as he let his flashlight beam swing listlessly back and forth. He didn't really expect to find anything; he was fairly certain that the grave robber, if that's what he was, had driven his car or truck in through the main gate—at least, that's what the tire tracks made it look like.

But why dig up a grave just to cut off the corpse's hand? Frank wondered, as he started into the woods along the side of the cemetery. The sound of the spring peepers was louder in the woods heading toward the wetland. The noise filled Frank's ears, almost crowding out the confusion of thoughts. Had the corpse been wearing a gold ring on its left hand that hadn't come off easily? Or had something else of value been taken, something they hadn't found out about yet? And if not, then what in the hell was the point of disinterring someone just to amputate their dead hand?

Once he arrived at the far corner of the cemetery, some distance from the scene of the crime, Frank stopped and, pressing his face against the cold iron rails like a boy staring longingly at the circus, watched as the detectives went about their work. They had the area illuminated with high-intensity, portable floodlights that cast long, wavering shadows over the ground as the C.I.D. people walked back and forth. With the sounds they made muffled by the distance, they looked eerily unearthly, almost like astronauts exploring the silent wasteland of the moon, as they combed the area for clues. Frank was sifting through his own list of possibilities for what had happened up there when, from behind, he heard a branch snap. Because his nerves were still wound up tight, it sounded as loud as gunfire. Turning quickly, he swung his flashlight in the direction of the sound.

"Stop where you are! This is the police!" he called out, not even sure anyone was there. Not willing to take any chances, though, he drew his revolver and let it track along with the beam of his flashlight.

The thick growth of brush and the close night muffled his voice, pushing it back at him as he started cautiously forward, flashlight in one hand, drawn revolver in the other. Dead leaves and branches crunched underfoot as he made his way slowly through the underbrush, constantly scanning left and right, tensed and waiting for the sound to be repeated. He was fairly certain the sound had been made by either the wind or an animal, but then he sensed a flurry of activity off to his right. Intervening brush blocked his view, so he got only a fleeting impression of someone running away into the darkness.

"All right!" Frank shouted. "Hold it right there!"

He raised his revolver and took a steady aim at the darker-than-night silhouette he glimpsed moving among the trees. Giving a slow count of three to see if the person would stop, Frank fired once into the air. As the booming echo of the gunshot died, he ran ahead, sweeping the area with his flashlight. The person was gone! Disappeared!

"Goddamn it!" Frank hissed, plowing through the underbrush, straining to hear the sounds of the person's hasty retreat. Had it been some curious bystander, maybe a kid drawn by the activity? Or had this been the person who had dug up the grave, returning to watch the investigation like a pyromaniac who returns to watch the house burn.

"What the hell's going on?" Norton shouted as he came running along the line of the cemetery fence toward where Frank stood in the woods, staring hopelessly at the impenetrable darkness. When Frank shined the light onto his partner, he saw that Norton's eyes were wide open, reflecting the light back like a frightened animal's.

"I saw someone over there. Get back to the cruiser and radio for some backup," Frank snapped. "Whoever it was didn't want to stick around and talk to me. It must have been the freak who dug up the grave."

"Where do you think he went?" Norton asked, peering into the dark and silent woods. If Frank hadn't known better, he would have thought Norton was stalling.

"I'd guess he's headed out toward Old County Road. Maybe he parked somewhere out there on the side of the road. If we can get a cruiser over to Deering Road and another at the end of Brook Road, we might be able to nab him. Probably ought to get K-9 out here, too."

With that, Norton turned and started back toward the cemetery gate to radio in, and Frank took off through the woods, vainly hoping he could run down whoever it was. He tried not to be discouraged by the person's sizable headstart; it was less than a mile to the main road by the most direct path, and something told him that whoever he was pursuing seemed to know where he was going.

As Frank ran, he kept glancing at the ground, looking for footprints, but the thick mat of dead leaves covering the forest floor looked undisturbed. Ducking under branches and running around trees, before long he wasn't even sure he was heading in the direction the person had run. For all Frank knew, the man he was after was already in his car and halfway to the state line.

Breathing heavily, the air stinging his lungs, Frank slowed his pace and started looking more carefully for tracks. As much as he strained his eyes and ears, though, he couldn't detect a thing, and started to suspect the whole thing was a figment of his overworked imagination, but he pushed onward, knowing that before long he'd come out somewhere on Old County Road.

And won't this look just great, he thought bitterly—having to walk back to town. So much for the concept of "hot pursuit."

The land sloped down through a soggy stream bed and then gradually rose. Ahead in the distance, Frank heard the sound of a vehicle passing by on the road. The engine whined loudly, filling the night before fading rapidly. He wondered if that was the person he was after, making good his getaway, or if it was a cruiser responding to Norton's call for backup. Either way, Frank had pretty much given up on the idea of catching whoever it was. He satisfied himself by thinking that it was going to be up to the C.I.D. unit to figure out the rest of this. As far as he was concerned, he would go back to the station, fill out the incident report, and that would be the end of it for him.

The end of it, he thought, unless, because he knew Elizabeth's family pretty well, the detectives asked him to stop by Junia and

Elspeth Payne's house in the morning to notify them about what had happened.

"Won't *that* be a whole barrel full of fun," he muttered, just as he broke out of the woods onto Route 22. Fortunately, the first car that approached was a cruiser, so he flagged it down. Ernie LaChance was the patrolman driving it, and after Frank explained what had happened, they drove back out to Oak Grove Cemetery and rejoined Norton. They finished out their shift drinking coffee and leaning against the cruiser as they watched the C.I.D. men do their work.

3.

Elizabeth was the kind of person who put a lot of faith in her first impressions of people; but for the first time since she could remember, she felt genuinely stymied by someone. Dr. Roland Graydon greeted her on the landing outside his office. Below her was the windowed breezeway that connected the garage to the large, very expensive-looking house on Shore Drive in South Portland.

Graydon was probably in his mid-fifties, tall and rather slender, with sandy brown hair. One of the first things she noticed about him was his penetrating, blue-eyed gaze, and, although not overtly handsome, his face was pleasantly attractive and masculine. He appeared to have a youthful energy about him, yet at the same time there was an aura of age and deep worry surrounding him.

"Elizabeth Myers," Dr Graydon said, as he extended his hand and gently shook hands with her. "I'm so glad to meet you at last."

His voice and handshake, his entire manner, were warm and comforting, but there was something about him, an undercurrent that made her feel—well, off balance. Perhaps, she thought, it was simply the confusion she felt from his initial greeting.

The wind off the ocean was warm and moist, and tangy with salt. The morning sun was warm on her shoulders, but the man's handshake felt even warmer—hot, almost, and too tight. She broke it off a bit abruptly.

"At last?" Elizabeth said, arching her brows. "We spoke for the first time last night, when you returned my call."

"Oh, yes—yes, of course," Graydon said, stepping back and holding the door open so Elizabeth could enter the office. He swung the door shut behind her, pushing back against it firmly. "For a second there you reminded me of someone else. I have another appointment in"—he stretched out his arm and glanced at his wristwatch—"an hour and fifteen minutes. I'm sorry. Please, make yourself comfortable." He helped her off with her light spring jacket and carefully hung it on the brass coat tree by the front door.

Smiling, but secretly wondering if she really needed a therapist who seemed as distracted as this man appeared to be, Elizabeth walked the length of the room, taking a few seconds to size up the office.

Graydon's office contradicted her initial impression of the man. Everything was neat and precisely placed. The desk was absolutely uncluttered, and set kitty-corner opposite the entrance. The bookcase covered one entire wall, floor to ceiling except for two windows, and was overflowing with books. A box of Kleenex and a tidy pile of magazines were on the coffee table at the other end of the room. Ringing the table was a plush-looking couch and two easy chairs, and on the wall behind the couch were several framed diplomas.

The single room should have felt more spacious and comfortable, but Elizabeth had an impression of being hemmed in. Even the blue sky and ocean, visible through the windows, didn't alleviate the sensation she had of confinement.

Although not quite as obvious as Elizabeth was about inspecting his office, Graydon was taking a few moments to study her, too. Following his momentary fluster at the door, he had assumed a firmly commanding presence, and now waited quietly while his visitor acclimated herself to the surroundings.

"Please feel free to have a seat in any chair, or you may lie down on the couch if you're 'traditionally' inclined," he said, sniffing with laughter at his own pun.

"I think I prefer to stretch my legs for a minute," Elizabeth said. "It was more of a drive out here than I had expected."

"It's a bit of a trick to find the house, too. I hope you didn't have any trouble," Graydon said pleasantly.

"Oh, no. Not at all," Elizabeth replied, although in truth she had missed the turn the first time. Walking over to one of the bookcase-framed windows and looking out into Graydon's back-yard, she was genuinely impressed.

The garage was built fairly close to the rocky shoreline, and the view out over the water was stunning. Elizabeth could almost feel the powerful push and tug of the tide as it sent tangled sprays of green water and white foam flying into the air.

"Would you care for coffee or tea?" Graydon said. "I have herbal tea if you like."

"I'm all set for now, thanks," Elizabeth said, still absorbed in the view. Watching the waves crash against the rocks, she felt, for a moment, a dizzying sense of impending danger, as if she were down there on the rocks, about to be swept away.

After everything she had been through, she just wanted to feel soothed and calm as she stared out at the beauty of the ocean. She hardly even gave Dr. Roland Graydon a second thought as she focused her attention on the swirling, swelling tide.

She found herself fantasizing that she would find a little cottage to rent on the shore somewhere, a place where she could just be alone with her thoughts. Maybe she didn't need to see a therapist after all, she thought; maybe all she needed was time and space to let her torn and frayed emotions heal.

"So then, Elizabeth," Graydon said, rubbing his hands together when she at last turned around to face him. "And please, if you're comfortable with it, I'd prefer that you called me Roland. Tell me a little bit about yourself."

Elizabeth took a long, deep breath and walked over to one of the easy chairs. Standing behind it, she let her fingers brush against the smooth material as she traced the outline of the flower print. Then, taking another deep breath, she said, "Well—where should I start?"

She glanced upward at the ceiling for a moment before continuing.

"I've been in therapy for almost a year now, ever since my daughter—" Her throat caught with a loud click, and she felt a warm rush in her eyes. (Damn it! Don't start crying already! she commanded herself.)

Graydon immediately picked up on her discomfort. "Why don't you start by telling me something about yourself," he said. "Where you were born, went to school—something of your background. I know you've been living in—you said Meredith, New Hampshire?"

Elizabeth nodded. "Uh-huh."

"And you mentioned working with Dr. Gavreau for the last year or so,'' Graydon said. He clasped his hands and rubbed them to-gether vigorously. ''But today let's not get into anything about why you *think* you need therapy. I just want you to relax. Let's take some time for you to get comfortable with me and my surroundings. Just tell me about yourself.''

Elizabeth ran her fingers through her hair as she came around to the front of the easy chair and sat down, heaving a heavy sigh. Taking his cue, Graydon sat down in the chair opposite her. Unlike Gavreau, he didn't instantly produce a notebook and pen for taking notes.

For the next half hour or so, Elizabeth gave Graydon a brief sketch of her life—how she had grown up in Bristol Mills, had majored in English at the University of Maine, where, during her junior year, she had met and married Doug, and how, after a few lean years following graduation, they had started doing all right once Doug found a good job teaching history at Lakes Region High School in New Hampshire. In all that time, though, she didn't once mention Caroline, simply because every time she even tried to broach the subject, her eyes would start stinging and her throat would close off.

Once Elizabeth had finished talking about her recent separation —and imminent divorce—from Doug, Graydon asked again if she would like something to drink. She accepted this time, and he went over to the counter, took two cups out of the cupboard, and poured them each a cup of coffee. When he returned to his chair, they were silent for several seconds.

''From everything you tell me,'' Graydon said, ''it sounds as though your life was fairly together. I mean, in terms of people who need help, I have clients—I prefer the word *client* over *patient*, by the way. After all, if we're human, which one of us isn't 'sick,' in some way? But as I was saying, I have clients who are much worse off than you appear to be. Is your problem simply that—well, things are changing, perhaps too fast for you right now, and you're having trouble handling those changes?''

Elizabeth laughed, but a thin laugh without a trace of humor. ''I think I can handle changes as well as anyone can,'' she said. ''I mean, even driving out here today, I saw so many changes around Portland. God, the Maine Mall has sprawled out to take over the whole countryside. I remember when it was just a cow field out there. Even in little old Bristol Mills, there are one, sometimes two houses wedged in between every house that was there when I was growing up. And the stores and traffic. Forget it!''

"But that has nothing to do with the way you feel," Graydon said pointedly. "I was talking about how you are handling these recent changes in your life."

"It's been . . . painful," Elizabeth said, blinking rapidly to keep the tears at bay.

"So if this separation from your husband isn't simply one or both of you 'growing out' of the relationship, what do you think caused it?" Graydon asked.

Elizabeth's eyes fluttered as her gaze went past the doctor and out the window. She couldn't see the ocean, just a square of bright blue sky; but she found it almost comforting, just knowing the ocean was out there. She imagined herself a tiny white dot of a sea gull, spiraling—free!—high above the raging surf.

"Well, you see," she said, her voice low and raspy, "my husband and I . . . lost our daughter."

Like a jolt of electricity ripping through her body, the memory of that night came rushing into her mind. She barely maintained control of her voice as she began to relate what had happened that night.

"It was late, well after nine o'clock, when Doug and I and Caroline started for home. We'd been visiting my parents during February school vacation and had planned on staying the whole week, but on Thursday afternoon, Doug started in, complaining that he needed some books that were back home for some lesson plans he was working on and that he wanted to leave for home—the sooner the better. I strongly suspected this was a ploy of his to get away from my parents' house, because I'd always known my parents—especially my father—didn't really like Doug."

"You say you *knew*," Graydon interrupted. "Had the two of you spoken about it?"

Elizabeth shook her head. "No—I just knew. There was always tension whenever we visited my folks. It kinda put me in a bind because I knew Doug didn't like to visit, but I wanted my parents to see as much of Caroline as they could, you know?"

Graydon nodded.

"Anyway, against my and Caroline's protests, after supper we packed our suitcases into the Subaru, intending to head back. But as evening fell, the blizzard the weathermen had been predicting all day finally hit. Within an hour, the roads were slick with a fresh coating of wet snow.

"I kept asking Doug if he didn't think we should at least wait till morning, till the roads were clear, but he insisted we start out then so he could have all day the next day to work on his lesson plan. Caroline, who *always* loved to visit Grammy and Grampy, tried to add her weight to the decision, but Doug held firm.

"We started out—I guess sometime just before ten o'clock. Caroline should have been asleep in bed by then, so she snuggled up in the backseat while Doug drove. I was sulking in the passenger's seat. I wanted to let him know how angry I was, but I didn't say anything because I didn't want to disturb Caroline. I guess I was afraid of what I might say once I got started.

"As usual, we headed up Route 22 toward Route 202, but a mile or so out of town, on Old County Road, Doug lost control of the car on a sharp corner in South Buxton. Maybe you know where I mean. There's a little church right there on the left."

Graydon shook his head and by his silence encouraged her to continue.

"Well, I always figured Doug's foot slipped off the brake and hit the gas, because I remember the engine started whining real loud. The car did a complete three hundred sixty turnaround as it slid off the road as smoothly as if the road had been greased. If it hadn't been for the head-high plow ridge, we would have gone careening down into a deep tree-lined gully.

"I remember I kept repeating 'Good move . . . *real* good move!' as I leaned into the back seat to comfort Caroline. She had woken up crying because she was confused by the sudden lurching motion of the car. I remember thinking at the time that it was a good thing she'd been wearing her seat belt. Once the car was buried in the snow bank, I asked Doug one last time if he would consider heading back to my folks—at least until the storm was over—but he remained adamant.

"Swearing and swatting his hands at the storm, Doug pulled on his gloves and got out of the car to inspect the situation. The front of the car was jammed deep into the plow ridge. The light from the headlights was diffused from underneath the snow, and when I got out of the car to join him, I clearly remember hearing the sizzle of snow, melting as it landed on the car hood, hot from the running engine. And then . . . then—''

Elizabeth fell silent as the full force of the terror of that night came roaring back at her like a train out of the darkness . . .

4.

"Goddammit!" Doug shouted, slamming his gloved hand against the fender hard enough to dent the metal. "Look at where the fucking car is!" He sucked in a short breath and then hammered his fist against the car again. "No sweat, though. I think if you can steer, I can push us out of here."

"Don't be ridiculous!" Elizabeth said. "I think it'd be a bit smarter to wait for a cop or a tow truck or something."

"How soon do you think that will be on this stretch of road?" Doug yelled. Elizabeth knew he was really angry at himself and his own half-assed driving, so she didn't shout back. After glancing at Caroline in the backseat and reassuring her that mommy and daddy were all right, and no, they weren't really arguing, she went around to the driver's door, got in, and sat behind the steering wheel. She knew there was no convincing Doug.

"Now don't go stepping hard on the Goddamned gas," Doug shouted, frowning deeply as he leaned down and braced himself to start pushing.

"You mean don't do what you just did, huh?" Elizabeth said under her breath.

The car rocked back and forth as Doug shoved against it. With the driver's door still open and her left foot out on the snowy ground, Elizabeth eased down on the gas, silently praying that the rear tires would catch and pull the car back onto the road, snow-covered as it was; then—maybe—Doug would calm down enough so that she could convince him to head back to Bristol Mills.

What happened next happened so fast that it was nothing more than a fuzzy, black blur illuminated by stinging spikes of light.

There was a sudden blast of flashing light in the rearview mirror. Turning, a scream already issuing from her mouth, Elizabeth saw bright yellow headlights, like the angry eyes of a demon, bearing down on her from behind. She yelled something—she didn't know what—and turned just in time to see Doug leap away from the car. Something slammed into the rear of the car like a pile driver. Elizabeth was thrown forward and hit her head hard on the edge of the steering wheel. More lights, brighter lights, exploded inside her head upon impact, and she was just barely conscious as the plow of the town highway truck scooped up the Subaru and carried it up and over the plow ridge as easily as if it were a Tonka toy.

She heard shrill screaming, but she was never sure if it was her own or Caroline's. All she knew was that—suddenly—she was flying through the wind-whipped snow, and then her flight abruptly ended with a chill when she landed face-first in the snow.

She knew she was screaming when she scrambled to her feet and watched, horrified, as the snow plow carried the family car down the hill and into the gully. The steep slope of the land was brilliantly illuminated by the truck's headlights and bright orange flashers. The taillights blinked intermittently bright red as the driver pumped the brakes. It might have been the shrill whistle of the storm wind or the snow plow's brakes, but Elizabeth was positive she heard Caroline crying out as the car and snow plow roared down toward the frozen stream. Caroline's last words echoed endlessly in the raging blizzard—

"Mommy! . . . Help! . . . Mommy! . . ."

Elizabeth stumbled forward as though she were drunk. Her arms flailed wildly, punching back and forth as she labored to push her way through the snow in the wake of the snow plow. The bright orange flashers on the back of the truck painfully stabbed her eyes as she watched both vehicles tumble down in slow motion over the drop. She watched in horrified silence as the plow flipped over, and its full weight came crashing down onto the Subaru's front end.

Elizabeth was still screaming when Doug caught up to her. She grabbed him by the arms and shook him, screaming her agony and terror as they both helplessly watched the car and truck finally stop their tumble and come to rest more than a hundred feet off the road.

In either her ears or her mind, Elizabeth could still hear Caroline's cries—"Mommy! . . . Help! . . ."

Looking down at the flattened wreck of the car, Elizabeth thought she saw Caroline's face in the rear window. Her eyes and mouth were nothing more than round, black holes in the blur that floated behind the glass.

There was a short burst of angry crackling as gasoline splashed from the truck's ruptured gas tank onto the Subaru. A blinding second later, the snow plow exploded. A huge ball of orange flame and billowing black smoke leaped into the night sky to be swallowed by the storm. Thicker smoke rolled out from under the overturned truck. Then there was a second, louder explosion as the intense heat ignited the Subaru's gas tank.

Before she passed out and fell to the ground, Elizabeth was dimly aware that Doug was no longer standing beside her. As darkness swelled around her, pulling her down, she was positive she could still hear Caroline's screams, echoing in her ears, even though she knew full well that the explosions and flames had silenced her daughter's cries . . . forever!

5.

". . . Then a snow plow came roaring around the corner, smashed into the car, and exploded." Elizabeth's voice hitched, but she forced herself to continue. "Caroline died instantly . . . At least, I find myself hoping so." Tears swelled in her eyes. She covered her face with her hands, muffling her voice. "I *have* to believe that!"

"Well," Graydon said, in the lengthening silence. He shifted uneasily in his chair. "The loss of a child is certainly tragic, and it certainly goes a long way in explaining why your marriage might not hold together."

Elizabeth's eyes glazed over as she looked up at Graydon, her mind dredging up—again—the horrors of that night. Tears flowed freely from her eyes. She reached blindly for the box of Kleenex on the coffee table, got a tissue, and then buried her face in it. Her shoulders shook and her lungs ached as grief and pain filled her, seeking an outlet. It startled her when she felt Graydon's hand come to rest reassuringly on her shoulder.

"The loss of a child—or *anyone* close to you—is something I feel certain no one can ever really get over," he said, lowering his voice until it was barely more than a comforting buzz. "Believe me. I know from personal experience. And I would chance to say that the agony stays with you your whole life . . . unless you find you can do something to get rid of the blocks that allow it to ruin your life. And—" He took a deep breath, sat back down in his chair, and rubbed his strong-looking hands together once he seemed assured the worse of Elizabeth's emotional outburst was over. "I believe that's what therapy can do. It can only help you if you're brave enough to face your grief, and then *do* something to settle it in your mind and overcome it."

When he said the word *do*, he brought his fist down into his opened palm so hard it made a loud, wet, smacking sound. Elizabeth was startled, but the sudden burst of positive energy she felt coming from Graydon, even in spite of her internal agony, made her smile slightly.

"Now I'm not saying I'm necessarily the therapist for you," Graydon went on, leaning back and glancing momentarily at the ceiling. "As a matter of fact, I always encourage my prospective clients to do a bit of comparative shopping. I can give you the names of several other highly qualified therapists in the area if you'd like."

Elizabeth wasn't sure why, but she instantly shook her head. "Oh, no," she said. "Dr. Gavreau recommended you to me, and I think . . . I think we can probably work well together. That is, if you're willing to work with me."

"I'd like nothing better," Graydon said quickly. He looked at her with an intense stare.

Surprised by his quick acceptance, Elizabeth frowned and regarded him carefully. "Just like that?" she asked, snapping her fingers.

"I'll give it careful consideration, then," Graydon said, smiling widely, "if it makes you feel better. After a day or two, why don't you give me a call to set up another appointment?"

"I will," Elizabeth replied. She was surprised that she was being so forward, but she took this as an indication that she was comfortable working with Graydon. When she stood up to leave, and

Graydon went to get her jacket from the coatrack, she wondered what it was that made her feel so inclined toward him. Maybe, she thought, it was simply that she felt a sense of empathy from him concerning her loss. He might help set her free . . . as free as those sea gulls she had seen, white specks circling against the blue.

6.

"What the fuck is this?" Frank snarled as he walked up to his partner, who was standing in the parking lot behind the Bristol Mills police station with Ed Phillips, the night dispatcher, and Chuck Willis, the desk sergeant. "You guys having a cops' convention or what?"

It was three o'clock in the afternoon, an hour before his shift began, and Frank had had to stop short to avoid running over the three men.

"This is something you'd sorta expect to have happen in Hitler's Germany, not Maine," Willis said, pointing to a freshly spray-painted piece of graffiti on the wall.

"Come on, Chuck," Norton said, snickering. "That ain't no Star of David. This here's a pentagram. It's something they use in witch-craft stuff, I think."

"When'd this happen?" Frank asked. He frowned deeply as he scanned the uneven five-pointed star.

All three men shrugged, and then Norton said, "Must've been sometime last night. I 'spoze we didn't notice it in the dark when we got off duty. Ed was the first one who spotted it this morning."

"Who in the hell would do something like this?" Willis asked, still scratching his head. Frank found himself wondering if Willis's habitual scratching was out of perplexity or due to scalp problems.

"It ain't nothing but a Goddamned prank, that's what *I* think," Ed said with a snarl.

Frank and Norton exchanged meaningful glances, and then Frank cleared his throat and said, "If you fellas have heard about what Norton and me found out to Oak Grove last night, you might think otherwise."

"What?" Willis asked. Yesterday had been his day off, and he had obviously not yet heard about the "incident" at plot 317. In as few words as possible, leaving out the more gruesome details, Frank filled him in.

"Well, then, Jesus H. Christ! No wonder," Willis said excitedly. For about three seconds, he stopped scratching his head, then he started up again. "I'll bet you, sure as shit, there's one of them witchcraft—what d'yah call 'em? Convents or covenants or whatever."

"You don't mean covens, do you?" Ed asked.

"Yeah—whatever," Willis replied. "I'll bet that's who did this."

"I think this is serious," Frank said, frowning as he squinted at the dripping red lines of freshly applied paint. The pentagram covered an area roughly six feet by six feet. "Someone tall enough to reach this high did it. I don't think it's any kid's prank."

"Come on, Frank, lighten up," Norton said, slapping him good-naturedly on the shoulder. "You're still just freaked out from last night."

Frank turned to his partner and was about to say something about Norton puking all over his shoes, but he decided to let it pass. Pointing at the muddy tire marks on the asphalt, he said to Willis, "I've got a report to write up and file before I head out, but if I was you, I'd get a lab tech to take a few snaps of these tire tracks. Who knows? Maybe one of 'em will match up with the ones we found out in the cemetery last night."

"You just drove over them," Norton said.

Cocking an eyebrow, Frank said, "Yeah, well I didn't see any of you guys flagging me away, either."

"Yeah, I'll get a tech out here right away," Willis said, running his fingertips over his ears; but he and none of the other men moved from where they stood as Frank turned and walked into the station to fill out his report.

THREE

Toys in the Attic

1.

During the drive home from Graydon's, Elizabeth had plenty to think about as she evaluated her new therapist. She was fairly certain she would work with him, especially since Dr. Gavreau had recommended him so highly; and anyway, it was just a doctor–patient . . . no, make that doctor–client relationship. Although the intimacy of a relationship like that could get quite intense, it wasn't as if they were getting married. She had to admit that the longer she had been with Graydon, the more she had come to recognize that he had quite a magnetic, almost hypnotic charm about him.

Just be careful, she warned herself.

When she got back home, just after three o'clock, she was relieved to find that both of her parents were out. Her mother had left a note on the kitchen table, informing her she had gone to Portland for groceries. Elizabeth crumpled up the note and tossed it into the wastebasket. Her father was probably working outside or gone for supplies.

She sat down at the kitchen table and let her mind wander as she gazed blankly out the window and over the field to the woods beyond. She already felt committed to work with Graydon, and she knew that this meant she would in all likelihood stay with her parents, at least for the time being. And that meant she would soon have to start looking for a job; she had no intention of freeloading off her parents indefinitely. Rather than rush the future or dwell too long and hard on the past, as Dr. Gavreau had told her, she decided— for now, at least—just to let things unfold in their own time, to see what would happen without her pushing one way or another.

The house was soothingly quiet.

Consciously breathing deeply and evenly, Elizabeth got up and went from the kitchen through the dining room and into the living room. She tried to open up her senses and let herself fully enjoy the tranquility. The clock on the mantel measured a steady, low *tick-tock*. The sound reminded her of those long-ago afternoons when she had sat in the living room, either doing her homework or else dozing on the couch. Long, yellow bars of sunlight angled across the floor and edged up over the faded wallpaper, casting long shadows of chair and table legs. Spinning motes of dust whirled like planets in her passing as she sat down on the couch, leaned her head back, and closed her eyes.

If she let herself, she could almost imagine that it *was* twenty years ago: that she had never grown up, never gone to college, never married Doug, and never given birth to . . .

"Aww, *shit!*" she said, jumping to her feet as soon as she thought the name *Caroline*.

She spoke aloud so suddenly, so sharply, her voice sounded foreign to her own ears, as though someone else in the room had spoken. Pacing back and forth across the living-room rug, she felt her eyes widening as they darted back and forth, scanning the quiet house as though looking for an unseen presence she had dimly sensed.

"Take it easy, there," she muttered to herself, even as she looked almost frantically at the familiar furniture, seeking an anchor to hold down the sudden flood of panic she had felt rising inside her like a tide. She rubbed her hands together, noticing they were clammy. The veins on the backs of her hands stood out like thin blue strings against her winter-pale skin. A thick, salty taste filled the back of her throat, and tears began to roll down her cheeks.

Was it thinking about Caroline that had started this? she wondered. Or had Graydon said something—or dragged something out of her

subconscious that had triggered this sharp, clear pain? Or maybe
. . . just maybe it was missing—

"—Caroline," she whispered, no more than a ragged, tearing
sound.

Here it's been a year and a half, she thought, and the grief and
pain are still as sharp as the day it happened. The wounds hadn't
healed or even dulled, and Elizabeth knew the pain would *never* go
away. She was going to have to learn to live with it and not let it
turn her into an emotional cripple.

Without knowing why, Elizabeth turned and started up the stairs,
but rather than going to her bedroom to lie down, she continued
down the hallway to the attic door. Flipping the wall switch by the
door, she undid the bolt lock, turned the handle, and started up into
the attic.

The smell of stale air wafted down the stairway and sent her
memories reeling. The attic had always been a special place for her;
she used to come up here and hide whenever she was upset and
didn't want anyone to see her.

Elizabeth also remembered the many rainy or snowy afternoons
when she and her sister Pam, or her best friends from school, Joanie
and Barb, had come up here to play or to paw through the boxes
and piles of accumulated junk. No, not junk—*treasures*! Old books
and magazines, her grandparents' musty old clothes, boxes of toys and
jigsaw puzzles, a trunk of old family letters and photographs, and
carton upon carton of old tools and useless gadgets, some of which
she could never identify.

Elizabeth walked slowly up the stairs, trying her best not to let
herself wonder how much Caroline would have loved to come up
here and explore!

Feeling warm with nostalgia, Elizabeth started going through the
boxes marked with her name and, for the next hour or so, the
memories that came back to her were almost dizzying. One of
the first things she uncovered was the dark blue dress and shoes she
had worn the night Frank Melrose had taken her to the Junior
Prom—the night they had driven out to Bristol Pond, instead of
going to the post-Prom party, and "gone all the way" for the first
time. The frilly lace was yellowed with age and seemed about to

crumble to nothingness as she touched it; the shoes she remembered as being fit for Cinderella now looked chintzy and sad. The dress was almost as hopelessly old-fashioned as her grandmother's wedding gown had appeared to her. She shook the dress out and held it up to her shoulders in almost total disbelief that she had once thought it was the most gorgeous thing in the world.

"Why on earth keep stuff like this," she muttered to herself as she refolded the dress and carefully placed it along with the shoes back into the box. Was it just so, years from now, as an old woman, she could come up here again and remember that she had once had a childhood? Or was it so someone else in the family could . . .

Someone else . . .

"No!" Elizabeth said tightly, the dust in the attic choking her throat. *"No!"* She clenched and shook her fists, telling herself that there no longer *was* a Caroline to come up here and explore.

The line of trash and treasure-seekers ended with her!

Elizabeth decided that, if she was going to spend very much time at home, what she should do is come up here and ruthlessly winnow everything, removing anything that no longer had a use. Why keep old clothes and shoes and broken toys and junk that no one would ever possibly use? Why accumulate all this—this *trash* that, once her parents and she were dead, would just have to be loaded up and carted off to the dump? Why spend *any* time thinking about the past when all it holds is suffering and pain and wounds that will never heal? Why go through the torture of looking through things she was never—*never*—going to share with Caroline? With tears blurring her vision, she turned to leave, but then, in the corner of her eye, she saw something. Fear choked her as she faced the stack of boxes over by the attic window.

The sun was touching the horizon in the west, and the light coming through the grimy window turned everything honey gold. A narrow shaft of sunlight, shining like an angled spotlight, hit a flat, rectangular box, and the single dust-filmed word it illuminated made Elizabeth's blood run cold.

ouija.

Casting a quick glance behind her to dispel the sensation she had that someone was watching her from the doorway, she walked over to the window and looked down at the box. The cover, name, and illustration were hazy beneath a thick coat of dust, making it look almost illusionary. Elizabeth had the fleeting impression that her hand would pass right through the box if she reached out to touch it.

Maybe I'm just dreaming, she thought, even though she could hear the fluttery hammering of her pulse in her ears. Didn't I get rid of this thing *long* ago?

Her hands were trembling as she stretched them out toward the box. She couldn't dispel the thought that, no matter how hard she tried, she wouldn't be able to pick up the box. Her fingers would glide right through it, through thin air. When her fingertips brushed lightly over the cover, leaving four thin lines in the dust, she almost convinced herself she could feel a faint tingling of electricity.

ouija!

The trembling in her hands intensified when she flexed her fingers and wrapped them around the stiff, dry cardboard and lifted the box. She tilted it a bit to one side and heard a hollow sound as the pointer shifted inside with an abrasive rasp.

Elizabeth couldn't resist a shiver of fear and . . . yes! she had to admit it—fascination.

It's still here! she thought. The ouija's still here!

Moving slowly, she sat down cross-legged on the attic floor and rested the box on her knees. She knew what she should do was just put it away and forget that she had even found it; but another part of her mind was stimulated, stirred up by the memories of using this.

Opening the box, she took out the board and pointer and sat there, studying them as though they were an immensely complicated puzzle. Her eyes darted back and forth across the fancy scrolled letters and numbers and the *yes* and *no* written in the corners.

"I'd get rid of that thing if I were you."

Coming so suddenly from behind her, her mother's voice made Elizabeth jump and scramble to her feet. The ouija board and pointer went flying and hit the floor with a clatter.

"Oh, God!" Elizabeth said, gasping as she patted her chest with the flat of her hand. "You scared the living daylights out of me!"

"I'm sorry," her mother said. "I thought you heard me coming up the stairs. I saw your car in the driveway and called out to you several times."

"I must not have heard you," Elizabeth said, still panting to catch her breath. The sound of her pulse pounding in her ears muffled and distorted her voice.

"Oh," her mother said, letting her gaze drop to the floor, "before I forget; Doug called again, asking for you."

Elizabeth started to reply, but all that came out of her was a heavy sigh.

"That's twice he's called," Rebecca said, her voice taking on a hard edge.

"What did he . . . did he want?" Elizabeth managed to say.

Rebecca shrugged. "Well, he says he's worried—concerned for you—but if you ask me, he sounded more angry than upset. I told him not to call anymore; that you would call him when you wanted to." She hissed with frustration and regarded her daughter with a pitying expression.

"I guess I should call him sometime, huh?" Elizabeth said softly.

"I think he has a lot of nerve, calling like that, trying to upset you!" Rebecca snapped. "Does he have any idea what you've been through?"

Elizabeth shrugged helplessly.

"Well, enough of that," Rebecca said. "What were you doing up here, anyway?"

"Oh, I was just going through some of . . . of my old things," Elizabeth said. She forced a tight laugh. "I'm surprised you saved some of this stuff."

"Well, I surely didn't mean to keep *that* old thing," Rebecca said, indicating the ouija box in Elizabeth's hands. She made no attempt to hide the disgust in her voice. "When I think of how you and Pam got yourselves so worked up, playing with that game."

"It's not exactly a game," Elizabeth said, somewhat defensively.

"No, I imagine it isn't," her mother replied. "Who was it you two used to say you were 'communicating' with?"

Feeling a flush of embarrassment, Elizabeth knelt down and picked up the board and pointer. She made a tight little laughing sound and said, "Oh, it was some guy named Max, remember? We were so convinced we were actually talking to him. What was it? He supposedly lived someplace in Texas—Dallas, I think. He told us he had killed himself." She shook her head and smiled weakly. "I guess it was pretty stupid the way we got so involved with it, huh?"

"I didn't think so at the time," Rebecca said sharply. "You had me scared half out of my wits the way you and your sister would go on and on about how you were trying to help Max . . . what was the phrase you used? Help him 'move on to the next plane.' Wasn't that it?"

Elizabeth nodded.

"And then, when you said he told you he *couldn't* move along until he got someone else to kill himself, God, you had me so worried!"

Again, more sheepishly, Elizabeth nodded. "Yeah. He told us the only way he could get out of the . . . the limbo state between being alive and dead was to get sort of crowded out by someone else who committed suicide." Biting her lower lip, she shook her head. The ouija board felt suddenly heavy in her hands. She wanted to put it down, to get rid of it, as her mother said, but for some reason she felt like she wouldn't be able to let go of it. She had the crazy notion that if she tried now to put it back on the shelf, it would stick to her hands as though it were covered with flypaper.

"Well," Rebecca said, shaking her head with disgust, "I would *think*, if this Max was a 'good' spirit, the best way for him to be released would be to help *prevent* another suicide, not cause one."

Elizabeth shrugged. "I think that's when Pam and I decided he was an evil person, and that he was trying to trick us."

"Into killing yourselves? Some trick!" her mother snapped. "Look, I've got a trunk full of groceries to unload, and I could use a bit of help putting them away."

"Sure," Elizabeth said, but even as her mother turned and started toward the attic door, Elizabeth couldn't bring herself to put down the ouija board and follow her. It was almost as if the childhood game—

. . . *No, it's not exactly a game!*

—didn't want to be left up here in the attic. Elizabeth couldn't stop the wave of goose bumps that rose up on her arms when she thought of trying to get in touch with Max again. Would he still be there after all this time? Was Max real, or had he been nothing more than a fabrication of her and her sister's childish imaginations?

"Are you coming?" her mother asked from the doorway.

"Sure," Elizabeth said. She quickly slipped the board and the pointer back into the box and followed her mother down the stairs. Excusing herself for a minute, she dashed into her bedroom and placed the game—*not exactly a game*—on top of her bureau and then went down to the kitchen to help her mother unload the groceries.

All the rest of the afternoon, though, and through supper and into the evening, Elizabeth couldn't stop thinking about the ouija board. At times, she even considered that maybe it was the reason she had come home so suddenly and why she had gone up to the attic this afternoon—maybe the ouija board had called her because Max *was* still around, and he had a message for her.

Finally, though, she pushed such a ridiculous notion out of her mind and, after watching a bit of TV with her folks, went up to bed when her parents retired a little after ten o'clock. She dozed but hadn't yet drifted off to sleep when she heard her mother and father talking in their bedroom, next to hers. Their voices were no more than muffled buzzings coming to her out of the darkness, but then her father's voice rose a bit louder than usual, and she clearly heard him say, "I don't see any reason for that!"

In the darkness, his voice sounded close to Elizabeth's ear as she waited, listening. Then her mother replied but, because she was keeping her voice low, Elizabeth couldn't quite make out the words.

"I say just let it be," her father said. "There's no reason to tell her about it. It'll just get her more upset."

Elizabeth had no doubt they were talking about something to do with her, and her father, at least, didn't want her to know. Lying there in her dark bedroom, she tensed up as she wondered what her father was keeping from her. After everything she had been through, what could possibly bother her so badly?

Her bedroom windows were open a crack to allow the warm night breeze to enter, and she watched the gauzy curtains waft gently in and out like bellows as she ran through several dozen "worst-case scenarios" . . .

Someone had died or was dying; one of her parents had inoperable cancer; Doug had told them something terrible when he had called this afternoon; or something terrible had happened to Doug; one of the aunts was seriously ill and wouldn't live long . . .

Whatever it was, Elizabeth was convinced *something* horrible had happened or was about to happen.

2.

No matter how many new houses and stores went up around Junia and Elspeth's house, Elizabeth knew that the aunts' family home would always stay pretty much the same, at least as long as the aunts were alive. The house was located on a three-acre triangle of land formed by the intersections of Old County Road, Saco Street, and Beech Ridge Road—right in the middle of what passed for downtown Bristol Mills. It was a century-old, three-story Victorian that had been weathered to the color of granite and was steadily falling into disrepair. Even back when Elizabeth was young, there had been rumors, especially among the younger children, that the place was haunted, but Elizabeth had always felt comfortable there because of the close relationship she had with her father's spinster sisters. She considered it her second home.

Whenever she entered the aunts' house, Elizabeth felt as though she had stepped back into the previous century. Antique furniture, dulled and worn by age, filled every room. One of Elizabeth's favorite pieces was the couch with curved wooden legs that looked like the hooves of some bizarre animal. In the living room were cherry-wood end tables and padded chairs. Lace doilies decorated every table and the backs of the couch and each chair. Faded but still beautiful handmade rugs were scattered around and did much to remove the chilly drafts that snaked along the floor. Paintings that were cracked and yellowed with age hung on the walls; and although the wallpaper in each room was old and faded, it seemed perfectly appropriate to the mood of the house.

The kitchen was a study in how life was lived at least fifty years ago. It gladdened Elizabeth to see that the aunts had still made no concessions to the twentieth century; they didn't have an automatic dishwasher or an electric stove, much less a microwave oven. Some of Elizabeth's fondest memories were of the times she had stayed overnight at the aunts' and sat up late, talking at the kitchen table with Junia.

If the house was aging but well-preserved, a survivor from another time, then the aunts themselves were approaching the miraculous. Of course, Elizabeth knew, if she compared them to photographs from twenty years ago, she would easily see that they had indeed aged; but both Junia, the youngest of the two, who was approaching seventy, and Elspeth, who would turn eighty-two on her next birthday, seemed to age one year for every five in the real world. Elizabeth toyed with the idea that, by surrounding themselves in an environment that didn't acknowledge the outside world, they somehow kept it—and aging—at bay.

It was late in the morning, and Elizabeth was sitting in her aunts' parlor with a steaming cup of tea and a few Fig Newtons on a plate on the table beside her. She had walked the four miles to their house because the day was sunny and warm, but even such a beautiful spring morning had trouble penetrating the gloom of the aunts' house. The curtains glowed with dull orange light, begrudgingly allowing the sunlight to enter.

Aunt Junia had just finished describing what had happened to her brother Jonathan's grave out at Oak Grove Cemetery the night before. Elizabeth's father, being Jonathan's younger brother, had also been notified about the incident yesterday morning by the investigating detectives. At last, she knew what her parents had been talking about last night that they didn't want to tell her.

"Why that . . . that's horrible," Elizabeth said. She leaned back on the couch and covered her mouth with her hands.

A tiny voice whispered in her head, *Thank God that's all it was*! She was trying not to think that Caroline's grave was out there in Oak Grove Cemetery, too—right next to Uncle Jonathan's. An image of that thick slab of polished pink marble with Caroline's full name—CAROLINE JUNIA MYERS—and the dates October 27, 1981– February 15, 1988, carved into it rose in her mind. She blinked her eyes rapidly and, just to have something to do, reached for her cup of tea. When she did, she caught a fleeting glimpse of motion out of the corner of her eye. Turning quickly, she looked from the parlor into the dining room, but, as far as she could tell, there was nothing—or no one—there.

"Why *anyone* . . . *how* anyone could do something like that is beyond me," Junia said. She leaned forward in her chair, her hands gripping both chair arms tightly. Her head swayed gently from side to side, as though it was barely supported by her thin neck, as she glanced over at Elspeth, who had fallen asleep in the chair by the window. Elspeth's eyes were closed, and her face looked waxy, almost translucent. Her chest rose and fell with her shallow breathing. "Of course, I haven't had the heart to tell Elspeth. I'm not sure she could deal with something like that."

"Well, Auntie," Elizabeth said, groping for something to say, "I'm sure there are a lot of kooks out there in the world." She had to fight to control her voice, even as she wondered almost frantically exactly what she had seen flit past the dining room doorway. She was sure she had seen something, and the feeling unnerved her.

"The detectives who are investigating it said they were pretty sure it was just some teenagers, pulling some kind of crazy prank," Junia went on. "But I just can't imagine the point of . . . of hurting a family like that, and doing something so morbid! It's so . . . so *evil*!"

Elizabeth was doing her best to fight back the waves of nervousness that were sweeping through her, but all she could think was, *What if it had been* Caroline's *grave they dug up? How would I handle something like* that?

"Of course, we've already spoken to Mr. Fraser, the cemetery caretaker, and he's arranged to have Jonathan reburied," Junia said softly. Whenever she spoke, she would glance over at Elspeth and watch her suspiciously, as if she thought her older sister was feigning sleep and was listening to their every word.

"But the detectives have no idea who did it . . . or why?" Elizabeth asked.

Junia shook her head sharply. "None. And I'm not entirely sure that finding out would even help. If it was—"

"It might help Jonathan rest better," Elspeth said. Her voice, no more than a faint stirring, startled Junia and Elizabeth, who both turned to look at her. She still sat with her head thrown back and her eyes closed. Elizabeth had to fight the impression that her elder aunt hadn't spoken at all; that she and Junia had imagined hearing her words.

"Elspeth . . . ?" Junia said, leaning in her chair toward her sister.

Elspeth didn't stir. Her breathing remained slow and shallow; her pale face was impassive.

"Our brother *is* resting peacefully, sister," Junia said, not even sure Elspeth could hear her. "At least as peacefully as you can expect for someone who killed himself. I'm not worried about him for a second."

At Junia's words, Elizabeth sat up in her chair, startled.

Jesus Christ! she thought, as a shiver ran up her back.

"Did I hear you right? Did you say Uncle Jonathan *killed* himself?" she asked. A wave of blackness threatened to sweep over her mind.

Junia nodded solemnly.

"How come I never heard this before?" Elizabeth stammered. "I never even suspected?"

"I always assumed you did know." Junia regarded her with a warm, faint smile. "I didn't mean to shock you. But what I'm more worried about," she said, turning to address her sleeping sister, "is, here's our favorite niece, Elizabeth, visiting us for the first time in—how many years? Too many, anyway. And we're upsetting her with this kind of talk. Fill me in on what you've been doing, Elizabeth. How's Doug doing? Why didn't he come over with you today?"

Junia's words only jangled Elizabeth's nerves further. She shrugged numbly as she considered the bombshell she was about to drop on the aunts—that she and Doug were soon heading for divorce court. After Junia dropped that bombshell about Uncle Jonathan's suicide, though, she thought maybe she shouldn't be so worried about relating unsettling things.

Even worse, she couldn't shake the persistent feeling that there was someone besides her and the aunts in the house . . . someone who was lurking in the hallway, staying out of sight, but never far away; someone who was listening to everything they were saying . . . someone who was watching and waiting. Never in her life had

Elizabeth felt so uncomfortable in the aunts' house, and that, more than anything else, bothered her deeply.

"If you, ahh . . . want to talk about getting upset," she began, after clearing her throat, "well, then—Doug and I are getting a divorce. I've come home to stay, at least for a while."

"Oh, my dear," Junia said, clapping her hand over her mouth. "I'm so sorry to hear that—I mean the divorce, of course. I'm thrilled you'll be around for a while, but tell me, what happened?"

Elizabeth took a deep, shuddering breath and said, "I think it's been a long time coming. Ever since . . ."

She let her voice trail away to nothing, unable to finish what she knew Junia—and Elspeth, too, if she was still listening—could complete for themselves.

Ever since Caroline died.

Elizabeth went on to tell them as briefly as possible what had happened. To spare them the bloody details, she left out certain facts she thought they would find unsettling.

All the time they were talking, Elizabeth felt distracted. Her attention was almost continually drawn away from Junia because she still kept getting fleeting glimpses of something moving out of the corner of her eye. It wasn't much—nothing she could really nail down except for a faint, almost transparent fluttery motion that made her think a spot of shifting light was darting in front of doorways or behind her or next to one of the aunt's chairs . . . wherever she wasn't looking directly at the time. She told herself it was just clouds intermittently blocking the sun, or maybe the shadow of a flock of birds flying around outside the house. Whatever was causing it, Elizabeth found the sensation disturbing, especially when she happened to glance toward the kitchen and was positive she saw a person walk by the open doorway.

"Is there . . . ?" she started to ask, but then she cut herself off. Of course there wasn't anyone else in the house! There *couldn't* be. The aunts never had visitors, other than close family.

"What is it dear?" Junia asked, arching her eyebrows.

Elizabeth thought her aunt was looking at her with an odd mixture of amusement and interrogation, and that made her feel certain Junia knew perfectly well what had been on the tip of her tongue; she was just *waiting* for her to ask.

"Would you excuse me a minute?" Elizabeth asked, chuckling nervously. "I have to go to the bathroom."

She stood up smiling, then left the parlor and walked quickly down the narrow hallway to the bathroom. She hoped just by getting up and doing something she could break the disquieting sensation she had that she was being watched, but the feeling continued unabated. Every step she took echoed dully in the hallway, sounding not like the sound of her own feet at all, but like someone else, someone in another room moving when she moved and stopping when she stopped, always just out of sight.

For a flashing, panicked instant, Elizabeth remembered the nightmare she had had the first night she was home. She was suddenly filled with the fear that she wasn't awake at all—that this was another nightmare! Her body tensed, and she fully expected to see the hallway suddenly telescope outward, adding new doorways on both sides like in *Alice in Wonderland.* Fear choked her as she looked up and down the length of the hallway; and as flooding panic rose in her chest, making a sickly taste fill her mouth, she was certain that every single door she could see would open up into the exact same room—

. . . the room she had dreamed about—

. . . the room where that old crone had been waiting—

. . . waiting and wanting desperately to show Elizabeth what she had inside her shopping bag!

When Elizabeth got to the bathroom door, no more than fifteen feet from the parlor, she reached out for the doorknob. Her fingers shook wildly, and she could feel a scream building inside her, wanting to burst out of her. One small corner of her mind was amazed that she wasn't screaming already. She was certain that, as soon as she touched the doorknob, she would see her hand pass through the doorknob and right through the door. When she started to imagine what might be on the other side of that door, what she might touch when her insubstantial hand reached through the dreamwood—or what might grab her by the wrist and not let go—she wanted to scream. She held back only out of a desperate desire not to worry or frighten the aunts.

The touch of her hand on the cold, unyielding brass doorknob helped snap Elizabeth out of her panic attack. With a slight rush of relief, she twisted the doorknob and, after sucking in a breath and holding it, walked boldly into the bathroom. Forcing such crazy notions out of her mind, she leaned over the sink and turned on the cold water faucet, letting it run until it was near freezing.

No, she told herself, letting her breath out slowly as she cupped her hands and splashed water on her face, this isn't a dream. It can't be! Wave after wave of chills danced up her back. It was only her overworked imagination, she told herself, tickled into action, no doubt, by all this talk about her Uncle Jonathan's body being dug up, his suicide, and . . . and . . .

—*Caroline*!

As Elizabeth stood leaning over the sink, she became aware of something else—a whispery trace of sound. Once she became aware of it, she realized it had been there for quite a while; she just hadn't consciously noticed it before. But now, in the silence of the bathroom, she realized she had been hearing voices, whispering softly on the edge of her awareness.

"You're losing it, girl," she muttered when she raised her head and stared at her reflection in the mirror. Water dripped from her face, giving her pale skin a glistening sheen. Smiling weakly and shaking her head, she reached for a towel to dry her face.

It irritated her that she would allow herself—in her aunts' house, of all places—to get so freaked out. If there was *anywhere* in the world where she should feel comfortable and secure, even more than in her own family home, it was here. The aunts had always been kind and loving. Elizabeth had known for a long time that they had singled her out as their favorite niece, and she had always reveled in that thought. But now—*this*! To let herself get so agitated in their home! It was almost a sacrilege!

Turning around slowly, she scanned the bathroom as she ran the towel over her face. When she looked back at the mirror, her throat made a strangled sound. Her stomach clenched with fear, and a wild, roaring rush of sound filled her ears, drowning out any hint of the vague whisperings. Then she began to scream. She was staring squarely at the reflection of someone she did not recognize. Her gaze was locked onto the eyes of a stranger, glaring back at her from the mirror—an unfamiliar face, watching her with a blank, almost deathlike gleam in her eyes.

Yes! Elizabeth's mind screamed. It's a woman . . . a girl!

The cold eyes stared not at Elizabeth's face; they were piercing right through her skin, looking directly into the core of her soul!

All feeling and strength left Elizabeth's body, and—still screaming—she watched the unfamiliar face slide out of view as she fell backward against the bathroom wall and slowly slid to the floor. She was only barely aware of the cold tile as she sat down, legs splayed, and listened to the steadily rising roar in her ears. She was only vaguely aware of footsteps shuffling down the hallway, echoing like the hammer-blows of distant thunder. Then the bathroom door swung open, an edge of it hitting her in the shoulder. In an instant, Junia was bending down beside her, running her cool, strong hands over Elizabeth's face and murmuring gentle, comforting words.

"There, there, Elizabeth. What in the world happened in here? Did you fall and hurt yourself?"

Forcing her attention to center, and aware that she had finally stopped screaming, Elizabeth looked up at her aunt, fearful that she wasn't going to recognize her face, either.

Maybe I really am losing my mind! she thought. *If I don't even recognize my own face in the mirror, I must be cracking up! Before long, I'll be playing with the toys in the attic for* real!

"Oh, dear, dear! I'll bet you slipped on that old rug," Junia said. Her voice was laced with concern and worry. "I've been telling myself for years I should get rid of it, and this is the final straw!"

"No—no," Elizabeth gasped, licking her dry lips with the tip of her tongue. "I didn't trip on the rug. I just . . . just bumped my knee on the sink. I—uh, sat down 'cause it hurt so much."

To her own ears, her words were slurred, but, at least as far as she could tell, she hadn't banged her head or been hurt in any way. It was the bolt of panic she had felt, seeing an unfamiliar face in the mirror, that still choked her. Spinning dots of white light weaved crazy spirals in front of her eyes.

"Are you sure dear?" Junia said. It wasn't much help, but she slid her arm behind Elizabeth's back and struggled to help her get to her feet.

"Yeah . . . I'll be all right. Give me a minute," Elizabeth said, as she stood and squared her shoulders. Her chest shuddered as she took in a deep breath. With an extreme effort of will, she let her gaze drift over to the bathroom mirror and was relieved beyond measure to see her own face reflected there along with Junia's deeply concerned expression.

"You look as white as a sheet," Junia said.

"Where's Elspeth?" Elizabeth asked, glancing worriedly out into the hallway.

"Still dozing in the parlor," Junia said. "She does that a lot lately." Still holding Elizabeth, who was very unsteady on her feet, Junia started guiding her to the door. "Maybe you should come into the kitchen. I'll get you a shot of brandy. That'll bring the color back to your cheeks."

Elizabeth was about to decline, then thought better of it and, side by side with her aunt, went down the narrow hallway to the kitchen. She sat down heavily in one of the chairs at the kitchen table and smiled her thanks after Junia fished out a squat bottle from under the counter, poured a generous amount of brandy into a tumbler, and handed the glass to her. Elizabeth made a quick "bottoms up" signal with her hand and took a sip.

"I keep it around for strictly medicinal purposes," Junia said. She cast a shifty glance at the parlor doorway and, lowering her voice, added, "I'd appreciate it if you wouldn't mention it to Elspeth. You know how she feels about having *any* distilled spirits around the house."

Elizabeth nodded, almost laughing aloud when she caught the unintentional wordplay—"spirits," indeed! That was exactly the feeling she had had, that there was a ghost, a presence in the house that was lurking, unseen in the darker, drafty corners.

Tilting her head back, Elizabeth let another swallow of the burning liquid splash down her throat. She had always preferred red wine or beer because brandy or any distilled liquor tasted more like battery acid than anything else to her; but after the flaming rush of fear she had experienced in the bathroom, Aunt Junia's "medicinal" brandy actually helped calm and steady her still-vibrating nerves. Smacking her lips with satisfaction, she put the half-emptied glass down on the kitchen table and smiled, and this time her smile was fuller and wider.

"My, my—that is *some* good medicine," she said.

"Heated up, it works wonders on a sore throat, too," Junia said. She grinned and then, after screwing the cap back onto the bottle, leaned down and put it back under the counter where she kept it hidden from her sister. When she straightened up, though, there was a hard expression on her face when she looked back at Elizabeth.

"But now," Junia said, lowering her voice, "I want the truth about what happened there in the bathroom."

"I told you," Elizabeth said. She found it impossible to maintain eye contact with her aunt. "I was just splashing some water on my face, and when I was reaching for the towel, I banged my hip on the side of the sink."

"I thought you said it was your knee," Junia said, frowning.

Elizabeth was about to protest further, but she knew—and Junia knew that she knew—that she had been found out in her lie. After another slug of brandy—this time to brace herself—she took a deep breath and said, "Can I trust you . . . not to think I'm crazy, Aunt Junia?"

"Of course you can! You *know* you can, dear," Junia said, with such warmth and gentleness it brought a warm flood of tears to Elizabeth's eyes.

"Well, my first thought . . . the one I hope is true, anyway, because otherwise it means I've *really* got some serious problems, is that your house is haunted." She snickered and glanced at Junia, but there wasn't the slightest trace of humor on her aunt's face. Elizabeth tilted the tumbler back and stared as though dazed at the small amount of brandy remaining.

"And what exactly makes you think that?" Junia asked pointedly.

After another deep breath, Elizabeth went on. "I don't mean your house is *really* haunted. I mean, that's impossible . . . I think. But ever since I got here this morning, I've had this . . . this sort of *feeling*—"

"Like you're being watched?" Junia said.

Elizabeth felt an electrical tingle throughout her body. Looking up at her aunt, she nodded. "Yeah . . . exactly," she said, marveling that Junia had picked up on it so quickly. "Like I'm being watched. A couple of times, I actually thought I saw someone, and when I was in the bathroom, I was positive I heard these faint voices, whispering as if in the next room." She shook her head with confusion and, shivering, cast a wary glance over her shoulder. "There isn't—I mean, there can't be anyone else in the house besides us, right?"

Junia shrugged and smiled. "I haven't the foggiest idea. Who do you think it might be?" she asked.

"I—I don't think it's anyone . . . Not really. But when I was in the bathroom, I . . . I—"

Elizabeth's voice cut off abruptly when the image of the face she had seen rose up in her mind. It was sharp and clear, but even now, with the numbing flood of panic receding, and the fire of the brandy soothing her nerves, she didn't recognize the face, even though she felt she should. The dimming memory of it was that it had looked more like a girl than a woman. Maybe someone in her early teens. Her hair had been long and blonde, but that and every other detail of her face was lost in the disturbing memory of how pale and drawn, how wrung of life she had looked. It was almost as if, even with her eyes open and staring unblinkingly back at Elizabeth, she had been *dead*.

"You saw something?" Junia said, her voice rising almost playfully.

Elizabeth bit down sharply on her lower lip and nodded. "Yeah—in the mirror."

"But you're sure you didn't recognize her?"

"No—I mean, yes. What I mean is, I feel like I *should* have recognized her," Elizabeth said. She shook her head and looked pleadingly at her aunt, wondering why she had said *her*. How did Junia know it had been a woman or girl? Elizabeth couldn't help glancing around behind herself again when she felt the hairs at the nape of her neck prickle.

Junia lowered her voice and, looking directly into Elizabeth's eyes, said, "Did it ever cross your mind that it might have been Caroline? That she might be trying to get in touch with you?"

FOUR
Old Flame

1.

The mere mention of Caroline's name sent a tingling chill up her spine.

"Could we—go outside? I think I need a breath of fresh air," Elizabeth said. She felt pressure coiling up inside her like heavy, black smoke.

"That might not be a bad idea," Junia replied, glancing toward the living room doorway. "That way we won't disturb Elspeth."

Once outside on the porch, they each sat down in one of the heavy, wooden lawn chairs that had been stored on the porch for the winter. The chairs were a grainy, faded white, and looked as if they had needed a fresh coat of paint for at least five years.

The traffic zooming by on Route 22 was much heavier than Elizabeth remembered it, but she still found the view peaceful and enjoyable. Sunlight poured through the huge maple trees, casting dancing shadows that made the front lawn and walkway look as though they were bubbling with activity. The warm breeze wafting from the south carried a moist, tingling smell of fresh growing things. Even the sound of passing traffic was lulling, rather than irritating. Aided by the brandy, Elizabeth's jangled nerves began to unwind.

But as pleasant as the early afternoon was, Elizabeth was still restless and uneasy in her heart. When she recalled how much she had enjoyed sitting here, sipping lemonade and talking with Aunt Junia, she couldn't stop thinking that Caroline would never be able to do this. As when she was exploring the treasures and junk in the attic, there were all these constant reminders of things Caroline was missing. Visiting with the aunts had always been something Elizabeth had appreciated; and she had always assumed Caroline would develop that same relationship with the aunts while they were still alive. She had never imagined that both Junia and Elspeth would survive Caroline.

"You know," Elizabeth said, taking another deep breath and looking up at the sky, "I just can't accept that Caroline doesn't— doesn't exist . . . somewhere." She squeezed her clasped hands between her knees, earnestly wishing she could shift her attention to something else. But she couldn't stop her thoughts from almost constantly revolving around Caroline and the things she was missing. Maybe, Elizabeth thought, coming back home was only going to make her healing all the more difficult because of the memories it stirred.

Junia reached out and gently gripped her arm. "There are a lot of things in life," she said mildly, "which surprise us when they happen."

Elizabeth took a shuddering breath and, not knowing exactly what Junia meant, closed her eyes and leaned back against the chair. She concentrated on feeling the spring breeze wash like water over her face. One small part of her mind, a part that got increasingly smaller as she got older, earnestly wanted to believe in . . . something— some kind of personal survival after death. But after the accident, she had lost any element of faith in a kind or even a benign universe. Things in life just happened—birth, death, accidents, misery, and happiness; they were all just the results of random activity. There was no wise, overseeing God who kept watch over things; there *couldn't* be, because if there were, how—in any conceivable way —could He justify taking away someone as precious, as innocent, as Caroline?

"You know," Junia said, her voice sounding dreamily distant, "the older I get, the stronger I believe that those who have passed on *do* experience a better existence than this one. And I'm positive they sometimes come back to visit those they loved who are still in this world."

With her eyes still closed, Elizabeth had a vague sense that she might be drifting off to sleep, but she focused her attention on her aunt's words and let them drag her back to awareness.

"You actually believe that?" Elizabeth asked.

"Yes, I do," Junia replied. "I'm convinced that death is only the beginning of a new and glorious adventure."

"But why—? Why would someone who's died do something like that, come back to where they used to live or whatever?" Elizabeth asked. The slug of brandy still warmed her belly, and she was feeling incredibly relaxed; she felt as if she were melting into the wooden chair. Her own voice had a muffled mellowness that soothed her in spite of the topic they were discussing. She thought how nice it must be to have faith in the idea of life after death—or in *anything*—as strongly as Aunt Junia apparently did in the continued existence of the soul.

"Souls can stay on the earthly plane for a whole host of reasons, you know," Junia said. "Some stay voluntarily; some involuntarily. I'm sure that, just as we who are still alive think we know their reasons for doing so, there are dozens, maybe hundreds of reasons to return that those on the other side have—reasons we aren't even aware of. Usually, though, I suspect a spirit will return to exact some kind of revenge or else to warn somebody—a loved one, usually, of some danger."

"But what makes you think Caroline might be trying to contact me?" Elizabeth asked. She opened her eyes and looked intently at Junia. As she had been by the bottle of brandy hidden in the cupboard, she was surprised by this conversation. Junia had always shown an interest in horoscopes and such, but Elizabeth had never even suspected that she had such a strong faith in religion or spiritualism or whatever you wanted to call it.

"I didn't say I *know* Caroline is"—Junia shifted her eyes, holding her hands up in the air and sweeping them around—"here."

Elizabeth grunted softly, closed her eyes again, and let herself float on the cushion of brandy. "But when I told you what I saw in the bathroom mirror, you said something about how it *might* be Caroline. Don't you think I would have recognized the face I saw —or whatever it was—if it was my own daughter?"

"Who's to say?" Junia replied. "You might have been so surprised, so scared, you didn't even recognize her face."

"I saw . . . enough," Elizabeth said, stirring uneasily on the chair. She wanted to open her eyes and sit up, but the brandy continued to press her backward into the chair. "The face I saw was an older girl—a teenager or something."

Junia sniffed. "Who's to say?" she repeated. "I'm not saying it was or it wasn't Caroline or anyone. I'm just suggesting that *if* it was Caroline, she might be nearby, trying to tell you something, trying to help you."

"And what do you think she'd—" Elizabeth cut herself off and suddenly sat bolt-upright in her chair. Her eyes snapped open as if she had been hit by an electrical charge. The sudden choking sensation she had was the only reason she didn't cry out or say out loud the thought that had popped into her mind.

—To exact some kind of revenge!

That's what Aunt Junia had said! If ghosts didn't return to warn someone of something, they came back to exact revenge for what's happened to them!

Maybe Caroline hasn't "passed on," Elizabeth thought, through a flood of panic; maybe now she's come back because she wants me to pay for what happened . . . maybe she wants me to die!

That's impossible! Elizabeth told herself, even as panic raged inside her. All of this talk is—it's impossible! It's crazy!

She fought to control her voice when she spoke—partly because she didn't want to hurt Aunt Junia's feelings about something in which she had obviously invested a great deal of faith—but she just couldn't bring herself to accept *any* of this. She didn't even want to be thinking or talking about it!

"Even if what you're saying is true," she said, measuring her words carefully, "that doesn't explain why I saw someone else's face in the mirror. It wasn't, it *couldn't* have been Caroline—"

Her throat went suddenly dry, and she could say no more. The warm smile on Junia's face never wavered as she leaned closer to her niece.

"I'm not saying it was or it wasn't," Junia said placidly. "And I certainly don't want to force my beliefs onto you or upset you, dear. You say you saw . . . someone. I'm saying, if it *was* Caroline, who knows why you didn't recognize her? Maybe you didn't see her as the six-year-old you knew her as. Maybe you saw what I guess would be called the 'spiritual essence' of your daughter. I don't know. I'd have to see it to know more definitely."

"Or maybe I just imagined the whole thing," Elizabeth said softly.

"Maybe," Junia said, smiling. "Life is such a . . . a mystery. I tell you, sometimes I'm not even sure whether I'm alive or dreaming or dead myself. How do *we* know—with certainty—what's real or not? But I'll tell you one thing." She leaned closer to Elizabeth and lowered her voice conspiratorially. "I could introduce you to someone who would be able to contact her for you so you could talk to her yourself."

"What—with Caroline?" Elizabeth said, almost a shout. Her first impulse was to laugh aloud and tell her aunt that maybe *she* was the one who needed to see a shrink. But the longer she looked into Junia's eyes, the more she saw the love and concern her aunt felt for her. It helped soften her reaction, and she finished, rather lamely, "I just don't—I *can't* believe anything like that is even possible."

Elizabeth raised her hands to her face and, shutting her eyes, roughly rubbed her palms against her forehead. The sudden darkness exploded with spirals of color. She watched with mounting horror as the rapidly unfolding designs expanded.

"I think my explanation makes a whole helluva lot more sense," Elizabeth said, her voice muffled by her hands. Uncovering her eyes, she looked pleadingly at Junia. "I think it's because I'm losing my mind because I'm so . . . so—"

"Come now!" Junia said, harshly. "We'll have no talk like *that* in this house!"

"It's true, though," Elizabeth said. Her voice shattered, and tears blurred her vision. "There wasn't anything in the mirror except my own face. What I saw there, and the feeling I had all day that there was someone behind me, no matter where I turned, someone was watching me . . . It's all just my imagination, just honest-to-God, going-crazy hallucinations.''

She raised her hands in front of her and shook them wildly as if she were desperately trying to restore the circulation. "And if I don't get some help, real soon, I . . . I don't know what I'll do!''

Saying that, she leaned forward and, covering her face with her hands again, began to sob deeply. She was distantly aware that Junia was patting her gently on the back; and her numbed senses barely heard her aunt as she crooned, "There, there dear. There, there. You may not believe me, but I *do* know someone who can contact Caroline for you.''

2.

Detective Harris looked up from his desk as Frank walked into his office, and pointedly asked, "What the fuck are you doing, Melrose—bucking for a gold shield or something?''

Frank smiled and shook his head. He still had a few hours before his shift began, but he excused his early arrival at the station by mentioning some paperwork that needed his attention. The Styrofoam coffee cup he was holding didn't fully protect his fingers from the near-boiling coffee, and he had to pass it from hand to hand as he stood in the doorway.

"I was just wondering if you had any leads with the Payne case?'' he asked, trying to sound casual before taking a slurping sip of coffee.

Harris frowned and shook his head with disgust before slapping his beefy hand onto the stack of reports he had been sifting through. "I'm awash in a raging sea of paperwork and madness,'' he mumbled.

"Hey, if you ever get tired of detective work, you could always become a poet,'' Frank said with a laugh.

"And you could become a fucking comedian,'' Harris said, almost snarling. "But to answer your question—bluntly—*no*. We don't have any leads. We conducted an area interview, but hey! On that stretch of road, there aren't all that many houses near the cemetery. Anyone out there at that time of night either was doing the digging or shouldn't have been there in the first place and is *never* gonna come forward.''

"Can't understand why," Frank said. "You're such a nice guy, and so easy to talk to.''

"Christ, you're regular David Letterman material, you know that?'' Harris said, scowling.

"I always figured that show was on way past your bedtime,'' Frank snapped.

"Don't let the doorknob bump your ass on the way out, all right?'' Harris said, looking back down at his work.

"Seriously, though,'' Frank said. "Nobody was passing by and saw anything, or remembers seeing anything suspicious out there that night?''

"Only one neighbor," Harris said with thinly veiled disgust as he riffled through the papers on his desk. "Dan Wood's house is about a quarter mile down the road. He said he *thinks* he saw a truck go into the cemetery that night just as he was coming home from work at the jetport. 'Least he thinks it was that night. He said he's so used to seeing teenagers go in there at all hours to drink or park or whatever the fuck they do for kicks these days that he stopped taking notice years ago.''

Frank sniffed and said, "Yeah, well, if I know Dan, I'll bet he was using the butt end of a whiskey bottle as a telescope, too.''

"We get leads, we check 'em all out, all right? You got any other suggestions on how I should conduct this investigation?'' Harris asked, smiling thinly.

"That's it so far, then, huh?'' Frank went on. "You didn't get anything back from the lab on those tire tracks or anything yet?''

Harris's chair made a ferocious squeak as he leaned back and hooked his thumbs through his belt loops. His sports coat hung open, exposing his shoulder holster. Glaring at Frank, he snarled, "Do you mind if I ask why the fuck you're so damned interested in all of this?''

"I dunno,'' Frank said as he looked down at the floor and

scratched behind his ear. "I mean, you know—finding something like that kind of did a number on me and my partner."

Harris frowned and, glancing quickly over his shoulder, said, "I don't see no Goddamned psychiatrist diploma on my walls. If you're looking for someone to tell your troubles to, I ain't the guy." He paused, then sniffed loudly and ran his hand back over his scalp. Suddenly pointing at Frank, he said, "Wait a fucking minute—the fact that you and the stiff's niece were high school honeys wouldn't have anything to do with this, now, would it?"

The bluntness of the detective's manner had always impressed Frank; but for the first time ever, being on the receiving end of it wasn't the least bit comfortable.

"Oh, no—not at all," Frank replied, sensing the transparency of his lie. "It's just—you've got to admit, this isn't your typical everyday small-town crime. I was just . . . you know, wondering if you were any closer to a suspect."

Harris shook his head and, jabbing his forefinger at Frank, said, "No, and shooting the shit with you all Goddamned morning isn't going to get me any closer, either. Tell you what, though, Melrose—if I come up with some hot lead, you'll be the first to know. All right?"

Frank knew he had already pushed Harris too far, so he accepted the kiss-off, backed out of the detective's office, and went down the hallway to the conference room. He couldn't help but wonder how Harris, when he had gone to notify Junia and Elspeth Payne as well as Elizabeth's parents yesterday about what had happened at Oak Grove, had handled something that required even a modicum of delicacy.

"Paperwork be damned," Frank said aloud as he got up and poured what remained of his coffee down the drain and tossed the cup into the trash. He knew all along that he had just been looking for an excuse to go out to Elizabeth's aunts' house and talk with them. If Harris or anyone else asked him why he was going out there, he'd tell them it was to smooth over what, in Harris's hands, might have been a fairly rough delivery of the news. But he was honest enough with himself to realize that, if nothing else, this would start to prepare him for his first face-to-face meeting with Elizabeth in nearly twenty years.

3.

Elizabeth was still wrung out and drawn from her emotional outburst when she heard a car pull into the aunts' driveway. Tires crunched on the loose gravel as the car stopped. The sound set her already overworked nerves on edge. When she looked up over the edge of the porch and saw that it was a police cruiser, and that Frank Melrose was stepping out, she almost stopped breathing. Feeling a wave of dizzy nervousness, she sat heavily back into the chair and hastily wiped her face with her hands.

Junia was in the house checking on Elspeth. She apparently hadn't heard the car drive in when she came to the screen door and reported to Elizabeth that Elspeth was fine, still snoozing in her chair by the window.

"Oh, my," Junia said, once she noticed the cruiser. She came out onto the porch, letting the screen door slam behind her as she started down the steps to the gravel walkway. "I certainly hope nothing else has happened," she muttered under her breath.

Elizabeth was shrinking back into the shadows of the porch, earnestly hoping Frank wouldn't look up and see her. She wondered if she still had time to zip into the house and pretend she hadn't seen him. It was just a matter of time until they met, but she wasn't ready to talk with him today; she would at least need a few minutes to compose herself.

All of her frantic planning instantly evaporated when she heard Junia say, "What a pleasant surprise, Frank. There's someone here who would love to see you."

Elizabeth's hands went cold, and a sheen of sweat broke out on her forehead as she listened to Frank's footsteps approach the house and start up the porch steps. After sucking in a breath of air, she forced a wide smile onto her face as she stood up and held out her right hand in greeting.

"Oh, my goodness," she said, using a tone of voice that seemed high and unnatural for her. "Well if it isn't Frank Melrose." Her first impulse was to give him a hug and kiss, as if that was the natural thing to do.

She felt thankful when Frank looked almost as confounded as she was as he took her extended hand and awkwardly but gently shook it. She wished it hadn't, but just the touch of his hand sent a pleasant tingle through her.

"My God—after all this time," Frank said. His voice sounded a bit tight and wistful. "You're looking . . . terrific, Elizabeth."

He held her hand a moment longer than she thought necessary, then released it. Elizabeth let it fall to her side as she stood there, feeling numb and awkward. "You look as though you haven't changed a bit," Elizabeth replied. As soon as the words were out of her mouth she cringed, realizing they could be taken either as a compliment or as a subtle put-down.

"You're in uniform," Junia said somewhat tightly, "so I take it this isn't a social call."

Frank was still looking squarely at Elizabeth, an urgent intensity in his eyes, but he shook his head and glanced over at Junia, his expression hardening. "Not serious business," he said. "Nothing like the visit you had yesterday morning from Detectives Harris and Jeffries. I—" Words failed him for a moment, so he simply shrugged and slapped his hands helplessly against his thighs. His right hand hit his holstered revolver. "I don't know exactly what I wanted to say except . . . I'm sorry something like that had to happen."

"I appreciate your concern," Junia said, her face warmed by a gentle smile.

"I wanted to let you know that, if there was anything I could do to help you out, you just let me know, all right?" Frank said. His eyes kept flicking in Elizabeth's direction. "And I wanted to reassure you that we're doing everything possible to find out who did it." It wasn't necessary to mention any of the details of the investigation, considering how little Harris had told him. He figured that dwelling on it too much might be counterproductive, anyway.

"You must've heard what happened . . . out at the cemetery the other night," Frank said, turning to Elizabeth.

Elizabeth nodded tightly, all the while thinking that if whoever had done that foul act had moved just one grave to the side, he would have exhumed Caroline. How would she have handled something like that, she wondered, especially on her first day back home after leaving Doug?

"Can I offer you something to drink, Frank?" Junia asked. "Some coffee or lemonade? Elizabeth and I were just about to have something."

"Coffee'd be nice," Frank replied, glancing at his watch. He looked over at Elizabeth, trying to gauge her reaction to the invitation.

"Have a seat right there," Junia said, pointing to where she had been sitting. "You and Elizabeth must have a million things to catch up on." With that, she disappeared into the kitchen, letting the screen door swing shut behind her.

The slamming door echoed in Elizabeth's ears like a gunshot as she went back to her chair and sat down. A heated flush raced over her skin as she wondered what in the hell she could say to Frank. As much as she wanted to resist the feeling, she had to admit that it was good—no, it was great—to see him again. Old flames, she told herself, probably never do die out entirely, but she was determined not to let this one even begin to be fanned into life. Things were confusing enough for her as it was.

"I'd heard you were back in town," Frank said, after clearing his throat. He came over and sat down in the chair Junia had indicated, but he didn't lean back or appear at all comfortable. "I was hoping I'd have a chance to see you. You're looking good."

"Thanks. So are you," Elizabeth said, thinking, *We already said this*.

"So how long do you think you'll be staying?" Frank asked.

Elizabeth shrugged. She could see that he was feeling as uncomfortable as she was, but that didn't make it any easier. She found herself remembering all those days and nights together, and the fun they'd had. Did he have such fond memories? she wondered.

"I don't know, for sure," she said. "It might be for a while. I've even been thinking about looking for work . . . at least until I get a few things sorted out."

Frank nodded as if he knew and understood everything she had to deal with. His face suddenly brightened. "Hey, you know, now that you mention it, Jake Hardy said something a couple of days ago about needing some more help at the hardware store. You might want to talk to him."

Elizabeth shook her head and laughed nervously. "I don't think I could work there. I mean, I don't know the first thing about carpentry and plumbing and stuff."

Frank shrugged. "Just a suggestion," he said. He didn't want her to bristle the way she used to, back before they broke up, and start accusing him of always telling her what to do.

"Thanks, though. I'll keep it in mind," Elizabeth replied. She glanced toward the kitchen window, where she could hear Junia as she bustled about getting the coffee pot going. She wished Junia would hurry back out to the porch, so that she wouldn't have to be alone with Frank; just recalling their times together made her feel as if she couldn't trust herself alone with him. Considering everything else she had had to deal with over the past few days, she wasn't ready for this. Actually, she wondered if she would ever be . . .

"Well," she said, casting her glance aside, "I see you haven't managed to keep yourself out of a uniform." The remark was meant humorously, as if just to cut through her own nervous tension; but she saw instantly that Frank misread her.

"Let's not get started on that, all right?" he said. The muscles in his jaw started rapidly flexing and unflexing. "What happened back then, happened." He snorted and shook his head. "Hey, we were just kids, and we thought we knew what we were doing."

"Oh, no—no. I didn't mean it like that," she said, suddenly flustered. Although she hadn't intended to remind Frank that it was his volunteering to serve in Vietnam right after high school graduation that had been the final wedge between them, she could see the old wounds reopening immediately. She didn't like feeling as though she had to be on guard against everything she said being laced with double meaning. A silence fell between them that began to stretch out uncomfortably long.

"So, I—umm—heard you've gotten a divorce from Doug," Frank said at last.

"Word travels fast."

"Once Betty Stevenson—you remember her, don't you?"

Elizabeth nodded.

"Well, once she hears something it burns through town like a brush fire in August." He paused a moment, searching Elizabeth's face for a reaction, then continued, "Is it true, though, or should I do my best to squelch this particular small-town rumor?"

"Squelch away if you'd like," Elizabeth replied somberly, "but—well, Doug and I are separated . . . and I'm fairly certain we'll be getting a divorce. We haven't—" Her eyes began to sting, but she continued undaunted, not allowing herself to cry. "Well, you know—ever since . . . Caroline—"

Frank nodded understandingly, but the ensuing silence threatened to be longer and more uncomfortable. It was all saved when Junia came bursting out onto the porch carrying a tray with cups, spoons, napkins, cream and sugar, a plate of plain doughnuts, and an urn filled with coffee. Frank stood up and pulled over the rickety table so she could put everything down and serve.

"It seems like just yesterday you two used to stop by the house and visit when you were out on a date," Junia said, smiling as she filled a cup and handed it to Elizabeth while Frank helped himself. She seemed about to say more, and Elizabeth was bracing herself for an embarrassingly direct question from Junia—such as, Why don't you two go out together again?—when a burst of static came from the cruiser.

"I'm not on duty yet, but maybe I'd better check that out," Frank said, placing his cup on the porch railing and dashing down the stairs to his cruiser. Opening the door, he reached inside and grabbed the microphone. Frank held the handset too close to his mouth for Elizabeth to overhear what the call was.

Junia, meanwhile, was casting meaningful glances back and forth between Elizabeth and Frank. Elizabeth had the distinct impression she was sizing them up to see if they still fit together as well as they had back in high school. What made her even more uncomfortable was feeling that she was thinking along those lines, too. She couldn't help but recall all those days—and nights—they had spent together. Maybe it was true—your first love is *always* your best. As much as she tried to keep such thoughts at bay, she found that, even after all these years and everything she had been through, she did still find herself attracted to Frank Melrose. Was it just physical, she wondered, or was there more?

Frank replaced the microphone and walked back toward the porch.

Looking up at Elizabeth and Junia over the railing, he said, "I'm sorry. I've got to go. There's been an accident out on Overlook Road. Thanks for the coffee, Miss Payne."

Junia nodded.

Glancing over at Elizabeth, Frank's eyes softened, even as she saw the sullen, hopeful glow in them. "And it was *really* good to see you again, Elizabeth," he said. His entire demeanor communicated that he would much rather spend the afternoon with her on the porch, rekindling their friendship . . . or possibly more.

"Same here," Elizabeth replied, feeling stupidly at a loss for words.

"So, maybe I'll see you around," Frank said, still not wanting to leave. He started for the cruiser, but then looked back at her and said, "Oh, and keep in mind what I said about Jake Hardy needing help. I'll bet he doesn't pay very much, probably just minimum wage, but it'd at least be something to do until you get your feet on the ground."

Elizabeth bristled and almost asked Frank who the hell he thought he was to say she didn't have her feet on the ground. Shifting uncomfortably in her chair, she wondered if her being at loose ends was *that* obvious?

"Yeah, maybe I will," she said, not even sure herself if she meant, Maybe I'll talk to Jake Hardy about a job at the hardware store, or, Maybe I'll see you around.

Frank got into his cruiser, started it up, and, after revving the engine, backed out of the driveway into the street. In a swirl of dust, he pulled onto Old County Road and was soon out of sight, heading out of town.

4.

After Frank left, Elizabeth and Junia had almost an hour to sit on the porch and further catch up with each other. The conversation skimmed around more sensitive issues, so Elizabeth never found an opportunity to press Junia further on her claim that she knew someone who could contact Caroline. Just before they went in for lunch, Elspeth woke up from her nap in her chair, feeling refreshed and alert. It bothered Elizabeth that her older aunt seemed to have no conception of the time she had been asleep; Elspeth acted as if there had been no more than a momentary lapse in the conversation when she joined Junia and Elizabeth in the kitchen for sandwiches.

Shortly after lunch, Elizabeth said goodbye to the aunts and left their house. Waving as she angled across the lawn toward the road, she forced herself to smile. The prospect of a three-mile walk home seemed fine, if only so she could clear her mind and let the morning's revelations and experiences sink in.

. . . As if they could!

Seeing Frank had been both awkward and tantalizing. She couldn't deny the warm feeling she still had for him even through the separation of years. She secretly gloried that he had been just as uncomfortable with her as she had been with him. That, at least, was one thing over which she felt she had a bit of control.

There were other things, though . . . things she couldn't accept that were definitely out of her control. Like the revelation of Uncle Jonathan's suicide. She couldn't imagine what might have led him to it. After she lost Caroline, she had felt as though she had some kind of reason to lose all faith and hope in life; but what could have driven Uncle Jonathan up to—and over—the edge?

Junia had offered no further information. Elizabeth had been only nine years old when her uncle had died—had killed himself. The only thing she clearly remembered was the impact the loss had on her father, mother, and aunts. She certainly had been too young for anyone to tell her the true circumstances of what had happened at the time, but then why over the years had she never even gotten a hint of the truth? Had Jonathan killed himself because of money problems, or personal relationships, or . . . or what? Now that Junia had so casually let her in on this dark family secret, was it something she could talk about with her parents, or should she simply go on as before, pretending ignorance?

And there were other, darker thoughts that cast chilling shadows over her mind . . .

In some crazy way that even the cops hadn't yet figured out, could Uncle Jonathan's suicide almost thirty years ago be connected somehow to the incident the night before last of someone digging up his body and removing his left hand?

Now that Aunt Junia had revealed the truth to her, Elizabeth actually found herself resenting her for it. She would just as soon have gone on in blissful ignorance about such long-ago family history. Maybe ignorance *was* bliss. She could very easily have lived the rest of her life without knowing what Uncle Jonathan had done, so why had Junia mentioned it now, after all this time? Like Aunt Elspeth, was Junia sliding into senility and had she inadvertently "spilled the beans"? Or had she done it on purpose . . . and if on purpose, exactly to *what* purpose? With her more recent tragedy, Elizabeth felt she had more than her fair share of misery!

But then, who the hell ever said life was fair? she asked herself as she walked slowly along the roadside. The afternoon sun was warm on her face, but it did little to remove the gnawing chill she felt around her heart because—worst of all—what in the name of Heaven had Junia meant, that she knew someone who could contact Caroline for her?

Walking west, Elizabeth had to avert her eyes constantly to avoid the glare from the road. Several people passing by in cars and trucks honked their horns at her, as if they recognized her, but they all drove by so fast she couldn't tell who anyone was. Why, if they recognized her, no one stopped and offered her a ride home mystified her, but she was content to walk and try to settle the emotional turmoil she was feeling. Maybe she should hike an extra ten or twenty miles.

When she realized she was in front of Hardy's Hardware, Elizabeth slowed her pace as she cut across the parking lot toward the gray, weathered store front. Wheelbarrows, lawn mowers, and cultivators lined both sides of the door, along with an assortment of rakes, shovels, and hoes. The store windows were plastered with posters announcing the upcoming Shrine circus and various other social events. A few of the posters were well out of date.

"This is ridiculous," Elizabeth muttered as she mounted the creaky steps and entered the store. It was just as she always remembered it from when she came in here with her father on errands; the little bell on a spring jangled when the top of the door pulled the spring down, and her nose was instantly assailed by a dusty aroma—a curious blend of old rope and wood. Like the aunts' house, Jake Hardy hadn't done much to "modernize" his store, in spite of the newer, fancier stores going up around town.

Do I really want to work here? Elizabeth wondered as she smiled a greeting to the young woman at the cash register. She didn't recognize her, but that was no surprise. The woman seemed friendly enough, but there was a touch of sadness at the thought that, for her, at least, this was probably the job she would have the rest of her life—a second income just to help her family make ends meet, or a bare subsistence salary for a divorced mother.

Is that my future? Elizabeth thought, feeling a cold touch of dread. In spite of everything I've been through, does it all come down to my spending the rest of my life working at some menial, low-paying, no-future job?

She hesitated for a moment by the counter. The woman at the register looked at her oddly.

"May I help you?" she asked, arching her eyebrows until her eyes looked like two big O's.

Elizabeth glanced nervously around, then—almost against her will—asked, "I was wondering if Jake was in."

The woman hooked her thumb over her shoulder toward a door marked EMPLOYEES ONLY. "He's out back. Lemme buzz him for you." She reached under the counter and pressed a buzzer, which sounded at the back of the store.

"Thanks," Elizabeth said, as she turned and started toward the door. She was halfway there when the door opened and Jake Hardy, looking older, balder, and certainly much fatter than she remembered, strode out. He was holding his hand up to his mouth and licking something from his fingers.

"Well, well, if it isn't Betsy Payne," he said, a smile splitting his face as he held out the hand he had just cleaned for her to shake.

"You're the only person who still calls me that, you know," Elizabeth said, as she mock-scowled at Jake.

"It's been so long since I've seen you," Jake said. "And I must say, you do look more like an *Elizabeth* than a *Betsy*. Where are those world-famous pigtails?"

Elizabeth blushed when she remembered how Jake had always teased her about her pigtails, threatening to tie them together whenever he saw her in the store or around town. "Gone," she said. "And so is my last name. My married name is Myers."

For a little while longer, anyway, she added mentally.

"I know that!" Jake said, chuckling as he rubbed his hands together. "I guess old habits die hard—'specially once you get to be my age. What can I get for you today? Your father need something out to the farm?"

Elizabeth shook her head and hesitated, not quite sure if she really wanted to go through with this. "Well, not really. I was—you see, I've moved back home, and—"

"That's right," Jake said, nodding. "I heard something about that from Betty Stevenson."

"Hasn't everyone by now?" Elizabeth said. "Anyway, I was looking for work and—well, I happened to bump into Frank Melrose today, and he said you might be looking for a little extra help. I'd be—"

"The job's yours if you want it," Jake said, cutting her off abruptly. "I can't pay you more than minimum wage to start. This time of year, what with everyone planting gardens and fixing up around the house, Ester and me been working fifty 'n' sixty hours a week. I got a couple of high school kids working part-time, but —well, you know how kids are these days. Do you know how to run a cash register?"

"I can learn," Elizabeth said brightly. She couldn't help but be surprised by how fast Jake had accepted her; it made her wonder what and how much about her current situation Jake had heard. The thought crossed her mind that quite possibly she had been set up by Frank, and that Jake was offering her this job simply out of some kind of misguided feeling of charity.

"I'll just bet you can," Jake said. "You always were a little whippersnapper."

Elizabeth didn't quite know how to take that, but clearing her throat, she said, "I've got to tell you, though, Mr. Hardy; I don't know the first thing about hardware. If someone came up to me with a question, I'd have no idea what to—"

"Don't you worry about a thing," Jake said. "Either Ester or me will be here whenever you are. Everything's got a price tag— at least it should. All you gotta do is ring up sales and bag things. And I'm sure you'll learn as you go along. There ain't all that much to it. You can start tomorrow, if you'd like."

Jake stood looking at her, waiting for her to say she'd take the job.

"Sure," she said brightly, after a slight hesitation. "Sounds great." She shook hands with Jake to confirm the deal. Just at that moment, she glanced toward the front of the store and was positive she saw the tail end of a police cruiser disappear around the corner of the store. She bristled, thinking instantly that it was Frank, checking up to see if she had taken his advice.

"Sounds great to me, too," Jake said. "We open at eight. Can you be here by a little before then? Say, seven-thirty?"

Having to get up that early made Elizabeth wonder whether she had just been given one more reason to think this might all be a mistake, but she smiled and said, "I'll be here."

"I'll need your social security number and, believe it or not, your birth certificate or passport so I can fill out this new form for the Immigration and Naturalization Service, to prove you're an American citizen."

"I'm pretty sure we can establish that," Elizabeth said with a laugh. Oh, one more thing, could you try to remember to call me Elizabeth?"

"Sure thing, Betsy," Jake said. He roared with laughter over that one.

Elizabeth considered stopping at the register to introduce herself to the woman who must be Ester, but she simply smiled as she passed by, figuring whatever Ester didn't know about her, Jake or —more likely—Betty Stevenson would fill in for her before seven-thirty tomorrow morning.

5.

Barney Fraser drove slowly out of town, heading west. He turned left onto Brook Road, sped up just a bit to get past Oak Grove Cemetery, then slowed down again. After glancing up and down the road to make sure no other cars were around, he drove onto a long-unused fire trail that entered the woods less than a half mile past the cemetery. Once he was in far enough so he was positive his car couldn't be seen from the road, he stopped, turned the engine off, and got out of the car. A deep, gnawing fear worked on his insides as he slipped his car keys into his pants pocket. Inhaling deeply and repressing a shiver, he started off into the night-shrouded woods.

The half moon rode low in the sky, casting thin blue shadows on the ground. Black slashes of trees stood out like claw marks on the sky. A gentle breeze clattered the branches overhead, making the night air feel colder than it was. Goose bumps broke out on Barney's bare arms when a voice suddenly came out of the surrounding darkness, booming like a distant peal of thunder.

"Do you have what I want?"

It sounded as if the man was standing less than a foot from him, and in darkness like this, Barney was sure he'd never know it even if they were nose to nose. He shivered wildly as his eyes darted back and forth, trying to pierce the inky blackness. All he could see were the dark lines of trees rising up against the starlit sky, and the darker black of the ground. Off to his left, he could hear a loud chorus of frogs in the wetlands behind the cemetery. He was just beginning to think he had imagined the voice when it came again, laced with menace.

"Well . . . do you have it?"

"Uh—yeah, yes, I have it," he said. His voice was wire tight; he was afraid it would crack. "I have it right here in this—"

"Give it to me," the voice said, low and demanding.

Barney tried to chuckle, but the only sound he could make was a tight wheeze. He held the paper bag he was carrying out in front of him and said helplessly, "How the hell can I give it to you when I can't even—"

His voice cut off when a bright circle of light suddenly snapped on, hitting him squarely in the eyes. The light instantly shattered into hundreds of watery diamonds as Barney's eyes reacted. Shielding his face with one arm, Barney took an involuntary step backward. He almost screamed when he bumped into something. His first thought was that he had hit against a tree, but then he realized it hadn't been hard and unyielding like a tree. He tried to scream when strong arms encircled his chest and squeezed him tightly.

"What the—?" he managed to say, but then a thick hand that smelled of oil and dirt clamped over his mouth. The rest of his protestations were lost in a muffled squawk.

"Take the bag from him," said the voice from behind the glaring circle of light. Not for a second did the beam waver.

Barney's mind flooded with panic as he felt the bag torn roughly from his grasp. The paper crinkled loudly in the darkness, sounding like a raging fire with no light. The hand covering his mouth was also covering his nose, and Barney was suddenly fearful that he would suffocate. He began to struggle against the person holding him, but it did no good. Whoever it was, was much stronger than he.

"If you promise to keep your mouth shut and speak only when you're spoken to, I'll tell my friend to let you go," the voice from behind the light rasped.

Barney nodded vigorously and was grateful when he felt the arms pinning him loosen up and release him. His legs almost gave out once he was supporting his full weight, but he locked his knees and took a deep breath to brace himself. In spite of his efforts, sour, black fear rose like bile in his throat when he saw the light begin to move forward. Then, from out of the stinging glare, a dark hand reached out. The person standing behind him handed over the bag.

"Who the hell *are* you, anyway?" Barney asked. "And what the hell do you want with this?" He was positive he would get no answer from the circle of light, but he had to ask . . . if only to divert this person's attention away from what was inside the bag.

"It's really none of your business," the voice from behind the light said mildly. "You had access to something I needed, and I'm pleased that you were so willing to . . . to cooperate with me."

The voice rumbled with low, mean laughter.

"Right," Barney said, feeling a wave of embarrassment when he considered how simply this unknown person had gained control over him and had made him do the horrible deed he had been asked to do—no, not asked to do . . . *told* to do!

"Well now," the voice from behind the light said, "you certainly wouldn't want me to show your wife those photographs?"

"You promised to give me those pictures . . . and the negatives," Barney said. His voice was trembling with suppressed rage and fear, but he didn't care. All he wanted was to exchange packages with this man and get the hell out of there! His car was parked out on Old County Road, where he had left it the night he had dug up

Jonathan Payne's grave and cut off his left hand, and he sure as hell didn't want the police happening by and getting a make on it. It wouldn't take Sherlock-fucking Holmes to put two and two together.

"But now that I've got what I want, I'm not so sure I want to give you those photographs," the voice from behind the light said. "I think I like our relationship just the way it is, you see, and if I gave you those photographs now, you might be tempted to go to the police and tell them all about our little deal."

"I'm not about to go to the police," Barney said, his voice cracking. "Why would I want—"

"Even if you didn't," the voice said, "I don't like the way the police are handling the whole case. I probably should have guessed that, in a small town like Bristol Mills, something like grave robbing would become the crime of the decade. There's been something about it in the Portland papers two days in a row, now. I just wouldn't feel comfortable, knowing there's a loose cannon like you out there."

"I'm no 'loose cannon,' " Barney said, almost wailing. "I've got my job, my family—my reputation to protect."

"You should have thought about all of *that* before you solicited that young man in Portland."

"I can't help it if I—"

But then Barney cut himself off because he had no idea how to finish his statement. So what if he had homosexual tendencies? Besides, he wasn't exclusively homosexual; he had a wife and had fathered one child. It was just that, every now and then, he had these . . . these urges to try something different and, at least until this whole business of AIDS started up, he had found that in some of the seedier sections of Portland.

"I . . . thought we . . . had a deal," Barney finally said.

"We did," the voice from behind the light replied. "And you used the correct verb tense—the past. I'm changing the deal, and I don't think you're in any position to argue."

The light shifted downward. Sweat broke out on Barney's forehead when he heard paper crumple and realized the man was opening the paper bag. For several seconds, there were no sounds other than the springtime chorus of frogs and Barney's stuttering heartbeat.

The flashlight beam dipped down into the bag and held for a few seconds; then the man's voice filled the night.

"What the fuck is this shit!"

"Wha-what do you mean?" Barney sputtered. He knew damned well what the man meant, but he knew he would have to run the lie as long as he could—hopefully long enough so he could get away from here.

"I told you to get me the *girl's* hand!" the voice shouted as the light swung back up and painfully stabbed Barney's eyes.

"That's . . . what you got," Barney said. His impulse was to start backing away, but he knew, as soon as he took the first step, those hefty arms would stop him from going any further.

"Are you trying to play me for a sucker?" the voice said, rumbling with hostile laughter.

"I don't take you for any . . ." Barney let his voice fade, unable to finish.

"This is an old *man's* hand!" the voice from behind the light growled. "How stupid do you think I am? You know, now that I think about it, the newspapers never did specify *whose* grave had been disturbed at the cemetery. I should have thought to check, but Barney . . . Barney!" He clicked his tongue several times. "I thought I could count on you."

"That *is* it! That's Caroline Myers's hand," Barney wailed, even though he knew he'd been caught in his lie.

"Oh, really?" the voice said. The next sound Barney heard was almost too faint to detect, but he knew what it was; the man had snapped his fingers as a signal. Before he could make a sound or turn to defend himself, he was grabbed from behind again. His arms were pinned painfully to his sides as the man holding him squeezed hard. Pinpricks of light shot across Barney's vision.

"What do you make of this?" the voice asked. Suddenly the flashlight beam was blocked by something crooked and black. Leaves on the forest floor crinkled underfoot as the man holding the light moved closer. Barney strained his eyes to see who this was, but all he saw was a darker than night silhouette.

"I don't want to cause any trouble for our friend here," the man holding Barney said, even as he gave Barney's chest a tighter squeeze, "but I'd have to say that sure as shit looks like an old man's hand to me."

"You don't . . . understand," Barney said, gasping desperately to inhale as the arms clamped tighter. "She's been . . . dead over . . . a year. Corpses shrivel up like that. Honest!"

"Why, why, *why* would you do something like this to me?" the voice said, lowering with intensity. "I thought we had ourselves a deal!"

"You're the one . . . wh-who changed it," Barney stammered, barely able to talk above his burning panic.

"Apparently not before you changed your end of it, though," the voice said.

"All right! All right!" Barney wailed. The arms holding him squeezed even tighter, compressing his lungs. Barney felt his feet lift up off the ground, and he began to kick futilely as he gasped, "Yeah . . . I . . . admit it . . . but when you . . . asked me to—"

"I didn't *ask* you, Barney. I *told* you to get me Caroline Myers's left hand!"

"I'm—sorry," Barney said. Tears flooded his eyes and began to run down his cheeks. "I—truly—*am!*"

He could hear his heartbeat growing steadily louder in his ears as the arms around him got tighter and tighter. The pressure built until his eyes felt as though they were going to explode out of his head.

"Why couldn't I count on you for something as simple as that?" the voice asked with a feigned tone of hurt feelings. "I figured, you being the cemetery caretaker, it wouldn't be all that difficult."

"I—couldn't—couldn't—do—it," Barney said. Glowing spirals of light were exploding on the insides of his eyes. A burning gulp of air wedged in his throat before each word. "Not—to—a —little—girl!"

"I'm really sorry about this, Barney," the voice said. The man's arms reached toward him out of the ball of light, but it wasn't his living fingers that brushed against Barney's cheek, smearing his tears. Barney saw to his horror that it was the hoary fingernails and cold, dead flesh of a man who had been buried upwards of thirty years that was stroking up one side of his face and down the other.

"And if I can't count on you to do what I *tell* you," the man purred as he probed at Barney's mouth with the dead man's fingers, "I know I could never trust you to keep from going to the cops."

"I—wouldn't," Barney managed to say, but that was all. No matter how much he wanted to draw in a deep breath, he didn't want to open his mouth with this rotting, dead hand pressing hard against his lips. Barney's face was infused with blood, and the hammering sound in his ears got louder and louder until it was all he could hear. The dead fingers pushed past his lips, between his teeth, as they were forced down his throat. Barney's chest hitched painfully as he gagged, trying to expel the rotten flesh, but it was being pushed down with a steady, unyielding pressure. A rank, sickening taste filled his mouth.

When the man behind the light spoke again, his voice was no more than a distant whisper that seemed to come from the end of a long, long, infinitely long tunnel. His words made almost no sense as Barney's mind rebelled at the thought of what was happening.

"I promise I'll bury you here in the woods," the man said as he jammed the dead hand as far as he could into Barney's mouth. "And from now on, I've learned my lesson; if I want something done right, I'm just going to have to do it myself."

Barney's mind formed words, but there was no way they could make it out of his mouth. He wanted to cry out, to plead for his life, to beg for mercy, to promise that he'd do it again and do it right this time; he'd get Caroline Myers's left hand—anything! *anything!*—if the man would just let him live!

But the decayed flesh filled his mouth and throat. The darkness of the surrounding woods was gradually replaced by a deeper darkness, a darkness that reached in from all around him and wrapped around his mind like black velvet gloves as it squeezed and squeezed. His stomach revolted as the rotting taste filled his mouth. When the hot vomit tried to surge out, the dead hand pushed it back.

The pressure squeezing Barney's chest intensified until it was a blazing iron band, pressing tighter and tighter. The last thing Barney Fraser ever heard was a loud *pop* that crazily reminded him of when, as a boy, he had been climbing a tree and the branch he had been standing on had suddenly given way. It was different this time, though, because Barney never knew it when he hit the ground.

FIVE

"Hey, ouija! We need yah!"

1.

Elizabeth swept the bedcovers aside, got out of bed, and walked over to her bureau. Looking around her bedroom, she was mildly surprised by the faint violet glow that edged everything, making the bedroom furniture look watery and dark, almost insubstantial. The gauzy curtains on the windows drifted back and forth with a whispery flutter, and the soft glow of moonlight covered the sills like a skimming of frost.

"I should have thrown this thing away long ago," she said, walking over to the bureau. Looking down at the ouija-board box; she reached out tentatively, fighting back the dizzying sensation she had that she was merely a spectator, watching her hands move. The soft glow of moonlight made the box appear illusory, and, like that time in the attic, she wouldn't have been surprised to see her fingers pass clear through the box.

She took hold of the box, surprised by the weight of it, and held it up close to her face in the dark.

In spite of the darkness, she could easily see and read the one word on the box—

ouija.

The letters, like the window sills, were edged with a faintly pulsating violet light. Elizabeth got the funny notion that each letter was somehow alive and, if she didn't watch them carefully, would slide off the box to the floor and scurry away from her. Carefully balancing the box to keep it level, she folded her legs and, in one smooth motion, sat down cross-legged on the floor.

—*Hey, ouija! We need yah!*

The words came to mind, making her chuckle as she remembered the old television advertising line for the game . . .

—*No, not quite a game!*

With just the soft moonlight filtering through her window, she thought there shouldn't be enough light to see by, but she had no problem making out the letters and numbers on the game board as she removed the box cover and carefully balanced the board on her knees.

Maybe I shouldn't be doing this, she thought as she took the teardrop-shaped pointer and placed it in the center of the board. Touching the tips of her fingers to the edge of the pointer, she pushed it around in several wide circles, as if it were an engine that needed to be revved up.

"I don't even know what I want to ask it," she said aloud.

Suddenly her eyes snapped into focus as she stared at her hands running the pointer around in wide circles. In an instant, as clear and as sharp as if someone had thrown on a megawatt spotlight, she no longer felt as if she alone was moving the pointer; the pointer was either moving under its own power or else someone . . . someone she couldn't see, was pushing the pointer, dragging her hands along with it. The felt pads on the legs of the pointer rasped against the board with a gritty sandpaper sound.

What to ask? What to ask? she wondered; but even as she formed her first question in her mind, she was aware that the pointer had already started spelling out a message. She squinted, trying to catch each letter the pointer paused over before darting to the next one.

W-H-E-R-E-H-A-

Whenever Elizabeth and Pam had played with the ouija, they always had to pause to write down each letter as it came; but now Elizabeth wasn't at all surprised that she immediately connected the letters into words that made sense.

V-E-Y-O-U-B-E-E-N

"Where have you been?" she repeated aloud. "Why—I've been right here, at home. I couldn't sleep, so I thought I'd see if maybe Max was still around."

Without pause, the pointer began making wide loops again, spelling out another message.

"Who . . . Who am I speaking to?" Elizabeth asked, feeling a subtle stirring of tension. She knew she would scream out loud— loud enough to wake up her parents—if the board spelled out M-A-X. Maybe there was a connection between Max and her Uncle Jonathan; maybe even back when she was a kid, she *had* picked up—subconsciously—that Uncle Jonathan had killed himself.

Or maybe, she thought, with a tingling chill, this *was* Jonathan.

But the ouija board didn't spell out Max or Jonathan or any other name. After one more lazy loop, it started jerking back and forth, and up and down with the jittery intensity of a seismograph. The letters followed rapidly one after another, with only a slight pause to mark between words.

Y-O-U-S-H-O-U-L-D-B-E-T-R-Y-I-N-G-T-O-H-E-L-P-H-E-R

"You should be trying to help her . . ." Elizabeth said. "Who—? Who should I be trying to help?" Before she could concentrate on the question to direct it toward the ouija board, the pointer again darted from letter to letter.

S-H-E-S-B-E-E-N-T-R-Y-I-N-G-T-O-G-E

Elizabeth's eyes and mind strained to absorb it all as the pointer darted like an angry bee from letter to letter.

T-I-N-T-O-U-C-H-W-I-T-H-Y-O-U

Elizabeth was beginning to feel as though the message was going to be completely lost when it snapped into her mind with near-photographic clarity.

"She's been trying to get in touch with you!" she whispered. "Who's been trying to reach me?" Her voice echoed with a hollow reverberation. Elizabeth had the distinct impression there was some-one leaning close to her ear, behind her, whispering.

The pointer zipped over to *yes*, in the corner of the board.

"Is this the someone I should be trying to help?" Elizabeth asked aloud.

The pointer shifted over to *no*, in the other corner.

"I don't understand," Elizabeth said, feeling a disorienting mixture of fear and confusion. "Do I need help?"

She stared down at the pointer, waiting tensely for it to begin to move, but it seemed to be glued to the board. Elizabeth gave the pointer a little nudge, but her fingers slid off the edge and came down hard on the board. The pointer didn't move. The board teetered on her knees, and she grabbed to steady it. Even that much motion failed to dislodge the pointer, which was stuck as though welded to the surface.

"Is someone I know in trouble?" Elizabeth asked, repositioning her fingers on the pointer and, gritting her teeth, trying to force it to move. She was tingling with expectation, but the pointer remained motionless.

A cold shock slammed into Elizabeth's body when, looking down, she saw not only her own hands, but someone else's reaching out of the darkness and resting on the other side of the pointer. Long, thin fingers, with dirt-encrusted fingernails that clicked on the plastic pointer, materialized from the elbows down out of the darkness, as if the night had suddenly solidified. Too frightened to look up, Elizabeth watched the skin on the backs of the hands as it peeled and curled away, shrinking as though melting or . . .

Burning!

Elizabeth watched the pale skin slough away like wet cardboard, exposing gray, brittle bones. She felt a violent tug on the pointer. The rasping sound began again, much louder. It sounded like the whining buzz of a chainsaw. Elizabeth watched, dumbfounded, as it spelled out another message.

Y-O-U-R-E-I-N-T-R-O-U-B-L-E-A-N-D-Y-O-U-D-O-N-T-K-N-O-W-I-T

The letters flew by so fast, her fear-numbed brain couldn't absorb the message. All she could do was stare, horrified, at the bony hands that reached out of the darkness of her bedroom and guided the pointer.

"Stop this! Stop it right *now*!" she yelled, but her voice was no more than a whisper lost in the roaring wind of terror whipping icy circles inside her.

No! Not wind, she thought, through the rising shrieks.

"Stop it! . . . *Please*," Elizabeth whimpered. She tore her hands away from the ouija pointer and covered her face, pressing hard against her eyes until they hurt. Flaming spikes of light jabbed her retinas.

"Stop it! . . . Stop it! . . . *Stop it! . . .*"

Elizabeth tried to stand up; she had to get away from the ouija board and those skeletal hands controlling it, but her body was paralyzed, caught in an iron grip that wouldn't let her go. Her mind was filled with horrifying thoughts of what those hands might do next—

. . . Reach out! . . . Grab her by the throat! . . . Strangle the life out of her!

A sudden pressure caught both of her wrists, and, as much as she tried to resist, her hands were pulled inexorably away from her eyes. The darkened bedroom snapped back into view, but what she found herself staring at was the ouija board. The skeletal hands were still guiding the pointer as it darted rapidly back and forth, spelling out the message:

M-O-M-M-Y-H-E-L-P-M-O-M-

The sound the pointer made on the board rose steadily louder until Elizabeth finally realized it wasn't metal on metal, or stone against stone . . . No! It was the sound of car tires, spinning frantically to gain purchase on a snow-slick road!

M-Y-H-E-L-P-M-O-M-M-Y-H-E-L-P

"*No!*" Elizabeth wailed as hot tears flooded her eyes, blurring her vision. "Who are you? Why are you doing this to me?"

The letters on the game board melted like chocolate on a sidewalk in August; but through the dizzying haze, Elizabeth's eyes followed the pointer as it spelled out over and over . . .

H-E-L-P-M-O-M-M-Y-C-A-R-O-L-I-N-E-H-E-L-P-M-O-M-M-Y-H-E-L-P-M-O-M

Elizabeth was spiraling down into a dizzying whirlpool of darkness when she snapped back to wakefulness. With a sputtering gasp that smoothly blended into a scream, she opened her eyes to find herself sitting cross-legged on her bedroom floor, the ouija board and pointer propped up on her knees.

2.

"I think there are two things you're going to have to do," Rebecca said, pointing her forefinger at Elizabeth. "Do you want to know what they are?"

It was a little after 3:00 A.M., and Rebecca was facing Elizabeth across the kitchen table. They each had a steaming cup of tea in front of them, but neither had taken a sip yet. The sky outside the kitchen window was black, and the dim light of the kitchen just barely kept the pressing darkness at bay.

Elizabeth's head was pounding, and even though it had happened over an hour ago, she still felt pale and drained after her nightmare.

Nightmare? she wondered. How can I call it a nightmare when I woke up doing exactly what I had dreamed I was doing?

Rebecca went on. "I think the first thing you have to do is give Doug a call. No, no—not now," she said, when Elizabeth glanced over at the phone. "But first thing in the morning. You've got to talk to him and try and patch things up between you. I think a lot of what's upsetting you is because—"

"It has *nothing* to do with what's happened between me and Doug," Elizabeth said. Her voice was low and surprisingly steady, but she couldn't bring herself to look up at her mother. All she could do was focus on her own hands, cradling the cup of hot tea, and remember those *other* hands she had seen—those skeletal hands that had materialized out of the darkness and guided the Ouija-board pointer.

"I think it has *everything* to do with you and Doug!" her mother said sharply. "I think you're feeling guilty that you've left him, and you're feeling—"

"I may have been the one to leave *physically*," Elizabeth said, "but *he's* the one who wanted me to leave. *I* never wanted a divorce."

"Make that three things I think you've got to do," Rebecca calmly said. "The first is to call Doug—"

"I can't do that," Elizabeth said sharply. "I can't! I won't!"

"Well, that may be," her mother replied. "But the second and most important, I think, is you have to stop lying to me."

"What are you talking about?" Elizabeth said. She sat up and looked squarely at her mother, even though the motion sent spikes of pain through her head and neck.

"You know *exactly* what I mean," Rebecca said firmly. "Look, Elizabeth—you're my daughter, and for that I'll love you unconditionally and forever; but if you're going to live here in my house, and if we're going to have any kind of honest, open relationship as one friend to another, not just mother to daughter, then you can't be telling me half-truths or outright lies."

"When have I ever—?"

Her mother cut her short by making a quick chopping motion with the edge of her hand. She grazed the side of her teacup and almost spilled it.

"You started lying to me and your father the night you showed up here on the doorstep, asking if you could spend the night. You told us that Doug had told you to get out of the house . . . that he told you he wanted a divorce."

"He did," Elizabeth said weakly.

"He most certainly did *not*!" Rebecca snapped.

"How do you know that?" Elizabeth asked, even as she flushed with embarrassment.

"Because I talked with him again this evening," Rebecca said matter-of-factly.

"He called again?" Elizabeth asked.

Her mother's voice had a steely, no-nonsense edge to it. "Doug told me that *you* were the one who started this talk about divorce, and that *you* were the one who walked out the door. So now I'm asking you to tell me the truth. Did you leave him?"

Elizabeth shifted her gaze back and forth, never letting it rest for long on her mother because the earnest intensity of Rebecca's eyes wounded her.

"Doug also repeated what he said before," Rebecca continued. Now it was her turn to find it difficult to maintain eye contact, so she stood up, walked over to the sink, leaned back against the counter, and folded her arms across her chest. She knew this wasn't a good time to confront Elizabeth, but she could no longer keep it to herself.

"What—?" Elizabeth asked. She could see that her mother was

upset, but all she could think was, *She knows what really happened that night! The bastard told her everything just to get even!*

Rebecca's lower lip trembled, her whole body shook as she spoke. "He said that you . . . you stopped him when he tried to save Caroline from the wreck. He insists that you . . . that you killed her!" She had to force the last two words out of her mouth, spitting them as though they tasted bad.

Elizabeth looked at her mother. As much as she wanted to put a lie to what Doug had told her mother, no words came to mind. In the shocked silence of the kitchen, Elizabeth heard a sound. At first, she thought she was remembering the hissing noise the Ouija pointer made as it ran over the board; but as it got steadily louder, so loud she was certain her mother could hear it as well, Elizabeth knew *exactly* what it was . . . the sound of tires, spinning futilely on snow-slick asphalt.

3.

Elizabeth had the driver's door open and was uselessly pushing with her left foot on the snowy road, trying to help Doug get the stranded car out of the snowbank. Her heel made deep skid marks in the slushy snow as her foot kept slipping.

When the flashing yellow lights of the oncoming plow lit up the inside of the car, she turned and saw the truck's headlights bearing down on her. A hot flood of panic filled her. Then, everything that happened next happened so fast. She didn't have time to absorb it all. She just reacted.

The snowplow scooped up the car and carried it over the snowbank and down to the trees at the bottom of the ravine. Elizabeth saw a flurry of motion as Doug dove out of the path of the oncoming truck. She heard someone—maybe herself, maybe Caroline—screaming just before her head hit the steering wheel. She was barely conscious when she was thrown clear of the car and landed facedown in the snow. In the raging confusion of the storm and her own blinding fear, she watched, horrified, as Doug struggled through the knee-deep snow in the wake of the car. When she caught up with him, she saw the truck carry the car down into the ravine, roll over onto it, and flatten it in mind-wrenching slow motion. The crunching sound of twisted, tortured metal filled the night, rising above the shrill whistling of the storm.

Elizabeth saw Caroline's face appear in the rear window of the car. Her mouth was a wide-open circle as she screamed in terror. With the ice-fingered winds of the blizzard screeching in her ears, Elizabeth thought she heard Caroline screaming . . .

"Help! . . . Mommy! . . . Help! . . ."

With those words shrilling in her mind, Elizabeth and Doug had started down the slope to where the car and truck had come to a stop.

And then, before the truck exploded . . . before the flames from the plow ignited the family car's gas tank . . . before Caroline's screaming was erased forever, *Elizabeth lunged out at Doug and grabbed him by the shoulders. She started shaking him, but not out of terror or desperation. The night crackled with a loud hissing sound as gasoline spilled onto the Subaru.*

"She's still alive!" Doug yelled, as he struggled to get out of Elizabeth's grasp and run down the hill to the flattened car. "She's still alive! I can—"

But then his words were cut off by the explosion of the plow's gas tank. Wicked orange flames bellowed out from underneath the overturned truck, and black smoke mushroomed up into the night sky. Elizabeth and Doug clearly saw Caroline in the backseat, futilely pounding on the rear window.

"I'm coming, baby!" Doug yelled, as he started again down the snowy slope. His arms pinwheeled wildly for balance. The wind buffeted him, almost knocking him over. In the lee of the hill, the drifting snow was up to his hips; he struggled as if plowing his way through a raging tide.

"Don't!" Elizabeth shouted. "Are you crazy? You can't do anything!"

Doug was slipping and sliding down the snowy slope, plowing up snow in front of him as he charged like a madman toward the wreck. The flames from under the plow's hood crackled wildly, peeling paint and melting plastic. Loud buckling sounds filled the night like gunshots, and glass shattered by the explosion gleamed everywhere, like diamonds thrown onto the snow. The flames underlit the overhanging trees and billowing smoke with a horrid orange glow that weaved and danced, casting dizzying shadows that gave the entire scene an otherworldly feel.

Elizabeth plunged after her husband, screaming at him that he would be killed, too. She tackled him from behind and brought him down just as the gas tank of the Subaru ignited. The second ball of flame erupted, filling the night, roaring over them like the blazing breath of a blast furnace. Shielded by Doug's body and pressed into the snow, Elizabeth was safe, but Doug screamed in agony as the roaring jets of flame ripped the skin from the side of his face.

Over and over, until Elizabeth thought he wouldn't be able to stop, Doug thrashed in agony on the ground, kicking clots of snow into the air. Seared flesh hung in raw strips from the left side of his face. The eyelid from his left eye was gone, and he looked at her with a horrifying, bulging-eyed stare, all the while shrieking, "I could have saved her! . . . You killed her! . . . You killed her!"

4.

"Could I have killed her?" Elizabeth asked her mother.

Looking over at the clock on the wall, she saw that it was already past three in the morning. Feeling completely drained, both emotionally and physically, she wished she had a bit of Aunt Junia's brandy on hand to help brace herself.

Rebecca's eyes glistened with tears after listening to her daughter's story. In the silence following Elizabeth's question—

"Could I have killed her?"

—Rebecca got up from her chair and went over to her daughter. Kneeling beside her, she hugged her tightly and willed with all of her strength that her daughter could find some relief, some small respite from her guilt and grief.

"I—I never realized . . . what happened," she said, licking her lips for moisture. "I . . ."

"So does that mean I *did* kill Caroline?" Elizabeth asked in a tortured wail. "That I wanted her to die, so I stopped Doug from saving her?"

Stunned into silence, Rebecca simply shook her head as she held Elizabeth close, feeling the sobs that racked her body.

"No, of course it doesn't, honey." she murmured. "But I'll tell you one thing—if that's how Doug felt, then I can't say I'm very surprised that you left him." She choked up as she gently raked her fingers through Elizabeth's hair.

Elizabeth opened her mouth to say more, but nothing came out.

"I mean," Rebecca went on, "how—how *could* he? How could Doug make you live with such guilt?" She shook her head in total confusion. "A man who says he loves you and who then can . . . can—"

"I *did* stop him from going down there," Elizabeth said, her voice no more than a squeak. "He was trying to save her, and I *stopped* him."

"But doesn't he realize he would have died if you hadn't?" Rebecca asked. She sat back on her heels and clenched her fists in frustration. Hot tears were coursing down her own as well as her daughter's face. "Even from where he was, the heat destroyed the side of his face. All those months of painful plastic surgery he had to have! And even after all of that, he still thinks he could have gotten Caroline out in time?"

Elizabeth snorted and ran the back of her hand under her nose. "He told me—told me afterward that he would just as soon have died with her that night," she said. Her voice hitched painfully, but she forced herself to go on. "He says Caroline was—was his only reason for living, and that without her . . ." Her gaze clouded as it drifted past her mother and out the kitchen window at the dusky night sky.

"And what—?" Rebecca snarled. "Does he think *you* never felt any pain, and grief? Does he think *he* was the only one who loved Caroline? That he was the only one who truly suffered when she died? *Christ!* When I think that I was *ever* nice to that man! That I talked to him just last night and tried to reassure him!" She pounded her legs with her fists.

"Why? What did you say to him?" Elizabeth asked.

Rebecca stood up slowly and went back to her chair. Shoulders slouched, she hung her head dejectedly.

"He never called the house," Rebecca said sullenly. "I called him, both the night you came home," she said, "and again last night. I just wanted to . . . to tell him how I thought you needed help, that he should call you or come here and try to patch things up between the two of you." She sighed heavily, like a wheezing bellows. "God*damn* him to *Hell*!"

"He has his own pain to deal with," Elizabeth said mildly. "And maybe—you know, the scars on his face and all are still a pretty vivid reminder of what he suffered that night."

Elizabeth knew she shouldn't be defending Doug. Over the past year and a half, she had lost or let slip away whatever love she had once felt for him; but she also didn't want to listen to her mother curse out the man she had once loved, the man who had been the father of her daughter. "He's had a pretty rough time of it, too, in the hospital after the accident and all."

Rebecca nodded in agreement, but she didn't unclench her fists, which were turning white at the knuckles.

"I know it's hard to see it that way," Elizabeth said, "but I think what he's blaming me for isn't just what happened to"—her voice almost broke, but she forged ahead— "to Caroline. I think he blames me for what happened to him, too. I don't think you realize how horrible it was, you know? There were burns over fifty percent of his face."

"I realize that!" Rebecca said. "In case you don't remember, your father and I came out to visit him nearly every day he was in the hospital. But doesn't he realize that if it hadn't been for you, he'd have died that night, too?"

"I'm sure he does," Elizabeth said, as she rubbed her eyes and shook her head. "I'm sure he does."

"But it doesn't stop him from blaming you for everything, does it?"

Elizabeth merely continued shaking her head.

Rebecca leaned back and took a deep, noisy breath. Running her hands through her hair, she let the breath out in a long, shuddering sigh.

"It's really late," she said. "You should be off to bed. You should get a few more hours of sleep anyway. You want to be fresh for your new job tomorrow."

"Oh, God—that's right," Elizabeth said with a start. "I have to be at Hardy's by seven-thirty."

"Your father'll be getting up in another hour, anyway," Rebecca said, glancing at the clock. "I might just as well stay up. I can take a nap later in the day."

Elizabeth stood up, but before she left the kitchen, she went over to her mother and gave her a long, tight hug. Tears were streaming down her face, and she could tell by the shaking of her mother's shoulders that she was crying, too. Somehow, distantly and dimly, that made her feel better . . . not much better, but better. At least for now, all she could do was be grateful that her mother had been there for her and try like hell not to think how badly she had let down Caroline!

"G'night, Mom," she said, kissing her lightly on the cheek. "And thanks . . . a lot."

"You know what I think the real miracle is in all of this," Rebecca said, smiling kindly as she held Elizabeth at arm's length and looked intently into her eyes. "I think it's simply amazing how well you've held yourself together through all of this. I know . . . I know it must have been absolutely horrible for you, but you've hung in there. You've been strong. I think you're a miracle."

A deep stirring of guilt twisted in Elizabeth's gut as she turned to leave the kitchen. As she mounted the stairs to her bedroom, all she could think was, *Maybe . . . hopefully you'll never have to learn the truth about the rest of it!*

5.

After an early-morning shower, which helped some but, she feared, not enough, Elizabeth left for her first day at Hardy's. Surprisingly, she was only five minutes late, and, as much as she wasn't looking forward to a day of selling monkey wrenches and screwdrivers, she found that Jake Hardy wasted no time making her feel welcome and comfortable at the register.

Once she got into the swing of the work, things weren't half as bad as she had thought they might be. She had always found Jake Hardy to be a cheerful man, and he had her laughing out loud much of the time as he explained the basic operations of the cash register. Between the few sales they had that morning, he kept up a good-humored, rambling discussion of things that had gone on in town over the past few years.

In the many quieter moments, when Jake left her alone at the register, she couldn't stop wondering how it *could* have been a dream when she woke up to find herself sitting on the bedroom floor with the Ouija board in her lap. She tried, instead, to focus on the more positive aspects, like the closeness and honesty she had felt between her and her mother.

By one o'clock, when Frank Sheldon, one of the high school kids who worked afternoons, came in, Elizabeth thought the job at Hardy's would prove to be well above the "tolerable" level. Then Frank Melrose dropped by during her lunch break and cast a cloud over the rest of her day.

Elizabeth's mother had packed her a lunch, and she was sitting in the back room, surrounded by cases of hardware and plumbing supplies, when she heard a light knock on the door. Before she could turn to tell the person to come in, Frank Melrose poked his head around the corner of the open door.

"Hi," he said, smiling widely. "Just thought I'd stop by and see how it's going."

Caught with a mouthful of tuna-fish sandwich, Elizabeth could do nothing more than nod and hurriedly swallow. She took a sip of milk when the food caught in her throat, making her cough, then swiped at her mouth with her napkin.

"Good . . . good," she said as soon as the coughing stopped.

"Great," Frank said. "I was just on my way to work." He eased the door open a bit more and tentatively entered the back room. "Mind if I come in?"

With so little sleep the night before and the memory of the messages from the Ouija board still working her nerves, Frank's appearance made her feel suddenly very vulnerable and insecure. Elizabeth's first reaction was to say, Yes I do mind! Yet she surprised herself by nodding and saying, "Sure—have a seat. I don't think Jake will mind."

Frank smiled as he pulled over a folding chair and sat down. There was a long stretch of silence between them as they looked at each other, both of them wondering where to start. Elizabeth thought she might start by thanking him for telling her about the job opening, but she remained silent after deciding she didn't want him thinking she owed him anything.

"I gotta tell you," Frank said at last, "I never thought I'd see the day when you'd be working in a place like this." He snickered and shook his head. "You always had such big plans."

He was embarrassed by his lame attempt to begin a conversation. The truth was, he had stopped by the store because he had to see Elizabeth again. Since talking with her at her aunts' house yesterday and finding out that she was planning on divorcing her husband, he had begun—as foolish as he knew it was—to think they might possibly pick up their romance where they had left off almost twenty years ago.

Elizabeth knew Frank well enough to see through his rather obvious attempt. No matter what she thought might happen between them later, once she was settled, she didn't want to say or do anything now to encourage him. Besides, the things that had split them apart were also still too clear in her mind.

"I guess a lot of things happen that we don't expect," Elizabeth said for want of a better response, then adding, "I mean, I was fairly certain that, once I was off to college, I'd get a phone call or a letter saying you'd been killed in Vietnam."

Frank scowled slightly. "But you didn't." He looked at her, trying hard to gauge her reaction, but all he could see was her blank, steady stare as she took another mouthful of sandwich. He leaned his elbow on the work table beside him and idly fingered through the box of loose bolts and nuts.

"You know," he said, once the silence began to get uncomfortable, "when I saw you yesterday, I couldn't help but start thinking about—you know, some of the things we used to do. Do you remember the time we double-dated with Skip Munroe and Gail Fisher, and drove out to Bristol Pond. What was it, sometime in early spring? March or April?"

Elizabeth chuckled in spite of herself. "I sure do," she said. "And the damned fools went skinny dipping! God, the ice was barely off the pond!"

"I thought we were going to lose Skip there for a while, too,"

Frank said. "Remember how he kept complaining how cold his dick was? That he was afraid it was going to drop off?"

Chuckling, Elizabeth shook her head with feigned embarrassment and said, "And his suggestion to Gail how she could help him get it warm again?"

" 'For future generations,' he kept saying," Frank added with deep laughter.

Before long, both of them were laughing out of control. "But you know," he sputtered, still laughing even though his face had gone hard, "it's too bad we can't stay like that all the time. I mean, happy-go-lucky, like we were back in high school."

Elizabeth suddenly stiffened as dark thoughts clouded her mind. Her voice was low with a tone of deep sadness when she said, "Well, life has a way of throwing curve balls at us, that's for sure. It's probably the people who try to stay the way they were who get hurt the most."

Frank saw the sorrow in her eyes; it was the same pain he had seen flitting in her glance yesterday out at her aunts' house. A sudden coldness tightened in his chest.

"And I think we only tend to remember the good times," Elizabeth went on, sounding almost wistful." . . . At least if we're lucky."

"It's tough sometimes, I know," Frank said, "when you start thinking about what could have happened."

Unable to stop herself, Elizabeth asked him directly, "Like how things would have been if I hadn't been so damned pig-headed about not wanting you to join the army?"

Caught by surprise, Frank was momentarily flustered, but then he slowly nodded and said, "Yeah—I think about that sometimes."

Hating herself for it, Elizabeth replied, "So do I . . . sometimes."

Frank shifted in his chair and made a move to come over her. He was filled with a desire, almost a need, to hold her, hug her, kiss her, tell her that even after all these years he still loved her . . . but he just couldn't do it. Too much had happened between then and now, and no matter what he felt, he couldn't expect her to still feel anything for him. It wouldn't be fair . . . to either of them.

"So does that mean you've forgiven me?" Frank said. "For joining the army and going to 'Nam?"

Elizabeth slouched back in her chair and closed her eyes for a moment. "You don't need my forgiveness," she said softly. "I mean—yeah, sure I was probably pretty irrational about it at the time, but I thought if you really loved me—I mean *really* loved me—you would have respected my feelings about how wrong the war was and not volunteered!"

Frank clapped his hands together. "And I felt just the same—that you should have respected my feelings—and I felt that I had an obligation to my country."

"Even after it was so clear that the war was wrong?" Elizabeth said, feeling the twenty-year-old anger swell up inside her.

Frank nodded and said, "Yeah—even then, if *you* really loved *me*."

Elizabeth burst out with a laugh and said, "And what did either of us know, about love or life or anything back then?" Frank didn't answer her, so she continued. "I mean, both of us, and all the kids we used to hang around with—who the hell did we think we were, acting like the world was our oyster?"

"It was, at the time," Frank replied. "And to tell you the truth, when I saw you yesterday, I didn't like what I saw—"

"And just what the hell is *that* supposed to mean?" Elizabeth snapped.

Frank held up his hands as though defending himself. "I remember you as a happy-go-lucky girl with a pretty good head on her shoulders and, as far as I could see, one hell of a future."

"And now . . . ?"

Frank shifted uneasily in his seat, almost regretting that he had stopped by the store; but he knew he couldn't back off now.

"I see someone who has been cheated—by life, by the world, circumstances, or whatever else you want to blame. I see someone I used to love, someone I still care about, getting the shit end of the stick and, worse than that, I see that person *letting* it happen!"

"Oh, is that so?" Elizabeth snapped. Putting her sandwich down, she glared at Frank. "And just who the hell are you to sit in judgment of me? What gives you the right—" She lowered her voice to an intense growl. "What gives you the right to say what I should or shouldn't do? Is that why you arranged with Jake for me to get this job? So I can start rebuilding my life the way *you* think it should be?"

"I never 'arranged' for you to get this job," Frank said. "And I just thought that—"

"You just thought that maybe if you got me a job I might feel —what—obliged to you? Is *that* what you were thinking?"

Flushing with anger, Elizabeth had to restrain herself from slapping him across the face.

"You don't know *shit!*" she said, her voice crackling with pain and rage as tears sprang from her eyes. "And you don't have *any* Goddamned right to sit here telling me how I should be living my life."

"That's not what I'm trying to do," Frank said, forcing calmness into his voice. "Look, I just stopped by for a friendly visit, okay? I didn't mean for us to get all worked up." He kicked back on his chair and stood up, preparing to leave, but he didn't really want to until Elizabeth had calmed down enough to see that he truly had meant no harm.

"Oh, yeah—yeah, sure!" Elizabeth said. Her voice was trembling, and her face had gone pale. "That's all I seem to hear from everyone—from Doug, from my parents, from you, and no doubt I'll be hearing it from Roland Graydon and everyone else I meet here in town. I've got to get back to being the lighthearted, lovable girl I used to be! Maybe I should grow pigtails again, and tell everyone to start calling me Betsy!" She snorted and stared at Frank, her eyes glistening with tears. "But that just isn't the way it's going to be! I've seen too much of what life can do to bring you down, to trample anything good right into the mud!"

"Elizabeth," Frank said, feeling helpless and fighting the impulse to embrace her. "Please . . . understand, I just want to be—"

"Look, Frank!" Elizabeth snapped as she slapped the table with the flat of her hand. It echoed like a gunshot. "I've already taken longer for lunch than I was supposed to, so why don't you just leave and let me get back to work, okay?"

"Sure," Frank said, as he backed up, feeling behind him for the door. "I'm sorry if I—"

"Forget it, all right?" Elizabeth said. She tore off a paper towel from the dispenser beside the sink and used it to wipe her eyes.

"Sure—okay. No sweat," Frank said. "Catch yah later."

He turned and, without another word, left the supply room, the door whooshing shut behind him. He felt like a fool, twisting with guilt and shame for having blown it so badly with Elizabeth. If—

Big "if," he told himself . . .

—he had entertained thoughts of rekindling their romance, he knew he had pretty much put an end to that.

It wasn't until later that afternoon that something else struck him, and once it was in his mind, he couldn't shake it. All through their shift he never mentioned it to Norton, but he couldn't stop thinking about it, and as tired as he was by the end of his shift, he was determined not to sleep until he found out one thing—who that man was that Elizabeth had mentioned.

What was his name? . . . Roland Graydon? Frank had never heard of him around town, but he sure as hell was going to find out!

SIX
The Old Crone

1.

"Are you feeling comfortable?"

"Sure, why shouldn't I?" Elizabeth replied. She let her gaze shift from the sky outside the office window to the man sitting directly across from her. "I mean . . . no—not really."

She had come to Graydon's office directly from work, but the rush to get there on time wasn't bothering her half as much as the anger left over from her lunchtime talk with Frank. She was still seething with hostility toward him, and it bothered her that she let *anything* he said get to her so much. It wasn't as though he had any control over her, or that she still loved him or anything.

Graydon leaned over the coffee table that separated them and patted her gently on her shoulder.

"I think it's safe to assume that's to be expected," he said, "but if at any time you start feeling *really* uncomfortable, just shift gears. Of course, you must realize that discomfort is often an indication that you're getting close to what's truly bothering you."

Elizabeth nodded agreement but said, "Dr. Gavreau used to tell me that, and that I wasn't going to work things through until I brought all of my pain up to the surface."

Graydon sniffed. "That may be," he said. "That may very well be, but at least for the first few sessions, I simply want you to talk about whatever you feel like talking about. I understand you were doing some dream work with Dr. Gavreau. Perhaps you'd like to tell me something about any dreams you've had recently.''

Elizabeth's discomfort spiked as she leaned back, closed her eyes, and tried like hell to clear her mind. The image of the purple-edged letters of the Ouija board sprang into sharp relief. She recalled the harsh rasping sound the pointer made as it scraped across the board. In spite of the warm office and comfortable chair, goose bumps rose on her arms when she recalled the spelled-out messages—

"You should help her . . ."

"She's been trying to get in touch with you . . ."

And the last, most frightening message, when she had asked who was trying to communicate with her:

"Caroline . . . Help . . . Mommy . . . Help!"

Elizabeth's hands were tingling, and, for an unnerving instant, she had the sensation that her fingers were still gently resting on the Ouija pointer, being dragged against her will by pale, skeletal hands as the pointer spelled out a new message . . .

What's the message this time? she wondered.

"Well . . ." she said, after taking a long, sucking breath. "Just recently I've been having this recurring dream about a room in a house . . ."

She opened her eyes and stared up at the ceiling, allowing her vision to go unfocused as she tried to reconstruct the imaginary room, only dimly aware of Graydon sitting across from her as she searched for the words to describe the dream.

"Do you recognize the room?" Graydon asked.

Elizabeth shook her head. "No—not really. I mean, it seems kind of familiar, but when I wake up, I couldn't say it was exactly this or that particular room."

"But you do have a sense that this room is . . . familiar," Graydon said.

"I think so," Elizabeth replied, "but what's unusual about the room is—" She wondered in a frantic rush of fear if she could *really* trust him.

"Yes-s-s?" he said, regarding her with a steady, reassuring expression.

"What's strange is how many doors there are leading into the same room. It's like, no matter where I go in this house, I keep coming back to that room. As if I can't ever escape from it.''

"Do you ever go into the room?" Graydon asked mildly.

Elizabeth nodded, even as she winced with the memory. "It's as if I can't avoid it . . . like I'm trying to get out of the house, but I always find myself back in that room."

"Always the same room?"

"Always!"

"Are there any furnishings in the room? Or people?" Graydon asked, shifting in his chair, and something—either the chair itself or a piece of paper in his pocket—made a faint crinkling sound. The noise reminded Elizabeth of the sizzle of a flame.

"There's an old woman—a . . . a witch, sort of, in there," Elizabeth said. As soon as the words were out of her mouth, she realized that the sound Graydon had made reminded her of something else—the crinkling sound the old woman's shopping bag made as she opened the top.

"Come over here, Elizabeth. See what I've brought you . . . See what I've got for you."

The words rang in Elizabeth's memory as clearly as if the woman were standing right there, unseen, behind her. She twisted her head slightly to see if, indeed, she and Graydon were alone.

"And do you recognize this *witch*?" Graydon asked.

"Well—she's not really a witch," Elizabeth said. "I mean, she's not dressed in black with a wart on her nose and all. I guess she's what you'd have to call an old crone, you know? Like someone out of an old-fashioned story or play . . . maybe something from a Dickens novel."

"Do you recognize her?"

Elizabeth bit down hard on her lower lip as she shook her head. Through the haze of memory, she could almost see the old woman as a distortion of her mother, or maybe Aunt Junia, or Aunt Elspeth; possibly a combination of the three. It might also be her projection of what she herself might look like as an old woman.

"No," she said, shaking her head stiffly, "but the last time I dreamed about her, she was trying to show me something she had in her shopping bag."

"And did you look inside?" Graydon asked pointedly.

"I didn't dare to," Elizabeth replied tightly, her voice getting increasingly high-pitched. She tried to fight down the dark surge of fear.

"Why not?" Graydon asked, pushing her. "What did you think you might see in there?"

Elizabeth shrugged.

"What are you afraid of seeing?"

"What's in the bag, I suppose," Elizabeth snapped.

"What do you think she might have in that bag?" Graydon asked. He was obviously not going to let her off the hook too easily.

Elizabeth exhaled noisily and said, "I . . . I'm not sure, but I know—even in the dream—that I don't want to see it."

"Okay, enough on that," Graydon said, sensing her extreme discomfort. "I want to do a little bit of association. Okay? I'm going to ask you a question, and I want you to say the very first word that pops into your head. The *very* first word you think of. And don't get flustered; if you draw a blank, we can just forge on ahead."

"Fine," Elizabeth said, nodding as she clasped her hands tightly in her lap.

Graydon cleared his throat and said, "When you're in that room, tell me; how do you feel?"

"Trapped!" The word sprang from Elizabeth's mouth even before she consciously formed it. After she said it, she felt flustered and tried to stammer out something else, but Graydon smiled, apparently satisfied.

"I suspect," he said, "that you already realize what this dream is trying to tell you. But *you* tell *me*—what is your subconscious mind trying to communicate to you by this dream?"

Elizabeth stirred uncomfortably in her chair. She wanted to remind Graydon that he had promised her she could shift gears if she began to feel uncomfortable, but she knew—Lord, God in Heaven! Did she ever know!—he had just said that to relax her initially.

After a long pause, Elizabeth said, "Well—I think in some ways, the room probably represents myself, and that I'm—Doctor Gavreau used to use the term 'blocking' for not letting the conscious mind accept something that, at least subconsciously, you already know."

Graydon nodded and, for the first time during the session, picked up his tea and sipped it. Elizabeth could tell by the face he made that it had gone cold.

"And . . . ?" he said, gently placing the cup down.

Elizabeth shrugged and glanced at her clasped hands. "I figure it probably has something to do with . . . Caroline . . . with her death," she said.

Again, Graydon nodded understandingly. "That's entirely possible. Either that or, perhaps, something you've been thinking and feeling since then."

"Like *guilt*, maybe?" Elizabeth said, surprising herself with the sudden intensity in her voice. "Because I couldn't—because I *didn't* save Caroline? Because I feel as though I let her down by allowing her to die?"

"That, too, would be entirely possible . . . and normal," Graydon said, in low, measured tones.

Elizabeth looked up at him and found him staring intensely at her. For just a flickering instant, before his expression softened, she experienced another wave of discomfort and distrust. She had the distinct impression he had been . . .

What had it looked like? she wondered, fighting back waves of rising panic. It was almost as if he had been *leering* at her, *gloating* over her discomfort, actually *enjoying* her misery! *Great way to start out our first session*, she thought, with a biting twinge of guilt. *Getting paranoid about my doctor!*

Graydon cleared his throat before saying, "My impression, Elizabeth, is that in some ways—in many ways—you've been very open and honest about how you feel about what happened to Caroline; but there are still some things that you have buried deeply inside your mind. Your recurring dream indicates that. Whenever anyone has a recurring dream, what a friend of mine calls 'psychic indigestion,' it indicates there are still some things you haven't been totally honest about."

Oh, great! Elizabeth thought. *First my mother, then Frank, and now him—all pushing me to be so Goddamned* honest *about what I feel! Can't they tell? I'm feeling lost, alone, and scared!*

It was only with great effort that she didn't get up, tell Graydon to fuck off and die, and storm out of his office. She'd had these feelings many times before with Doctor Gavreau, and she knew what they signaled.

"I think it's—" She halted, as if strong, unseen hands had suddenly wrapped around her throat.

"—fairly obvious," Graydon finished for her.

She looked at him with fear-widened eyes but could make no sound other than a gasp.

"I suspect what you're 'blocking' is not what happened that night," Graydon said. "You seem to have the sequence of events fairly clear in your mind. If anything, perhaps *too* clear. I think what you haven't dealt with is how you handled Caroline's death. What you did afterward."

"I did what any parent who loves a child who dies would do," she said. Her voice rasped like . . .

. . . Like the felt-padded legs of the Ouija pointer, scuffing over the board.

"I was devastated! It ruined my life, my marriage, my hope for the future . . . even what little faith I had in God. It ruined *everything*!"

"Were you hospitalized after the accident?" Graydon asked. His voice was still even and measured, and that only increased Elizabeth's feeling of hostility.

"Do you mean was I thrown into the looney bin?" she shouted.

Graydon calmly shook his head and said, "No—I mean were you hospitalized as a result of your own injuries . . . the night of the accident?"

"Only overnight," Elizabeth said. She took a deep breath and let it out slowly. "My husband—I might have told you—was seriously burned when the car and truck exploded. He was trying to get down to the wreck because he—we—could see Caroline in the backseat, trying to get out of the car."

Graydon nodded as he listened.

"More than half of his face had third degree burns," Elizabeth continued. "Even after plastic surgery . . . well, he isn't back to normal yet. The damage was extensive—a lot of nerves were destroyed."

"So he doesn't look—" Graydon said.

"Normal," Elizabeth said, interrupting him. "No, he doesn't. The left side of his face is all twisted scar tissue." She shivered.

Graydon stroked his chin and nodded thoughtfully. "And do you feel responsible in any way for what happened to him?"

Elizabeth cringed back into her chair as a cold rush swept through her. An uncomfortable silence filled the room. She knew she had to say something.

"Is what happened to—your husband's name is Doug?"

Elizabeth nodded silently.

"Are you still blaming yourself for what happened to Doug, as well?"

Closing her eyes momentarily and shaking her head tightly, Elizabeth said in a raw whisper, "No." When she opened her eyes and looked at Graydon, her vision was blurred with tears.

She wanted to say more. She wanted to tell Graydon that, if it hadn't been for her, Doug would have died along with Caroline that night. Doug had run toward the wreck; all she had done was stop him. She also wanted to tell Graydon that she had suffered enough, and that she didn't like him pulling everything—every dark and twisted secret—out of her. She was tired of dredging up her grief and guilt like this, but words failed her, and she looked down at her hands, folded tightly in her lap.

Running her fingers through her hair, Elizabeth closed her eyes and took several deep breaths. The pain and suffering Doug had gone through because of the burns on his face were nothing compared to the mental torment she experienced as she sat by his bedside in the hospital day after day, silently grieving over Caroline as she waited to see if his skin grafts would take. She remembered too vividly the thick pads of bandages on Doug's face—how, when the nurse came to change them, they pulled away, soaked through with sticky, yellowish fluid. She remembered how even the slightest facial movement sent random nervous impulses racing through Doug's whole face, more often than not making what might have begun as a smile turn into a ghoulish grimace of agony.

Those months of pain and waiting were still clear and sharp in her mind. But worse than all of that were the things Doug had said to her once the bandages were removed and his face had healed well enough so that he could speak clearly. Each word had been like a razor, stinging as it sliced her, as he poured out his bitterness and hatred.

"I went through . . . a lot," Elizabeth said at last to Graydon. She wanted to push those painful memories aside, but more and more, she came to realize that they would always be there—that they had become a necessary part of her.

"I was on some pretty heavy-duty medication by then. Antidepressants. That's when I started seeing Doctor Gavreau," she said.

Her hands tightened in her lap until the knuckles were bloodless; then she slowly unfolded her hands, rolled her sleeves up to her elbows, and held her arms out over the table, exposing her wrists.

"That's when I did . . . this," she said. Her voice was shaking badly, and she couldn't stop herself from trembling.

Graydon's face was unmoved as he looked at the thick, white lines of scar tissue crisscrossing the insides of both of Elizabeth's wrists. His breath caught for just a second, but his expression never wavered. Certainly, she thought, he's had to deal with suicide attempts before today! When he cleared his throat and spoke, his voice sounded steady and calm.

"I think it's . . . terrible when grief can be so . . . so deep as to drive a person to such an extreme act," he said, looking Elizabeth straight in the eye with an intensity that was so strong she couldn't help but wonder what *his* private pain was.

"I was . . . a wreck," she stammered. "I felt as though I had lost everything of meaning in my life, and I—" Her voice faltered, but she went on. "I just didn't want to live any more. But do you want to know the craziest thing about it all?"

She looked at Graydon, feeling an almost overwhelming desire to burst out laughing.

"Up until the time I cut my wrists, everything I had felt and done had seemed . . . seemed like the normal thing to do, if you know what I mean."

Graydon's silence encouraged her to continue.

"I mean, the grief and crying without stopping, and the depression. Everyone told me that it was normal—to be expected—and that, with time, I'd get over it. But do you know, after I cut my wrists and I was sitting on the kitchen floor in our house . . ." Her voice trailed away, and her eyes dimmed with the memory. "The afternoon sun was streaming into the kitchen, making big yellow squares on the linoleum. And I was just sitting there with blood pumping out, all over my legs, soaking into my jeans, just waiting to feel weaker and weaker until I dimmed out, when I was suddenly filled—I mean my whole being was *overflowing*—with this feeling that Caroline was right there in the kitchen with me, and that she wanted me to live! A friend of mine happened to stop by just then and found me, and he—I mean, she—got me to the hospital fast enough. But *that's* when I knew I was crazy! I felt so positive my dead daughter was still there beside me, taking care of me!"

Elizabeth heard Graydon mutter something under his breath, but couldn't tell what; it sounded something like, "Perhaps she is," but he didn't repeat himself, and she didn't ask him to. Leaning back in his chair, Graydon took a deep breath and smiled sympathetically at her. Elizabeth thought his complexion had turned a shade or two lighter, and, unlike his smiles earlier in the session, this one seemed more forced, more controlled. Whatever he was thinking or feeling, he never betrayed it in his voice.

Glancing at his wristwatch, he said, "I see we're just about out of time, but I think we've made quite a bit of progress for one day." He sighed and shook his head. "You certainly know how to end a session on a powerful note."

Elizabeth shrugged, wanting to say more but not knowing what. She carefully rolled her sleeves back down to her wrists.

Picking up his now ice-cold tea, Graydon stood up and walked over to the sink, where he dumped it. After rinsing the cup and placing it upside down in the drainer, he went over to his desk and glanced at the calendar.

"If it's convenient for you, this time next week would be fine for our next session," Graydon said without looking up.

"Sure," Elizabeth said, her voice strained. She wondered how shaken up he was by the revelation that she had attempted suicide. "This time next week it is."

Graydon penciled in the time and then, coming around the desk, took her jacket from the coatrack by the door and helped her on with it.

"I'll see you then," Graydon said, as he opened the office door and nodded his farewell.

Elizabeth started down the flight of stairs to the driveway. Once she was at the car, she hesitated for a moment before getting in and driving off. She couldn't rid herself of the feeling that the session had ended too abruptly, that there was still some unfinished business between her and Graydon. It was almost as if he had had something more to say to her—something urgent—but had been shaken by her revelation and had either forgotten or thought better of it. Looking back up at the office door, she fully expected to see Graydon standing on the platform, looking down at her. It surprised her to see the office door shut, and Graydon gone. Feeling suddenly very fragile and alone, she got into the car, started it up, and drove away. But all the way home, she couldn't stop wondering if maybe seeing Dr. Roland Graydon *wasn't* the best thing for her right now . . . maybe Graydon wasn't the therapist for her.

One thing for sure—she certainly had a lot to think about.

2.

Frank was staring straight ahead at the winding stretch of Beech Ridge Road, busily chewing the inside of his cheek as he drove the cruiser back to town. It was almost five in the morning, and they had just finished responding to a resident's complaint of someone racing a car up and down the road, squealing their tires on every turn. The joyriders were gone by the time the two officers had arrived. Frank was so preoccupied that he barely heard his partner's question.

"So what the hell are you interested in this—this Grayson guy for, anyway?" Norton asked. "Did he do something?"

The steering wheel played loosely in Frank's hands as the road unscrolled in front of his headlights. He was tired as hell, and his mind was churning with thoughts . . . and memories.

"Well—? What'd he do?" Norton asked.

"Huh? . . . Who?"

"This Grayson guy you've been askin' about," Norton said. "What the fuck's got you interested in him?"

"What—do you know him?"

Norton shook his head. "Naw—I don't know no fuckin' Grayson."

"His name's Graydon . . . Roland Graydon," Frank said. "He's a psychiatrist in South Portland."

"Whatever," Norton said. "Why're you checking up on him?"

"No special reason," Frank replied, still distracted.

As he slowed and signaled for the left turn onto Fork Road, Norton gave him a light punch on the shoulder. "Just can't keep away from it, huh?"

For an instant, Frank thought his partner had guessed his intention to drive past Elizabeth's family home, but then Norton shook his head and added, "God, I'm never gonna forget that night! How 'bout you?"

Frank realized Norton was talking about the incident in the Oak Grove Cemetery a few nights ago, so he decided not to correct his mistake. As the cruiser approached the Payne house, Frank didn't even slow down, but shifted his gaze up to the house and was surprised to see a light on downstairs, glowing pale yellow in the predawn grayness.

Who would be up at this hour? he wondered.

They drove down Mitchell Hill Road and, for Norton's sake, Frank slowed in front of the Oak Grove Cemetery near the intersection with Brook Road. Norton kept going on about what they had found out there that night, but Frank barely noticed his partner's words. His mind was mulling over what he intended to do before heading home for some well-deserved rest.

Before his shift, he had started running his unofficial check on Roland Graydon. So far, at least, other than the basics—that Graydon was a psychiatrist, unmarried, who lived and practiced in South Portland—he had come up dry. There was no record of him ever being arrested, except for a speeding ticket a little over three years ago. As far as the state was concerned, Graydon was clean as a whistle.

Still, Frank didn't like the feeling he had about all of this. He knew his suspicions about Graydon were probably entirely based on some twisted kind of jealousy he felt simply because, in the heat of his argument with Elizabeth, she had mentioned Graydon's name.

But it was significant, he thought, that of all the names Elizabeth *could* have mentioned, she had chosen Graydon's. Short of asking her directly why this particular name would come to her first, he was just curious to see if he could find any connection that might prove important.

"Yeah," Norton said, "that sure was the weirdest thing *I've* ever run into. And now that Fraser's gone missing, I'd say we can—"

"What?" Frank shouted. He was coming up on the stop sign where the road joined Old County Road. When the cruiser slid to a stop, he turned and faced Norton. "What was that about Fraser?"

"Oh, yeah—that's right," Norton said, snapping his fingers once. "You were off playing with the computer, looking up that Grayson guy during the briefing. I mentioned it to you earlier tonight, but you're so fucking out in the zone, you probably didn't hear me. Yeah—Fraser's wife reported that he never came home yesterday. Something about a phone call he got, and then he took off sometime after supper. From what Betty says, Barney and his wife don't have all that hot a relationship, but whatever—he hasn't shown in twenty-four hours, so I guess they're calling him officially missing."

"Jesus Christ," Frank whispered. "Jesus H. Christ!"

The cruiser idled at the stop sign. Glancing into his rearview mirror, Frank saw the brightening morning light glancing off the cemetery's wrought-iron fence and the rows of shadow-cast tombstones. Everything was bathed in a thin wash of gray light.

"What did Harris have to say about it? Does he think Fraser might have had something to do with what happened out there?" He hitched his thumb over his shoulder in the direction of the cemetery.

Norton snapped his gum in his mouth and shrugged. "Beats the shit outta me," he said. Then, pointing in the direction of downtown, he added, "You gonna head back to the station? Or are we gonna sit here and admire the dawn? I can hear those Dunkin' Donuts callin' my name."

"Yeah—sure," Frank said as he pulled out into the road, driving straight into the rising sun.

He was feeling stunned, almost dazed. Until now, he hadn't even suspected any connection between what had happened in the cemetery and Roland Graydon; but now, just because the two along with Barney Fraser had been mentioned so close together, Frank started wondering if there might not be some connection, however tenuous. If his background check on Graydon turned up *anything* suspicious, or even mildly interesting, he'd be sure to pass it on to the investigating detectives.

3.

Much later that day, Elizabeth drove out to Oak Grove Cemetery. She sat in her car in front of the gate, the engine running as slanting sunlight streamed in through the windshield and warmed her face. It did little to drive away the chills that raced like tiny claws up and down her arms and neck. Glancing at her wristwatch, she saw that she still had almost an hour before she had to be back at Hardy's Hardware to finish her afternoon shift.

OAK GROVE CEMETERY

The black slashes of the letters stood out vividly against the washed-out blue of the sky. Simply mouthing the words made Elizabeth's stomach churn with acid. Her pulse was racing.

Straight ahead, the rutted dirt road rolled up over the hill and disappeared from sight. On both sides of the car, she could see silent row after silent row of tombstones, the names and inscriptions casting long shadows. She was grateful that, at least from where she was parked, she couldn't see all the way up to the crest of the hill where Caroline's gravestone stood. She didn't need to see it. The name and dates etched in the pink marble were neon-bright in her memory.

Why had she even bothered to come out here? she wondered. She knew damned well that she didn't have the courage to go up there. Not yet, anyway. Since coming home, she had driven past the cemetery a couple of times every day, but speeding by in a car was one thing; even *considering* going up there to visit the family plot was quite another!

Muttering a mild curse at her mother for even suggesting that she should go by the grave and pay her respects—the third thing Rebecca had told her she had to do—Elizabeth looked up at the sun-washed crest. The thick tombstones cast long shadows over the spring-fresh grass, chilling her as she struggled to resolve the conflict that was raging within her. She knew she should be bold and just drive right up there, get out of the car, and go to Caroline's grave. She should visit her daughter's grave! But she couldn't bring herself to do it!

What am I so afraid of?

What could possibly happen?

Is it just my own guilt and grief that are keeping me from visiting Caroline?

Or is there more? Something my dreams and fears are only hinting at?

She considered driving into town first to buy some flowers to put on the grave. Maybe she should also get some for her recently reburied uncle . . .

Who had committed suicide! she thought, unable to repress a shiver. She realized she was rubbing the scar tissue on the inside of her left wrist with the flat of her hand and quickly stopped it.

If only her mother hadn't mentioned it—this morning, of all times!!—at breakfast, she thought bitterly. She figured she probably could have gone right on pretending that the grave wasn't even up there. As long as she couldn't see it, then it wasn't a real threat! She could have kept telling herself she didn't feel those jolting little twinges every time she drove by the cemetery. Actually, she had started taking the long way around to get home, just to avoid going past this cold, black gate. She knew it was what Doctor Gavreau and Doctor Graydon would call "avoidance," but maybe avoidance wasn't quite as bad if you were aware you were doing it.

"Then again, maybe not," she whispered.

A car came around the curve of Brook Road, heading toward town. The driver slowed down and gawked at her, no doubt having heard about what had happened out here a few nights ago and wondering if she had anything to do with it. Elizabeth turned and smiled as she waved to assure whoever it was that everything was all right. She wasn't a grave robber, casing the place to disinter some more corpses. As she watched the car pull up to the stop sign, she jumped with surprise when, out of the corner of her eye, she saw sudden motion. Something loomed up close beside her by the side window. After the initial flood of panic, she saw that it was her own reflection in the sideview mirror. Heaving a sigh of disgust, she swatted the mirror out of her way.

"So, Elizabeth old girl," she said. "Can you do it? Do you *dare* do it?" She gripped the steering wheel with both hands, took a deep breath, and focused again up the road to the crest of the hill. The palms of her hands began to ache. She could almost imagine that her hands were frozen there, locked in place; she wouldn't be able to let go and get out of the car even if she wanted to. As she stared up the road, her heart gave a cold flip when she saw a car come up over the crest of the hill, heading out of the cemetery toward her.

Oh, shit! Am I blocking the road for a funeral procession or something?

It was just a single car, but the cold fear inside her got worse when she recognized whose car it was!

"Oh, Jesus—Oh, Christ!" she muttered as a blade of bright pain slipped up under her ribs. "Doug . . . you Goddamned bastard!"

Fumbling to shift the car into reverse to get out of his way, she jerked the steering wheel too hard to the right. The car lurched sharply, then spun around, ending up in the shallow gully beside the dirt road. She whimpered softly as she jabbed the shift into drive, jolted the car forward a few feet, then snapped it into reverse again and stepped down hard on the gas. The tires whined loudly and almost caught hold, but she knew when the car suddenly sagged to the right that she had buried the wheels in the soft ground.

While she was doing all of this, she glanced up and saw to her horror that Doug had parked his car, gotten out, and started walking slowly down the slope toward her. He had his hands shoved inside his pants pockets and looked for all the world like a casual, happy-go-lucky guy out for a pleasant springtime walk. Elizabeth wondered if he had recognized her car yet and was enjoying her dilemma.

"Well, well, well," Doug said, smiling as he leaned down into the open car window. The scarred left side of his face twitched and twisted into a pained-looking grimace. His left eye looked oddly bigger than the right one, staring at her unblinkingly from the folds of ruined flesh.

The slanting sunlight cast deep shadows into the sickly brown wrinkles on the left side of his face. A soft wash of shadow made his drooping left eye look dark and penetrating even as his right eye sparkled with merciless glee. Placing both hands on the car door, he pushed against it as if he meant to roll the car over.

"History *does* have a way of repeating itself," he said with a laugh. His breath washed over her like a chilled autumn breeze.

"You're the history teacher," she replied softly. "You'd know better than I do."

Glancing in both directions over his shoulders, Doug said, "I don't see any oncoming snow plows. Do you think I can trust you to steer straight while I push you out?"

"Go to fucking *hell*!" Elizabeth snarled, surprising herself. It took all of her will power not to reach out the window and slap him across the face.

The right side of Doug's smile twisted upward even further, giving him a horrifying look. Then, in an instant, his mouth hardened into a taut line and he said, "I'm *already* in fucking hell, Elizabeth. *You* should know. You put me there!"

"Just leave me the Christ alone, will you? You *bastard*!" she snarled as she tried again to slam the shift into drive. Instead, she got it into park. When she stepped down hard on the gas, the engine whined loudly. Sputtering with anger, she threw the shift back into reverse and hit the gas again, but only succeeded in burying the wheels deeper into the mud.

Doug's laughter cut her deeply, but she stared straight ahead, avoiding his gaze. Tension crackled like summer heat lightning in the air around them. Finally, unable to take it any longer, she turned and looked squarely at him, something she had found difficult to do ever since the accident.

"What the hell are you doing out here, anyway?" she asked, in a heated flush of anger. "I thought you had a job!"

"In case you don't remember," Doug said in an irritatingly slow and measured tone, "I have a daughter who's buried out here. I drove over from Laconia to put some flowers on her grave, if that's all right with you." He leaned in close to her. "And by the way, I didn't notice any fresh flowers from her mother out there!"

"Aren't you supposed to be teaching?" Elizabeth asked him.

Before Doug could answer, a thought struck Elizabeth with numbing intensity: what if he had followed her to Bristol Mills the night she left him? What if he had been in the area the whole time? No, she told herself; that was impossible. Her mother had said she had talked to him twice on the phone since that night. But Laconia wasn't all *that* far away from Bristol Mills. What if Doug *had* been coming out here all along? What if *he* had something to do with what had happened to Uncle Jonathan's grave?

"How—uh—long have you been around town, anyway?" Elizabeth asked, unable to keep her voice from shaking.

"I drove out just this morning, if that's any of your business," Doug said sharply. "What the hell's it to you?"

"Goddamn you!" Elizabeth said. Her rage and frustration were turning into tears, but the last thing she wanted was for him to see her crying. Blinking her eyes rapidly, she looked away and rubbed her eyes with the back of her hand. "Why don't you just leave? There's enough room so you can get around me," she said.

"Elizabeth . . ." Doug said, his voice suddenly soft and soothing. Reaching in through her open window, he placed his hand gently on her shoulder. Elizabeth's first panicked thought was that he would suddenly clamp his hand around her neck and start to squeeze the life out of her. Holding her breath, she waited, but Doug did no more than touch her lightly, caressingly, as he spoke.

"I'm . . . sorry, Elizabeth," he said, his voice going low and gravelly. "I . . . I shouldn't have said that."

There was a long silence that Elizabeth finally broke when she said, "There are a lot of things you and I shouldn't have said to each other. Too much. But it's too late for that now."

Just as much as she didn't want him taking out his anger and frustration on her, she also didn't want even to hint that she desired a reconciliation—no matter *what* her mother or anyone else said! Too many things *had* been said, and there were too many scars that were worse and deeper than the ones that had ruined his once-handsome face or the ones that laced the insides of her wrists. Scars too deep and calloused to heal.

Elizabeth's vision blurred as she looked straight ahead up the slope, past Doug's parked car toward where she knew that block of polished pink marble stood. And then the thought she'd had before hit her again, this time so hard it took her breath away in a sharp gasp.

Maybe he *did* do it! she thought, feeling herself cringe under his touch. Maybe he came out here late that night and dug up her uncle's grave! It had happened the first night she was back in Bristol Mills. Maybe this was his way of terrorizing her, of knocking her off balance, by doing something so horrible so close to Caroline's grave! This was his way of getting even . . . of destroying what few shreds were left of her sanity!

"Impossible," she whispered.

"Huh?" Doug said.

Snapping back to what was happening, Elizabeth shook her head to clear away such a ridiculous thought. Of course it was ridiculous! Doug could never do something like that. An act like that was . . . was crazy, completely insane; and while Doug certainly had been upset, maybe even a bit unbalanced, by Caroline's death, he *certainly* wouldn't do anything as extreme as that just to upset her— if, in fact, the grave robbing had been done to upset her. She had to believe that the incident at the cemetery and her arrival home weren't in the least bit connected.

"Just leave me alone . . . *please*," Elizabeth said, still not daring to look at him directly. "I've got enough problems without you hanging around. I can take care of myself . . . if you'll just leave me the Christ alone!"

Doug quickly withdrew his hand from her shoulder as if he had gotten an electric shock. He started to say something but then remained silent. For emphasis, Elizabeth stepped down hard on the gas and let the car's engine roar.

She sensed him moving away from the side of the car, and she turned to watch, tracking him with a narrowed gaze as he walked slowly up the hill to his parked car. Without a backward glance, he got behind the steering wheel, started the engine, and drove down the hill. Even when he slowed to pull around where Elizabeth's car was mired, he didn't bother to glance at her. From the side, all Elizabeth saw was the ruined half of his face as, eyes straight ahead, he drove past her and out onto Brook Road. He barely paused at the stop sign as he took the left-hand turn toward Route 22.

"And stay away!" she shouted as she hammered both fists onto the dashboard. "Stay the Christ away from me and Bristol Mills! *Do you hear me? Goddamn you to hell!*"

She was crying as she watched her husband's car round the corner onto Old County Road and disappear from view.

4.

Wind whistled through the open windows as snow drifted onto the sills and spilled onto the floor of the darkened bedroom. Elizabeth shivered, but not so much from the cold as from the look the old woman was giving her. It was a look that cut through flesh and blood and peered intently at the core of her soul.

"Are you *sure* you don't want to see what I have in my shopping bag?" the woman asked, leaning close to Elizabeth and freezing her with the cold, hawklike gleam in her eyes. She was smiling, but her expression could just as easily have been that of a hungry wolf.

Behind her, all around her, Elizabeth heard the snaps and creaks of the old house as it stood up against the swirling blizzard outside. She choked on her reply and could do no more than shake her head in desperation.

"Please . . . take a look?" the old crone begged. "I got it *just* for you."

Elizabeth's ears filled with the sound of crinkling paper as the woman raised the shopping bag and held it out to her. The expectant, pleading look in her eyes made Elizabeth's breathing hot and labored.

No! Not crinkling paper! Flames! Fire!

"No, I . . . I can't look! I don't want to look!" Elizabeth pleaded. She tried to look away but felt herself pinned by the woman's icy stare. "I . . . don't want to . . . see."

"How do you *know* you don't want to if you don't know what it is?" the old woman crooned.

For a dizzying instant, Elizabeth felt as though she were gazing into a mirror at a nearly unrecognizable reflection of herself.

"You don't *know* what I have . . . do you?" the woman asked, almost accusingly. Her face shifted subtly and took on the cast of the evil witch in *Snow White*. Her features seemed starkly underlit, as though the lighting were coming from below her. The hissing wind lifted the strands of her hair, making them twine like a knot of serpents.

"It's something . . . *nice*," the old woman purred. "Something special . . . Something you'd just *love* to see again!"

Harsh red light cast thick, ink-black shadows on the woman's face, highlighting her face with blood-red curves. Her cheeks and brow stood out in sharp contrast, wavering in the flickering light. A wicked gleam danced like flames in her rheumy eyes.

"I *don't* want to see it!" Elizabeth shouted. She swung her hands wildly at the large shopping bag the woman was holding up to her, but it was as futile as trying to swat a mosquito in the dark. Somehow, Elizabeth's hands couldn't make contact with the bag, even as she knew the woman was bringing it closer to her. As the old woman began to open the bag, the paper crinkled as loudly as a roaring fire.

Elizabeth thought crazily, *How can she be carrying a fire in a paper bag?*

She suddenly felt someone's hands . . .

Whose hands? she wondered, feeling a cold, dark pull centered in the pit of her stomach. Certainly not the old woman's! She was holding the shopping bag!

But *someone's* hands roughly gripped Elizabeth's head and started to pressure it inexorably forward and down, forcing her to look. Elizabeth tried to shut or avert her eyes, but they felt as though they were stitched open. The light and the heat rising from below her grew steadily stronger as the mouth of the bag gaped wider and, against her will, she looked down . . .

. . . and saw the woman's cracked and wrinkled hands, carefully unfolding the top of the bag . . .

. . . and saw, inside the bag, a pulsating, orange glow that stung her eyes and made them water . . .

. . . and saw the face rising from the core of the flames, floating like a chip of wood on a sea of fire. It was a face Elizabeth recognized immediately!

Oh my God, Caroline!

Her daughter's features were restfully composed, just as Elizabeth had always imagined Caroline *should* have looked, lying in her pink-satin-lined, polished white coffin. But Elizabeth knew that Caroline's face and body weren't at all composed or at peace. She had been fried in the blast-furnace heat as the two vehicles' gas tanks exploded; her entire body crushed and burned beyond recognition.

"See . . . ?" the old woman croaked. "See what I have for *you*?"

Unable to turn away from Caroline's face, Elizabeth saw it loom upward at her out of the raging flower of flames. Heat and light hammered her face, feeling strong enough to melt her own flesh and bones down to ash. And then, as spikes of terror drove through Elizabeth's mind, she saw Caroline's eyes open slowly. Her eyelids fluttered; her lips began to move. Elizabeth knew with heart-squeezing horror that it wasn't just an illusion produced by the madly flickering flames. Caroline's face was struggling, twitching with agony as she twisted her lips, trying to form words, trying to force her burned vocal cords to vibrate. Caroline was trying to reach her! She was trying to tell her something!

". . . *Help . . . Mommy . . .*" Caroline said. Her voice rang with that same crystal-clear sweetness Elizabeth always remembered. Just hearing it wrung her heart between cold, clammy hands.

"*. . . Help . . . Mommy! . . . Help! . . . Mommy! . . .*"

With a roaring intake of breath, Elizabeth yanked herself out of the dream and found herself sitting straight up in bed. Her eyes were wide open, staring fixedly at the glow of moonlight on her windowsill. In her blurred vision, the sills did look snow-covered. Outside, a steady breeze rustled the leaves of the maple tree in the backyard. Holding both hands firmly over her mouth, Elizabeth forced back the scream that was surging like a wild beast inside her, trying to break free.

SEVEN
Night Hunter

1.

The last thing Henry Bishop wanted was trouble because he was hunting out of season; but when that damned raccoon broke into his chicken coop three nights in a row, he figured, "Fuck the law! I'm going after the bastard!" When the ruckus started sometime after midnight, he put on his plaid jacket and his battered Bean boots, grabbed his 4-10 shotgun and his high-powered flashlight, and headed out the door. He considered bringing Murf, his hunting dog, with him but decided against it.

"Stay here, pal," he said, pausing a moment to scratch the dog behind the ears before opening the back door and starting out across the yard. The night air had a sharp chill to it, and he pulled his collar up tightly against his throat. Faint moonlight glimmered on the path from the house to the chicken coop.

The noise from inside the hen house was deafening as the chickens scrambled wildly around. Several ran out into the hen yard and started beating themselves against the chicken wire. A flurry of feathers and down filled the air and drifted against the edges of the cage like snow, gleaming white in the moonlight.

"Goddamned *bass*-turd," Henry muttered as he stormed over to the hen house and flung the door wide open. The air inside was filled with a swirling dust of dried chicken shit, grain, and feathers. Henry choked and sputtered when he entered.

"Come on, you Goddamned sum-bitchin' coon!" he shouted. He scowled as he swung the flashlight beam back and forth. The cone of light was practically solid from the raised dust.

The hens were running and flapping every which way, and in the swirl of activity, Henry didn't at first see the raccoon. Then, over by one of the rounded hen doors, he caught sight of a bushy, bunched up shape. The animal was surprisingly large, but Henry felt a measure of satisfaction when he saw the thick, striped tail. The animal stared unblinkingly up at him, its eyes reflecting back the beam of light with a glittering green glow.

"You've et your last fuckin' bird," Henry growled. He raised the shotgun to his shoulder and braced the flashlight alongside the gun barrel as he sighted down the bead; then, holding his breath, he gently squeezed the trigger. The blast from the gun was deafening as it kicked back hard against Henry's shoulder. If it was possible, the chickens scrambled and flew in an even wilder frenzy. Hazy blue smoke hung heavily in the dusty air, like smoke from a pile of burning leaves. As Henry's vision cleared and he looked to where the raccoon had been, he was surprised not to see the buckshot-mangled body splattered in the corner.

"Well suck my hairy bag," Henry muttered as his eyes darted back and forth, looking for any trace of the raccoon.

The buckshot had blown a gaping hole in the side of the coop. Henry swore to himself when he considered the repair work he would have to do . . . but not before he took care of that mother-fucking raccoon!

"You sum-*bitchin'* coon!" he sputtered as he shouldered open the coop door and barrel-assed back outside. He practically ripped the outside-cage screen door off its hinges when he went into the hen yard. Frantic with fear, chickens beat against his legs and scrambled in the dirt as he waded through them over to the small doorway into the coop. He fully expected to see the wounded animal sprawled on the ground outside the door. It didn't take him long to realize that the bastard must have turned and run the instant before he pulled the trigger.

"You ain't gettin' far, though," Henry snarled. He smiled grimly as he shoved the chickens out of his way and bent down to inspect the ground. A dark red splotch of drying blood glistened on the wooden ramp. He touched it with the tip of his finger and smiled when he felt it was warm and fresh.

Straightening up, he shouldered his shotgun and went back to the house. Flinging open the door, he whistled for Murf, who, excited by the noises coming from the hen house, bounded out the door, almost knocking him over.

"Hold on there, shit-for-brains!" Henry shouted as he grabbed the dog by the collar and yanked hard. "I want yah to get a good whiff of the prick before we head out."

It took Henry a lot of effort to hold Murf back while trying to carry the flashlight and shotgun, but after bringing Murf out to the coop and letting him sniff around the doorway, he turned him loose. In a flash, Murf took off into the night-drenched woods baying like a lunatic. Henry's only problem now was to keep up with him. Cradling the shotgun in the crook of his arm and lighting his way with the flashlight, he followed Murf into the woods.

The dog's wild barking echoed eerily in the night, and Henry couldn't help but wonder if one of his neighbors, having heard the commotion and the shooting, might call the police or game warden. He knew Kendall Payne, who lived on the farm next to his, probably wouldn't; but Murf had taken off in the direction of the housing development going up in the woods on the other side of Henry's property, and he knew damned well those friggin' yuppies wouldn't hesitate to call the cops if they heard gunshots and Murf's barking, especially if it woke up one of their spoiled little yuppie-brats!

"Fuck 'em! Fuck 'em all!" Henry muttered as he ran as fast as he could through the thick woods. Branches, suddenly illuminated by his flashlight beam, leaped out at him like hands from the dark and just as quickly whisked away. Henry's boots pounded heavily on the forest floor, crushing last year's leaves. He realized it was useless to try to track Murf in the dark, but the old dog was keeping up such a racket, Henry figured he'd have no trouble finding him once he treed the wounded raccoon. As long as the bastard doesn't turn and fight, he thought. He knew raccoons weren't quite as nasty as fishers, but once they were cornered, they could give even an experienced dog like Murf a pretty good tussle.

Before long Henry's lungs were burning with exhaustion. Murf's baying didn't sound any closer. If anything, it was further off. Henry started to wonder just how wounded this raccoon was. He knew the woods didn't go on forever. He had already passed behind the new yuppie housing development, so if he kept going in a straight line, he figured he'd come out on Old County Road, maybe up near where it joined Deering Road, out behind Oak Grove Cemetery.

"Dammit all!" Henry muttered over and over. "Dammit all to hell!"

Slowing his pace, he took in huge, burning gulps of air, not even sure whether he was cussing the raccoon and Murf for leading him on such a merry chase, or his own drinking and smoking that made a chase like this such an effort. It hadn't been this tough back when he was, say twenty—or even thirty. Cocking his head to one side he listened and heard Murf, still baying like a hound from Hell as he raced effortlessly through the woods; but then, when Murf's howling suddenly cut off with a sharp, rising yelp, Henry froze in his tracks. A teasing chill raced up his neck as he strained forward and listened.

All around him, the woods were deathly quiet. Deep shadows and weak moonlight shifted under the trees. Henry was a hunting man; he had spent plenty of nights out in the woods, so he would never have said it was *fear* he felt tingling his gut; but something made him feel . . . well, cautious. It wasn't like Murf to stop his barking like that. If he had the raccoon treed, he'd be roaring as he leaped into the air, jaws snapping, trying to get to the animal scrambling up into the higher branches. Christ! Henry thought, they should be able to hear him all the way to the fucking game warden's office!

"Goddamned sum-bitchin' coon!" Henry muttered as he swung his flashlight around in a wide arc. Off to his left, he caught a green glimmer of something. Thinking it might be the wounded raccoon, Henry approached, his gun held level and steady. It turned out to be nothing more than a discarded Heineken bottle. Damned uppity teenagers, sneaking out here and drinking Heineken in the woods. Shit! Budweiser had always been good enough for him and his friends! Kids these days sure thought they had class! Henry picked up the bottle and threw it into the night. He waited until he heard it thump to the ground.

Henry froze where he was, listening, hoping to hear Murf at least snuffing at a hole in the ground or a hollow log where the raccoon had gone to ground, but the silence of the night was like an extra layer to the darkness. Eerie shadows thickened in the underbrush.

Placing his tongue up against his top teeth, Henry let out a short, shrill whistle. It echoed back out of the darkness, sounding much too close.

"Hey boy! Murf!" Henry shouted, when repeated whistles produced no response.

Henry didn't like what he was feeling and thinking; he was suddenly quite sure that something had happened to Murf—something bad! It couldn't have been that wounded raccoon, though; it would take more than a sum-bitchin' raccoon—even a desperate, wounded raccoon—to get the best of Murf. Of course, there was always the chance that a bear or a bobcat had run him down; or that in the dark Murf had fallen into a ravine and hurt himself; or just maybe he really had run off so far that he was truly out of earshot.

Henry whistled again and called the dog's name, even louder. He took a deep breath of relief when he heard a response, a faint chuffing sound. It sure as shit sounded like Murf, but either he was far off or else he had his head stuck inside a hole or log nearby. The sound was heavy and muffled, as though Murf was . . .

"You all right, boy?" Henry shouted. His voice echoed back out of the darkness. The ringing echo indicated he had misjudged his direction and was closer to the cemetery and Brook Road than the Old County Road.

Without warning, Murf started barking, loud and steady nearby. The sudden sound made Henry jump, but after a moment, he got a fix on the direction and, lighting his way with the flashlight, followed the sound. Before long, he found Murf. He was down in a narrow ravine, his face buried in the dirt as he scrambled wildly to dig up something.

"There yah are, you sum-bitch! Good boy! Good boy!" Henry shouted. "Y'got 'em!"

The forest floor was spongy underfoot, and Henry slipped as he started down the slope to where Murf was furiously digging. Leaves and dirt flew high into the air from between Murf's hind legs as he dug, growling deeply in his chest.

Henry scrambled to his feet and approached Murf cautiously from behind. Murf was digging so intensely, he seemed not even to have noticed Henry approaching. The shower of flying dirt and debris made it difficult for Henry to see exactly what Murf was doing, but when he was about ten feet away, he jerked to a stop and trained his flashlight on what the dog had uncovered. His heart stopped for just an instant and then began a rapid-fire pattering.

This was no animal's burrow Murf was ripping into; Henry saw that right away. He also saw, but didn't immediately recognize, the face. Actually, recognition didn't sink in until much later, once he was running toward his house to contact the police. All Henry saw and recognized now was the exposed face, chest, and belly of a dead man. Murf's claws had already torn away the man's clothes. Beneath thick smudges of dirt, the pale skin gleamed an eye-aching bone white. The man's glazed, open-eyed stare cut through Henry like a laser beam.

"Jumped-up Jesus Christ, Murf! Back off! Get the fuck away from that!" Henry shouted. His voice was ragged with mounting fear.

He knew better than to approach the dog. Murf was in such a frenzy, he might just as easily turn on his master and attack him. Unable to think of anything better to do, Henry pointed his shotgun into the air and pulled the trigger. The report startled Murf who, whimpering, immediately backed away from the body and cowered in the brush.

"Com'on! Com'ere, you sum-bitch!" Henry growled. He was trembling inside because of what he had found, but he knew he had to keep his voice firm so Murf would know who was still in charge here.

As Murf grudgingly obeyed, cowering over toward his master, not for a second did the dog take his eyes off the partially exposed body. He kept looking at it for all the world like he wanted to go back to it and savage it some more. Henry wondered if dogs, like tigers, could acquire a taste for human flesh.

"Get your bloody ass over here, boy!" Henry said, his tone low and steely.

When Murf was close enough, Henry grabbed the dog by the collar and yanked hard on it. Aching lungs be damned! he thought as he turned and started running as fast as he could back to his house, hauling Murf along beside him. He had the clarity of mind to let the butt of his shotgun drag on the ground, leaving a nice, clear trail he and the police could follow back to the body; but every step of the way, he expected to see that dead man's glazed eyes suddenly loom out at him from the surrounding darkness.

As the memory of that death-frozen face worked its way into his numbed mind, Henry nearly stumbled and fell when he realized— finally—*who* he had found. He had read about it just that evening in the *Portland Evening Express*. The dead man was none other than Barney Fraser, the Oak Grove Cemetery caretaker who had been reported missing.

2.

"Hey, it's not like I'm in any trouble or anything, right?" Henry said, after greeting the policemen at his front door. Frank and Norton arrived five minutes after his call to the police station, reporting his discovery. "I mean, all I did was find the poor guy, you know? It's not like I killed him!"

"Henry, nobody's saying you killed anyone," Frank said patiently. "Calm yourself down, will you? You look to me like you could use a stiff drink." Frank knew Henry quite well and had always considered him a fairly even-tempered person; right now, though, he seemed completely rattled.

"You want one, too?" Henry asked, his eyes brightening.

Frank and Norton shook their heads. "Can't," Frank replied. "We're on duty."

"Oh, yeah—sure," Henry said. His gaze drifted over to the kitchen cupboard where he kept a bottle of whiskey stashed, but decided not to have anything, either; he didn't want his breath smelling of booze when he talked to Detective Harris. He knew Harris from a few poker nights at the fire barn, and he didn't care for him all that much.

"When d'you think Harris will get here?" Henry asked nervously. His tongue flickered over his upper lip, as if he could taste a trace of whiskey there.

"He'll be right along," Frank said, glancing at his watch.

"Huh," Henry grunted. He looked down at his shoes and shook his head. "Never would've gotten into any o'this if I'd 'a killed that sum-bitchin' coon."

"Just save it till Harris gets here, all right Henry? No sense repeating yourself," Frank said.

"Yeah, but you ain't gonna—I mean, I ain't in any trouble for huntin' out of season, am I? I mean—that sum-bitchin' coon's been after my hens for weeks now, and I don't wanna—"

"Henry," Frank said, with less patience. "Will you calm down, for Christ's sake? I think we've got a bit more to worry about than someone out hunting at night, all right?"

Headlights washed across the front living-room windows as another car pulled into the driveway. Chained out beside the barn, Murf started up a long, loud howling. All three men went out onto the front steps and greeted Detective Harris and Jeremy Keller, the lab technician who was with him. Even before they finished shaking hands, Henry was pouring out his story, completely forgetting his private vow to talk slowly and clearly so he wouldn't get tripped up on any small details he might overlook. He'd seen enough cop shows on TV to know that some little screwup could land *him* in jail on a murder charge.

"Tell you what," Harris said, once he had the gist of the situation. "Why don't you just take us on out there so we can have our own look around?"

"Yeah, but—I ain't in any kind of trouble, am I?" Henry blurted.

"Did you kill Barney Fraser and bury him out there in the woods?" Harris asked.

Henry sputtered and shook his head. "'Course I didn't."

"Then I'd say you haven't got a worry," Harris said. "So let's take ourselves a little walk."

With flashlights glowing, illuminating the trail Henry had scraped with his rifle butt, they headed out to the makeshift burial site. The lab tech was loaded down with equipment, which, along with the dense underbrush, made for slow going. Angry at being left behind, Murf barked all the louder, and they could hear him long after they were out of sight of the house. Henry wondered if Murf wanted to come along so he could finally nail that raccoon, or so he could have another munch on Fraser's decaying corpse.

"Never woulda gotten into all 'a this if I'd a'killed that sum-bitchin' coon," Henry repeated several times as he walked along beside Frank. Harris and the lab tech followed behind them, and Norton trailed last behind everyone else. Night sounds of frogs and birds filled their ears as they made their way through the thick growth of trees and underbrush.

Looking up at the sliver of moon, Frank said, "I'd guess we're going to end up out behind Oak Grove Cemetery, if we keep heading this way." He glanced over his shoulder at Harris but couldn't see his face clearly enough to judge his response. They continued to walk in silence, except for the noise their boots made on the forest floor.

When they crested a small rise, Henry called a halt and, aiming his flashlight beam down the slope, said, "Right over there by that old deadfall." He cringed when he caught a glimpse of the pale flesh and torn clothing. The dead man's face rose up in his memory like a misty ghost. He tried like hell not to think about how Murf had been gnawing so avidly on the body. Shit like this was *bad* if it made a man question his dog's loyalty.

"You can either wait up here and watch," Harris said, "or you can head on back home. I'll stop by later if I have any further questions for you."

For several seconds, Henry didn't move; then he glanced over at a large tree. Hitching his thumb at it, he said, "I'll hang around close by." He walked over to the tree and eased himself down against the gnarly trunk. Harris stayed with him for a few minutes to ask him a couple more questions and jot the answers down in his notebook. This time, Henry considered what he said more carefully. His biggest concern, still, was getting nailed for hunting out of season, but Harris never mentioned it, so he figured it was best if he didn't, either.

Once Harris had gone back down to where the body was, Henry tried to relax as he watched the police set about their work at the scene. They marked the area with POLICE LINE tape, took hundreds of photographs, and poured plaster casts of any footprints and scuff marks they found. After a while, Frank radioed for the State Medical Examiner to come out so they could remove the body to the hospital for an autopsy. At first, Henry was interested in what the men were doing, but before long, he got bored; with that, his attention began to wander.

At first, Henry had hoped that this discovery would make him some kind of town hero—the person who had found the missing cemetery caretaker; but before long, he started seeing how all of this could turn into a ripe, royal pain in the ass. Over the next few days—weeks or months, more likely—he'd probably be bugged to death by *everyone* around town asking him to relate exactly what had happened. The prospect was getting increasingly less pleasant.

Muttering under his breath, Henry began to curse a whole host of things . . .

First off, he cursed that sum-bitchin' coon! Why the fuck hadn't he steadied his aim better and blasted the fucker right there in the coop? Who cared if he'd splattered his whole coop with coon blood and shit? If he'd gotten one clear shot, none of this would be happening.

Next, Henry cursed fucking Murf and his fucking nose! Why the Christ did he have to smell out Fraser's body and then go and dig it up? And the way he had gone after the body! Christ! Fraser was practically torn to ribbons by the dog's claws and teeth! Something like that could make a guy wonder what they put into those cans of dog food!

Finally, and most of all, Henry cursed his own fuckidy-damned bad luck! Why couldn't someone else have found Fraser's body . . . say, next spring sometime? The corpse wasn't even on Henry's land, so if someone else had found it, Henry would have been simply one more curious neighbor, asking for details and gossip about what had happened and when and why!

Of course, as he sat watching the police work, Henry also couldn't help but wonder who the hell *had* killed Barney Fraser and buried him out here; but *that*, at least, he figured, was the least of his problems!

3.

Kendall Payne was sitting at the kitchen table, eating a quick lunch before heading back out to the barn. His hands and elbows were smeared with oil and grease from working on the tractor. As he chewed the sandwich Elizabeth had made for him, he made small, satisfied sounds in the back of his throat.

Elizabeth was at the counter, mixing up a batch of brownies for desert and racking her brain, trying to think of something to start a conversation with her father. Since she had arrived home, she hadn't had a good opportunity to talk with him. He always seemed too busy, too preoccupied with work to take the time to talk with her the way her mother did. Even though they had had their differences over the years, Elizabeth had always felt a deep and abiding love for him; and she had always felt it returned. Now, with her mother away for at least an hour or two, she was hoping they'd get a chance to talk before he went back to work.

"Wasn't that something about Barney Fraser?" she said, just to break the ice.

It was Thursday, her day off, and she was grateful for the break from all the gossip she had heard at Hardy's about Henry Bishop's discovery. Dozens of bizarre explanations were circulating, with stories ranging from darkly whispered rumors of Barney's closet homosexuality and that he had been killed by a male lover who accused him of giving him AIDS, all the way to a Mafia hit connected to something, never specified, to do with his job as cemetery caretaker. When the unsubstantiated story began making the rounds that the autopsy had discovered dead human flesh—not his own—in Barney's mouth and throat, talk about a secret group of black-magic practitioners and Satanists swept through the town like a fire.

"Don't know what to think of it," Kendall said gruffly. He took a long drink of beer and then wiped his mouth with his napkin. "Barney always seemed like a nice enough fella, but who's to say?"

Elizabeth continued, "He might have been the one who dug—who did that to Uncle Jonathan's grave!"

And by moving just one grave over, could have done the same thing to Caroline!

Her father grunted. His eyes narrowed, as if with remembered pain, but he said nothing as he took another bite of sandwich.

Elizabeth hated the way she was stumbling to get the conversation going, and then the last thing she wanted to have happen, did; the phone rang just as she was walking over to the table to sit down with her father. Huffing with frustration, she turned and picked up the phone.

"Hello?" she said, glancing at her father, who was looking at her with raised eyebrows.

"Hi, Elizabeth," the voice on the other end of the line said. It had been years since she had talked to him on the phone, but Elizabeth instantly recognized Frank's voice.

"Oh . . . hi," she said, not caring if she betrayed the disappointment she felt. Her first impulse was to say, *I thought we had nothing else to say to each other after that argument in Hardy's backroom*, and then hang up.

"You're not busy, are you?" Frank asked.

"Not at all," Elizabeth replied, turning her back to her father and cupping the phone close to her mouth in case she lost her patience and told Frank to take a flying fuck at the moon or something.

"Look," Frank said, sounding almost breathless. "I don't want to waste your time or anything, but I was wondering if I—if you would like to go out sometime . . . say tomorrow night?"

Elizabeth started to reply, but all she got out was, "I—"

"Maybe we could go out to dinner or something," Frank said. He sounded hurried. "There are a lot of nice places that've opened up since you've been around. There's a really nice Chinese restaurant, the Panda Garden, out on Forest Avenue. Or maybe we could take in a movie or something."

Elizabeth hesitated, feeling anger welling up inside her. Her first impulse was simply to say *no thanks*. That would have been easiest and cleanest because, bottom line, she had absolutely no interest in even seeing him again, much less picking up where they had left off twenty years ago. After unnerving herself by getting out the old Ouija board, she had vowed *not* to start digging up, much less start living in, the past. No matter what she had for pleasant memories of growing up in Bristol Mills, the more recent past was laced with too much misery and pain. She *prayed* that those wounds would heal up and be gone soon; she certainly didn't need to open up any new ones!

On second thought, *why the hell not?*

No matter what bad things had come between her and Frank, she knew he was a decent sort of person. There probably wouldn't be any harm if they went out on a—well, the word "date" almost made her chuckle aloud; she was too old to be going out on a date! But what was the harm if she went out to dinner or to a movie with him as a friend? If nothing else, she should see him at least once so she could apologize for overreacting that day in Hardy's backroom. She knew damned well that she had unloaded emotions and reactions on him that should have been directed elsewhere . . .

Like maybe right back on myself, where they belong, she thought with a guilty twinge.

"Uh . . . sure," she said, surprised by the tentativeness in her voice. "I think that'd . . . be fun."

She glanced over her shoulder when she sensed that her father was getting up from the table and clearing his place. She wondered if he had overheard her conversation and figured out what it was about.

"How does tomorrow night sound?" Frank asked.

Elizabeth watched her father as he rinsed his plate at the sink and then put it into the dish drainer. Shrugging even though she knew the gesture was wasted, she said, "I get out of work at five o'clock. Why don't you stop by around—oh, say six-thirty? That'll give me a chance to get ready." She turned to face the wall again but could feel her father's gaze boring into her back.

"I'll see you then," Frank said, and hung up before Elizabeth could say anything more. Listening to the steady drone of the dial tone, she cradled the phone and, cringing, turned to face her father.

"'S that who I think it was?" Kendall asked. His brow was furrowed, casting deep shadows over his already grease-streaked face. His mouth was set in a thin, hard line.

"That was Frank . . . Frank Melrose," Elizabeth said simply, forcing herself to sound casual and uncaring.

"From what I heard, it sounded to me like he asked you out for a date," Kendall said.

Biting her lower lip, Elizabeth nodded.

"'N' it sounds like you accepted?" He looked down at the floor for a second, then back at Elizabeth, his scowl deepening.

Elizabeth blushed under the gathering storm of her father's disapproval. But she also felt defensive and almost said aloud, *Hey, wait a minute! What the hell's going on here?*

"Dad," she said, trying to color her voice with a hint of laughter. "I think I'm old enough to decide for myself who I want to go out with. Besides—"

"It ain't that simple," her father said in a low, measured tone. "You're still a married woman. I don't think something like that is—is proper."

Elizabeth flushed with anger. Only with effort could she refrain from shouting at her father—as she *had* as a teenager. He wasn't even trying to see things from *her* point of view! Why in the hell did *everyone* think she needed so damned much advice about what she should and shouldn't do?

"Doug and I are separated, Dad," she said evenly, "and nothing will change my mind. I want a divorce because as far as *I'm* concerned our marriage is over . . . it's *dead!* Can't you understand that?"

In the hollow silence that followed her outburst, a blinding panic filled her as she remembered the night Caroline died . . .

4.

The night was filled with the tortured sounds of twisting metal and ear-shattering explosions . . . a searing jet of orange flame ripped upward, into the storm clouds . . . a shrill voice, sounding feeble and helpless against the razor-sharp blast of the blizzard, cried out . . .

"*. . . Help! . . . Mommy! . . . Help! . . .*"

"You ain't *not* married till you get legally divorced!"

Her father's voice snapped Elizabeth back. She shook her head as though she had been blindsided.

"Till you're divorced, you ain't got no right to be going out on no Goddamned date with Frank Melrose or anyone!"

"Come on, Dad!" Her voice was high and shaky. "For crying out loud. It's just Frank Melrose. He wants to go out for dinner tomorrow night. It's not like I'm going to jump into bed with him!"

She felt a moment of satisfaction when her father's face registered shock.

"No—I never said nothing 'bout jumpin' into the sack," he replied gruffly. "I just said it ain't proper for a married woman to be runnin' around with another man."

"Do you want the truth, Dad?" Elizabeth asked.

"I always 'spected you'd tell me the truth," Kendall said. "'N' I assume you always did." His strong workman's hands clenched the edge of the countertop. Tendons and grease-stained knuckles stood out like mountains on the backs of his hands. Elizabeth wondered how such hands could ever be soft and loving.

Sucking in a hissing breath of air, she pulled out one of the chairs and sat down, slouching. Unclenching her own fists, she folded her hands in her lap. Tears welled up in her eyes.

"Dad—" she said, barely above a whisper. She sniffed loudly. "I haven't been *married* to Doug, not in the real sense, since long before . . . Caroline died. If I was really honest with myself, I'd have to say even before Caroline was born, but definitely after that."

She paused, blinking madly as she looked at her father. Kendall stood there watching her with almost no expression on his face. Finally, he cleared his throat and said, "Havin' children changes lots of things, but it don't necessarily mean—"

"It changed *everything* between me and Doug," Elizabeth said. There was a strain of resignation in her voice. "Look, Dad, I hate to pop any illusions you might have had, but Doug and I had been drifting apart for years—*years*! He had his work and I had mine, at least until Caroline was born. And then I was just stuck home, taking care of this . . . this baby!"

She was surprised that she could talk about Caroline in such a detached way. But something in her father's steadiness gave her the strength to see things just a bit more objectively and not get so lost in her emotions.

"That's natural, for the woman to be home, raisin' the children," her father said. "That's the way it's always been."

"Come on, Dad," Elizabeth said. "Let me ask you, then, what was the sense of spending all that money to send me and Pam to college? Did you think I needed a diploma so I could stay home and raise children? I could do that without a high school diploma, for crying out loud.'' She shook her head as though amazed, but her father's expression never wavered. ''Dad, that kind of thinking may have worked back when you and mom got married, but times have changed. Most families need two full-time incomes just to get by.''

Her father started to reply, but she cut him off with a quick wave of her hand. ''But I don't want to get side-tracked. I'm talking very specifically about *my* marriage—me and Doug—and I'm telling you, straight out, we weren't *married*, not in the true sense, for years!''

'''N' I 'spoze, like everyone else these days, you can just toss aside your marriage vows like that, huh?'' her father said, snapping his fingers.

Elizabeth ran her lower lip under her teeth and bit down hard as a surge of guilt rippled through her. Her eyes misted over, and she found it impossible to look directly at her father. When she spoke, her breath came in short, gulping gasps that punctuated every other word.

''After Caroline . . . was born . . . I think Doug loved her . . . more than he did me.'' Tears carved warm, wet tracks down her cheeks. ''He lost himself—in her.''

''A parent's 'spoze to love his child,'' Kendall said mildly, even though his expression remained as hard as stone.

Elizabeth shook her head vigorously. ''Not the way Doug loved Caroline,'' she said, gaining a measure of control over her voice as her anger at Doug flared up. ''I don't mean sexually or anything, but it was like . . . like he thought she was a part of him. So much of his love went out to her that, after a while, there just wasn't any left over for me.'' Her shoulders shook, and she grabbed a napkin from the dispenser to wipe her eyes.

''Don't you think you're bein' a little hard on him . . . and on yourself?'' her father asked.

Elizabeth blew her nose into the napkin, then crumpled it up and squeezed it into a tight ball. ''No,'' she said. She caught herself just before she mentioned that she was seeing a psychiatrist, just in case her mother hadn't told her father. ''I mean, you know, from talking to people and all, I realize that mothers and daughters can feel . . . like they're in competition for the husband's love. It happens all the time. But by the time I realized Doug was putting so much of himself into Caroline, I—'' Her eyes flickered upward at the ceiling before she finished. "I just didn't care any more."

"So when she died . . ." her father said.

Elizabeth nodded and looked down at her hand clutching the balled-up napkin. "When she died, he blamed me for . . . for everything," she said. Her throat rasped loudly on the last word, but she forced herself to continue. For the first time in her life she said something she had always thought but never dared to express aloud:

"And as much as I loved Caroline and miss her so much it hurts, I'm *glad* she died for this one reason." She choked and sensed her father stiffening at her words. "I'm glad because, after she was dead, Doug and I didn't have a single reason to stay together!"

5.

"You sure as hell seem to have an inordinate amount of interest in this case," Detective Harris said to Frank, who was standing beside him as he drew a cup of coffee from the urn in the police station's conference room.

Frank nodded curtly and said, "I just want to stay current on what's happening. After all, it isn't every day someone gets murdered in town, and . . . well, because I was the one who responded to both calls, out at the cemetery and then when Henry found Fraser's body, I'm just kinda curious."

Harris leaned back against the countertop and took a slurping sip of coffee. The steam curled up like smoke around his face, and Frank wondered how the hell the man could drink coffee that hot. Iron gut, probably; just what it takes to be a detective!

"And what, exactly, makes you think these two incidents are even remotely related?" Harris asked pointedly.

Frank shrugged. "I think it's safe to assume—"

"Uh-uh," Harris said, wagging his forefinger under Frank's nose. "Remember what *assume* makes—an *ass* out of *u* and *me*."

"It doesn't take fucking Sherlock Holmes to see that they're connected," Frank said, his anger rising at Harris's cocky attitude. "There's some wacko around town doing this stuff. I saw the preliminary autopsy report. Fraser had shreds of human flesh—*dead* human flesh—on his teeth and in his throat. You know damned well that anyone who would dig up a corpse and cut off its hand could just as likely use that dead hand to choke someone to death.''

"You know," Harris said, glancing up at the ceiling. "You're making me kinda curious as to why you'd get interested enough in all of this to bother to read the autopsy report. Did you already get your detective's shield?"

"The whole thing has me a little nervous, all right?" Frank snapped, unable to keep the edge out of his voice. "This isn't your everyday, run of the mill 'accidental death.' "

"And what exactly *is* your 'run of the mill' death?" Harris asked laconically.

Frank ignored him as he pushed his point. "I figure Fraser was a suspect in the grave robbing, given that he had access to the cemetery and all. I *assume* you questioned him rather thoroughly."

Harris's cold stare didn't reveal a thing.

"But now, knowing that Fraser was involved with . . . well, you saw it yourself—there were at least two other sets of footprints out there besides Fraser's and Bishop's. That says to me there was some kind of . . . of conspiracy going on."

Harris chuckled before taking another sip of coffee and swallowing noisily. "You're getting to sound downright paranoid, Melrose," he said. "Did you ever consider taking a bit of a vacation? Maybe you should see a shrink about this problem you got."

"Well what would *you* call it if not suspicious?" Frank said, his voice rising to a shout.

"Circumstantial," Harris said, shrugging.

Frank shook with frustration; it was like talking to a brick wall. "Okay—sure, disturbance of a corpse is classified as only a misdemeanor, but now there's murder involved, and I—" he cut himself off.

"You were about to say . . . ?"

"Look," Frank said, loosening his stance and backing a few steps away from Harris. "This whole thing has me worked up because . . . I think it involves a friend of mine."

"You don't mean to say you've been withholding information, do you?" Harris asked sharply.

Frank shook his head. "No . . . no. I don't know who's doing this. I'm talking about Elizabeth Myers. You know—Kendall Payne's daughter. She's just moved back home."

"Yeah, yeah," Harris said with agitation. "You and she used to be cozy. I know all about that. Get to the fucking point."

Frank held his hands up helplessly and let them drop, slapping his thighs with a loud *crack*. "I'm not sure I know what the point is," he said, "but I'm wondering if your investigation has included certain things."

"Such as . . . ?"

"Such as her husband, Douglas Myers," Frank said. "From what I've heard, she left him a couple of weeks ago. It crossed my mind that maybe he, you know, flipped out about that and has been doing this—I don't know, bribing or blackmailing Barney to dig up Elizabeth's uncle's body to . . . to—I dunno, to terrorize Elizabeth and her family, for revenge or whatever."

Harris placed his coffee cup on the counter and silently considered for several seconds what Frank had said; then he snorted, shook his head, and said, "I think what I said earlier still holds. You need a fucking vacation. You're sounding 'looney tunes.'"

"You don't think digging up bodies in the cemetery and killing someone by strangulation with a corpse's hand is fucking 'looney tunes'? Are you telling me you haven't checked out her husband? You haven't run down his background and where he's been for the past week or so?" Frank felt a hot rush of blood to his face and neck.

Harris shook his head and held up his hands as though helpless. "I ain't telling you doodly-squat. And anyway, you seem to be putting things together pretty well on your own. Here—" He reached for his hip pocket, took out his badge case, and attempted to hand his detective shield to Frank. "Go ahead. Take it. You've earned it."

"For Christ's sake, Harris! I'm just concerned, if that's all right with you. Okay? People's feelings are involved here! Elizabeth Myers was—is a good friend of mine, and I don't like feeling as if there's someone out to get her."

"Like maybe the—*boogeyman*?" Harris said. His voice was mocking as he raised his hands like claws and slashed them toward

Frank's face. "Or maybe Frankie Krueger, or whatever the hell his name is?"

"Barney Fraser sure as shit must've met the boogeyman," Frank snapped. His fists doubled up, and he wanted like hell to punch the smirk off Harris's face.

"Look here, Melrose," Harris said as he slipped his badge back into his pocket. "Honestly—I appreciate any leads you can give me with this because, frankly, we haven't met with a whole shitload of success. But the last fucking thing I need is some paranoid bullshit about some . . . some black-magic conspiracy to get this friend of yours who hasn't even been in town more 'n a couple of weeks—all right?"

"I just wanted to tip you off about her husband, Douglas Myers," Frank said. "In case you hadn't gotten anything along that line."

"I appreciate it," Harris said, nodding. He picked up his coffee and, tilting his head back, took a huge swallow that drained the cup. He tossed the empty Styrofoam cup into the trash can, turned, and left the conference room without another word to Frank.

As Frank watched Harris leave, he didn't feel even the slightest bit better about any of this. He knew one thing for damned sure—from now on, when he wasn't on duty, he was going to do a bit of investigating on his own . . . if only to convince himself that Elizabeth was and would remain safe.

EIGHT
First Date

1.

"I didn't know you were interested in such reading material."

Speaking so close behind her, the voice startled Elizabeth, who was kneeling in front of the ASTROLOGY/OCCULT section in the Maine Mall Booksmith. She looked up and was even more surprised to see Dr. Graydon smiling down at her.

"No, I was . . . uh, just checking out a few things," Elizabeth stammered as she stood up and brushed her hands nervously together. "My aunt does astrological readings, and I was just looking to see if there was anything she might like."

"I see . . . I see," Graydon said, nodding. His eyes narrowed as he scanned the aisles of the bookstore. "Are you out shopping by yourself?"

"Actually, no," Elizabeth said. She, too, glanced up and down the aisle. "I was—that is, a friend of mine and I were going to the movies at the Mall Cinema, but the early shows were sold out."

"Oh—what were you going to see?"

Elizabeth smiled weakly. "We hadn't really decided."

"There's one movie, I think it's playing across the street now, called *Firewater Pond*. It was filmed here in Maine. There was quite a bit about it in the papers last summer."

"Oh," Elizabeth said, nodding knowingly, "maybe we'll check

157

it out." She stood up on tiptoe and finally caught a glimpse of Frank, over by the mysteries. She wanted to signal to him, but he was intent on scanning the shelves.

"So," Graydon said, "did you find anything here for your aunt?" He leaned forward and let his eyes wander back and forth over the shelves. "My, my—there *are* some quite interesting titles here. Look at this one—*Mysteries of the Hidden World*. And these—*Conversations with the Dead* and *Practicing the Black Arts*. Indeed!"

Elizabeth couldn't quite read the expression on Graydon's face. Was he genuinely interested, or was he being teasingly skeptical of her interest in such things? She wanted to repeat that she, truly, had been looking for a book for Junia, but decided to let it drop. She felt thankful when, just then, she saw Frank glance up. She signaled him to come over to her.

Graydon saw her expression brighten, and he turned to look where she was looking. His eyes narrowed when he saw Frank walking toward them. "Oh, is this your friend?"

Elizabeth nodded just as Frank joined them.

"Frank Melrose," she said, "I'd like you to meet Roland Graydon."

She wasn't sure, but she thought that, as soon as she said Graydon's name, Frank stiffened.

"Dr. Graydon, this is my . . . friend, Frank Melrose."

"Pleased to meet you, Frank," Graydon said as the two men shook hands.

Frowning, Frank nodded and said, "Same here."

"I was just suggesting to Elizabeth that you go see the movie that was filmed here in Maine last summer," Graydon said smoothly. "It's supposed to be quite funny."

Frank nodded again and smiled widely, but Elizabeth could tell he was putting it all on; she could sense that he had snapped into his "cop mode" and was studying Graydon, although she had no idea why he would be at all suspicious of Graydon.

"Well, I must be going," Graydon said, glancing at his watch. "Nice to see you, Elizabeth." He smiled as he shook her hand. "And nice to meet you, Frank."

"Same here," Frank replied. His voice was low and controlled.

Graydon turned and strode from the bookstore at a brisk pace. Once he was out of sight, Elizabeth let her breath out with a whoosh.

"Friend of yours?" Frank asked.

She could tell just by the way he was looking at her that there was a lot of weight behind his question, but for the life of her couldn't figure out why. Could it be simply that Frank had a spark of jealousy?

"He's a doctor . . . someone I've been seeing," Elizabeth said and, because she didn't want to say any more, let it drop. Frank didn't pursue it any further, but she did notice that he looked down the aisle again, as though expecting to see Graydon lurking there, watching them.

"We probably ought to head over to the theater early to make sure we get tickets," Frank said.

As they started walking toward the exit, Elizabeth couldn't shake the feeling that Graydon *had* ducked around the corner and was hiding somewhere nearby, watching them. Was Frank's reaction just making her paranoid? Or had there been something . . . strange about Graydon, something that unnerved her? Maybe she just felt awkward, surprised at meeting up with her therapist out in public. He seemed so different, outside the confines of his office.

"So what would a doctor be doing in the occult section of a bookstore?" Frank asked. "I thought people like that didn't go in for that wacky kind of thing."

The question startled Elizabeth. They were walking down the hallway toward the exit, and all the while she thought she could feel a harsh, cold stare boring into her back.

"What do you mean?"

"I mean, you were kneeling down in the section," Frank said, "and it makes me wonder if Dr. Graydon was heading down there himself before he noticed you."

"I didn't know you were watching," Elizabeth said. She shook her head and used the motion as an excuse to scan the hallway behind them, unable to shake the feeling she was being watched. "You cops," she said, hissing with frustration. "Don't you ever go off duty?"

"I just notice these things," Frank said with a shrug.

"Dr. Graydon had seen me and just came over to say hi. That's all. Why are you making such a thing out of it?"

Frank didn't answer as he held the door open for her and then followed her out into the warm, spring night. Only when the door whooshed shut behind them did Elizabeth no longer feel as though they were being watched. Walking back to Frank's car, though, she felt a light chill run up her back. Now that she thought about it, it *had* seemed a little strange that Graydon would start pointing out book titles to her. Had he been prodding her, testing her in some way, maybe so he could get some kind of insight into what kind of person she was?

Dammit, no! she thought. There was nothing weird or threatening about Graydon! It had just been coincidental that they had bumped into each other.

As they walked across the parking lot, Elizabeth moved closer to Frank; and when he automatically placed his arm around her shoulders, she had to admit that it felt good . . . very good.

2.

"I probably shouldn't have even brought it up," Frank said. "I didn't mean for you to get upset about it, that's all. Do you want to go someplace for a drink?" he asked.

Elizabeth let her breath out slowly as she looked at the creeping traffic. "I dunno," she said. "I'm not so sure I'm in the mood for it anymore."

"Oh, come on," Frank said. "The night is young and so are we . . . well, sort of."

He jostled her shoulder good-naturedly before rolling down his side window to let the warm spring air swirl into the car. In spite of the heavy exhaust, he inhaled deeply. He was cursing himself for even mentioning the incident out at the cemetery, but the EXHUME ELVIS bumper sticker on the pickup in front of them had prompted a remark that she had taken the wrong way.

Elizabeth looked at him with what she thought was an earnest pleading in her eyes, but right now she wasn't even sure *what* she wanted—

Did she want him to tell her more, tell her everything he knew about what had happened out there, and why Barney Fraser had been killed? Frank hadn't come right out and said so, but there had been something in his voice that had hinted that he knew more than he was letting on.

Or did she want to forget he had even brought up the incident? Like he said, he hadn't wanted to put a damper on the evening which, surprisingly for her, had gone much better than she had expected. Throughout the meal at Panda Garden, their browsing at the bookstore, and all during the movie, she had actually had flashes of the "old Frank." Several times she had to catch herself from thinking that they *were* still sweethearts. So why ruin a fun evening?

"It's just that when you . . . when you put everything in such stark, black-and-white terms," Elizabeth said, unable to hide the quaver in her voice, "it sounds so—so *dangerous*."

"Look, Elizabeth," Frank replied. "I'm not going to bullshit you, all right?" He slapped the steering wheel with the flat of his hand. "You know damned well that the last thing I want to do is get you all worked up about this, okay? On the other hand, I don't want you to be blind to anything. *If*—and that's a big if—there's something going on that you should be aware of, I want you to know about it." He paused a moment and swallowed with difficulty. "I want to be able to protect you from it."

He felt her bristle at that, so he hurriedly added, "I don't mean it like *that*—" He looked at her. The bright lights from the traffic made her skin glow vibrantly. "I just don't want anything to happen to you. I think you've had your share of shit to deal with, all right?"

Elizabeth chuckled softly and, in spite of herself, felt herself warm up to him. She had always known that, underneath his rather rigid exterior, Frank was just a soft-hearted fool. The uniforms had always seemed like a thin shell he adopted to protect himself, his emotions, from the pain of the real world.

"I just can't imagine why . . . anyone would want to do something like that—dig up my uncle's body! . . . Just to get at me?" she said. The quaver had returned to her voice, but Frank didn't seem to notice.

"There are a lot of weirdos in the world, babe," he said.

"I never thought there'd be nuts like *this*, though," Elizabeth said. "Not in a town like Bristol Mills."

"You didn't seem to enjoy the movie very much," Frank said, trying again to shift the conversation.

"Oh, yeah—I did. I thought it was really funny."

"So what's the problem?" he asked pointedly. "Want to grab a beer at Stoover's?"

"I dunno . . . maybe," Elizabeth replied. Her gaze shifted out the side window. All the lights seemed to blend and melt together.

Her mind was filled with worries and concerns. She was positive Frank had answers to some of her questions, but she didn't want— she didn't *dare*—to ask him certain things . . .

—Like what *really* happened out there in the graveyard last week?

—And *who* was involved with Barney Fraser . . . Who would *kill* him and bury him in the woods? And why? To shut him up about what had gone on out there?

—And what, if anything, did the police know and weren't saying? What were they doing about it, especially if she *was* in some kind of danger?

Frank switched the radio on, cutting into the middle of Joni Mitchell singing "Both Sides Now." As soon as he heard it, he smiled and turned the volume up.

"Ahh—remember this?"

Elizabeth grunted and shrugged, her eyes still fixed on the snarled traffic around them.

"Well, something's bugging you," Frank said. They had finally made it to the turn onto Maine Mall Road, but the light was red, and they were still stuck behind EXHUME ELVIS. As soon as the light changed to green, Frank turned right and pulled around the truck.

"No," Elizabeth said, sighing as she shook her head. "Nothing's *bugging* me."

"If it's anything I . . ." Frank said, but he let his voice trail away. His brow was furrowed with concern as he drove through the sets of lights and then slowed for the turn onto Running Hill Road.

Biting her lower lip, Elizabeth took a deep breath and looked out at the deep night, grateful to be leaving the lights of South Portland behind. She was wracking her brain, trying to think of something to say. It seemed as though every time she was with Frank, everything she said had a double meaning. Shivering, she looked out at the night-shadowed woods whipping past her window, and she wondered if she was truly in danger, or if she was letting Frank's paranoia get to her.

"It just feels so . . . so *funny*," she said, chuckling softly, "to be out on a date with you again." She hoped it sounded like that was what she had really been thinking. "I mean, after graduation, I pretty much thought I'd never see you again."

"Funny how life can do stuff like that to you, huh?" Frank said, smiling as the steering wheel played loosely in his hands. The car took the curves of the road with a smooth, fluid ease.

Elizabeth grunted, thinking that Frank, like her, wasn't saying what was really on his mind. They rode for a while in silence, both of them staring ahead at the pools of yellow light from the headlights, illuminating the road. They passed several well-lit houses, and Elizabeth wondered if the same people had lived there when she was growing up.

"So, tell me," she said, as she settled back in the car seat, forcing herself to relax. "How come you never got married?"

Frank's mouth twitched into a thin smile. He didn't take his eyes off the road for a moment as he said, "What makes you think I *never* got married?"

Elizabeth laughed aloud, feeling the tension between them lessen. It was rather funny how she and Frank were always tiptoeing around each other, cautiously probing and questioning, and then dropping the bombshells.

"Do you actually think you could have gotten married without me hearing about it from *someone*? I mean, my mother told me when you were going out with Linda Martin for a while—"

"Yeah," Frank said, with stifled laughter. "—For a while."

"Did you love her?" Elizabeth asked, realizing as she did that it was none of her damned business.

Frank shrugged and quickly glanced at her. His face had a pale cast to it from the dashboard lights. "I suppose I did . . . but I guess not enough to marry her."

"Probably because the love of your life had broken your heart back in high school, right?" Elizabeth said, glancing at him from the corner of her eye.

She laughed loudly, and Frank joined in with her; but when he muttered, "Absolutely," there was a little more conviction in his tone than Elizabeth cared to hear.

Frank slowed for a stop before turning right onto Route 114, heading toward Bristol Mills. As they neared the intersection in the center of town, Elizabeth wanted to ask him if he'd mind stopping by the aunts' house to visit—for old time's sake. Before she could say anything, Frank, without even clicking on his turn signal, turned left onto Beech Ridge Road and then right onto Bristol Pond Road.

"I can't believe you," Elizabeth said, both amused and nervous as the car's shocks rattled and swayed on the bumpy dirt road. Looking out the windshield, she could have sworn she really *was* back twenty years ago. No matter what changes had taken place in the center of town, Bristol Pond Road, at least, was *exactly* as she remembered it.

Frank was smiling wider now, his face glowing in the dashboard lights as he navigated the curves of the road. He slowed down to less than five miles per hour.

Off to their left, Elizabeth caught a glimpse of velvety black water. The sweep of stars overhead cast the land and water of Bristol Pond into inky darkness. Pointed pines stood up against the sky like jagged fangs. As dark and foreboding as the spot looked, though, she had too many pleasant memories of the place to feel really nervous. She wondered if high school kids still came out here to "go parking." There weren't any cars on the slight crest of the hill overlooking the pond—the traditional place for necking—but then again, this was a Tuesday night. Maybe the pond was busier on weekends.

"Just like always, you didn't even ask me if I wanted to come out here," Elizabeth said with mock indignation. "Is that all you can think about—sex, *sex*, SEX?"

"I promise you I won't put it in all the way," Frank replied with a burst of laughter, using one of the lines he had actually thought she would believe back in high school. He leaned toward her, his eyebrows arching upward in a wicked, Jack Nicholson leer.

"One of the Great American Lies," Elizabeth said, shaking with laughter.

"Yeah," Frank replied, "just like 'No new taxes'!"

On pure instinct, Frank drove straight to *their* spot and killed the engine and headlights. The night dropped down on them like a feathery curtain. Elizabeth looked from Frank to the view in front of them. Rolling down her window, she stuck her head outside and inhaled deeply of the resinous air. In the dusky starlight, the surface of the pond looked rippled, like a gray washboard, almost as if the water were frozen.

"How many times on a date did we end up out here?" Elizabeth asked, turning to Frank. She could hardly see him in the darkness and, for a panicky instant, had the scary thought that Frank wasn't beside her at all; it was someone else sitting there in the dark car. Her heartbeat started racing as she stared at him, trying to pierce the darkness to see his face.

"Not enough, if you ask me," Frank said, not realizing the relief that flooded Elizabeth when she heard his voice.

"Let's go down by the water," she said suddenly. Before he could respond, she had popped open the car door. The dome light momentarily stung their eyes. As Elizabeth stepped out into the night, it was like diving into dark, cool water. The night breeze hissed in the tall pines, making the branches creak and snap. There was a lonely, eerie feeling about the place which Elizabeth had always both cherished and feared.

She heard Frank's door open and close, and then the crunch of his shoes on the gravel as he came around the car toward her. She wasn't surprised—or disappointed—when he reached for her out of the darkness. His hands touched her shoulders and then slid down to encircle her waist. She shivered and didn't resist as he pulled her up close from behind. His hands moved down to the swell of her hips. *Just where he always used to put them*, she thought, with a twinge of memory twenty years old.

God! How can it have been that long? she wondered as she twisted around to face him. Without a word, they hugged for a moment. When they broke off, they turned together and walked slowly down the beach toward the water's edge.

The air close by the pond was moist and clean smelling. Elizabeth smiled when she remembered how, when they had brought a blanket down here on the night of the Senior Prom, they had been so fearful that some other couple might arrive and discover them. That night they had made love—gone all the way—for the first time. It had hurt that first time, and for a while Elizabeth had been fearful that she would never enjoy the act of making love; but with time and experience she had come to recall that night with a warm sentimentality.

"You know," Frank said, his voice barely a whisper as he stopped her and brought his face close to hers in the darkness, "I—I've thought about a hundred different things I'd say to you if I ever came out here with you again."

Elizabeth made a soft sound deep in her throat. Her mind was a roaring blank; she could think of nothing to say. She, too, had often wondered about Frank, but never in her wildest dreams had she thought they might actually come out here again . . . together. As far as she had been concerned, their relationship—and friendship—had ended long ago, no matter how many pleasant memories had fueled it.

She let herself melt into Frank's tightening hug. "You're the one who said it was funny how life can do stuff like that to you," she whispered huskily.

They were standing at the sandy edge of the pond. Frank gently lowered his face to hers and gave her a long, moist kiss on the lips. The tip of his tongue darted playfully against her lips, and Elizabeth opened her mouth slightly. The sensation caught her by surprise— a curious mixture of familiarity and strangeness, as if she had kissed this man just yesterday and as if he were a total stranger. Responding cautiously, she let her hands gradually tighten around his waist as she pressed her hips tightly against him.

Sweet Jesus, this is ridiculous! This is class-A crazy! she thought, even as their kiss lengthened and their embrace tightened. She could feel the hardening of Frank's crotch as it pressed roughly against her belly. She told herself, even if this *wasn't* wrong, it was too soon, too fast. In spite of that, she started moving her hips gently back and forth with an easy, sensuous glide. Warm, moist heat spread throughout her body, and she had the dizzying thought that this was how it should have been all along.

Their lips separated for a moment even as their breaths washed warmly over each other's face. Elizabeth tilted her head to one side, and with that invitation, Frank kissed a line along the edge of her jaw and down her neck. Elizabeth's view of the sky got hazy when she felt his hands slide up and begin unbuttoning her blouse. Stars swam like watery diamonds when she felt Frank's lips travel lower. In an instant, she was on fire, and only distantly did she blame him for remembering how she liked to be touched.

"You don't know how long I've dreamed about this," he whispered. His breath was hot in her ear as she arched her head back, letting his lips travel wherever they wanted to go . . . down . . . down.

"I . . . I . . ." was all she could stammer as she felt him gently lean her backward and, supporting her with his strong arms, lay her down on the sand. Slowly, lovingly, he eased her out of her clothes and then, after taking off his own, covered her with a long, passionate embrace. For Elizabeth, at least, the lovemaking was almost as frightening as it had been the first time. This time, though, it was not out of fear or ignorance; it was because, as he entered her, she realized that it had been much too long since she had surrendered herself so completely to a man . . . or had a man surrender himself so completely to her.

3.

"Well, so much for your word of honor," Elizabeth said an hour later, once they were dressed and walking hand in hand up the beach, back to the car. She swung their hands playfully back and forth as she and Frank both kicked the sand in arcing fans in front of them. The slight chill of the night air cooled the sweat on her skin, making her shiver; but whenever she remembered their passionate lovemaking, she felt a warm, comfortable stirring in her stomach.

"What do you mean, I didn't keep my word?" Frank asked. He glanced at her and smiled, feeling a rush of confidence as he tightened the grip on her hand.

"I mean—" Elizabeth began, then stopped in her tracks and jabbed his chest with her pointed forefinger. "You said you wouldn't put it in *all* the way! Ahh . . . men!" She shook her head with mock disgust.

Frank shrugged as he laughed and said, "You're not worried, are you? I mean, you did say you couldn't get pregnant, right?"

Elizabeth felt suddenly deflated. She let her hand drop to her side and sighed heavily. Frank had told her that, other than Linda Martin, he had not been "sleeping around"; and, in spite of her own failing marriage, she had remained faithful to Doug—until tonight, at least. It galled her that his first concern seemed to be whether or not she could get pregnant, as if that was a threat hanging over them.

"Haven't you realized yet, Frank? There are no free rides," she said bitterly. "You have to pay for it *all* . . . eventually."

"I'm sorry," Frank said. "I didn't mean it like that."

"I know you didn't," she said. She tried to sound mellow, but her voice took on a deep rasp as another, older pain, thankfully duller than the more recent pain of Caroline's death, rose in her mind. After they had made love, she had told him about the "complications" that had arisen when she delivered Caroline—complications which insured she could never get pregnant again. Back then, she had thought that losing the physical potential of having more children was the worst thing she would ever have to face . . .

Until the night Caroline died!

He drove her straight home this time, with no more detours; but when they pulled into the driveway of her parents' home, he was grateful that she didn't get right out and go up to the house.

"Well," Elizabeth said, smiling at him in spite of the chill that had settled between them. "This wasn't exactly what I had in mind for tonight."

She glanced at her watch. It was a little after eleven o'clock. Her parents would be in bed by now, but they had left the front-porch light on. The glow from it faintly outlined Frank's face as she looked at him. He had a satisfied smile, but she thought there was also a pained tightness around his eyes.

"Maybe we can do it again sometime," Frank said. "Only next time, I'll try to remember to throw a blanket into the backseat."

"Frank . . ." Elizabeth said, drawing out his name because she wasn't exactly sure what she was about to say. Before she could say more, the night suddenly echoed with a rolling, distant boom that made both of them jump.

"What in the name of God was that?" Elizabeth said, looking nervously around. "It sounded like a cannon or something."

Frank was just as confused as Elizabeth. He leaned over the steering wheel and looked up at the night sky. When the sound didn't reoccur, he shrugged and said, "I dunno. The flight path for the jetport goes over town sometimes. Maybe it was an airplane . . . or maybe just thunder."

"It doesn't look like it's going to rain," Elizabeth said, staring up at the spread of dusty starlight. They waited in silence to see if the sound would come again. When it didn't, Frank cleared his throat and said, "Anyway, you were about to say . . . ?"

Elizabeth looked at him but said nothing.

Frank was watching her expectantly, fearing what she might say. Once it was obvious she was struggling to put her thoughts into words, he took a deep breath and said, "I know, I know. You were about to remind me that you're still a married woman, and that you don't think you should be dating me, much less making hot, passionate love to me on the beach, right?"

"Well—sort of," Elizabeth said. The roaring boom was still echoing in her ears, and she couldn't stop wondering what it might have been. She looked up at the house to see if either of her parents had awakened.

"But you *are* going to be getting a divorce, right?" Frank asked.

Elizabeth nodded but said nothing as her mind roiled with things she could—and should—say.

"And once you do—well, maybe then I can start hoping we can spend some time together."

"It's not that," Elizabeth finally said, her voice taking on a hard edge. "I mean, if I want to, I can go out with whomever I wish to—now. It's just that . . ."

"That you don't want to go out with me, is that it?" Frank asked. "Tonight was a one-shot deal. Kind of like one last time for old time's sake, huh?"

She heard the tremor in his voice, and it hurt her deeply.

"No—I mean, yes . . . I mean—I don't know," she stammered as confusion swelled inside her like an ocean tide. "I don't know what to think right now. I mean, going out tonight—even what we did out at the pond . . . It was good—it was *great*, but—'' She held her hands helplessly up in front of her face. ''I just don't know! I don't know *what* I feel or think anymore!''

''Then it isn't because of what I said earlier?'' Frank asked. ''You know, about all that crap that's been happening around town?''

Elizabeth shrugged. ''Sure that stuff has me worried. I can't help but wonder if maybe it *is* directed at me and if—''

''If it was,'' Frank said, assuming an iron-edged tone of voice, ''who do you think it might be?''

Elizabeth was stunned. She sat back in the car seat and took a deep breath, letting her lungs fill to capacity before she let the air out in a long, slow whistle.

''Is this something your husband might do?''

''Doug . . . ?'' Elizabeth said, followed by a short burst of laughter. ''No! Don't be ridiculous!''

Frank rubbed his hands together and said, ''Hey! I don't know him. I mean, I've met him a couple of times, but how would I know what he could or couldn't do?''

''Well, you can be damned sure Doug wouldn't do something like *that*!'' Elizabeth said. ''No matter how upset he was about me leaving him, he just . . . he just wouldn't.''

''You're absolutely sure of that?'' Frank asked, pressing the point.

Elizabeth turned to him as she felt a rush of anger. ''What the hell is this, an interrogation?''

''No,'' Frank said, shaking his head. ''Not at all. It's just that . . .''

''Maybe that's what all of this has been about, huh?'' Elizabeth said. ''Maybe you just wanted to *see* me on official business, and you thought if you could lull me by taking me out to the movies— and the *pond*—that you could pry some information out of me! Is *that* what you had in mind?''

''Now *you're* being ridiculous,'' Frank said with anger and hurt in his voice. He wanted to say more but fell silent.

Taking his feeble denial and his silence to mean that that had been his intention exactly, and that she had found him out, Elizabeth sighed sadly and said, ''And to think that I let you . . . that I let *myself* get suckered in!''

She reached for the door latch. The car door clicked open, and the dome light came on; but before she could shift to get out, Frank reached across the seat and grabbed her wrist.

"It wasn't that at all! You've got to believe me, Elizabeth!" he said. His grip on her arm was firm but not painful.

"I'm not so sure I do," she snapped back. The bright light inside the car hurt her eyes, and she found it impossible to look straight at him. She was trembling with anger. "And to think that I joked with you about trying to 'take advantage of me'! That's *exactly* what you were trying to do. Getting laid was the easy part! Will you please let go of me!" She struggled to break his grasp, but he held on.

Frank's voice trembled as he spoke. "If that's what you think tonight was all about—" he stammered, but then words failed him. He wanted to pull her to him and smother her with kisses, if only to convince her that he hadn't had any ulterior motives tonight—other than the obvious. Beyond that, he wanted her to know that, even after twenty years, he *did* still love her . . . more than ever!

"What the hell do you *think* I'm supposed to think, then? You tell me!" Elizabeth said, her voice hissing with anger and hurt. "You make me feel as though . . . as though *everything* is a setup just to get me to talk."

"It isn't," Frank said. "It wasn't. You've got to believe me." He felt a slight measure of relief when she stopped pulling away from him. Easing the car door shut enough to turn off the dome light, she leaned back in the seat and took another deep, shuddering breath. Frank let go of her wrist and settled back in his own seat, feeling flushed and confused. He hated the way she could do that to him.

"So tell me the truth. Do you suspect that Doug had something to do with what happened out there?" Elizabeth asked. "I'll bet you do, and you think I'll be able to help you find something out about it, right?"

Frank shrugged and looked at her helplessly. "I have no idea what leads the detectives are checking out. Look, Elizabeth, I was unfortunate enough to be one of the patrolmen who was out there that night; but after that, as soon as the detectives arrived on the scene, it was all out of my hands. I went back to the station and filled out an incident report, and that's it as far as I'm concerned. Except . . ."

"Except what?"

"Except I don't think it's over," Frank said softly. "And I think if there's even a possibility that you are in danger of . . . of something, then I want to help."

Elizabeth was still simmering, but she controlled her anger as she asked, "So then why even mention Doug? I mean—why even bring him up?"

Frank forced a tight laugh but checked his impulse to reach out and take her hand, gently this time. "Like a lot of things I've said to you in the past, it was just me, saying things without really thinking them through. I'm pissed at myself for spoiling tonight. I wanted it to be perfect."

Elizabeth sniffed loudly but couldn't deny the sincerity in his voice.

"It's just that, as soon as I even mentioned what had happened," Frank continued, "you said something kinda off-handed about how you thought it might be directed at you, and—quite honestly— that's what has me worried, too."

"Do the detectives working on the case think it's directed at me?" Elizabeth asked. Her voice was constricted, and she looked at him with terror-filled eyes that glinted in the dark.

"They aren't exactly forthcoming with what's going on," Frank said with a light laugh. "I don't know. Jesus Christ, Elizabeth! You get me so worked up I can't even think or talk straight. As far as I know, you don't have anything to worry about, okay? Believe me, if I *knew* you were in any kind of danger, I'd tell you. I was just asking, casually, if you thought your husband could have done something like that—to get even with you or whatever. It was a simple, innocent question, and I should never have even brought it up."

"But if you suspect Doug, then why don't you suspect me, as well?" Elizabeth asked. "I mean, nothing even happened out at the cemetery until I came home. How do you know I'm not the one who dug up my uncle's body?"

"I don't *know* it wasn't you," Frank replied simply.

"Oh, great . . . just great! Who are you, Inspector Clouseau? 'I suspect everyone; I suspect no one!' "

"I don't *suspect* anyone!" Frank said, his voice taking on an edge. "I filed my report, and that was the end of it for me. Look, Elizabeth, I don't want you to think that I had any ulterior motives about tonight, all right? I just—it's been so long since I've seen you, and I just wanted to spend some time with you. I want to spend more time with you because I still—"

"Don't!" Elizabeth said quickly, looking at him in the darkness of the car. She reached out and touched the side of his face, stroking his cheek with her fingertips before letting her hand drop back into her lap. She couldn't stop the trembling building up inside of her as her mind raced to process everything she was thinking and feeling about tonight . . . and all those other nights twenty years ago. She knew that if she didn't say or do something soon, she was going to explode into tears.

"Elizabeth . . . *please*," Frank said. He reached for her and tried to pull her close, but she held back.

She clenched her hands into tight fists just to stop them from shaking. "Let's not ruin anything else tonight, all right?" she said tightly. "I had a good time. I really did, and I don't regret anything that happened."

"I do," Frank said.

Elizabeth knew immediately that this was his own clumsy way of apologizing for all the wrong things he had said, tonight and all those years ago.

Leaning over toward him, she gave him a quick kiss on the cheek and whispered, "Thanks," even as she thought that, if she had *any* sense left at all, this would be her last date with Frank Melrose. She opened the car door to get out, but just as she put her feet on the ground and began to stand up, a blaring sound filled the night, making her jump. She banged her arm on the open car door. "Shit!" she shouted, as sharp bursts of sound cut through the darkness like swift slashes of a knife.

"The town fire horn," Frank said calmly. Elizabeth was still cursing her hurt arm, but he hushed her with a quick wave of his hand and said, "Shush! I'm counting the code."

Elizabeth leaned down into the car as Frank counted the series of blasts on the fire horn. When there was a long pause, marking the end of the first cycle, they waited tensely for it to begin again so Frank could make sure he had gotten it right. He counted each blast with a light tap on the steering wheel. When the second cycle ended, he looked at her and said, "It's three-three-five."

"Holy shit!" Elizabeth said. "That's the code for Brook Road! It must be somewhere nearby!" She straightened up quickly and glanced around the yard, suddenly fearful that the fire might be in her parents' house or the barn out back.

Frank got out of the car, too, and looked around. Just before Elizabeth ran out to the backyard, he called her name and pointed up the road toward town.

"Look," he said.

Elizabeth turned and saw a flickering glow of orange above the dark border of trees that lined the road. Thick smoke, looking soft gray in the moonlight, masked a long stretch of the starry sky.

"Come on," Frank said, as he slid back behind the steering wheel and waved her into the car. "Let's go see where it is. Maybe we can help."

With a whining squeal of tires, Frank backed out of the driveway, and they raced into the night up Brook Road.

4.

Henry Bishop woke up to the sound of a floorboard creaking. He shifted around as he sat up in bed, listening intently to the silent house, waiting for the sound to be repeated. For several tense seconds, he held his breath; when the sound didn't come again, he told himself to forget about it and go back to sleep. If there was any problem, like a prowler or burglar, Murf would be barking his ass off. With a sigh, he sank back into a tangle of sheets and blankets that were long overdue for a washing.

"Sum-bitch . . ." he muttered as he scrunched up his pillow and buried his face in it.

But now that his sleep had been disturbed, it wasn't all that easy to drift back off. No matter how much he reassured himself that he had no reason to be nervous about burglars or anything else, he couldn't settle down again. He lay there, staring at the ceiling and wondering how in the hell such a small noise like a squeaking floorboard could wake him up.

"Ahh, *fuck* it!" he muttered. He swung the bedcovers aside and got out of bed. "Might's'well go down stairs for a nip or two. That'll help me get back to sleep."

Without turning on the light, he shuffled across the bedroom floor and into the hallway, all the while imagining the smooth taste of a glass of whiskey. Once he was at the top of the stairway landing, though, he noticed something that made him freeze in his tracks. From downstairs, coming from the kitchen, he saw the faint flicker of what looked like candlelight. Either that, or else he had left a light on and his eyesight, adjusting to the darkness, was making it flicker. His hand reached out blindly for the hallway wall switch; then—again—he heard a floorboard downstairs creak.

"What the be'*Jee*zus?" he hissed. He tried to reassure himself that he must have left the light on in the kitchen; but, as best as he could remember, he had turned everything off. Besides, the light he could see really *was* flickering, so it couldn't be just his failing eyesight.

Moving as silently as he could, he went down the stairs, noticing for the first time in his life how damned many of the steps squeaked. He wished he'd made it a practice to keep one of his shotguns in his bedroom, but his guns and ammunition were in the hall closet by the front door. If there was an intruder, Henry knew he was going to have a hell of a time getting the gun and loading it without being found out.

And where the fuck was Murf? Henry wondered all the way down the stairs. Murf should've been barking his sorry ass off!

At the foot of the stairs, Henry paused, trying to think through very clearly the next few steps he should take. Should he go for the shotgun in the hall closet, or just barge on into the kitchen and tackle whoever the fuck was in there? Surprise might work in his favor . . . then again, the intruder might have a gun of his own.

Glancing back and forth between the closet door and the kitchen entry, Henry suddenly had any and all decisions taken out of his hands when a deep, resonant voice spoke from the kitchen.

"Ahh . . . there you are, Mr. Bishop. I was wondering when you'd get around to coming downstairs."

Henry was totally taken aback. He could do nothing more than stammer senselessly. His eyes were bulging out of his head as he watched the flickering glow of light get brighter.

"Henry . . . Do you mind if I call you Henry? Don't be shy. This is your house, after all. Come right on in here so we can have a little talk. Will you?"

"Who the hell are you, 'n' what in the name of *fuck* are you doin' in my house?" Henry snarled as he took several hesitant steps forward. The entire kitchen was suffused with a warm orange glow that might have been downright cheery if Henry hadn't felt such a tight knot of tension deep in his groin. He entered the kitchen and saw the dark silhouette of a man standing by the sink. He was keeping one hand behind his back; that hand obviously held the candles, which were blazing, creating a yellow aura all around his black silhouette.

"'N' what in the fuck'd you do to my dog?" Henry snapped, as the realization came that *something* must have happened to Murf; otherwise, by now this guy—whoever the fuck he was—would have been torn to bloody pieces . . .

Like Barney Fraser's body in the woods, Henry thought, unable to keep the memory of that horrible, dead, pale face out of his mind.

"Have a seat, Henry. Please, have a seat," the man said, indicating with a wave of his arm the solitary chair at the kitchen table. Henry didn't have any company other than Murf, so he had never seen the need for a second chair. In spite of his impulse to charge the man, wrestle him to the floor, and then pummel the living piss out of him, Henry did as he was told and sat down.

"I want to know who the fuck you—"

"I'll do the talking, if that's all right with you, Henry," the silhouette said. The voice was firm and commanding, and, against his will, Henry found himself nodding his agreement.

"Now, the first thing I want you to do"—as the man spoke, he slowly withdrew his hand from behind his back—"is sit right there. Don't you even think of moving a muscle, all right?"

Henry couldn't believe what he saw. The man wasn't holding candles. No, not at all! Only after several seconds did Henry realize what the object was; at first, he was simply entranced by the five flickering points of light. A numbingly cold rush coursed through his body, instantly freezing his muscles, when he saw that the man was holding a black, twisted-looking thing that sure as shit *looked* like a withered human hand, cut off halfway between the wrist and elbow. A little spur of bone protruded from the bottom, glowing like dull metal; the fingers curled like a claw, and on the tip of the thumb and of each finger, a tongue of flame flickered softly. Each burned with an oily blue core, like the flame of a gas stove.

"Wha—?" Henry said aloud, even though it took a great effort to move his jaw. "What the . . . fuckin' hell—?"

The light from the five fingertip candles underlit the intruder's face, but Henry was damned if he recognized the man, who was holding the hand off to one side so that only half of his face was illuminated. The other half was cast into deep shadow.

"Scratch your head," the man commanded.

"Huh—?" Henry said, even as he tried to raise his own hand. He was shocked to discover that he couldn't budge it—not an inch. It was as if his hand had been Super-glued to his pants. Henry tried harder, but the effort only made sweat break out on his forehead. His whole body shook with a deep, useless tremor. He stopped trying once he realized that he was immobile and that any struggle was useless. Chilling fear rippled through him even as his leg and back muscles seized up.

"What the fuck'd—you do—to me?" Henry wailed, only slightly grateful that he could still move his mouth to speak.

As the man waved the horrible candles in a wide arc, the flames made soft little puffing sounds in the draft. He brought the light so close to Henry's face that he could feel the shimmering waves of heat it gave off. The cloying stench of burning flesh filled Henry's nose. If he had had control of his neck muscles, he would have turned away and gagged. As it was, his revulsion merely twisted like heavy, black smoke in his mind.

"I have . . . *control* over you," the man said, lowering his voice to a deep, thundering boom. "It's that simple." He turned and walked out the mudroom doorway, returning a moment later with a rusted five-gallon gasoline can in one hand, the flaming human hand in the other.

"What . . . are . . . you . . ." Henry said. Each word felt as though it were being pried out of his mouth with a crowbar. Strong, frigid hands were squeezing up his jaws, and every effort to move his muscles sent blades of pain slicing through his body.

"You must recognize this," the man said. To help Henry see, he raised the horrible five-pointed candle to illuminate the can he was holding. "This is a gasoline can." He gave the can a quick shake and smiled at the heavy sloshing sound it made. "Sounds just about full, too."

". . . I . . ." Henry began, but then he gave up the effort of trying to speak as his neck muscles contracted into painfully hard knots.

"I'm just going to open the can," the man said, "and—oops! I seemed to have spilled a little on the floor here. How clumsy of me!"

Henry's eyes felt cemented in place, but he tried to force them to move so he could see what this madman was doing. He watched, horrified, as the man splashed more than a little gasoline around on the kitchen floor, right up to Henry's feet. When the can was empty, the man put it down beside the gas stove.

"Now, then, Henry," he said in a mockingly smooth voice. "I assume your gas stove has a pilot light." He raised one of the burner covers and looked inside. "Ahh, yes—there it is." Puffing his cheeks, he blew the pilot flame out. Picking up the other burner cover, he did the same, carefully replacing the covers.

Reaching into his coat pocket, he took out a pack of cigarettes and a Bic butane lighter. Placing them carefully on the kitchen table, within easy reach of Henry if he could have moved his hand, the man pointed up to the wall and said, "You can easily see the clock?"

Unable to speak or nod, Henry simply glared hatred and fear at the man. He tried to consider *why* this was happening to him, if maybe it was some terrible dream from which he would soon wake up, but more than that, he was wondering *how* this man was doing this. How was he making it so that Henry couldn't move a finger, couldn't even speak? It was almost as if, the instant he had seen the five fingers flickering with blue flame, he had begun to lose his strength and will . . . as if he had been hypnotized, somehow.

"It's just about eleven-fifteen," the man said. "In another fifteen minutes, it'll be time for Johnny Carson. Do you like to watch Johnny Carson?"

Henry, of course, couldn't respond. His vision had begun to swim as tears filled his eyes.

"There, there," the man cooed. "Don't cry! You're a grown man, and grown men don't cry. Besides, if you cry, you won't be able to see what time it is, now, will you? Do you know what I want you to do, Henry?"

From deep inside his chest, somehow, Henry made a soft gagging sound.

"Oh, I see," the man said. "You want to know what's going on. Well, I suppose, since you'll be dead soon, there's no harm in telling you. You see, Henry, you pissed me off." The man jabbed him in the chest with his pointed finger. Surprisingly, Henry didn't feel a thing. "Do you want to know how you pissed me off?"

He leaned so close to Henry's face that Henry could feel the warm wash of his breath over his numbed skin. The five points of light danced in the watery spheres of his eyes, waving in and out, leaving long tracers, like comet tails.

"Well—I'll tell you how. You and your half-assed mutt . . . What did you say his name was? Murf? Well, don't you worry about Murf any more. He's beyond your—or anyone's—help now. But you know, Henry, you *really* pissed me off when you reported finding that body out there in the woods. You know . . . Barney Fraser? Well, that created for me"—the man glanced over at the stove for a second—"some problems. Now, you don't know me, but I'm the kind of man who, when I meet up with an obstacle or a problem, I don't waste my time worrying or fussing over it. No, I *do* something about it. And tonight, I'm going to *do* something about *you!*"

The strangling sound inside Henry's chest got a bit louder. The man shook his head and clicked his tongue. "My, you are putting up quite a struggle, but it won't do you any good. You see, you won't be able to move until you do what I tell you you're going to do. Do you understand?"

Tears were running freely down Henry's cheeks, now, as much for Murf as for himself.

"You see, Henry," the man said, waving the hand with the burning fingertips in front of Henry's face, "this gives me power over weak minds such as yours. *Control!* All I want from you is a simple thing. I just want you to sit here and watch the clock. Sounds easy, doesn't it? I think even someone as stone stupid as *you* will be able to remember that. And when it's eleven-thirty, time for Johnny Carson, I want you to take a cigarette and light it. Easy enough? It doesn't matter if you don't smoke. You will . . . oh, yes—you will *smoke*!" He laughed, deep and hollow.

The man moved back over to the stove and, holding the flaming hand well away, twisted all four burner knobs to ON. The kitchen instantly filled with the hissing sound of gas as it poured, unlit, through the gas line and into the kitchen.

The man wrinkled his nose at the smell. "Remember, now, Henry. Don't disappoint me," he said as he went quickly to the door. "Keep your eyes on the clock, and in fifteen minutes, sit back, relax . . . light up and have a smoke."

With that, the man, still carrying his five points of light, snapped on the overhead light in the kitchen and ducked out of the house, slamming the kitchen door shut behind him. Henry was left squinting in the suddenly bright kitchen as the sickening smell of gas got stronger and stronger.

As much as Henry tried to fight the icy grip that held his body captive, he couldn't take his eyes away from the sweeping red second hand and the slow progression of the minute hand as it moved steadily downward. Sweat stood out like dew on his forehead and cheeks, and spidery lines of moisture ran from his armpits down his sides to his belt. But he couldn't muster even the slightest movement of his muscles. His mind was raging, roaring, commanding himself to look away, not to watch the clock, and not to think about what he had been told to do! He knew he could resist. It was impossible that this man—whoever the fuck he was!—could have any kind of control over him. It was simply impossible!

But finally, Henry saw that the minute hand was pointing straight down. He felt a warm rush of release in his left hand. His entire arm tingled with burning pins and needles as he flexed the fingers. Totally against his will, he reached for the cigarette pack the man had left on the table, shook out a cigarette, and placed it in the corner of his mouth. His fingers were trembling violently as he grasped the cigarette lighter, put his thumb on the flint striker wheel, and snapped it once, hard.

Henry never heard the scratching sound the lighter made; it was lost in a single, mind-numbing roar, like a cannon going off inside his head. The kitchen and the entire house exploded as the gas-filled house ignited. The gasoline the man had sprinkled on the floor burst into flames, and burning wood, glass, and household items blasted outward. Henry was already dead by the time his body, clothes engulfed in flames, slammed into the kitchen wall. Within seconds, the house was a raging inferno.

NINE
Jonathan's Hand

1.

Elizabeth's parents woke up with the blast of the fire horn, and they along with several other people from the neighborhood joined together and watched as the firemen fought the flames. Henry's old house went up fast, filling the night with loud, crackling sounds and hammering heat. By the time dawn approached, blending the eastern sky from black to sooty gray, the fire was pretty much out. The charred remains of Henry's body were found in the smoldering ruins, and Elizabeth and Frank watched as the ambulance crew covered what was left of him, placed it on a stretcher and then in the vehicle, and drove away.

The firemen continued to spray water on the embers as investigators began to pick through the ashes. Onlookers were already saying how the fire must have been caused by a gas explosion to flatten the house as it had. Elizabeth and Frank also heard several people say that the fire seemed suspicious, since Henry Bishop would never have been so foolish as to blow himself up like that. Some people conjectured that Henry had been the one to discover the body of Barney Fraser, and wondered aloud if the two events were connected somehow. Elizabeth's own suspicions deepened when Frank pointed out that Detective Harris had been on the scene throughout the night.

Around seven o'clock, exhausted from the events of the night, Frank drove Elizabeth home. She watched from the front porch as he drove away, strong in her determination never to date him again. With sunlight streaming in her window, she finally got to bed, but sleep didn't come easily. Other thoughts besides Henry's horrible death plagued her, keeping sleep at arm's length, and when she finally drifted off to sleep, it was thin and disturbed.

Elizabeth began having vivid, erotic dreams that replayed her and Frank's lovemaking on the beach at Bristol Pond, but as they made love again in her sleep, a raging fire was consuming the forest all around Bristol Pond. The dream-night was filled with the thundering roar of flames that slashed like flashing blades against the starry sky, hammering heat making Elizabeth's dream body feel as though her flesh were burning. Clearly, it was Frank she was making love to in her dreams, but at one point, the features of Frank's face subtly melted into those of an older man—the rotting, gray-fleshed face of her Uncle Jonathan. She woke up screaming, her body slick with sweat.

For Frank, staying up all night hadn't been as tough as it had been for Elizabeth; he was used to working all night and then going to sleep early in the morning. But today was different: after such a great time with Elizabeth, the spectre of Henry Bishop's horrible death—the death of someone he knew and liked—affected him deeply. Worse, Frank couldn't stop thinking about what he had overheard at the fire . . . like the possibility of a connection between Henry's death and his discovery of Fraser's body. Unable to sleep, Frank considered calling Elizabeth, but was still tormented by the things he had said—and felt he *shouldn't* have said—to her the night before. He had no regrets about what they had done. It was just that when he opened his mouth and tried to explain himself to her, he always seemed to get so flustered! Their conversation in his car outside her house just before the town fire horn had sounded bothered him the most. He wanted to tell her now that he had *never* intended to use her for sex or to get information about her husband or for anything else; he wanted to tell her *everything* before what they had—and what he hoped they would have—slipped away . . . forever.

He knew he had told Elizabeth a "little white lie" when he said he was off the case as soon as the detectives had arrived at the cemetery that night. Certainly, he couldn't investigate it officially . . . but because he was *unofficially* checking into the backgrounds of Douglas Myers as well as Roland Graydon, telling her he "wasn't involved" was enough of a lie to make him feel a bit uncomfortable. He was angry at himself for even hinting to her that he was concerned for her safety, but the truth was, he was absolutely convinced that the person who had dug up and mutilated her uncle's body had done this specifically to attack *her*.

Harris's words rang in his memory: "*You should never ass-u-me anything!*"

That afternoon, Frank made a quick detour past Hardy's Hardware, slowing down just enough so that he could see through the glass front door whether Elizabeth was at the cash register, but she wasn't, so he drove on.

If Elizabeth *really* was in any kind of danger, he would warn her once he had some hard evidence, whether Detective Harris was willing to help or not!

2.

He took three steps back from his handiwork. The ritual had been performed according to the ancient custom. The illumination from the flames cast an eerie glow. By using the power of the relic, contact had been made. He would receive the information he desired. Oily smoke and mist resolved into a figure which began to speak . . .

3.

The sun was low in the sky as Frank and Norton drove the cruiser out past what was left of Henry Bishop's house. The area was blocked off, and the firemen and investigators were still sifting through the ashes for evidence of what had caused the fire. Like a finger pointing at the sky, the chimney stuck up through the ruins.

"So, did you get to slam some ham last night?" Norton asked.

Frank shifted his gaze to his partner, hoping his expression communicated his disgust.

Apparently Norton read it as confusion, because he added with a nudge and a wink, "You know—with Elizabeth Myers . . . last night. Did you screw her?"

"I don't see where that's any of your Goddamned business," Frank replied, barely able to control his anger. He stepped down hard on the accelerator and sped past the scene of the fire. "And anyway, how the fuck did you even know I took her out last night?"

Norton shrugged. "Someone—I forget who—mentioned they saw the two of you at the fire at Bishop's house last night. Damn!" He looked over his shoulder as they pulled away and added, almost wistfully, "Wish I'd been here to see it go up."

"*Who?*" Frank snarled, slamming on the brakes and making the car swing heavily to one side as the tires left twin, black strips on the asphalt. Trembling with rage, he turned and faced Norton. "Who *happened* to mention it?"

"I . . . I can't remember," Norton stammered, once he realized this wasn't a casual locker-room discussion. "It was—I dunno, either Ed or Chuck. One of 'em said you were out there with her and you looked kinda . . . kinda tight, you know?"

"I'll tell you one thing, pardner," Frank said, jabbing Norton in the chest with his pointed forefinger. "If you or *anyone* else thinks it's their business to go talking about what I do or who I'm with off-duty, they're gonna be bleeding-ass sorry. You think you can remember that?"

"Hey! Come on! Lighten up, will yah?" Norton sputtered. He forced a chuckle entirely devoid of humor. "I was just kidding, for Christ's sake! I didn't mean anything by it."

"You damned well better not!" Frank said. He popped the gear shift and stepped on the gas. The cruiser roared to life, leaving behind close to twenty feet of rubber on the road and a thin haze of bad-smelling blue smoke that rose up like ground fog. Frank nervously chewed the inside of his cheek, trying not to imagine how great it would have felt to pound the living shit out of Norton right there on the spot!

Throughout the late afternoon and early evening, there was a marked absence of the usual bantering conversation between Frank and Norton as they cruised around town. They responded to several calls, all of them minor, and the hours passed by slowly until around eleven o'clock, when they drove past Oak Grove Cemetery for the fourth time that shift. Because of what had happened out there recently, they had been asked to keep a close eye on the place for *anything* that looked suspicious.

"What the fuck do you expect to see, anyway?" Norton asked when Frank slowed the cruiser down to about five miles per hour. The hours of no conversation beyond what was required while they worked had made Norton nervous. He sounded tired and irritated —or else scared, Frank thought, maybe from remembering the discovery they had made up there not so long ago.

Frank didn't bother to look at him, and kept his eyes scanning the gently rising slope and the fringe of woods beyond. Soft moonlight gave the landscape a cold, white glow, as if it were skimmed with frosting. Since the night of that discovery, the cemetery gates had been locked, but Frank knew that wouldn't stop anyone who was determined enough to cause trouble.

And exactly what kind of trouble? he wondered.

"You know what they say about a criminal returning to the scene of the crime?" Frank said gruffly. "Well, I'm just betting whoever dug up that body a couple of weeks ago isn't done yet. Not after all this shit with Henry and all. I'll just bet some night he's gonna come back here to do it again . . . or something else. And when he does, I'm gonna nail his ass!"

Norton sniffed. "Yeah—sure." He looked at his partner with irritation. "First of all, it was probably Barney Fraser who did it. And now that he's dead as rat shit—"

"There were others involved," Frank said softly.

"Yeah, sure," Norton replied, shaking his head. "And anyone'd have to be a damned fool to come back here now."

"I'd say he *has* to be a 'damned fool'—or worse—to do what he did," Frank said.

"Yeah, well—"

Frank stopped the cruiser opposite the cemetery gates and stuck his head out the window. A warm breeze played through his hair as he looked up the rutted dirt road that ran over the crest to the grave site. He shivered as he wondered exactly what in the hell *had* been going on up there that night. Why would anyone—*how could* anyone—do something like that? It went way beyond the casual "Well, it takes all kinds to make up this world" response that cops usually resorted to when trying to explain some of the unusual things they encountered in their work. Whoever had dug up that body and cut off the dead man's hand was sicko in the extreme! And if he was responsible for Barney Fraser's murder and the fire at Henry Bishop's house, it only made things worse!

"D'you see what I see?" Frank asked, catching a glimpse of . . . something, up there on the hill. He purposely kept his voice low so that he wouldn't betray the jolt of surprise he felt. He wanted to stay calm so that he could gauge Norton's initial reaction.

Norton leaned forward so that he could see past Frank, but hardly seemed to look at all before shaking his head and saying, "I don't see a Goddamned thing 'cept a bunch of gravestones. Come on. Let's get a move on."

"Up the hill there," Frank said. "Doesn't that—holy shit!" His first impression was that it was a trick of the moonlight, reflecting off the polished tombstones. There was a hazy, blue glow that flickered dimly at the crest of the hill, hovering like a strangely illuminated mist above one of the graves. "That almost looks like a . . . like a kid standing on top of the gravestone there."

"Yeah—sure," Norton said, stifling a laugh. "Maybe we got ourselves a gen-u-ine UFO. Better call—what's his name there. That writer guy I saw on Donahue who said he was kidnapped by aliens and experimented on and all. Maybe they're stealing corpses now." He shifted to one side of the seat and let out a soft, squeaking fart.

"Or maybe it's just swamp gas," Frank said. His tone of voice didn't at all reflect the humor of his attempted joke. "But I think we ought to check it out."

"Come on, Frank," Norton said, letting his frustration show. "I've been riding with you all night, and you've barely said 'boo.' My bladder's about to burst if we don't get back to the station so I can take a leak."

"What? Have you suddenly gone delicate on me? All of a sudden you can't piss on the side of the road?" Frank said, as he stared up the hill. It was maddening how, whenever he thought he clearly saw the silhouette of a child perched on one of the tombstones, he would blink and the illusion would be gone. Maybe he had been right; it was pretty swampy behind the cemetery . . . maybe it *was* just fox fire.

"Oh, sure. That'd look great," Norton said gruffly. "Bristol Mills's finest, whizzing on the roadside. What, are you looking for something to write me up on, just 'cause I teased you a little about Elizabeth?"

"Well, I'm gonna check it out," Frank said, bristling.

Norton's reply was lost beneath the sound of the cruiser's tires scrunching in the dirt on the shoulder of the road as Frank cut across it and pulled up under the black, wrought-iron gateway.

"This is total bullshit," Norton muttered. His voice sounded wire-tight, but Frank couldn't tell if it was because he had to go to the bathroom so bad or because he was remembering what they had found up there.

"I just wanna have a look around," Frank said, not daring to look away from the faintly glowing silhouette at the top of the hill. He got out, unlocked the gate and swung it wide open, then got back into the cruiser and drove slowly up the rutted dirt road. The closer he got, the more teasing the flickering light became. The shimmering figure of a child—a young girl—wavered and then vanished. Frank's body went cold when he realized he was looking at the same spot he had investigated a couple of weeks ago—Jonathan Payne's grave.

"Holy shit!" Frank muttered, as the slow realization worked its way into his mind.

Rather than drive all the way up the hill, Frank stopped the cruiser. Both he and Norton sat there, staring ahead in disbelief. The intervening tombstones blocked their direct view of whatever it was burning up there, but they both could clearly see a light, shining weakly near Jonathan Payne's grave. The flickering blue glow cast long, black shadows that stretched out and soaked back into the night. Frank's breath caught in his chest when he saw a dark shape shift against the night, only now it looked like a man's figure.

"Motherfucker! There's someone up there!" he whispered.

"You sure?" Norton asked as he strained forward to see into the darkness.

"Radio in what's happening and get some backup, *pronto*!" Frank said. "I'll start up the hill. After you call in, circle around behind."

He cut the engine and popped his door open. In spite of the warm spring night, a wave of chills swept up his back. The muscles in his shoulders tensed into hard knots as he stepped out of the cruiser and eased the door shut with a soft *snap*. Loosening his revolver in its holster, he came around the side of the car and, crouching low, dodged between graves as he started up the hill toward the flame. He couldn't see the dark shadow of a person anymore, and he began to hope it had been an illusion, created by the flames; he wasn't so sure he wanted to meet up with whoever was responsible for what had been happening around town lately.

The wavering shadows of the tombstones, cast by the fire, made it difficult to see clearly, and Frank stumbled on the uneven ground, silently cursing any noise he made. He wanted to scan the area to see if there was anyone else around, but he couldn't take his eyes off the glowing area of light. He still couldn't see exactly what was burning, but his heart felt squeezed by cold hands as he wondered what—and *who*!—he would find up there. He bent down low behind a tombstone, just outside the area lighted by the fire, and eased his revolver from its holster. Gripping it tightly, he tensed, waiting until Norton swung around behind and got into position.

From behind him, Frank heard the sudden slam of the cruiser door. It echoed as loud as a gunshot in the still night. With a quick glance back, he saw that Norton had started out and around so that he would come up on the site from the other side, but Frank knew it was already too late. If there had been someone up there, the noise had certainly alerted him.

Bursting out from behind the tombstone, Frank dashed up the hill to close the distance. He was just in time to see a person disappear out of the sphere of light, to be instantly swallowed by the surrounding night. There was no sound of running feet other than his own, so he wasn't sure if there really had been someone there, or if it had merely been his overwrought nerves. Holding his revolver ready, he crouched and swept the surrounding ring of darkness.

"Stop right there!" he yelled. His voice bounced back from the gravestones. "This is the police!"

The night was silent. Once Frank was positive the person—if he had been there at all—had gotten away, he looked behind him at what was burning beside the grave. The cold tightness in his chest got so tight it was almost impossible for him to breathe.

"Holy Mother of Jesus!" he heard Norton say, as he crested the other side of the hill and came around from behind Jonathan Payne's tombstone.

Frank could do no more than grunt as he stared for several silent seconds at the blue-tipped flames. Then he looked at his partner, and his anger suddenly flared. "Do you think you could have made any *more* noise?" he shouted. "You sounded like a fuckin' bull moose coming up the hill! You scared him off, for Christ's sake!"

"I didn't see or hear a thing," Norton said innocently, casting a glance around.

"Well, whoever it was must've run right through you because he was headed in your direction."

"I didn't see a thing," Norton repeated, his voice tighter and higher than usual as he stared past Frank to the fire burning behind him. "But look at that, will you! Can you fuckin' believe this?"

Frank realized he was still pointing his revolver in Norton's general direction, so he lowered the gun and slipped it back into its holster. Nodding grimly, he said "Yeah—I can believe it." He drawled his words, hoping his own nervousness didn't show when he turned and looked at the fire as well. "I'd say even you have to agree now that we're dealing with one helluva wacko!"

They looked down at the gravestone where the fire was still burning. A severed human hand had been stuck into a fresh mound of soil above the grave. The tips of the fingers and thumb had been dipped in some kind of flammable liquid, and five small blue flames danced above the shriveled hand. A heavy, oily-smelling smoke curled up from the end of each finger and disappeared into the night sky. Shadows weaved sickeningly on the ground and colored the dead hand a deep gray. But what struck the deepest spike of terror into Frank was the name he read on the tombstone. The reflection of the light from the five flames glowed with a bright rose color on the polished marble, casting the inscription into deep, inky shadows.

CAROLINE JUNIA MYERS
OCTOBER 27, 1981–FEBRUARY 15, 1988

4.

Still exhausted from recent events, Elizabeth felt the need to start her afternoon session with Graydon lying down on the couch.

"I'm feeling pretty wiped out," she said. "There was a fire at the house next to ours. Our next-door neighbor, a friend of my parents, died. They're saying there must have been a leak in his gas line, and a spark or something touched it off."

"Oh, that's right," Graydon said, nodding. "I saw something about that on the news. The man was killed, I think I heard."

"After the explosion, the house burned," Elizabeth said. "I just hope he . . . didn't suffer."

"It's such a shame," Graydon said. "But I sense that this isn't all that's bothering you." He looked at her with a penetrating stare. "Perhaps you've been having some dreams you'd like to discuss, for starters?"

Biting her lower lip, Elizabeth shook her head, pushing aside the paranoid thought that Graydon was, somehow, reading her mind. "No. Not really."

"Well, then," Graydon said, sitting back comfortably in his chair, "what do you feel like talking about?"

"How about Caroline?" Elizabeth said, surprising herself with the thought that it might actually be less painful than some of the other things on her mind.

"Sure," Graydon replied, not missing a beat. "We can talk about Caroline if you'd like."

"What would you like to know?"

Graydon shrugged and said, "It's not what I'd like to know; it's whatever you'd like to tell me."

Placing her fingertips contemplatively on her chin, Elizabeth let her gaze drift out the window as she pondered for several seconds. When she didn't speak, Graydon interrupted her silence.

"Let's try a little different approach. How about if we talk about what you would like to say to Caroline if you could. What would you tell her if she were here, right now?"

Elizabeth laughed aloud to cover up the jolt of fear that shot through her. "You know," she said, "that's not such a bad idea, considering what my aunt said to me the other day." She looked at Graydon, who simply sat there listening. "My Aunt Junia asked me if I would like to get in touch with Caroline."

"How interesting," Graydon said, shifting forward in his chair. "This is the same aunt you were looking for astrology books for at the bookstore the other night, correct?"

Elizabeth nodded.

"And how exactly did she propose to do that, to let you *contact* your daughter?"

"Well, you have to understand," Elizabeth said, "my aunts, both of them, Junia and Elspeth, are getting along in years, and sometimes I think they're not—you know." She tapped the side of her head. "Not all there. But Junia told me she could introduce me to someone who could contact Caroline in the spirit world."

"So . . . what do you think about that?" Graydon asked. His eyes narrowed, and Elizabeth didn't like the way he was looking at her, as though he could see clear through her.

"You mean about the spirit world and all of that?" she asked, arching her eyebrows and sniffing. "I have no idea! I suppose I'd have to say I think it's a bunch of bullshit, but—" She finished by shrugging.

"But let's just say, for discussion's sake, that if you *could* speak with Caroline, what would you say to her?"

Elizabeth's next breath caught in her throat like a fishhook, and as much as she tried to stop it, her eyes started to sting as they glazed over. The tips of her fingers got cold and started to tingle, and she started breathing in fast, light gulps, as if the room didn't have enough air.

"I . . . I don't know," she stammered, forcing herself to breathe more evenly and deeply, "I just don't know."

"Let me ask you this, then," Graydon said, as he rubbed his hands together and leaned slightly forward. "Do you believe that there is life after death? In any form?"

By taking the discussion onto the abstract level, Elizabeth thought she might be able to deal with it a bit more easily, but still words failed her and she shrugged helplessly.

"I just don't know," she finally said. "I mean, I'm pretty sure I don't buy the straight church line about Heaven and Hell and all of that."

"But what about life after death? What do you think about existence on a spiritual plane. Do you believe in that?" Graydon asked. He was pressing the point so hard Elizabeth couldn't help but wonder why. "Do you believe in *any* aspect of spiritual existence, or are you simply what we'd call a 'here and now' kind of person."

In spite of her stinging eyes, Elizabeth looked at him and, blinking back the tears, said, "Dr. Graydon, what I've been through has pretty much weakened or destroyed any faith I might have had in any kind of religion."

"Beyond all that," Graydon said, "in a more general sense— do you believe in personal existence after death?" He leaned forward even further; so much so that, from Elizabeth's angle, it looked as though he were about to topple out of his chair. Was he just pushing her for the sake of discussion? Or was he probing with a purpose?

After a thoughtful pause, she said, "I guess I'd have to say that's just something we'll all find out . . . eventually."

Graydon laughed softly and added, "Yes . . . sooner or later. Pascal's wager—have you heard of that?"

Elizabeth shook her head.

"The proposition is that, if you make a bet that there's some form of afterlife, you can only win because anyone who says there isn't an afterlife, after he dies, will never know there isn't one. Thus, he can't win his wager."

"Sounds like a lot of intellectual bullshit," Elizabeth said.

"Well then, let's get back to my earlier question," Graydon said. "What would you like to tell Caroline if you could talk to her?"

Elizabeth took a deep breath and let it out slowly, trying to clear her mind. "I think I'd—" she began, but before she could say more, her voice choked off. Forcing herself to go on, she continued, "I'd want to tell her . . . how sorry I am."

"For what?"

Twisting her hands in her lap, Elizabeth had to fight back the impulse to get up off the couch and run from the office. She felt disoriented and dizzy, and everywhere she looked, her vision got too intense. Dazzling lights and sharp, scary details jumped out at her. Everything was terrifying to look at, and her pulse was making a feathery hammering sound that reminded her of a bird frantically beating its wings and body against an unseen windowpane.

"I'd tell her I was sorry . . . for not trying to save her," she finally managed to say.

"You mean from the car wreck?" Graydon asked. "Because you feel as though your husband may be right—that you were responsible for her death?"

Biting down hard on her lower lip to keep from screaming aloud, Elizabeth nodded.

"But from what you told me about the accident, there was no way either you or your husband could have gotten to her in time," Graydon said softly.

"Doug . . . tried to get to the car," she said, her voice little more than a gasp.

"But you told me the gas tank exploded before he was even halfway down the hillside," Graydon said. "And he would have been killed as well."

Elizabeth nodded tightly, running her teeth over her lower lip. "Yes, but . . . I stopped him. I saw what he was trying to do, and I held him back."

"Because you knew of the danger?" Graydon asked pointedly. "Or because you didn't want him to even *try* to save her?"

Elizabeth stiffened as though a megawatt jolt of electricity had slammed into her body. She was only dimly aware of the two hot streams of tears running down her face as her mind filled with the memories of that night.

"I'm sure you must see that your need to apologize to Caroline is rooted in something you feel was lacking in your relationship with your daughter when she was still alive. Do you agree?"

Elizabeth cast Graydon a quick, angry glance. She was thinking how Dr. Gavreau had never been so confrontational.

"I . . . I don't think there were any . . . any really major problems between me and Caroline," she said.

"I'm not saying there were," Graydon replied. "I want you to search your own feelings, your own memories of Caroline, un-colored by the tragedy that occurred. Look back at how you *honestly* felt, say, when she was born."

"I was happy . . . I was ecstatic," Elizabeth said, even as the slight quaver in her voice betrayed her memory of the deep postpartum depression she had experienced and the "complications" that had eliminated her chances of ever having more children. She had always told herself that, just knowing Caroline would be her only child—*ever!*—only made her all the more precious.

"And what about your husband—Doug," Graydon said. "How did he handle this new addition to your family?"

The lie, that Doug—like her—had been as happy and loving as ever, was on the tip of Elizabeth's tongue, but in the silence before she spoke, all the darker, more hateful memories came rushing back upon her. She knew Graydon would detect the lie if she spoke it.

"I'd have to say that his—my relationship with Doug changed quite a bit right after Caroline was born," she said, squirming as she considered how far Graydon was willing to push all of this.

"For better or for worse?" Graydon asked.

"Certainly not for the better," she said, her voice a twisted hush. "Doug did more than dote on Caroline; she became just about everything to him."

"At the expense of his relationship with you?" Graydon asked.

"Absolutely," Elizabeth said, nodding. "I think, to be honest, I'd have to say that. But to be fair—"

"There's nothing *fair* about a marital relationship," Graydon said rather harshly. "As much as we would like to think there is, there just isn't! Ninety-nine times . . . no, make that a hundred times out of a hundred, one partner or the other feels taken advantage of or used or abused or whatever!"

Graydon spoke with such vehemence Elizabeth couldn't help but wonder what personal pain he had suffered to make him so hateful, so negative about marriage. Sure, she could admit—to herself and to him—that she and Doug most definitely drifted further apart after Caroline's birth, but the split between them had started long before Caroline was born.

"I know, I know," Elizabeth said, feeling strong barbs of anger and knowing they were directed as much at herself as they were at Graydon. "And you're going to tell me that we're dealing with the old Electra complex, right? That I have all this built-up resentment for Caroline because I think she took my husband's love away from me, right?''

"I'm not *saying* anything," Graydon replied. "I merely want to direct the conversation to areas I think will be fruitful for you."

"But I—well, what I think you're implying is . . . what? That I buried all of my resentment for my daughter because of what happened to her?"

"Do you think there's any truth to that?" Graydon asked pointedly.

Elizabeth shrugged. "I don't know. I mean . . . sure, I guess I felt like I was in competition for Doug's love and attention, but I realize the love between a husband and wife is very different from the love between a parent and a child."

"You can say that quite easily in general, intellectual terms, but how do you feel about it personally—specifically? Why do you feel as though you have to *apologize* to Caroline?"

A rush of panic swept up inside Elizabeth's chest. Her hands went suddenly cold and tingly again.

"You want the truth?" she asked.

"Nothing but," Graydon said, smiling broadly.

"I feel I have to apologize to her because when I really search my feelings about what happened that night and how I reacted, I still wonder if maybe I *did* stop Doug—on purpose—because I *did* want Caroline to . . . die."

Rubbing his hands together, Graydon stood up and walked over to the kitchenette. "I respect you for saying that," he said. "It takes a great deal of courage to say something like that." He poured himself a fresh cup of tea. When he held out an empty cup toward Elizabeth, she shook her head tightly and said, "No thanks."

Walking back to his chair, he sighed as he sat back down. When he sipped his hot tea, Elizabeth noticed how delicately he held the cup. Veins and tendons stood out starkly from the back of his pale hand. She wondered whether he would get a tan with warmer weather coming, or if his skin maintained this winter-sallow complexion all year round. There was something almost unnerving about him that she realized for the first time; it was as if he was a person who abhorred the sunlight at all times.

"And do you think—I suppose you must have talked this over in great detail with Dr. Gavreau—that this feeling you have, that you purposely allowed your daughter to die, has anything to do with your attempted suicide?"

Elizabeth sighed deeply and shook her head. "Boy, you don't waste any time getting to the point, do you?"

Graydon took another sip of tea and smiled. "No. That's my approach to therapy, at any rate. I realize it may be uncomfortable at times—"

"I'll say it's uncomfortable," Elizabeth muttered.

"But as much as I believe the mind and personality are very delicate machinery, I don't think it does either you or me any good to pretend we don't see something so obvious . . . what at Al-Anon they call 'the elephant in the living room.' "

"Am I that transparent?" Elizabeth asked, feeling suddenly quite vulnerable. She couldn't stop her voice from trembling. "Is what I'm holding back or hiding from myself so obvious?"

Graydon shook his head. "No—I don't want you to feel that way, but if we're to have a productive relationship, we can't very well ignore such an obvious conclusion. You know, when people begin therapy, they sometimes think they have to dig deeply to uncover some long-hidden, deep dark secrets; but quite often the real problem actually *is* the one that seems most obvious. We're not *all* bundles of hidden, tangled secret drives, you know."

"And is that what you're telling me?" Elizabeth said, her voice shaking almost to the breaking point. "That it's no secret that I wanted Caroline to die?"

"I didn't say that. I'm simply throwing out topics to discuss," Graydon replied. "Feelings of competition—especially between a mother and daughter, or between a father and son—are normal; I'd say even natural. If something horrible happens, it would be reasonable to think that the subconscious guilt you feel could lead you to—"

"To try to kill myself?" Elizabeth said.

"Possibly," Graydon said. He stretched out his arm and looked at his watch. "I hate to say it, but we're about done for today. How do you feel about what we've been discussing?"

Elizabeth took a deep, shuddering breath. "I guess I've got plenty to think about until next week," she replied, as she shifted around on the couch and stood up shakily.

"Until our next session, though, I want you to consider that," Graydon said, also rising from his chair.

"What?" Elizabeth said, unable to control the trembling of her voice.

Lowering his voice and looking at her with a dark, intense stare that was almost cruel, Graydon said, "If you could speak with Caroline . . . what you would say to her."

"You know," Elizabeth said, lowering her eyes and laughing nervously as a wave of dizziness swept through her, "just now I thought of another reason. It might be that I just want to have a chance to . . . to say good-bye."

5.

The next morning, unable to get the strange goings on at Oak Grove Cemetery out of his mind, Frank wasn't so sure it would do any good to talk to Elizabeth about the horror he and Norton had found in front of Caroline's grave. If Harris and Lovejoy decided to inform her, then let them. It might be best if he stayed out of it entirely—except unofficially.

Unable to sleep past noon, as he usually did, Frank got up and drove into Portland, figuring he could do some research at the Portland Public Library. He made his way up the steps to the second-floor entrance and went directly to the reference desk on the first floor, where a frail, elderly man was standing at the desk, sorting index cards. The name plate on the desk read WILLIAM BAKER.

"I was wondering if you could help me find some books on magic," Frank said, as he opened his wallet and flashed his police identification.

"Do you mean like magician's tricks—hocus-pocus?" the librarian asked, waving his thin fingers in the air as if he were about to make a book on the subject magically appear. "Or are you talking supernatural magic, like witchcraft and stuff?" His voice was so cracked with age it made Frank wonder if it was the result of breathing book dust all his life.

"Witchcraft and stuff," Frank said, closing his I.D. and slipping it into his hip pocket.

"Some general reference material, or are you looking for some particular topic?"

"Well," Frank said, his mouth twitching into a lopsided grin, "this is kind of a crazy request."

Rolling his eyes ceilingward, Baker said, "Believe me, after working here as long as I have, I've probably seen and heard it all."

"Well, then," Frank said, clearing his throat, "how about supernatural—you know, magical—uses of a severed hand, like from a dead person?"

The reference librarian regarded Frank with an odd mixture of amusement and suspicion. His bushy white eyebrows jiggled up and down as he finished jogging the handful of index cards into place. Putting them to one side, he said, "Well, now, either this is a remarkable coincidence, or else you've been reading the newspapers about what happened up there in Bristol Mills, huh?"

Frank casually leaned his elbows on the desk edge. "I'm Frank Melrose, a police officer from Bristol Mills," he said. "I'm involved in the investigation."

"You don't say," Baker said. "What the devil is going on up there, anyway? Do you have any ideas?"

"Some," Frank said, offering nothing more.

"Anything we have on something like that would be in our occult section," Baker said, as he came around the desk and waved for Frank to follow him. He continued to talk to Frank over his shoulder as he walked slowly down a narrow aisle of green metal bookcases. "I think that, next to the Stephen King novels, more books disappear from this section than anywhere else. I dunno— maybe they teleport out of here or something." He chuckled softly to himself.

"No doubt," Frank said, keeping his voice to a low whisper.

Baker finally stopped in front of a section of books and, waving his thin hand in a broad arc, said, "Well, whatever we've got would be here."

The shelves did look rather sparse, with dozens of books leaning in random disarray. Every shelf was less than half full, and most of the books there looked as dusty and worn as Baker himself. In most cases, the titles printed on the spines had long since faded.

"I think more general information, like what you're looking for, would be on this shelf," Baker said. He reached up, grabbed two books at random, and handed them to Frank, who shuffled them back and forth as he read the titles aloud.

"*Mysteries of the Unseen World. Magic and the Supernatural.* Yup. I guess this looks like the stuff."

Baker backed away and said, "I'll be at the reference desk if you have any other questions." Before turning away, he gave Frank another intense once-over.

"Police work should always be this easy," Frank said, laughing to reassure Baker that everything was all right. "Thanks for your help."

Once Baker left, Frank leaned against the bookcase and began riffling through the pages of *Magic and the Supernatural.* Checking the index for the word *hand*, he found a section titled "The Hand of Glory," and, marking the place with his forefinger, he carried both books over to a nearby chair at a table and, taking out a notepad, settled down to read.

Within half an hour, after two more trips to the shelves for a few more books, Frank learned more than he had ever cared to know about the magical preparation and uses of a dead person's hand, commonly called the Hand of Glory. He found references to the Hand of Glory in three different books. All three texts said that the hand should preferably be that of a hanged man, that all of the blood must be drained or squeezed out of the hand, and that the hand was to be dried out and treated with a variety of herbs and other things. One text even specified that the hand was to be dried in the sun from July 3 through August 11, the "dog days," when Sirius, the "Dog Star," rises and sets with the sun. The whole point of it, Frank discovered, was to mix the fat extracted from the hand with wax to make a candle. This candle, then, when burned, supposedly blinded anyone but the magician who held it, and allowed the magician to rob either the blinded person or his house.

Nowhere in his reading did Frank find any reference to soaking the tips of the fingers and thumb of the Hand of Glory in an oily substance and using them as candles; but, by the time he was through with his research, he didn't think that was necessary. His conclusion didn't need to be based on whether or not he thought any of this magical mumbo-jumbo *really* worked. All he needed to know was that someone who lived either in or near Bristol Mills believed in this stuff—believed in it enough to be trying some of it! And the bottom line was, whatever warped reasoning was behind it, it seemed pretty Goddamned clear that it *was* directed straight at Elizabeth and her dead daughter!

TEN
Another Warning

1.

The sky was lowering with rain clouds blowing in from the west as Elizabeth walked out of work late Thursday afternoon. She took a breath, deeply inhaling the moist-smelling air, and started across the parking lot, intent on heading home before the rain started. Looking up at the fast-moving clouds, she realized she would be in for a soaking by the time she got halfway home; so she turned toward downtown instead, figuring she'd go to the aunts' house and visit for a while before calling home for a ride. It had been over a week since she had seen the aunts, and one of the few promises she had made to herself was that she would visit them as often as possible now that she was back home.

"I had a hunch I'd see you today," Junia said, swinging open the screen door to allow Elizabeth to enter. "Just after lunch, I told Elspeth that we'd be seeing you before the day was over. Come in, come in and have a cup of tea with us." She leaned out and looked up past the porch roof at the darkening sky. "Looks like you just made it, too."

"Yeah," Elizabeth said, as she came into the kitchen and took her accustomed seat at the table.

Junia let the screen door slam shut with a bang, then directed her

voice toward the living room doorway and called out, "Elspeth—
your niece is here to visit."

When there was no response, Junia walked over to the doorway
and glanced around the jamb. Looking back over her shoulder, she
smiled and said to Elizabeth, "She's fallen asleep again. Oh,
well—the sleep can't hurt her." With that she walked over to the
sink, filled the tea kettle, lit the burner, and placed the kettle on to
boil.

"I understand you and your fella went out on a date a few nights
ago," Junia said as she sat down opposite Elizabeth. "Did you have
fun?"

For an instant, Elizabeth considered telling Junia the truth, that
she intended never to see Frank again, but instead she simply
shrugged and said, "Sure. We had a lot to catch up on. But that
was the same night Mr. Bishop's house burned."

"Oh, yes," Junia said, covering her mouth with her hand.
"Wasn't that horrible? But I'm glad to hear you and Frank are back
to—"

"We're not," Elizabeth said, simply but sharply.

Junia instantly read in her response that there was more to it, but
she let it drop. While waiting for the kettle to boil, they chatted
pleasantly about a variety of subjects. Elizabeth kept the discussion
away from her sessions with Graydon, Henry Bishop's death, and
her relationship—or *non*relationship—with Frank Melrose. Junia
talked of neighbors and innocuous local events, such as the patch-
work quilt she was working on for the church fair and how grateful
she was that spring had arrived and she could work outdoors on her
rose bushes.

Outside, the darkness gathered swiftly as the clouds lowered. A
strong breeze blew up from the west, and, before the tea kettle had
begun to whistle, plump raindrops were splattering against the
kitchen window. Junia snapped on the overhead light, and a warm,
yellow glow flooded the room. Safe in her aunt's cozy kitchen,
Elizabeth thought that any disturbing thoughts and feelings should
be kept at bay, but when the water in the tea kettle began to boil,
the shrill whistle jangled her nerves.

Junia got a package of store-bought chocolate-chip cookies from the cupboard and brought them, along with tea cups, a honey jar, and a pitcher of milk, over to the table.

Once she was settled back into her chair and had taken a nibble of a cookie, Junia smiled and said softly, "So now tell me, dear, have you thought any more about what we talked about last time you were here?"

Momentarily confused, Elizabeth looked dumbly at her aunt. Junia smiled and added, "You know, about letting my friend try to help you."

In a rush, Elizabeth remembered Junia's mention of a friend of hers who might be able to contact Caroline. She almost said *I have all the help I need already*, but took a bite of her cookie instead and chewed; her gaze drifted to the rain-splattered window as she struggled to phrase a reply. When she took in a sharp breath, she inhaled a cookie crumb and ended up having a brief coughing fit. The tea was too hot to sip, so she got herself a glass of water at the sink while Junia looked on. After gulping down several mouthfuls of water, Elizabeth sat back down at the table, still wondering what in the world she was going to say to her aunt.

"I—really hadn't thought much about it, I guess," she managed, even though her voice sounded fragile to her own ears. "I've been pretty much occupied with . . . other things."

Her mind was filled with echoes of the conversation she had had with Graydon three days before, and she couldn't help but wonder if this was just a bizarre coincidence or if—somehow—that conversation and her aunt's suggestion were connected.

"Well, I realize it's a rather . . . unusual thing to ask," Junia said, "but I want to reassure you that I think she can help you. If you would like to speak with Caroline, that is. I know Claire would do everything she can to help."

"Do I know who this 'friend' of yours is?" Elizabeth asked.

Junia shook her head. "I doubt it. Her name's Claire DeBlaise. She lives up in Raymond and I met her only a few years ago myself. Actually, I'm not sure exactly when it was, but I do know it was long after you had moved away from home."

Elizabeth shivered as she took her cup of tea and sipped at it. In her imagination, she was already following this conversation along the same lines she had followed with Graydon; but where

Graydon had been inconclusive, insisting he was throwing this out only as a therapeutic point of conversation, Aunt Junia was being very specific and very sincere, telling her exactly what she wanted to do. It came down to the same questions: Did she believe there was any possibility at *all* that it could be done? Could she—or *anyone*—contact Caroline? Or did she think that dead is dead, and that any contact with the dead had to be no more than woolly-headed wishful thinking, outright deception, or—perhaps worst of all—self-delusion.

"And this friend of yours—Claire . . . she says she can do this?" Elizabeth asked, her face feeling as if it were chiseled out of ice. "Do you really think she can do what she says?"

"I can't speak for you, dear," Junia said, lowering her voice and leaning toward Elizabeth across the table, "but I know that when I've sat with Claire, she's said things that she absolutely could not have known, things that could *only* have been known by me and . . . the person I was contacting."

Elizabeth wanted to ask her aunt who she had contacted, but thought better of it. She had always wondered why Junia had never married. Her mother had told her that, when Junia was young, she had had a lover who was killed during World War II. Elizabeth wondered if that was who Junia had been speaking to "on the other side."

"And if I . . . if I *did* want to give this a try," she said softly, "is there—I mean, would it cost me anything?"

Junia let loose a short, braying burst of laughter. "Of course it wouldn't! Claire doesn't do this for money. She's been given a gift, the gift of allowing spirits of those we say are dead to enter her and speak through her. To accept money for sharing such a gift would be . . . well, it just wouldn't do." She shook her head, her eyes going momentarily unfocused. "No—it wouldn't do at all. Would you like me to give her a call?"

Elizabeth hesitated as conflicting thoughts cascaded wildly in her mind. The reasonable thing to do, she knew, would be to put a stop to it right now—thank Junia for her concern and tell her that she didn't want to dabble in *anything* occult. She had learned her lesson back when she had fooled around with the Ouija board, and the spirit of Max had told her and her sister to commit suicide.

She surprised herself when she nodded in agreement and said, "Yeah—I guess so . . . Why not?"

"Okay, dear," Junia said, pushing herself away from the table and standing up. "Let me just duck into the living room to check on Elspeth, then I'll give Claire a call. You just sit here and enjoy your tea."

With that, Junia hurried from the kitchen, the sound of her feet scuffing like sandpaper on the hardwood floors. Elizabeth smiled weakly as she shifted back in her chair and pretended to get comfortable. She couldn't deny the thoughts that nagged at her, the feelings that, spurred by Graydon's "theoretical" discussion, she was allowing herself to be suckered into some crazy-ass spiritualist stuff. The chances that Aunt Junia's friend Claire—or anyone, for that matter—really could communicate with the dead were remote, perhaps impossible. Even if this Claire DeBlaise wasn't an outright charlatan, Elizabeth figured she would end up sitting in a darkened room, waiting for the table to start tapping or something like that, and then would be told that the spirits, apparently, weren't willing to communicate.

But what if it works? she thought, even as waves of gooseflesh rippled up her arms. If she put aside her intellect and searched her feelings, she could feel a slim ray of hope.

What if this woman really *does* have an ability, and what if I *could* speak with Caroline? What would I say to her?

Elizabeth found herself already phrasing questions for Caroline in her mind.

"It's all set for tomorrow night, if that's all right with you."

Junia's voice burst suddenly from behind her, startling Elizabeth. She turned around and looked up at her aunt as she came back into the kitchen.

"Tomorrow . . . Friday? Umm, yeah, sure," Elizabeth said, not really thinking. "I don't think I have anything planned for tomorrow night."

"Good, then," Aunt Junia said. "She's expecting us around eight o'clock. I'll have Helen Saunders stop by to stay with Elspeth while we're out. Can you pick me up sometime between seven and seven-thirty?"

Still feeling numb, and thinking she was probably a complete fool for getting involved in any of this, much less for encouraging Aunt Junia's belief in such nonsense, Elizabeth gulped down the last of her tea. She brought the empty cup over to the sink and then asked if she could use the phone to see if her mother would come and pick her up.

She walked down the hallway to use the phone in the entryway so she wouldn't disturb the still-sleeping Elspeth. With each footstep, the unnerving sensation that she was being watched got stronger and stronger. Glancing over her shoulder, she saw that it wasn't Junia, watching her from the kitchen, but seemingly someone lurking in the darkened corners of the hallway, always just out of sight . . . just out of reach.

As her nervousness steadily increased, Elizabeth paused by the bathroom, both tempted and afraid to peek in at the mirror over the sink. Who might she see reflected there? she wondered. Whose death-pale face would be looking out at her from the glass?

Finally, bracing her shoulders and sucking in a deep breath, she walked past the bathroom door to the phone in the hallway. As she dialed home and spoke briefly with her mother, who said she'd swing by within half an hour, Elizabeth could feel the almost physical contact of unseen eyes peering at her from *somewhere* in the house. No matter which direction she looked, it always felt as though there was an indistinct presence behind her, and cold, unblinking eyes were watching her . . . staring at her . . . drilling into the back of her head.

2.

Elizabeth decided to wait outside on the back porch for her ride while Aunt Junia helped Elspeth with her afternoon bath. When she heard the crunching of tires on the gravel driveway above the splattering sound of rain on the porch roof, she looked out expecting to see her mother's car. Her throat tightened when, instead, she saw the rain-slick two-tone blue of a town police cruiser. At first she thought it was Detective Harris, coming by to ask her or her aunt some more questions. Then the driver's window slid smoothly halfway down to reveal Frank, looking up at her with a thin smile.

"Hi," he said, with a forced cheerfulness.

"Hi, yourself," Elizabeth replied, before turning to glance nervously at the kitchen door, as though expecting help to come charging out of the house. When none seemed forthcoming, she looked back at Frank and asked, "So what brings you around?"

Frank shrugged. "Just passing by. I thought it was you I saw waiting out here, I just kinda wondered what was up."

Elizabeth wanted to be mad at him for intruding on her like this, but there was something about his friendly smile that warmed her, and she couldn't help but smile back. If he did give her a ride home, she thought she might ask him to fill her in on what Detective Harris hadn't told her.

"I walked over here after work," she said, resenting that she felt she needed to explain herself to him.

"Rain kinda caught you, huh?"

"Yeah," Elizabeth said, nodding. Her eyes kept flicking up and down the road, looking for her mother whenever she heard the hissing of tires on the wet asphalt, but Rebecca was nowhere in sight.

"I was just waiting for a ride," she said at last.

"I can drive you home if you'd like," Frank said brightly. His smile seemed warmer, more honest now, but there was still an edge in his voice that made Elizabeth think he was offering his help just a bit too fast.

"My mother's already on her way," she said, glancing at her wristwatch. "She should have been here by now. Thanks anyway."

Frank nodded but made no move to back the cruiser onto the road. The engine idled smoothly, and, for a little longer than was comfortable, the only sound was the steady *slap-slap* of Frank's windshield wipers and the splatter of rain on the roof and road.

Finally, unable to stand the silence any longer, Elizabeth asked, "Is there something *I* can help *you* with?"

"I've been meaning to give you a call," Frank said, biting his lower lip.

Elizabeth looked away when she found she had nothing to say.

"Why not call home and see if your mother's left already," Frank suggested. "I'm heading out your way, anyway."

Elizabeth opened her mouth to say she'd just as soon wait for her mother, but Frank cut her short.

"I really do want to talk to you. And no—it's not about . . . us."

After considering a moment, Elizabeth flashed Frank a "hold on" signal with her hand and dashed back into the house. She hurriedly dialed her mother on the kitchen phone and, luckily, Rebecca hadn't left yet. Elizabeth told her not to bother coming out into the storm and hung up and went back outside. Pulling her jacket collar tightly around her neck, she ran down the steps and around to the passenger's door and got into the cruiser.

"Whew!" she said, wiping streams of water from her face. "I wasn't expecting this kind of weather."

"Maybe we should change the poem to say, 'May showers bring June flowers,' " Frank said, laughing as he shifted the cruiser into gear and, cocking his arm over the back of the seat, backed out into the road.

Elizabeth tried to settle down and relax. The steady rhythm of the wipers was almost soothing, but still, she felt wound wire-tight. The bunched-up muscles in her shoulders and neck just wouldn't unwind.

Frank started driving down Main Street, holding the steering wheel loosely with both hands, and he was smiling gently, as though privately pleased with himself. But Elizabeth could sense that there was something bothering him in spite of his cheerful exterior; there was a held-in-check tightness about him that, try as he might to hide it, Elizabeth could feel. Maybe she knew him just a bit too damned well!

"So what is it you have to talk to me about?" she asked.

Frank was silent as he slowed for the left turn onto Brook Road. Elizabeth couldn't help but notice that, in his silence, his eyes drifted up to the black iron gate of Oak Grove Cemetery as they drove slowly past. Low black rain clouds hung like funeral curtains over the tombstone-littered hill, and the twin-rutted dirt road was mired with running streams of rain water, and the grass that only yesterday had looked so green and spring fresh now looked gray and beaten, as though winter had never left.

"Well . . . ?" Elizabeth said.

Frank grunted, cleared his throat, and took a deep breath.

"This doesn't have anything to do with what Detective Harris was asking me about the other day, does it?" Elizabeth asked.

"Harris? When did he talk to you?" Frank snapped. His hands clenched the steering wheel so tightly the knuckles turned white.

"He came out to the house a few days ago and was asking me all sorts of questions. He said something else has happened. Tell me—what?"

Frank considered for a moment, then nodded. "Yeah," he said, his voice low and resonant. "Something else has happened. Look, Elizabeth, I don't quite know how to say this."

"Well you'd better hurry up," Elizabeth said with a grim smile, "because we're almost to my house."

"Let's go around the loop once, then. This is important."

"Does it have anything to do with Caroline?" Elizabeth asked. Her voice cracked on the last word, and she felt a passing wave of dizziness.

"It's . . . important," Frank said.

"Just tell me! What's so *damned* important?" Elizabeth said sharply.

They rounded a curve in the road. Straight ahead they could see the white siding of Elizabeth's family home. Frank took a deep breath and said, "I think I know who was out at the cemetery that night."

Elizabeth sagged back into the car seat and watched, almost helplessly, as they got closer to the house.

"Keep driving," she said, surprised that there was enough air in her lungs to force out *any* words. When Frank drove past her parents' house, the familiar, comfortable surroundings slid silently past her in the rain with the dissociated distance of a dream landscape. Turning and watching the front porch fall behind her, Elizabeth had the sense that the house, not she, was slipping away. In a momentary flash of fear, she could imagine a bent, withered figure standing in the darkened shelter of the porch as she held up a wrinkled shopping bag and slowly opened the top . . .

"Want to see what I have in here now . . . ?"

Frank turned left onto Nonesuch Road, named after the river it crossed, then turned right onto Mitchell Hill Road. For an uncomfortably long time, the only sounds in the cruiser were the wipers slapping back and forth and the steady whir of the heater. In spite of the heat in the car, Elizabeth felt cold, steely fingers wrapping around her throat and squeezing . . . squeezing ever so slowly.

"So . . . tell me," Elizabeth finally said. Her voice croaked, like the old crone in her nightmares.

"This isn't official . . . in any way," Frank said. "And I'm only telling you this as one friend to another." He was sawing his front teeth over his lower lip, and there was a tightness, a distance in his eyes that Elizabeth found unnerving.

Getting a grip on herself, she straightened up in the car seat and said, "Okay—fine. I won't hold you to it in a court of law. Will you just tell me what the hell is going on?"

Frank flashed her a harsh glance and said, "I wouldn't joke about it if I were you. I think you're in trouble—a lot more trouble than you realize!"

"You told me that before."

"Well," Frank began haltingly, "after the first incident . . . you know, I wasn't so sure, but now—"

"Cut through the bullshit, Frank, and tell me!" Elizabeth said, her voice threatening to break with every word. "First Harris and now you are saying *something* else happened. What the fuck was it?"

"Yeah . . . there was something else," he said. He eased over onto the dirt shoulder on a stretch of road with no houses on either side and slipped the shift into park. Twisting around and resting his arm on the back of the car seat, his fingertips just touching Elizabeth's shoulder, he faced her.

"Last Monday night," he began, his voice low and halting, "someone was out by your Uncle Jonathan's grave again. We're pretty sure it was the same person, because of what we found."

Elizabeth was just about to ask what it was they had found, but then, with a jolt of horror, she realized what it must have been. She gasped and then said, "His . . . hand?"

"Yeah," Frank said. "Whoever it was left your uncle's severed hand out there."

"Oh, my Christ!" Elizabeth whispered.

"There's more," Frank said. "A lot more. He didn't just leave it on Jonathan's tombstone, you see. He was doing some kind of

. . . of magical ceremony or something. Norton and I almost caught him, too, but he got away. Do you know what a Hand of Glory is?''

Flooding with fear as she stared out at the rain-drenched trees, Elizabeth numbly shook her head and rasped, ''No.''

''I did a bit of research on it. It's got something to do with certain magical rituals. Usually, at least in the old days, when people actually believed in this kind of stuff, the Hand of Glory had to be that of a hanged man. It was used to get control of someone so the person using the Hand could . . . I guess sort of hypnotize him so he could then rob his house.''

''If someone was using my uncle's hand for something like that, then I'd guess at least one person still believes in this stuff,'' Elizabeth said. She almost said something about Aunt Junia's arrangements for her to meet with a spiritualist friend of hers, but then she thought better of it.

''There's more,'' Frank said grimly.

''Jesus Christ—what is it?'' she said, even as she wished to heaven none of this was really happening.

''The magical ritual, at least as far as he got, was done at—'' Frank stopped and took a deep breath, but before he could continue, Elizabeth interrupted him.

''—At Caroline's grave!'' she said.

Frank nodded and slid his hand firmly onto her shoulder. He could feel her trembling, and his heart went out to her.

Elizabeth let out a sharp gasp, only distantly aware of the tears that were flowing from her eyes. Frank's words drove into her ears like a sledgehammer.

''No . . . did he . . .''

She couldn't finish the terrifying thought she had, but Frank knew what she meant. Shaking his head, he said, ''No—he didn't . . . dig her up. But you see, the hand was stuck into the ground over Caroline's grave. He had soaked the fingertips in something flammable because they were burning, like candles.''

''Oh, *Jesus*!'' Elizabeth gasped. A sudden gust of wind blew some wet leaves against the cruiser's windshield, where they stuck like fat leeches.

''I haven't figured out exactly what was going on,'' Frank said, assuming a commanding tone of voice if only to keep from feeling too deeply what Elizabeth was feeling. "I mean, you can bet that Harris and Lovejoy are working on it, but still, you've got to understand, what happened out there is not that serious a crime—"

"What do you mean 'not that serious'! Jesus Christ, Frank! Someone . . . someone *desecrated* my daughter's grave, and you're telling me it isn't *serious*?" Slouching against the car seat, she buried her face in her hands.

"I didn't mean it that way," Frank said soothingly, wishing—as always—that he could say the right words to her. "It's just that—you have to keep in mind that there's quite a bit of other work these detectives have to do. Even something as . . . as horrible as this is classified only as a misdemeanor by the state."

"You mean to tell me that performing a black-magic ritual over my daughter's grave is like a . . . like a Goddamned speeding ticket? Jesus!"

"All I'm trying to do is explain why Harris and Lovejoy can't put all of their time into investigating this," Frank said. "There are plenty of other more serious crimes committed that they—"

"How can you say this isn't serious?" Elizabeth burst out. Her voice was raw and broken. "What are you talking about? Someone dug up my uncle's body, for Christ's sake! They cut off his left hand, and now they're doing some kind of ritual over my daughter's grave, and you try to tell me it isn't serious!"

If it hadn't been pouring rain, she would have gotten out of the car right then and walked away, no matter how far she was from home. A numbing chill was gnawing at her gut like sharp, animal teeth. Deep muscle tremors rumbled inside her like an earthquake; she didn't dare move, and she knew that if she looked at Frank she would completely dissolve.

"What can it . . . What does it mean?" she asked. Her voice warbled faintly as she fought to control it. She stared blankly ahead at the rain-slick road.

Frank wanted to be sympathetic and tell her comforting lies, but he knew he couldn't. This was the part of police work that he hated the most—being "professional" when a close, personal friend was involved.

"What it means is, there's at least one honest-to-Christ class-A wacko in town or nearby who's doing shit like this," he said, forcing his voice to stay measured and even. "And there's no doubt in my mind that he's directing it right at you."

"But . . . *why*?" Elizabeth asked. Her eyes were wide with fear and shock as she turned to him.

"That's what I want to find out," Frank said. "Who's doing it and why."

"You keep saying 'he.' How do you know it's a man?"

"From the evidence—the footprints we lifted that night out at the cemetery and some other clues, Harris is fairly certain there's at least one man involved—possibly two—but there's really no way of knowing conclusively with the evidence we've gotten so far. But I want you to think about it a minute. Is there someone—anyone —you can think of who might be mad enough at you to do something like this?"

Elizabeth gave her head a quick, tight shake. "The only one I can think of is Doug, but he wouldn't—"

"I know you got upset with me the other night when I suggested he might be involved, and I'm not saying it *isn't* him, but can you think of anyone else who could have . . . well, enough hatred for you that he—*or she*—would be trying to terrorize you this way?"

Elizabeth's breathing came in short, shallow gulps. The tips of her fingers were tingling as thoughts and fears collided in her mind. She was gripped with the sudden fear that she was going to pass out.

"*Someone* is doing this, and I'm not entirely convinced it's because he honestly believes this black-magic bullshit really works. I think it's just as likely he's doing it to try and freak you out, maybe so much so that you'll—"

"Go crazy," Elizabeth said raspily. "Or maybe kill myself or something."

"Maybe," Frank said, stroking his chin thoughtfully.

"You said this . . . this Hand of Glory had to be that of a hanged man, right?" Elizabeth said. She knew she was a breath away from completely shattering.

Frank grunted and nodded.

"Did you know that my Uncle Jonathan killed himself?" Elizabeth said. "I just found out this last week. My Aunt Junia told me that they found him hanging from a rafter in his barn."

"Jesus H.," Frank said. "I never knew that. I mean, it was—how long ago? I remember when he died, but we were just kids—what, nine or ten years old? I'd never heard he killed himself."

"Neither had I until just a few days ago," Elizabeth said, a slight measure of control returning to her. "He didn't leave a suicide note or anything, and the family kept it pretty much hushed up. I mean, all my life, I never even had an inkling."

"So—who would know something like that?" Frank asked.

Elizabeth shrugged. "I dunno. I suppose just my family—you know, my mother and father and aunts. The police must've been told, too, but they must have helped my family keep it hushed up. I suppose there might be something in some old records or something, maybe a police report that anyone who might be interested could look up."

"That's not unreasonable," Frank said. "Especially in a small town like Bristol Mills, where everybody seems to know everybody else's business. But you'd think there would have been at least some gossip about it."

"None that I ever heard," Elizabeth said. "That must rule out Doug, because if I didn't know, he certainly couldn't have."

"I'm not going to rule out *anyone* until I find out who did it, and can prove it," Frank said. "But you know—all of this is getting us nowhere fast. I mean, as cruel as it sounds, what we're talking about isn't going to amount to a hill of beans for either your uncle or your daughter. What we've got to be concerned about is your safety, because if this *is* directed at you . . ."

Elizabeth held up her hands in a gesture of helplesss frustration. "I don't even know what we're looking for! I don't suppose whoever's doing it is going to start sending me little pieces of paper with black dots on them as a warning or whatever, is he?"

Frank looked at her until she was forced to look away. He wished that the tiny voice whispering inside his head, saying that maybe *Elizabeth* was the one doing all of these weird things, would just shut up; but it wouldn't. If he looked at this objectively, it seemed entirely plausible that she had become so distraught over first losing her daughter and then getting divorced that her mind had snapped. She was, after all, seeing a therapist. Maybe she was the one who was full-tilt-boogie "looney tunes."

Clearing his throat, Frank said, "You know, I've also been wondering if your therapist, Roland Graydon, might be involved."

Elizabeth couldn't have been more stunned if Frank had fired his revolver at her, point-blank. She stared at him wide-eyed, not really believing what she had heard.

"You've got to be kidding!" she said, after a brief burst of laughter. "Graydon? What the hell are you talking about, Frank?"

"I'm talking about who I think might be doing all of this—for whatever twisted reason."

"You can't be serious!" Elizabeth said.

Frank shrugged as he nodded. "I couldn't be more serious."

"That's a pretty irresponsible allegation," Elizabeth said. "I met the man for the first time in my life just a couple of weeks ago. Anyway, all of this began happening before I started seeing—Hey, wait a minute! How the hell did you even know I was seeing a psychiatrist in the first place?"

Frank said simply, "I met him with you that night at Booksmith, remember? And since then I've done a bit of research on him. It wasn't hard to discover that he's a therapist, so I figured you were seeing him professionally."

"So you've been checking up on me behind my back?"

"Look here, Elizabeth. You may not think so, but I honestly believe you're in some kind of danger. I don't know for sure who's doing it or why, but there's been too many things falling into place here."

Elizabeth snorted with laughter that didn't come at all close to breaking the tension in the cruiser. "You're starting to sound like a paranoid, Frank," she said. "Maybe *you* should make an appointment with Dr. Graydon for yourself."

"I plan to talk to him, all right . . . just as soon as I can. And if I get enough evidence, I'll nail him."

"I don't see how you can even suggest that he's involved!" Elizabeth said, torn between laughter and an explosion of anger. She wanted to lash out at Frank.

Maintaining a low, steady voice, Frank said, "I can suggest it because, in doing an area survey, we did get a description of a car in the area of Oak Grove that night. It matches Graydon's car.''

"You mean someone got the license-plate number and everything?" Elizabeth asked, trembling with rage.

"No—but the make and color are a match. The car was parked in a vacant lot out on Route 22, right next to an old fire road that comes up from behind the cemetery. Coincidentally, it's fairly close to where Henry Bishop found Fraser's body. Barney Fraser obviously was murdered, and I'm not entirely convinced Henry's death was an accident, either.''

"I thought cops didn't believe in coincidences," Elizabeth said, unable to disguise her sarcasm.

"We don't," he said, "but we also don't pretend there aren't connections when we see them.'' Glaring at her, Frank shook his head with disgust and continued, "Look, Elizabeth, if you want to be blind to all of this, then fine—but I think you're a damned fool not to look at it for what it is. Sure, I don't have enough proof to truly suspect anyone. But let me ask you this—how much do you really know about this Dr. Graydon?''

Elizabeth sighed deeply. "Well, I certainly know he isn't the type who would get involved with any kind of black-magic bullshit.''

"How do you know that? Tell me, what exactly *is* the type?"

Elizabeth shrugged, speechless.

"See," Frank went on, "you don't even know. You have no idea. I've been checking into this stuff some, and one thing I'm finding out is that no one can know for sure who's involved. All I'm saying is, there's a lot of weird shit going on, and you can never tell. You can't judge this Dr. Graydon's or *anyone's* personality superficially as either being or not being the *type*.''

Elizabeth tried to push aside the uneasy thoughts Frank's words stirred in her. Snickering, she jabbed at Frank and said, "Come on! Take me home. I'm already late for supper. If I listen to very much more of this, I'm going to start suspecting even *you* might be involved! After all, if we're looking for connections—*coincidences*, if you'll allow me to use the word—you were the one who discovered what was going on out there both times.'' She stroked her chin thoughtfully and glanced at Frank from the corner of her eye. "How do you think *that* looks?''

"Okay, fine; go ahead and make light of it if you want," Frank said, totally frustrated.

"I'm not making light of it," she replied earnestly. "Keep in mind what you keep telling me; all of this seems to be directed at me!"

"And I'll tell you something else—whether you like it or not, I'm gonna keep on watching you and checking out everything— and every*one*—I have to until I find out who's doing it . . . and why!"

Elizabeth laughed again, louder this time as she lightly gripped Frank's arm above the elbow. "Somehow," she said, even as her stomach twisted with a cold dread, "I just *knew* you were going to say that."

PART TWO

Look!
The dead have risen!

These creatures are all inferior to us,
and what you see is only smoke and shadow;
so then raise your eyes!
—*Autobiography of Benvenuto Cellini*

Methinks that what they call my shadow
here on earth is my true substance . . .
Methinks my body is but the lees of
my better being.
—Herman Melville

ELEVEN
Seance

1.

The rain that had begun the day before was still pouring down on Friday night when Elizabeth and Junia left Elspeth in the care of Mrs. Saunders and drove up Route 302 to Raymond to meet Claire DeBlaise. As they drove, the glare of the streetlights made the slanting sheets of rain look like drifting snow, while hammer-fisted gusts of wind buffeted the car, making it difficult for Elizabeth to keep straight on the slick surface.

After turning right off Route 302 onto Route 85, they drove a few miles to the right-hand turn onto Egypt Road. What an appropriate name for the road a psychic lives on, Elizabeth thought with a faint stirring of humor. After driving a mile or so down the road, Junia tapped her lightly on the arm and said, "That's her house, there on the left." Elizabeth should have felt relief that the drive was over, but a deep, cold tension coiled up inside her when she thought about what she and her aunt proposed to do tonight.

Slowing for the turn into the driveway, Elizabeth's first thought as she looked up at the house was that it wasn't at all what she had been expecting. At best, she had imagined Claire's house would look like the house from *Pyscho*, but it turned out to be a pleasant little ranch with a two-car garage connected to the house by a breezeway. The outside light was on, and there was someone waiting in the doorway as they got out of the car and hurried up the walkway. The downpour drenched them during the short walk to the breezeway door.

Like her house, Claire DeBlaise was not at all what Elizabeth had been expecting. Aunt Junia had told her Claire was a young woman. Elizabeth had assumed she meant younger than herself, which could still mean she would be considerably older than Elizabeth. Elizabeth had built up a complete stereotyped image of an elderly woman, maybe in her sixties, most likely with long, thick, curling black hair, several pounds overweight, with fleshy jowls, thick pancake makeup, and hooped, Gypsy earrings. As she and Junia crowded into the entryway out of the storm, Elizabeth thought the sprightly woman with bright blue eyes and fiery red hair who greeted them might be Claire's daughter.

She realized her mistake when the woman smiled and extended her hands in greeting to Junia.

"I'm so glad you could make it," Claire said, gripping both of Junia's hands and shaking them. Her voice had a pleasant lilt, as if she were singing her words. "And in such weather! I was waiting for a call to say you were going to cancel."

When Claire gave Junia a warm embrace, Elizabeth noticed that the woman's hands looked unhealthily thin and pale; the skin was almost translucent, and the sprinkling of freckles seemed to hover in the air above the surface of her skin.

"And this is your niece, Elizabeth, whom you told me about," Claire said, standing back and giving Elizabeth a quick once-over. "Welcome to my home." She stepped to one side, watching and smiling warmly as Elizabeth helped Junia take off her dripping raincoat.

"Here, let me take both of those for you," Claire said, holding her hand out for Elizabeth's coat as well. She hung them on a coat rack. "I can put on some coffee or tea if you'd like."

In spite of the bone-deep chill she felt, out of nervousness Elizabeth shook her head and said, "None for me, thanks."

"No, thank you," Junia replied.

"Well, maybe later. As soon as you're comfortable, we can begin in the sitting room. I call it that," she added, addressing Elizabeth directly, "because *seance*, in French, means 'sitting.' "

"Oh, I didn't know that," Elizabeth said, nervously shifting her weight from one foot to the other. Her hands were trembling. Casting a wary glance at Claire, she flushed with embarrassment that she was letting her nervousness show.

And what have I got to be nervous about? she thought as she looked around the dimly lit house. *After all, we're only here to try to contact my dead daughter!*

"Well, let's make ourselves comfortable, then," Claire said, starting down the hallway toward the living room.

Elizabeth glanced at her aunt, but Junia apparently either didn't notice her tension or else chose to ignore it. Casting her eyes downward, Elizabeth followed along behind.

Although from the outside, Claire's house had appeared thoroughly modern, Elizabeth at least wasn't disappointed in her expectations about the inside. The living room, she saw, was filled with either beautifully restored Victorian furniture or else perfectly detailed replicas. A gorgeous hand-carved clock tick-tocked on the mantel and scroll-footed couch, mahogany end tables, and heavy oak bookcases made the living room seem slightly crowded but comfortable. Being inside Claire's house was like being instantly transported back to the nineteenth century. Even the air smelled curiously old-fashioned but not stale or dusty.

After passing through the living room, Claire paused in front of a double doorway. Then, with a sweeping hand gesture, she swung the doors open and indicated that they had arrived at the "sitting room." She stepped back to allow Elizabeth and Junia to enter first.

"Oh, my . . . this is beautiful," Elizabeth said, unable to resist the charm of the Victorian decor.

"Why thank you," Claire replied, nodding as she watched and gauged Elizabeth's reaction.

Elizabeth's preconceptions about the house were confirmed even further. In the center of the room was a claw-footed oak table covered by a lacy white tablecloth. Surrounding the table were seven chairs, all made of dark wood, with thickly padded seats. The windows were draped with heavy curtains that had just a hint of a design worked through the dark blue material, and the wallpaper was an old-fashioned Victorian "mirror" design. Two wall sconces with tiny bulbs shaped like candle flames bracketed an ornately framed picture of a British pastoral landscape from the last century.

Claire gently closed the double doors behind them. The latch made a faint *click* which, to Elizabeth's mind, had too much of sound of finality. The heavy drapes on the windows deadened the sound of the rain beating against the house. As Elizabeth and Junia walked slowly toward the table, their footsteps on the carpeted floor hissed unnaturally loud.

"Please—have a seat," Claire said. "Wherever you like. I want you to feel completely comfortable before we begin."

"And what is it—exactly—that you plan to do?" Elizabeth asked, turning to look at Claire. She was standing by the door, her hands folded in front of her as she squinted and silently surveyed the room. She appeared to be taking slow, measured breaths.

Eyes widening, Claire looked directly at Elizabeth; then she shrugged. Her eyes twinkled in the soft light from the sconces. "What *I* want to do has very little to do with what might happen in this room tonight," she replied with a hushed note of reverence. "If the spirits are willing, you will be conversing with them— through me. You see, I am a medium—a clairaudient. The spirits speak inside my head, and they use my mouth as if it were their own." She laughed softly. "You see, I always felt as though my name, Claire, which means *light*, more or less predestined me to become a . . . a messenger of the True Light. Spirits of the departed who haven't yet passed on to the higher planes of existence use me as an instrument to speak to loved ones still here on the earthly plane."

As much as she liked Claire on first impression, Elizabeth's first thought was, *Yeah, sure!* She smiled thinly and asked, "Where would you like us to sit?"

"Wherever you feel comfortable," Claire said pleasantly. "If you feel drawn or directed to a particular chair, please sit there. We can begin as soon as you're feeling comfortable."

"Sure," Elizabeth said. She knew she wasn't going to start feeling any more relaxed until all of this was over. She pulled out a chair for Junia, then sat in the one next to her. Her hands were slick with sweat as she folded them on the table in front of her and took a shallow, shuddering breath.

Claire walked over to the wall switch, a dimmer switch, and put the lights almost all the way down. The deadened quiet of the room increased as it got darker, and after a moment, Claire came over to the table and sat down directly opposite Elizabeth.

"Now, I don't know exactly why you're here, Elizabeth," Claire began. "All your aunt told me was that you wished to contact . . . someone—someone who is no longer among us."

"It's my dau—"

"Ut-ut," Claire said, waving her forefinger in front of Elizabeth's face. "The less I know about you and what you want, the more likely we are to get in touch with whomever you're looking for. If you would, please place your hands on the table, palms down and fingers spread."

Elizabeth did as she was told. Looking down, her hands were nothing more than dark, indistinct smears against the white of the tablecloth.

"Now just relax," Claire said, her voice lowering to a lulling croon. "Open up your heart, and fill your mind with thoughts of the loved one you wish to contact."

A ripple of chills danced up Elizabeth's spine when Claire's hands slid soundlessly across the table toward her. As they touched fingertips, Elizabeth was sure she felt a tickle of electricity pass between them. She told herself it had to be just static electricity in the tablecloth, or else her keyed-up imagination, when she saw a faint blue spark jump between their fingers.

"Now I want you to take several deep breaths, Elizabeth," Claire said softly. "I can feel that you've been greatly upset lately, but I want you to forget everything that's been troubling you. Clear your mind and open it to new, higher levels of awareness and love, and your heart will follow."

Elizabeth labored to take several deep, even breaths, but all she was conscious of was the nervous fluttering sound her throat made every time she exhaled. Her body was tingling from excitement and expectation even as she told herself not to let imagination or wishful thinking carry her away.

Claire whispered, more softly, "That's good . . . that's very good. Breathe deeply . . . evenly. Now, as clearly as you can, I want you to say in your mind the name of the person you wish to communicate with. Not aloud. Just in your mind. Repeat it several times.''

Resisting the sudden, frightened urge to cry out, Elizabeth scrunched her eyes tightly shut to hold back the tears that were forming. She phrased Caroline's name in three, distinct syllables and thought it repeatedly . . .

Car-o-line . . . Car-o-line . . . Car-o-line . . .

The rain continued to batter the side of the house, but as Elizabeth concentrated on her daughter's name, the sound dropped even further into the background until it was nothing more than a lulling hiss . . .

Like the wind in the grass, Elizabeth thought, vaguely aware that her mind was drifting. With a sudden start, she shook herself erect in the chair, thinking she had almost fallen asleep.

"Calmness," Claire said softly. "Fill your heart with calmness and love. Open your mind so the spirits will feel welcomed.''

Is she just trying to hypnotize me? Elizabeth thought. Either this is a complete scam, or else this woman is a positive nut-case!

"The spirits won't come to us if there is any agitation in the mind of anyone in the room," Claire said. The musical tone in her voice drifted like a dancer in and out of Elizabeth's awareness.

Bracing herself in her chair, Elizabeth slitted her eyes open and watched the hazy form of Claire across the table from her. She held her breath, expecting to see her do something, make some kind of motion that would indicate she was pulling a trick. But, in spite of her mounting suspicions, which could just be nervousness, she couldn't deny the tingling charge she had felt from Claire's fingertips. Even now, as she looked down at their hands reaching across the tablecloth and touching, Elizabeth could feel—if not an actual charge, at least the sense of a charge building up, like a thunderstorm brewing just over the horizon.

Elizabeth wondered if there was truly anything "spiritual" happening in the room, or if her expectations and suggestibility were making her feel things that weren't there. Just as she and Pam had convinced themselves that a disembodied spirit named Max was controlling the Ouija-board pointer, she could be telling herself something was actually happening.

"Is there anyone here who wishes to speak with Elizabeth?" Claire asked. Her tone of voice shifted subtly, making the request sound almost like a command.

For several heartbeats, Elizabeth waited, wondering what would—or could—happen. What in the name of God was she doing here in the first place? This whole charade . . .

Is that what it is? A charade?

. . . is just a waste of time.

Turning her head to the side, Elizabeth chanced a quick glance at Junia. She saw that she was slouching in her chair, her chin resting on her breastbone, her hands folded in her lap. Elizabeth couldn't even tell if her aunt's eyes were open or closed. She tingled with fear when she had the sudden impression that her aunt's eyes were indeed open, and that she was staring unblinkingly back at her. For just an instant—an instant that crackled with fear . . .

Like a thunderstorm on the horizon . . . moving closer!

. . . Junia's face shifted, transforming subtly into that of . . . *The old crone!*

A quick sip of breath entered Elizabeth's lungs like fire. Her arms and legs jerked with tension, and deep tremors shook her muscles. She was suddenly convinced that the old woman in her nightmares was a distorted vision of Aunt Junia, and she was filled with the paranoid fear that all along her subconscious mind had been warning her to beware of Aunt Junia!

"Let the spirits come," Claire said, her voice no more than a sing-song whisper. "Let the spirits speak—through me—to Elizabeth."

Elizabeth glanced quickly back at Claire, then at Junia. A chilled rush of fear swept through her as she strained to hear the sound of her aunt's breathing and couldn't. Her instant, panicked thought was that Junia had died and was sitting there, staring glassy-eyed and sightless at the table. The darkness of the room made it impossible to tell as Elizabeth leaned toward Junia, trying to detect the gentle rise and fall of her chest. Finally, she saw a faint stirring of Junia's blouse and, sighing with relief, eased herself back into her chair.

"Elizabeth is here, waiting to speak with you," Claire said, apparently unaware of Elizabeth's rising agitation. "She wishes to speak to someone . . . someone who might have a message for her."

Again silence and a hushed expectancy filled the room. Elizabeth heard a stirring sound, the faint rustle of cloth against cloth. She wasn't sure if it was Claire or Junia, but she pushed aside her paranoid thoughts and, forcing herself to close her eyes again, filled her mind with her daughter's name . . .

Car-o-line . . . Car-o-line . . . Car-o-line . . .

"I feel it," Claire said. "I can feel it. There is definitely a presence here." Her tone of voice lowered and hardened.

With her eyes shut tightly, Elizabeth thought Claire's voice was coming from somewhere other than across the table; it seemed to be behind her, all around her, muffled by the walls and closed doors. Pinpricks of fear rushed through her, but she told herself not to open her eyes and look. She scrunched her eyes so tight she saw weaving light patterns blossom and dissolve in the darkness.

Car-o-line . . . Car-o-line . . . Car-o-line . . . Come on, honey! . . . Talk to me, baby! . . .

Elizabeth was paralyzed by the memory of how Aunt Junia's face had appeared dead and how it had shifted so subtly into that of the old woman in her dreams. Wave after wave of numbing cold rippled through her.

"There is *definitely* someone here, Elizabeth," Claire said. "Someone who wants to reach you."

Every time she spoke, Claire's voice dropped down another register, until she now sounded more masculine than feminine. "There's someone here who wants to see you . . . Someone who has to talk to you."

"Is it—"

Car-o-line . . . Car-o-line . . . Car-o-line . . .

"Shush," Claire said, her voice deep and resonant, almost dreamy.

Gooseflesh rippled up Elizabeth's arms even as she told herself this was just the power of suggestion at work. It wasn't reasonable—it wasn't *possible* to communicate with spirits of the dead. This whole thing was just a performance, and she was being a gullible dupe!

Claire spoke again. This time her voice rose up high, like a little girl's. "I . . . want . . . to . . ." There was a strained effort with each word, as Claire struggled to speak, almost as if strong hands were covering her mouth and squeezing her throat.

But before Claire could say anything more, something exploded into Elizabeth's awareness like a shotgun blast close to her head. It came so suddenly, so clearly, she honestly couldn't tell if Claire had said it aloud or if the voice was inside her head. Each word was spoken with the precise tone of Caroline's voice.

"*. . . help . . . mommy . . .*"

No! Impossible! Elizabeth thought. *It can't really be Caroline's voice!*

Her hands clenched into knotted fists, and she squeezed until her hands went numb right up to her elbows. Her pulse pounded in rapid, heavy, hammer blows. Sweat broke out on her forehead, and her breathing came fast and sharp.

That hadn't been Caroline speaking! It couldn't have been!

But Elizabeth was filled with the undeniable sensation that there *was* someone in the room besides the three of them. She didn't dare open her eyes to look, afraid of what she might see in the darkened room. She certainly hadn't heard anyone enter, but there was the feeling of a presence behind her . . . above her . . . surrounding her, and it was as real as Claire's and Junia's presence. She remembered having that same sensation at the aunts' house—of unseen eyes watching her, glaring at her from shadowed corners of the room. Fear coursed like a raging river inside her.

Do it! she commanded herself, even as she trembled. *Open your damned eyes and look!*

Straining with the effort, Elizabeth forced her eyes open to narrow slits. She was shocked when that didn't break or even dull the illusion that *someone* was in the room with them. Horrified, she looked over at Claire, sitting opposite her. She knew it could be, it *had* to be an illusion generated by the dark room and her wound-up imagination, but she was *positive* Claire looked . . . different, somehow, as though she had shrunk in size and become much younger. She looked almost like a little girl.

"Help! . . . Mommy! . . . Help! . . ."

The words came again, louder and clearer, but still Elizabeth couldn't tell if Claire was actually speaking them aloud or if they were inside her own head. Her breathing was raw, stinging like razor cuts as each gulp of air shredded her lungs. Her body was trembling so violently that she expected to hear her chair and the legs of the oak table chatter like machine guns on the floor. Her hands felt welded to the tablecloth, and she was fearful that she wouldn't be able to move them or to control her muscles no matter how much she wanted to.

"*Mommy! . . . Help! . . . Mommy! . . .*"

"Jesus Christ!" The words formed in Elizabeth's mind, but she had no way of knowing whether or not she had spoken them aloud. "Oh, my sweet Jesus *Christ!*"

"*Help! . . . Mommy! . . .*"

Is that you, baby? Are you here with me?

Elizabeth's eyes bulged with each surge of her racing pulse. Pressure built unrelentingly behind her eyes, and she was convinced her head was going to explode. She looked frantically around the darkened room, trying to find something tangible to latch her terrified gaze onto, something to anchor her here in the real world and keep her mind from spiraling into blackness. She could feel a powerful force, gathering just outside the curtained windows of Claire's "sitting room." It was as though a huge and hungry beast was pressing its fanged mouth and hell-fire glowing eyes against the glass . . . wanting her! Wanting to rip her to pieces!

"*Help! . . .*" wailed the voice. "*Help! . . . Mommy!*"

Each time the voice spoke, it became more shrill, until it approached a whining buzz.

"*Mommy! . . . Help . . . Mommy! . . .*"

Suddenly the room was filled with a shrieking scream that blotted out those two repeated words along with every other sound in Claire's house. Every muscle in Elizabeth's body contracted simultaneously. Her mind was a swirling confusion. She wasn't even aware of what she was doing when she kicked back her chair and stood up. She doubled up, groaning with pain, and hunched over the table. Clenching both hands into fists, she brought them down time and again as hard as she could onto the oak table. Each blow crashed like an echoing cannon shot of thunder.

"*Help! . . . Mommy! . . .*"

The voice, screaming, filled the "sitting room," spiraling higher and higher until Elizabeth was convinced it wasn't a real voice at all; it was the eternal reverberation of her daughter's screams as the pressing weight of the snowplow came down on top of her . . . the terrified, final screams of her daughter that should have been blotted out forever when the gas tanks of both the snowplow and the family Subaru exploded.

Elizabeth looked up to see Claire and Junia staring at her with horror-filled expressions, and she realized that she was the one who had been screaming.

2.

An hour later, Elizabeth, Junia, and Claire were sitting in the living room with all of the lights on, sipping tea while Elizabeth tried to calm down. She felt a small measure of reassurance when she saw the love and concern in both women's eyes, but her gut was still twisting with cold dread.

"I—I'm sorry I reacted like that," she said, looking down at the floor, blushing with embarrassment. "I just don't know . . . what came over me."

"I don't know what to say," Claire replied. Her knuckles were pure white as she raised her hand to her mouth. "I mean, I did sense the presence of *someone* there in the room, but I felt as though I couldn't draw him—or her—in. Actually, just before you jumped out of your chair and started screaming, I was about to stop everything. I was convinced we weren't going to get through." She smiled warmly and tenderly at Elizabeth. "Believe me, dear, I had no idea you were feeling it so . . . so strongly. I would have stopped sooner had I known."

At a complete loss for words, Elizabeth shrugged and smiled thinly. Junia reached over and patted Elizabeth gently on the arm. Looking at Claire, she said, "This is so unusual. I mean, I always thought it was the medium who went into the trance."

"Usually that is the case," Claire said, "but—" She held her hands up helplessly. "I just don't know. I've never experienced anything like this before. It could mean . . . any number of things."

Elizabeth shivered violently. In the prolonged silence that followed, she rubbed her shoulders and forced herself to ask, "Such as—?"

Claire's eyes jumped back and forth between Junia and Elizabeth. Finally, after taking a deep breath, she said, "I'm not entirely sure. I suppose it could mean that you are much more psychically attuned than you realize, or that you might have been in direct contact with the spiritual entity, and your mind just couldn't handle it."

Elizabeth shook her head back and forth as Claire spoke. "I don't think so," she said, her voice twisting up high and tight. "I mean, I never . . . never—" She stopped herself, unsure of what she was trying to say.

"I just don't want you to worry, dear," Claire said, looking deeply concerned, almost pained. "I'll grant you that you gave me quite a fright when you screamed like that. It certainly isn't what usually happens, but if there's something that's been bothering you very deeply, you must understand, a seance could, I suppose, trigger a quite unusual reaction."

At a loss for words, Elizabeth just nodded.

"I appreciate it if you don't want to talk about your personal life, Elizabeth," Claire continued, "but if there's something bothering you . . ."

"I lost my—daughter," Elizabeth said. A sharp hitching in her throat almost made her choke. "She died about a year and a half ago, in a car accident."

"I see," Claire said, nodding knowingly. "And it was she you wanted to contact."

Elizabeth nodded. "I think I—"

"You know, many people are knocked back at their first genuine contact with the beyond," Claire said warmly. "And I think it's important that you realize that. Probably the one thing that works against us most is our own fear. We generate it, usually out of ignorance. But if you are willing to try again sometime, let me know, all right?"

Unable to speak, Elizabeth nodded again.

"It's only knowledge and love that helps us rise above our ignorance and fear," Claire said. She glanced at the clock on the mantle and stood up swiftly. "Well, it's getting late and I'm sure you two aren't looking forward to that long drive home. Are you feeling calmed down now?''

"I think so," Elizabeth said shakily. She and Junia got up and followed Claire out to the kitchen, where they put on their raincoats and prepared to leave. When Claire swung the door open for them, a cold gust of wind blew rain into their faces. Claire quickly leaned over and gave Elizabeth a tight hug, patting her lightly on the back. "You give me a call if you want to try again," Claire said softly. "And please—whatever you do, don't let your fears get the better of you, all right?"

"Thanks," Elizabeth said, her voice no more than a gasp. "I'll try not to." She followed Junia out into the rainy night and down to the car.

3.

Still feeling dizzy and embarrassed by her outburst, Elizabeth pulled out of Claire's driveway onto Egypt Road and headed down Route 85 to Route 302, She noticed something that she hadn't been aware of, at least not consciously, on the drive out to Claire's. With the windshield wipers slapping back and forth and her headlights trying to force back the rain-swept darkness, she saw, no more than a hundred feet down the road behind her, a pair of headlights wink on. The reflection in the rearview mirror stung her eyes, and she remembered—now—that there had been headlights behind them almost the entire drive out to Claire's house.

"What the—" she muttered. She stepped down on the gas as she sped away, and the headlights sped up right along behind her.

Was there someone following her, she wondered, or was she just overreacting after her scare at Claire's seance? How could it be the same car? Who would even be interested in following her? It had to be just a coincidence. As one car had turned off the road, another had simply fallen in behind her. What this had to be was just another car that had happened to get behind her.

But the more she thought about it, the more she convinced herself that it was the same set of headlights, keeping the same distance behind her just as it had all the way from Bristol Mills.

"Jesus Christ," she said softly to herself.

Junia was chilled, sitting hunched up inside her raincoat, waiting for the car's heater to kick in. She stirred and, picking up on Elizabeth's agitation, said, "What is it, dear?"

"I . . . no—nothing."

She was about to tell Junia about her suspicions but then thought better of it and simply shook her head. "No, I was just . . . remembering what happened at Claire's." She glanced over at her aunt and forced a weak smile. "I'm so embarrassed about it. I . . . I really don't know what came over me."

"There, there," Junia replied, feeling for Elizabeth's hand on the steering wheel and patting it gently. "You were overexcited, and considering what we were trying to do, it's more than understandable. Claire understands these things better than you realize, you know."

"Oh, I know that," Elizabeth said, nodding. "She seemed very nice."

She glanced into the rearview mirror again. The headlights were still keeping pace behind them, neither dropping back nor pulling ahead to pass. Whoever it was, if the car *was* following her, was certainly not losing her on the twisting road. Elizabeth considered playing a game of speeding up and slowing down, just to see what the other driver would do, but she decided against it, not wanting to upset Junia.

"You know, though," Elizabeth said, speaking more to keep her mind occupied with something other than who might be following her and why, "I still can't believe neither one of you heard what I heard." Her eyes kept dancing back and forth between the road ahead and the rearview mirror. "The voice seemed so . . . so clear, at least to me."

"Oh, I'm not all that surprised," Junia replied. "Like Claire said, quite often the spirits don't speak directly through her but use her simply as a . . . a . . . What's the word I want?"

"A conduit?" Elizabeth said mechanically. She slowed the car when she saw up ahead the stop sign at the intersection of Route 302.

"Right," Junia said, "a conduit—they use her as a conduit to speak directly to the subject. But I suppose sometimes the only direct contact could be telepathic. Sort of like mind-reading. It's entirely possible that the spirit, whoever it was—''

"She called me . . . *Mommy*," Elizabeth said, her voice hitching painfully in her throat.

"Maybe it *was* Caroline, speaking directly to you inside your head. Claire said she sensed you have a high psychic potential." As Junia spoke, she stirred in her seat. Elizabeth felt a dart of panic when her aunt casually glanced over her shoulder at the headlights behind them. It was as if she had sensed her niece's concern about the car that was following them. Apparently satisfied, Junia turned and looked straight ahead at the road again.

As she approached the intersection, Elizabeth reached for the turn signal, but then decided against it, just to see what the car behind her would do. There was no traffic on the road, so after angling the car to make it look as if she intended to turn right, she quickly wheeled to the left and started down Route 302, stepping hard on the gas and keeping as close to the speed limit as was safe, considering the slick road conditions.

A hard lump formed in Elizabeth's throat when she saw the car take the left hand turn without using its turn signal as well. She silently cursed the rain-smeared rear window, which reflected the glaring streetlights and made it difficult for her to see clearly what kind of car was tailing her.

"So I'm not surprised you would hear something that neither one of us heard," Junia said. "*Especially* if it really was Caroline, trying to get through to you."

"Do you honestly think something like that is possible?" Elizabeth asked, unable to hide the quaver in her voice. "I mean—it just seems so . . . so—unlikely."

"I wouldn't have introduced you to Claire if I didn't think it was possible," Junia replied, smiling at her niece in the darkened car.

As they passed through the sprawling mall section of North Windham, Elizabeth purposely slowed to less than half the speed limit and pulled into the right-hand lane, hoping the car would pull out and pass her. Lights from stores and restaurants reflected brightly on the wet pavement.

"God*damn* it!" Elizabeth muttered when she saw the headlights stay right where they were, between one and two hundred feet behind her. All she could think about was what Frank had said to her yesterday—that someone was after her, and that she was in trouble!

"Oh, I wouldn't be too disappointed," Junia said kindly. Elizabeth realized her aunt, still unaware of the car following them, had misread her reaction. "Actually, I was thinking about someone else I could introduce you to. A man named Eldon Cody. He's got a method of contacting the—"

"Would you like a cup of coffee?" Elizabeth asked suddenly, seeing the golden arches of McDonald's up ahead on the right. She thought she had a good idea how to lose the car tailing her—if it *was* tailing her. She was driving slowly enough in the right-hand lane so that she could easily make the turn without using her blinker, and she hoped to force the driver behind her—whoever it was!— either to make an obvious sudden turn and give himself away or else to continue on his way.

"Isn't it too late?" Junia asked. Her eyes reflected the bright yellow light of the McDonald's sign. "I wouldn't sleep a wink if I had any caffeine."

Hell, I probably won't sleep a wink as it is, so what does it matter? Elizabeth thought.

All she said aloud was, "I think I'd like a cup, though."

At the very last possible moment, she jerked the steering wheel to the right and sped into the entrance. She slowed almost to a stop. Staring long and hard at the rearview mirror, she tensed, waiting to see the pursuing car go by. Before it did, though, she felt forced to keep moving so she wouldn't raise Junia's suspicions that something was wrong. She rolled down her window, thankful that the wind wasn't blowing the rain straight in on her, and drove around back to the ordering window.

"May I take your order, please?" a voice said, rattling the speaker on the metal post in front of the lighted menu.

Elizabeth was barely aware of the request as she leaned forward, craning her head around as she tried to see the taillights of her follower disappear down the glistening road. No cars went by, and she wondered with a flush of anxiety if she had missed it or if the driver behind her had had enough time to pull over to the side of the road, and if he was sitting out front, just waiting for her. She tried to cover her agitation as she turned to Junia and said, "You're sure you don't want anything?"

Junia shook her head.

"Just a cup of regular coffee, then—with cream and sugar," she said, scanning the road in front of the restaurant for any sign of the car. She was trying to convince herself that the car had indeed sped by just at the moment they had passed behind the building, but she couldn't quite accept that. She could easily imagine the car, idling in the breakdown lane just in front of the McDonald's entrance.

"Would you like an apple pie with that?" the tinny voice asked, sounding bored, almost mechanical.

"Ahh, no . . . no thanks," Elizabeth said, all the time thinking, *Who the hell would be following me on a night like this? And why*?

"That will be fifty-three cents, please," the metallic voice said. "Please drive up to the window."

The muscles in Elizabeth's leg were beginning to cramp as she stepped lightly on the gas and eased her car ahead to the window. She paid for her coffee and, after dumping a packet of sugar and two creams into it and stirring, pulled away from the window. She approached the exit onto the road with anxious caution. Her heart was fluttering in her throat and her free hand clenched the steering wheel in a death grip as she forced herself to look to the left to see if the car was there.

Nothing.

Because it was so late and such a stormy night, the long stretch of road was empty except for a northbound sixteen wheeler and, way off in the distance, just cresting the hill as it headed toward her, a pair of headlights that couldn't possibly belong to the car that had been tailing her. After coming to a complete stop at the McDonald's exit, she took a sip of coffee and waited as the distant car approached and went whizzing past. Its tires sounded like tearing paper on the wet pavement.

Once the car's taillights had disappeared down the road, Elizabeth let her breath out in a long, slow hiss. When Aunt Junia looked at her questioningly, she covered it up by pretending to blow over the steaming coffee to help it cool. Finally, she pulled back onto Route 302, intending to follow it down to Foster's Corner, where she'd pick up Route 202 back to Gorham and then Bristol Mills.

As she approached the lights at the intersection where the Dairy Queen used to be, though, her heart skipped a beat when she noticed a dark car parked close to the road in the Shell service station on her right. The gas station was closed for the night, and the car's headlights were off, but she could see a plume of exhaust, spewing like a tiny tornado from its tailpipe. The windshield was streaked, as though the wipers had been turned off recently. Trying not to appear too obvious—either to Aunt Junia or to whoever the hell was in that car—Elizabeth slowed down and stared over at the idling car. She wished to hell she could see the face of the person behind the steering wheel, but the dark figure was nothing more than a black blur behind the rain-streaked window. She sensed more than saw his head turn to track her as she went slowly past.

Elizabeth's first impulse was to pull right over into that gas station and angle her car so that her headlights shined directly in the side window and onto the driver. Let *him* see what it feels like, she thought. Let him *know* she knew he was following her. And make it Goddamned clear she wasn't about to be intimidated.

But the traffic light was green, and the last thing Elizabeth wanted to do was alarm Junia. She knew that if she was in trouble, that was one thing, and she would just have to deal with it; but if at all possible, she didn't want to involve—or endanger—Aunt Junia. She pressed down hard on the accelerator, and the car sped down the road. A cold tightness gripped her chest when, in her rearview mirror, she saw a pair of headlights wink silently on and pull out, falling in behind her.

"You *bastard*!" she muttered.

"Is something the matter, dear?" Junia asked.

Looking at the headlights behind her, which had dropped back and were following her at exactly the same distance as before, Elizabeth covered up by saying, "Oh, no—no. For a second, there, I thought that car was going to pull out right in front of me."

"I didn't even see it," Junia said, twisting to look over her shoulder.

"Umm—I guess only fools would be out on a night like this, huh?" Elizabeth said, trying to turn it into a joke, if only to lighten her own mood.

But as she cruised down Route 302 toward Foster's Corner, she

:ept well under the speed limit; not because of the wet roads, but ›ecause she no longer cared that the car was right there behind her. She calmed herself as best she could, resolving that she would handle hings as they came. Worrying about who this was and why he was ‹ollowing her would only work to unbalance her, and she couldn't ›fford that.

The car stayed with her all the way to Bristol Mills, but long ›efore she had passed through downtown Gorham, Elizabeth no ›onger wondered who it was. The more she thought about it, the :learer it became. There was only one possible answer. This wasn't ;omeone "out to get her," as Frank had said. That was indulging n paranoid thinking. No—Elizabeth was positive who it was, and ıs she drove down Main Street to Junia's house, she vowed, first hing tomorrow afternoon—when she knew she could get him on he phone at work—she would call Frank up and tell him just where he hell he could go!

4.

"Hello. This is Officer Melrose," Frank said, picking up the ›hone in the squad room.

"Frank," the voice on the other end of the line said, and with :hat one word, Frank knew who it was. His mind flooded with :houghts and speculations as to why she was calling.

"Hey, Elizabeth. What can I do you for?" he asked.

"I think you've probably got a pretty good idea what you can *do* me ‹or," she said. "You can take a flying fuck at a rolling donut, okay?"

Elizabeth's cold, controlled tone of voice was like a slap in the ‹ace. For a moment, Frank was confused. Hadn't they ironed out ›verything yesterday afternoon before he dropped her off?

"Umm—I'm sorry," he said, clearing his throat. "I'm not ex- actly following you."

"Oh, that's rich, Frank—real rich! *Following* me! I get it! You're ›ust too hilarious!" Elizabeth said. Her mock laughter crackled like ‹ire over the phone line.

"Uh, look, Elizabeth," Frank said, scratching behind his ear. "I was just heading out on patrol. Is there something I can do for you?" He glanced up at the clock on the squad-room wall and saw that it was already ten minutes into his shift. Norton had called in sick yesterday, and Frank assumed he wouldn't be in today, either.

"You can start by leaving me the fuck alone, all right?" Elizabeth snapped. Her voice was steely and hard. "I remember what you said yesterday—that like it or not you're going to be watching out for me. I didn't think you meant it that literally, but I certainly don't want to feel as though every time I turn around, I'm going to see you lurking in the shadows."

Frank sighed deeply and said, "Elizabeth—you're not making sense. What the hell are you talking about?"

"Last night . . . ? Or don't you remember? Driving out to Raymond and back . . . ? A little house on Egypt Road? I *know* that was you who followed me."

"I *what*?" Frank said sharply. "Last night I was on my usual shift from three to midnight. I don't—"

"Frank, you can cut the bullshit with me, all right?" Elizabeth shouted. "I know it was you who followed me when I took my aunt out to visit a friend of hers last night, all right? I know that was you parked in that gas station waiting for me, and I know it was you who—finally—pulled off just before I drove into my aunt's driveway, okay? All I'm asking you now . . . No, I'm not asking you, I'm *telling* you—if you don't stop following me around like a frigging watchdog, I'll talk to a lawyer and have a . . . an injunction or whatever thrown at you to keep you away from me! Can I make myself any clearer?"

Frank's face tightened into a hard, unsmiling expression as he stared blankly at the institutional green wall of the squad room. "No, Elizabeth. You couldn't be any clearer," he said softly.

"Good!" she replied. "I'd really appreciate it."

Frank listened as she hung up with a click. For several seconds he just stood there with the receiver pressed against his ear, listening to the steady, insectlike drone of the dial tone. Usually that sound irritated the shit out of him, but now—for some reason—he found it almost comforting, almost a distraction from the question that was raging inside his mind . . .

Who the Christ is trying to terrorize Elizabeth? . . . And why?

TWELVE
Visiting Caroline

1.

"You never let me explain about Eldon Cody," Aunt Junia said when Elizabeth came to visit the next day. The rain had stopped during the night, and a warm, spring-fresh breeze rustled the leaves, casting deep green shadows over the lawn. The world seemed refreshed and vibrant, truly alive.

Perched on the porch railing, Elizabeth was gazing out at the small downtown area, watching the sporadic traffic rumble by. The warm breeze carried the full promise of summer coming on fast, and she was filled with pleasant memories of sitting in the shade of the porch as a child, sipping lemonade as she watched the heat haze ripple along the road.

"I—what did you say?" Elizabeth asked, shaking her head as she drew her attention back.

"Eldon Cody . . . remember?" Junia asked, smiling. "I thought I mentioned him to you last night, on the drive home."

"Umm, yeah—I think you might have," Elizabeth replied although, searching her memory, all she had from last night's rainy and dark drive was the heart-squeezing terror she had felt every time she looked up and saw those headlights, glowing in the rearview mirror.

"He's someone else who might be able to help you," Junia said.

Lowering her voice and casting a suspicious eye toward the open kitchen door, she finished in a whisper, "You know—in contacting Caroline."

As usual, Elspeth was dozing in the living room. Junia's secretiveness made Elizabeth wonder if Junia's involvement with occult and spiritualistic things was another dark secret—like her hidden bottle of brandy—that she had to hide from her older sister. Although she didn't feel anything close to humor, Elizabeth chuckled and said, "After what happened at Claire's house, I'm not so sure I want to mess around with stuff like that anymore."

"Oh, that's too bad," Junia said suddenly, as she covered her mouth with one hand and opened her eyes wide with embarrassment.

"What?"

"Well, you see," Junia replied, casting her eyes downward, "I thought you told me it was all right to go ahead and get in touch with him." She shook her head as if she had an ear full of water. "Maybe I'm just getting old, but I could have sworn you said you thought it was a good idea. Anyway, I've already called him and arranged for you to go out and see him on Sunday afternoon."

Elizabeth stopped herself before she snapped, *Well you can just call him again and tell him we won't be there*, and, looking at the honest embarrassment in her aunt's eyes, she felt a powerful surge of affection for the old woman.

"He lives in Standish, on Black Hill Farm," Junia went on. "And from what I've heard, he's done some pretty remarkable things."

"Like what?" Elizabeth asked, her gaze shifting back out over the town. The view looked and felt as though a black cloud, heavy with rain, had passed between her and the sun. She shivered, dreading her aunt's response and knowing she should stop the whole thing right now; she should admit to Junia that she hadn't really wanted to go to Claire's in the first place, and that she sure as hell wasn't interested in this Eldon Colby or Cody or whatever the Christ his name was. Especially not after what had happened at Claire's!

"He's got this new method of communicating with the departed," Junia said. "I haven't seen him do it, mind you. I've only heard about him through a mutual friend of ours, but . . . well, when I spoke with him this morning, he told me not to mention anything about his method.''

Elizabeth almost said, *Sounds like horse shit to me*, but then thought better of it.

"Because of something going on at church, Mrs. Saunders won't be able to stay with Elspeth on Sunday, so it turns out I won't be able to go with you," Junia said. "I can give you directions to his house, though. I told him you'd be by sometime early in the afternoon.''

"Gee, thanks," Elizabeth said, bristling at the thought of practically being forced to do this alone. If it had been *anyone* besides Aunt Junia, she knew she would have told that person to go to hell! Aunt Junia's forwardness bothered her, though; it didn't seem like her, and Elizabeth wondered if maybe she, like Elspeth, was starting to show her age.

"There was one thing he did say, though," Junia added.

Elizabeth looked at her, arching her eyebrows questioningly. "I'm not so sure I want—"

"He said you should bring two blank cassette tapes with you."

"What?" Elizabeth said, unable to hide her surprise. She couldn't deny the uncomfortable feeling that she was being railroaded into all of this.

"That's what he said," Junia replied firmly as though, now that she had said her piece, that was the end of the discussion. "He said for you to bring two blank cassette tapes, and for your own good, make sure they haven't been opened."

For my own good, huh? Elizabeth thought bitterly. *That's the whole problem with practically everything that's happened since I got home: everyone's telling me what I should be doing for my own Goddamned good!*

2.

Elizabeth helped her aunts with supper that evening, and, throughout the preparation, eating, and cleaning up of the meal, neither Elizabeth nor Junia again mentioned anything about Claire or Eldon Cody or engaged in any other kind of occult talk. Maybe, Elizabeth thought, it was because Elspeth stayed awake until after ten o'clock, by which time Elizabeth had to head home, and Junia had to keep quiet about such things around her sister; or maybe it was simply because everything was settled, and there was nothing left to discuss.

After ten, Elizabeth excused herself, saying she had to get home so she would be fresh for work the next morning. She wasn't really the least bit tired, but didn't want to exhaust either one of her aunts, or overstay her welcome.

Elizabeth didn't know why, but as she approached the turn onto Brook Road, she began to feel tense and restless. More than a week ago, her mother had told her there were three things she wanted her to do. First, call Doug and talk to him, which Elizabeth had no intention of doing. She knew she couldn't avoid it simply by putting it off, but so far her mother hadn't mentioned it again.

The second thing was to stop lying to her mother. That comment had cut Elizabeth deeply, because she felt more than a little guilty. She convinced herself that they were nothing more than "little white lies," but why couldn't she just be direct and honest with everyone, all the time?

The third thing was perhaps the most difficult to accept or even contemplate—it was visiting Caroline's grave. Although Elizabeth hadn't told her mother about it, she had tried, that day she had bumped into Doug at the cemetery; but for some reason she was positive she wouldn't have been able to go up the hill to the site. The thought that she didn't even dare go visit her daughter nagged at her mind constantly day and night.

Elizabeth knew she had to eventually go out there. The least she could do was place some fresh flowers on the grave. She also knew damned well she couldn't go there now—not after the sun had set! But as she slowed for the turn onto Brook Road, the turn that would bring her past the Oak Grove Cemetery gate, the stinging pain of loss gripped her heart. She was suddenly seized by a blind fear of even driving past the cemetery, so instead of turning left, passing it, and going home, she headed straight out Route 22 toward Buxton. She knew she was just fooling herself by excusing her action as just her need for a long drive, but that didn't make her turn around.

Heading west on Route 22, Elizabeth watched the road unscroll lazily in front of her headlights, feeling a small measure of relief when she didn't see another set of headlights come up behind her and stay there, dogging her tail. At one time a car did approach from behind, but, not being in any mood to fool around, she slowed down way below the speed limit until the impatient driver passed her—honking his horn angrily and crossing a double line, no less!

"Where are the Goddamned cops when you really need them?" she said to herself. She chuckled at the thought of Frank, pretending he hadn't followed her out to Claire's house and back the night before.

As the taillights dwindled and then disappeared around the curve, Elizabeth gasped aloud when she realized where she was heading. She slowed the car to a stop at the side of the road, then killed the engine. Slouching forward over the steering wheel, she stared blankly at the intersection up ahead. From out of the darkness, a night bird sang and then fell silent. The night closed down around Elizabeth. She was aware only of her ragged breathing and the rapid *thump-thump* of her heartbeat, pulsing in her ears.

She was parked about a hundred feet from the spot where, only a year and a half before, she and Doug had watched in horror as the Buxton town snowplow scooped up their Subaru and carried it down the hillside and off into the dark night. She snapped off her headlights and just sat there, staring ahead into the swelling night.

"Jesus Christ," she whispered as her focus blurred. In the haloed blue glow of the streetlight, she could see the front of the church that stood to the left of the intersection. The road ahead, forking left and right, was silvery with moonlight, and the breeze wafting in through the car window sent a chill dancing up her arm.

Elizabeth licked her lips as she recalled the events of that horrible night. Her mind filled with sharp bursts of color and deafening noise, and every image was ghoulishly underlit in flashes of brilliant light. Elizabeth swallowed with difficulty, her throat as dry as if she had just now inhaled those flames that had consumed her daughter.

"Come on, Elizabeth," she whispered, surprised at how distant and distorted her voice sounded to her ears. "Get your stupid ass *out* of here!"

She wanted to start up the car and drive the hell away from there, but she couldn't will her hands to move from the steering wheel. Through her tears, her eyes were focused on the lit intersection ahead. Everything got hazy with dim light, and she almost convinced herself that she had been magically transported back in time. With just a little kick of imagination, she could see that the moonlit landscape ahead of her was really covered with blowing, drifting snow.

Elizabeth's pulse raced faster and faster as she imagined—*soon! right now!*—that she would see headlights appear in her rearview mirror. It wouldn't be Frank Melrose, following her; it would be her own Subaru, with Doug at the wheel . . . herself sitting in the front passenger's seat . . . and Caroline, strapped safely—*so she thought!*—in the backseat.

"No . . . *No!*" Elizabeth said, her voice tight with tension. "*Stop it! Stop it right now!*" Her fingernails pressed into the plastic rim of the steering wheel.

But there was no way to stop the rush of her imagination! She had to sit there, replaying the accident in her mind, overlaying it onto this warm spring evening. She stared ahead in stark horror, waiting breathlessly, watching their Subaru speed down the road from behind her, approach the intersection, and, just as it started to take the curve, slide into the head-high plow ridge. The flashing lights of the snowplow appeared from around the curve ahead of her. She and Doug scrambled out of the way as the plow swept the car up over the snowy embankment. She could see the flashing lights of the plow underlighting the branches of the trees as it bulldozed the car down into the ravine. She wondered as she stuck her head out the window—*out into the blizzard that had been raging then*—whether she would be able to hear the shrieking crush of metal, the roar of the explosions, the tormented echoes of her own screams . . . and Caroline's . . . ?

Help! . . .

Mommy! . . .

Then the intersection began to glow with yellow light, bleeding out of the darkness and quickly overwhelming the faint blue glow of the streetlight. A jolt of horror seized her as she stared helplessly ahead, her mind filling with a cold blast of terror.

Is this really happening? Can I really be seeing this?

Her eyes were stinging. Her lungs burned from lack of air. She tried to take a breath but couldn't.

Is it possible? she wondered, as fear, sharper and stronger than anything she had ever felt before in her life, gripped her. *Can I really be seeing what happened on that night? Do the ghosts of people who died suddenly and violently reenact the scene of their deaths in the place where they died?*

The steadily brightening yellow light infused the night, exploding and swelling until it looked like dawn bursting over the scene. In the harsh light, Elizabeth could see every detail of the intersection in mind-numbingly sharp clarity. The rippling grooves of tree bark—the deep blackness of every shadow under each clapboard of the church—every curled and peeling strip of paint on the church doors and windows—the pebbled smoothness of each crushed stone in the asphalt surface of the road . . . *everything* stood out in bright relief and cast ink-deep shadows . . . shadows as dark as death.

"Help . . ."

The single word zipped through Elizabeth's awareness like a feather, blown and tossed on a gale-force wind. The flood of light intensified. Unable to blink her eyes or look away, Elizabeth noticed something reaching up over the tufted grass from behind the crest alongside the road. Something . . . something white and thin . . .

". . . Mommy!"

. . . was reaching, clawing up over the embankment. Elizabeth clearly saw . . . *something* trembling like a bleached branch in a strong wind as it struggled upward, clawing toward the night sky.

"Help! . . . Mommy! . . ."

"Oh, my God!" Elizabeth heard herself say. "My *God! No!*"

Even as the words slipped from her mouth, they disappeared in the roaring, rushing noise that filled the night. Elizabeth wanted to scream, but there wasn't enough air in her lungs to begin to make a sound. From over the far edge of the road, she saw a hand!—a human hand!—reaching up, groping, clawing at the night as though the hand could snag onto the blackness of night, as if the night were a dark, funereal curtain, and pull that hand's owner up . . . up and back into the world. The flood of yellow light got brighter, jabbing Elizabeth's eyes like fiery spikes.

"No! *It can't be!*" Elizabeth wailed, staring at the clawed hand struggling to reach upward. She watched in horror as the fingers worked futilely, clenching and unclenching in spastic twitches.

Suddenly, Elizabeth's ears filled with a blasting sound that shook her. Light exploded into a blinding glare, and then, with an air-sucking roar, a trailer truck zoomed past her parked car. The suction of its passing shook the car as dust and small pebbles blasted through the open window, stinging the side of Elizabeth's face. She raised her hands to protect herself, thinking in one mind-freezing instant that the truck hadn't passed her by; it was, even now, crushing down on top of her, and she—*like Caroline!*—would die in a fiery explosion that would rattle the nearby church's doors and blow out its windows.

The truck was already a hundred feet or more down the road, the whining of its engine trailing behind it with a quickly diminishing wail, when Elizabeth snapped back to reality. A stinging coldness spread out from the pit of her stomach as she groaned and collapsed forward, barely aware of the pain when she banged her forehead against the steering wheel. All of her misery came out in one long, tortured groan, and she cried so hard her chest and stomach hurt. Her eyes felt bathed in acid.

Elizabeth lost all sense of time as she hunched over, crying out her pain and misery. The night, so recently alive with menace and terror, settled peacefully back into a dark lull. She knew if she looked up toward the intersection she would see no trace of the accident of a year and a half ago, and she realized that she had only imagined seeing a white hand . . . reaching up into the night . . . *reaching for her*! And as she looked through the fish-eye lens of her tear-filled eyes, she told herself that Caroline was gone . . . dead and gone . . . *forever*!

"Forever . . ." she rasped. Her throat sounded as if it were lined with sandpaper. "I'm sorry, baby! You've *got* to believe me, honey. I'm sorry! I never *wanted* you to die!"

Her voice hitched painfully in her chest as a flood of sour-tasting acid kicked up from her stomach into her throat. Unconsciously, she loosened her aching hands from the steering wheel and, with the fingertips of her right hand, started to rub the inside of her left wrist, where she could feel the puffy welt of scar tissue.

"You *have* to believe me, honey," she whispered, her voice almost a snakelike hiss. "Your father's not the only one who misses you! Baby, I wish I had died that night instead of you! I just wish I could have . . . could have said good-bye.''

3.

When Norton still hadn't shown up at the station by three-thirty, Frank called his home. Frank couldn't shake the feeling that Norton was faking it for another day off. He didn't sound all that bad over the phone—certainly not as bad as he said he felt. Frank figured he was just pulling a few extra days off for personal reasons, and wasn't about to clue in the police chief to his suspicions. Actually, he was looking forward to the prospect of patrolling alone tonight. He had gotten rather tired of working with Norton; enough so that he was even considering a request for either a different shift or a new partner. This would give him plenty of time alone . . . to think.

And he sure had plenty to think about.

Frank wanted to think about Elizabeth's situation from as many angles as possible, and not be blinded by the feeling he had for her. Most of all, he wanted to understand what she was going through and help her as best he could—probably in spite of herself, he thought, bitterly remembering their recent phone conversation.

Since she had accused him of following her and her aunt out to Raymond and back, Frank had been bordering on panic. He knew it *hadn't* been him, and he was tormented, wondering who the hell it *had* been! He hadn't told Elizabeth the truth, figuring if that's what she thought . . . no amount of convincing was going to change her mind; and secondly, he might be better able to watch her and help her if she thought, however wrongly, that he was the problem.

But this latest development only reinforced his conviction that Elizabeth was the object of some crazy person's obsession. Certainly, anyone who would dig up a corpse and cut off its hand, use that hand to choke the local cemetery caretaker to death, and then use it as a five-flame candle on Elizabeth's daughter's grave had to be considered dangerous. Frank was also convinced that the fire at Henry Bishop's house had *not* been accidental. As far as he could tell, Harris and Lovejoy's investigation was going nowhere, partly due to the lack of clues and partly because they were swamped with other work. Investigating Barney Fraser's murder had to take precedence over everything else, even the "supposed" threat to Elizabeth. Frank was thankful that—so far—he hadn't been brought into the official investigation because, just as he thought he would be more help to Elizabeth if she thought he was the one following her around, he thought he might do better work if he wasn't directly involved with the investigation.

After finishing up some paperwork, he got into his squad car and drove through town, heading out to Brook Road. Like every other patrolman, he had been told to keep a watchful eye on Oak Grove Cemetery. Although it would be nice to have some backup handy if anything happened, Frank particularly didn't miss Norton whenever he drove out this way.

Throughout the evening and on into the night, things around town were fairly quiet. Frank picked up two speeders north of town on Route 22. About eleven, Frank took another spin out past Oak Grove Cemetery just to have a look around. With a bold confidence which he figured insured nothing would happen, he pulled up in front of the cemetery gate, got out, unlocked it, and then cruised up and down the rutted cemetery roads. Everything was peaceful and quiet; no sign of any disturbances . . . not even late-night partying teenagers.

On the crest of the hill at the far end of the cemetery, well away from Caroline Myers's grave, Frank parked, snapped off his headlights, and killed the engine. For several minutes, he just sat there, listening to the static on his patrol radio and letting his confused thoughts cascade through his mind. The serenity of the cemetery didn't help him sort anything out, however, because his eyes kept shifting over to the knoll where Caroline was buried. He felt a bit unnerved whenever he considered what, if she could talk, she might have to tell him about what was happening.

Finally admitting that he wasn't going to come to any resolutions tonight, he radioed in his intention to head back to the station for a break. Just as he was reaching for the ignition key, a car moving down Brook Road caught his attention. It slowed as it approached the cemetery gate and pulled over to the shoulder of the road.

Based on nothing more than a policeman's hunch, Frank decided to wait and see what the driver did. "Who knows," he whispered, squinting as he watched the car down by the cemetery gate. "Might get lucky."

The sloping hillside was dusted with a faint skimming of moonlight that cast long, thin shadows between the tombstones. The streetlights lining Brook Road glowed with thin blue light, and even though it was a warm, pleasant spring evening, the wind moving between the tombstones had a chilly hiss in it.

Frank felt a jolt when he recognized Elizabeth Myers's car as it crept forward and finally came to a stop directly in front of the cemetery entrance.

"Goddamn son of a bitch," he muttered, studying the idling car, waiting—and dreading—that the driver would turn and enter the unlocked cemetery. Is this the story after all? All along it's been Elizabeth!

Of course, before now he had considered that Elizabeth might be involved more than he cared to admit; but he had never allowed himself to follow that line of thinking very far because . . . it simply was too terrible to contemplate. He couldn't help but think how much Elizabeth had changed over the years. Certainly, everyone changes as they get older, and in the line of duty he had seen how life has a way of hardening and testing people, often past their breaking points. Until now, Frank hadn't allowed himself to admit the depth of the changes he had seen in Elizabeth. He knew it was foolish to think she was immune to change; but if there was any kind of fairness in the universe, she would have remained the happy, pleasant, and trustworthy person he had known all those years ago.

"Whoever said life is fair," he said aloud, letting his thoughts take form on the night breeze that blew in through the open car window. Faintly, he heard the steady rumble of Elizabeth's car, down by the gate.

Sure, it was possible that after everything that had happened to her—first losing her daughter and then her marriage—her mind could have snapped and gone sailing around the bend. In the short time they had spent together recently, especially while they were out on their date, she had seemed withdrawn, tense, at times openly hostile to him. Maybe she had been harboring all of these black secrets all along—that she had dug up her uncle's corpse, that she had killed her accomplice Barney Fraser, that out of revenge for the discovery of Fraser's body she had burned Henry Bishop in his house, and that she had performed that magical ceremony on her daughter's grave. Christ, she might even have been responsible for her daughter's death! Maybe all along she's been privately teasing and taunting him to find her out.

You're getting paranoid, old buddy, he thought, but there was no pushing aside the nagging thought of how upset, how outright pissed Elizabeth had sounded when she accused him of following her. Did she have anything to hide? And if she wasn't involved, then what the hell was she doing out here this late at night?

All the while, Elizabeth's car sat immobile at the entrance to the cemetery. Its engine idled smoothly, the cones of light from its headlights illuminating the dirt shoulder of the road in crisp detail.

"So what are you gonna do, babe?" Frank wondered aloud as he stared down at the car. "Come on, do *something! Anything!*"

He wished to hell the cruiser wasn't so visible on the crest of the hill, but he knew he couldn't start it up and back out without being discovered. If Elizabeth hadn't already spotted him, she would as soon as she drove into the cemetery. Frank had no doubt which grave site she would go to if she did. Was this simply a late-night visit to her daughter's grave . . . or something far worse?

The night pressed in on Frank. He prayed that Elizabeth would pull back onto the road and drive away. She hadn't seen him yet, and—for now—he wanted to keep it that way. Even if she *was* responsible, he just wasn't ready to deal with it tonight. He knew he had to keep his edge on this, and if Elizabeth got any more suspicious of him, he wasn't going to get any further. When—or if—the shit came down, he wanted to be able to help her out any way he could. Everything that had happened out at the graveyard had occurred between ten o'clock and midnight, so one thing he decided—unless it all came down in the next few minutes—was that from now on, when he patrolled, he would stake out the cemetery for a few hours every night . . . just to see what the hell else was going on.

It had been almost five minutes since Elizabeth first parked down by the gate, and still she hadn't done anything. Choking fumes of exhaust drifted up the hill and stung Frank's nose, masking the fresh smell of the night air. Frank strained to see but couldn't detect any hint of motion inside the car. For a moment he wondered if the car was empty; maybe Elizabeth had—somehow—gotten out without his noticing and had gone for a walk. Maybe she was creeping up behind him . . . Whatever the answer, it sure as hell looked as though there was no one sitting behind the steering wheel.

"Come on, man, stop it with those crazy thoughts," Frank said to himself. "This whole thing is making you nuts."

Without warning, the car's engine started racing as the driver revved it up. The car strained with each whining roar, but still it didn't move forward. Exhaust billowed out into the night, rising like a sheeted ghost before dispersing.

"Leave, Goddamn yah! Leave!" Frank hissed in the direction of Elizabeth's car. "Go on! Get the fuck out of here!" The palm of his hand was aching from the grip he had on his revolver.

He knew damned well he wanted to see Elizabeth drive off instead of pull around and start up the cemetery road. Had she just been waiting to see if the coast was clear and was now going to come up the hill? If she did, she sure as hell was going to notice him sooner or later.

"Go on! Get the fuck out of here!" Frank said, almost loud enough for her to hear if her window was open.

From below, Frank heard a loud *clunk* as the car shifted into gear. He almost whooped out loud with joy when he saw Elizabeth's car pull back onto the road and disappear around the curve, leaving behind nothing except the lingering smell of exhaust.

Straightening up in his seat, Frank let his withheld breath out in a long, shuddering sigh. He released the pistol's grip and rotated his arm to relieve the knotted tension in his shoulder. He knew that not much had changed. Whatever reason Elizabeth had had for stopping by the cemetery tonight—even if it was only an attempted visit to the grave of her daughter—there was still a murderer on the loose somewhere. If the murderer wasn't Elizabeth, and if it wasn't just a matter of time before she was arrested, then Frank knew, sure as shit, that she was the next most likely victim!

4.

It was well past midnight when Elizabeth got home after her drive out to the accident site and her second failed attempt to go into Oak Grove to visit Caroline's grave. Her parents were already asleep, so after changing into her nightie and opening the bedroom window to allow the gentle night air to circulate into her room, she settled down in bed. Sleep came slowly, creeping up on her like a black panther in the night, coiling and hunching, but it didn't strike. Elizabeth had too many things to think about.

As she tossed and turned in bed, she sifted through a barrage of thoughts and impressions, trying to make sense of them. Some—like that withered, white hand she had seen reaching up over the edge of the road, clawing toward the light—were very clear . . . *too* clear, actually. She knew *that* had to have been the product of her stressed-out imagination, but others—like the overpowering swells of loneliness and grief, and her sudden mistrust and anger at Aunt Junia for arranging the appointment with Eldon Cody—were real enough. They reverberated in her memory like distant echoes fading into a deep well of blackness . . . gone but certainly still strong enough to leave a stinging last impression. The white hand could not have been real! Her overwrought imagination had taken something, perhaps a twisted tuft of grass or a fallen tree branch, and magnified it into something horrible. Or even if by some horrible chance there really had been someone lying there on the side of the road either injured or dead, that was still no reason for her to think that it had been *Caroline's* hand or had anything to do with Caroline.

No, she told herself repeatedly, as she shut her eyes tightly and begged for sleep to come, she was letting her grief manifest itself; she was taking purely innocent things and twisting them into horrible, scary images. Like seeing the hand, she knew she had convinced herself that she had actually heard Caroline's voice at Claire's house. It was nothing more than an echoing memory; it *couldn't* have been real!

"Help! . . . Mommy! . . ."

And everything else—from the time she first realized she was heading out to the accident site right up until she pulled away from the cemetery gates, unable to force herself to go up to her daughter's grave—was nothing more than twisted, dark imaginings. Graydon ight throw out some fancy clinical term for it, such as "guilt rojection" or "hallucination," and even *that* was scary enough, think that she might actually *be* losing her mind.

"But I'm *not*!" she whispered, her face buried in the well of her illow. "I'm *not* losing my mind! I'm *stronger* than that!"

Rolling over onto her side, she opened her eyes and stared blankly the moonlit curtains framing her bedroom window. The night air ad a warm, earthy aroma to it, reminding her of the freshly turned il . . .

. . . Of a recently dug grave!

Elizabeth shivered and, turning onto her back, pulled the blankets tightly under her chin. As she did, she felt a drag on the blankets, most as if something was on the bed, pinning the blankets down. er first thought was a pleasant memory, of when she was younger, nd her cat, Friskie, had slept on her bed. He had always resented ny movement under the blankets once he was settled down for the ight, and he would claw the bedspread whenever Elizabeth rolled ver in bed.

But Friskie was long since dead, buried out behind the barn under e apple tree. As far as Elizabeth could remember, there was nothing n her bed that would pin down her blankets, unless she had tucked em in wrong. Sighing with frustration, she sat up to straighten em out. When she saw what was lying in bed beside her, her reath froze in her chest, stifling any sound she tried to make.

No! her mind screamed. *This can't be real!*

She stared in horror at the dark shape that was stretched out on e bed beside her. The hazy moonlight cast an indistinct glow in e room—enough to see by but certainly not enough to make out ny details. All Elizabeth could see was a small, dark, human figure, s features lost in shadow, lying curled up beside her on the covers. could have been either a very old woman or a young girl. On the azy white of the pillow rested a dark, oval that looked like a erson's head!

It's just a trick of the light, she told herself, even as panic flooded er mind. She must have left her nightgown on the bed, and it now oked like the rough outline of a person in bed with her. The circle n the pillow was just the depression where her head had been.

But then why can I feel the weight on my bed? she wondered.

Her blood was chilled, and her muscles were frozen. The tendon
in her neck strained as she tried unsuccessfully to turn her head an
get a better look at what was there beside her.

It certainly isn't someone! Not a person! her mind screamed. *Ho
could it be?*

But as she watched with steadily mounting horror, the shape of
the bed moved subtly, like dark ice melting in a hot, tropical night
The sheets rustled and the bedsprings creaked as the weight—no
her own—shifted. Elizabeth's throat closed off in terror as she
watched the rounded dark head rise slowly up from the pillow. A
indistinct nimbus of frizzy gray hair framed the face as it turned
and looked at her with eyes that glowed like hot coals. A dimmed
red fire stared at Elizabeth from the darkness.

". . . No . . ."

The shape sat up. The figure, pitch black against the dark bedroom
wall, continued to twist and rise until it was floating off the bed
hovering above Elizabeth like a heavy column of curling, black
smoke. Every muscle in Elizabeth's body twisted and screamed as
she tried to shake off the paralyzing terror that pinned her helplessly
to the mattress. Drifting above her, the black shape leaned forward
and down, pouring a wash of cold air over Elizabeth's face. The
angry red glow in the eyes grew steadily brighter as the dark face
came closer and closer to her. Even when it was no more than six
inches from her, Elizabeth couldn't make out the slightest detail
other than the angry, blazing eyes. It was as if she was looking into
the very heart of space—a cold, black vacuum with no shape and
no content other than those two heated pits of flame.

In a single, roaring *whoosh*, the head leaning over her burst into
flames. Blades of searing orange and yellow fire tore at Elizabeth's
face, and she was engulfed by a hundred blades of roaring flame
that sliced her, reached for her, tried to pull her in. Wave after wave
of heat hammered against her like solidly placed punches.

". . . No . . ." she said, her voice nothing more than a whimper

The head had become a rapidly diminishing black ball framed by
coiling white hair floating in the middle of the withering sphere of
heat and light. As Elizabeth's stinging eyes adjusted to the sudden
glare, she could see a person's features underlit by the raging fire

She found herself staring, eye to eye, into the grinning face of her dead daughter!

"*. . . No! . . .*"

The word ripped from Elizabeth's chest with a force that felt as though it had shredded flesh and splintered ribs. Her hands reached feebly to her throat, and she was deadly certain she would feel the warm wash of fresh blood flowing down over her chest. Not a single muscle in her body would obey the commands of her brain. The pressure in her head increased until she was certain she was about to explode, consumed by the heat and flame; but then, with a roaring intake of breath, her body jerked into a sitting position on the bed. She let out a single, gravelly growl—more a pained whimper than a scream—as she slammed her hands against her head and pressed them tightly against her throbbing temples.

"*. . . No! . . . Goddamn it, NO!*" she wailed out loud.

In that instant, her awareness snapped, and she found herself panting as she stared in almost total shock down at her bed. There was not the slightest hint of any dark shape lying on top of the covers or hovering above her near the ceiling. No face staring at her. No raging flames. The flesh of her throat and chest was solid and whole, and there was no outpouring of blood and exploded lungs and ribs.

Tears of relief and agony flooded Elizabeth's eyes.

THIRTEEN
White Noise

1.

"Mr. Cody—? Your wife told me I'd find you out here," Elizabeth called out as she walked across the wide stretch of field toward the man working along the fence-post line. She kept her eyes on him, but he, after giving her a curt nod, turned away and resumed his work.

Several hundred yards across the sloping field, a thin slice of the Saco River glimmered silver in the sun. The grass was nothing more than a tangled yellow mat left over from winter, but between the tufts new green was thrusting upward. Overhead, the sky arched a bright blue without a single puff of cloud. The air was tangy with the smell of new growth. As nervous as she was about meeting this man—and as much as she had considered not even coming out here—Elizabeth couldn't *not* respond to the beauty and peace of such a Sunday afternoon.

"My name's Elizabeth Myers. I was supposed to meet with you this afternoon, Mr. Cody," Elizabeth said, once she was standing beside him. She felt as though she should shake hands with him, but saw no opportunity.

"Yup, but y'can call me Eldon," the man said, without even a glance back at her. He had a pinch bar in one hand and, levering it with his shoulder, was pulling a string of barbed wire as tight as he could while wielding his hammer to nail the wire to the rough-cut fence post. "You any good at poundin' nails?" he asked, grunting with effort.

Elizabeth smiled thinly and nodded at the grizzled old man. "Sure," she replied.

Without another word, Eldon gave her the hammer and a nail and then, stepping to one side, gripped the pinch bar with both hands and pulled back until the wire was taut.

"There yah go. Give it a whack!" he said. His face flushed red with strain . . . as Elizabeth placed the small, horseshoe-shaped nail up against the barb and drove it in with two solid, accurate blows. When Eldon released the tension on the wire and saw that it was going to hold, he smiled, wiping his forehead on the sleeve of his frayed plaid work shirt.

"Thanks," he said, making no effort to take the hammer from her. "So, you must be the woman Junia Payne gave me a call 'bout."

"You can call me Elizabeth."

"Sure thing . . . Elizabeth," Eldon replied.

His eyes were such a dark brown that they looked like two little balls of black rubber. His cheeks were weathered like leather and stubbled with a short white beard that looked at least two weeks overdue for a shave. When he smiled, his teeth, brown-stained and rotting, stood out in his mouth like spindly tree stumps. He was dressed like a typical Yankee farmer, with bib coveralls, plaid shirt, and mud- and manure-crusted rubber boots. In spite of his taciturn exterior, there was something that was immediately likable about him, and Elizabeth's smile widened.

"Junia Payne is my aunt," Elizabeth said, still feeling a need to shake hands. She wasn't at all confident about how to proceed with this conversation now that the preliminary challenges had been made and met. Narrowing her eyes to slits, she looked over her shoulder at the long line of newly strung barbed wire that ran a good two hundred yards before it jagged to the left, back toward the barn. All in all, she guessed Eldon had enclosed roughly half of a five-or six-acre area.

"Stringing barbed wire's usually a two-man job," she said. "Do you mean to tell me you did all of this by yourself?"

Eldon wiped his forehead and nodded. "T'weren't easy," he said, "but I can't afford no hired help now that the boys are all growed up and gone. Farmin's been my life, but it sure as hell ain't no livin'." He held out his hand to take the hammer back from her before adding, "'Course, if you don't have anything else planned for th'afternoon, I might ask yah to help me finish this up."

Looking ahead at the line of still unstrung posts, Elizabeth considered for a moment before saying, "I don't have anything special planned for this afternoon . . . other than what my aunt spoke to you about. I'm not exactly dressed for farm work, though." She was grateful, at least, that she hadn't worn a skirt as she had originally planned.

"To tell yah th'truth, I certainly'd 'preciate some help here. I've done the bitchly part, down along the slope," Eldon said. He used his sleeve to wipe his forehead again and let his breath out in a long, rising whistle. Rotating the shoulder he had used to brace the pinch bar, he added, "T'ain't as young's I used t'be."

"Who is?" Elizabeth said, unable to stop herself from thinking, *Well, Caroline isn't getting any older!* She was grateful when she saw Eldon's deeply wrinkled face widen into a smile. "Do you want me to pull the wire or do the nailing?"

Handing the hammer back to her, Eldon said, "Looks t'me like you got nailin' down just fine. Soon's I saw yah comin' toward me 'crost the field, I could tell you were a farm girl."

"Really?" Elizabeth said, half suspecting Eldon was about to make a joke about his psychic abilities. "And how'd you know that?"

"By the way you walked," Eldon said simply.

Elizabeth looked at Eldon, wondering what it was he was supposed to do for her. Junia certainly hadn't supplied her with any facts, and Eldon looked so much like a typical Maine farmer, she couldn't quite fathom how someone like him would have an interest in spiritualism or anything else occult; he certainly didn't look like someone who had any particular psychic abilities.

Then again, who is the type? she asked herself, remembering Frank's comments about Graydon. "So much for stereotypes," she muttered, as she unslung her purse and laid it down on the fresh grass. Without another word, she rolled up the sleeves of her fresh, white blouse and started working alongside Eldon.

As they strung the barbed wire, which Elizabeth had done more of as a child than she cared to remember, Eldon said very little. She figured it was up to him to talk if he wanted to, but the next two hours passed mostly in silence, broken only when Eldon commented on the fine job she was doing—"'Specially for a woman."

All during the time they worked, Elizabeth's curiosity steadily rose. She wondered why he had asked her to bring blank cassette tapes and what—exactly—he planned to do for her. How could such an apparently hard-working, practical man be interested in *anything* supernatural, unless Sunday mornings at the local Baptist church could be considered "supernatural"?

The sun was lowering in the west and there was a slight chill in the air when Elizabeth drove the last nail into the last post. Her arm was aching from the palm of her hand right up to her shoulder, and there was the thick pad of a blister on the heel of her palm. Her body was sticky with sweat, and she promised herself a very long, hot shower when she got home.

"I cain't tell yah how much I 'preciate th'help," Eldon said, as he picked up the nearly empty spool of barbed wire, slung it onto his shoulder, and started across the field toward the barn. Exhausted, Elizabeth followed along until he pointed over to the place where she had first joined him and said, "Yah might wanna pick up your pocketbook 'fore it gets too dark."

As tired as she was, she ran over to where she had left her purse, scooped it up, and, slowing her pace to a casual walk, started up the slope toward the barn. In spite of what Eldon had said about having done the worst part down by the river, her sneakers and jeans were caked with mud and grass stains, and her blouse was sodden with sweat and grime. She figured her face must be just about as dirty as her hands, but in spite of all that, she was feeling good, exhilarated, after a few hours of honest, hard labor, and content that she had been able to help him out.

As she came up into the dooryard, she knew Eldon was inside the barn by the sounds of clanging metal that echoed from the wide-open doorway. It sounded as though he was running a length of chain over some metal; the noise rang out like rattling gunfire. Leaning her head inside, Elizabeth blinked her eyes rapidly, trying to adjust to the darkness. Her nostrils filled with the smell of fresh cow manure and musty hay; and she marveled at how, for probably the first time in her life, she thought of the identical smells in her father's barn with pleasantly nostalgic thoughts.

"Be right wit'cha," Eldon's voice called from somewhere down the line of cow stalls. "Just gotta take care o'this."

Preferring to stay in the sunlight, Elizabeth backed out into the dooryard and, placing her hands on her hips and stretching back, inhaled deeply. Already, her knotted muscles were softening in the warmth, and she found herself thinking that—no matter *what* happened with Eldon Cody—she wasn't about to let this terrific feeling be ruined.

A looming shadow shifted within the barn doorway. Elizabeth tensed for an instant, then relaxed when she saw Eldon walk out, squinting in the bright sunlight.

"Well," he said, running his work-grimed hands through his thinning hair as he looked out across the field they had just finished refencing, "I hope you brung what I asked yah to."

Elizabeth was only momentarily confused; then she shook her head and said, "Oh, yeah—sure. I have the blank tapes."

"Com'on, then, 'n' we'll see what we can git."

Elizabeth halted on the walkway, and Eldon turned and looked quizically at her.

"Somethin' the matter?" he asked. His voice and expression were as hard as nails, in spite of the welcoming gleam in his eyes.

"Well, I was just—you know, I have no idea what you plan to do," Elizabeth stammered as she twisted the strap of her purse nervously in her hands.

Eldon snorted with laughter and, shrugging his shoulders, said, "Why, I'm gonna help you so's you can talk to your dead daughter. Com'on in'ta the house, 'n' we'll git goin'."

2.

Frank knocked on the front door several times before he saw motion through the gauzy white curtain and heard the steady approach of footsteps. He could tell by the smallness of the silhouette that it was Suzie Norton. Stepping back to allow the screen door to swing open, he smiled widely and said, "Howdy, Suze."

The woman in the doorway regarded him with a fluttering of eyelids and her own friendly smile.

Suzie was quite an attractive woman, with long brown hair and very clear, green eyes that were always sparkling. Considerably younger than Brad, probably no more than twenty-five, she still had the figure of a schoolgirl, with a slim waist and large, rounded breasts. Frank always felt just a bit uncomfortable in her presence because of all the bragging Norton did during the long, boring night shifts, about Suzie's bedroom expertise. Over the years, Frank and Suzie had developed a teasing repartee between them, and Frank sometimes found himself wondering how far Suzie would go if he decided to make a serious move. He would of course never *really* try to get his partner's wife into the sack, but still . . . the fantasies were sometimes fun.

"Well, well, well," Suzie said, letting her words drawl as if she were a Southern belle. Her tongue darted out between her teeth as she stepped back and regarded Frank from head to toe. "I certainly *do* hope you're not thinking 'while the cat's away . . .' "

Although it was early afternoon, Suzie was wearing a thin nightgown that clung to her figure. Frank smiled and, shaking his head, said, "As much as I'd like to, Suze, you know I'm saving myself for marriage. No, I just stopped by to see if Brad was feeling any better."

A confused frown crossed Suzie's face, and, cocking her head to one side, she sniffed and said, "Is this some kinda joke I'm not getting?"

Frank shrugged. "I don't think so. I just wanted to see how Brad was feeling. I haven't talked to him for a day or two, now, and I—"

"What the hell are you talking about, Frank?" Suzie said. Her frown deepened. "Brad left for work over an hour ago. He said he was putting in extra hours, helping you with . . . he didn't say exactly what, but he said he was working with you on something."

"For Christ's sake," Frank said, scratching his head. He looked away from Suzie for a moment, his first thought being that Brad was seeing another woman on the sly (he was pretty sure that was Suzie's first thought, too).

"I'll have his *balls*, that rotten son of a bitch!" Suzie muttered, her face noticeably paler, and her eyes glistening as tears began to form. She seemed somehow diminished in size, and Frank's first impulse was to hug her for reassurance.

"Well—hey, all I know is, this is the third day I haven't seen him," Frank said. It twisted his gut to see the pain and dark suspicion in Suzie's expression, so he added, "But when I do, I'll sure as hell find out what's been going on."

"You aren't keeping anything from me, are you Frank?" Suzie said, her voice softening. Her lower lip trembled when she spoke, and Frank could tell it took a lot of effort for her to keep from crying. He reached out and placed his hand gently on her shoulder. It felt thin and frail beneath his hand, and his heart ached for her. "You know I wouldn't lie to you, Suze," he said simply.

Suzie sniffed loudly, and her expression hardened again. "If I find out you've been keeping something from me, I'll get even with you—right after I'm through with Brad!"

"It's not what you think," Frank said mildly, even though he only half-believed it himself.

Suzie sniffed again as she twisted her shoulder out from under Frank's grip. He let his hand drop to his side, and for several seconds, the two of them just looked at each other in tortured silence. Finally, Suzie nodded and said, "Yeah—sure it isn't." She stepped back into the house and, still looking squarely at Frank, swung the door shut in his face.

"Catch'cha later," Frank said to the silhouette behind the door-window curtain, then walked down the steps back to his cruiser. As he got into the car and pulled out of the driveway, he could feel Suzie's harsh gaze boring into the back of his head. He felt her pain and confusion, but he told himself to leave it at that—there was no reason to get involved any deeper than he had to. If there was something going wrong between Suzie and Brad, it was none of his damned business. If there was anything else going on, some screwup at work where Brad might need some disciplinary action for taking off time not owed to him—well, that was the chief's responsibility.

All Frank knew was that he wasn't about to be a buddy-fucker and tell everyone at the station that Brad was AWOL.

As he drove back to town, though, Frank couldn't help but wonder what in the hell Brad *was* up to. It was stupid to jeopardize his position on the force by calling in sick just so he could skip work for a few days. Frank had no idea if Brad had something going with another woman or if it was something else. Whatever it was, it had to be something Brad wanted to keep to himself. He certainly hadn't mentioned anything to his partner. As far as Frank could remember, Norton hadn't been acting differently lately, so he tried to push it all aside, telling himself it was probably something minor, and even if it wasn't minor . . .

"What the hell! Forget about it," Frank muttered to himself as he pulled into the police station parking lot. He had concerns of his own, and they were much more important. Whenever he saw Brad next, he'd ask him what the hell was going on. He'd get the truth out of his partner, so he decided to leave it at that for now.

3.

After taking a few minutes to wash up in Eldon's bathroom, Elizabeth joined him in the living room. Afternoon sunlight cut across the worn-out rug and reached partway up the wall, illuminating the faded design of the wallpaper. Motes of dust drifted into the bar of light, were momentarily bright, and then winked out as they floated into shadow. Elizabeth thought *that's all any of us are*—tiny specks of dust, sailing aimlessly in the void. *For our brief instant, the sunlight lights us up, and then*—*blink*—*we're gone.*

But gone where? she wondered. *Where do we go? What happens to us? And more to the point, what the hell can this old farmer tell me about it all?*

"I wanna do a little demonstration first, if yah don't mind," Eldon said.

"Well, before we start, I was just wondering—"

Eldon raised his eyebrows and looked at her. "Yeah?"

"What I mean is—well, this whole thing has me sort of confused," Elizabeth said, shaking her head. "I don't understand how—or *why*—someone like you can be involved in . . . in whatever you want to call it.''

Eldon's face remained impassive as he looked at her. Then he cleared his throat and said gruffly, ''It's called E. V. P.—electronic voice phenomenon. The *how's* simple. I got the equipment and desire to do it. 'N' it works, so I do it. I won't be makin' any claims as to how it happens, but I know it does.'' He squinted as he looked at her, his eyes asking for her understanding, and although she was still confused, Elizabeth nodded.

''Now as to the *why* of it,'' Eldon continued. ''Well . . . I guess that ain't so hard to understand. I spoze, just like some folks go to church 'n' some folks read astrology or whatever 'n' others don't believe in anything, this is what gives my life meaning.'' He folded his rough workman's hands in front of his face, looking almost as if he were praying. ''But unlike a lot o'that stuff, what I do is different 'cause it works . . . *every* time.'' A thin smile flickered across his face, then dissolved. ''But the best way's to see and hear it bein' done, so let's get a move on.''

''Uh, yeah—okay,'' Elizabeth said. Still confused, she looked squarely at Eldon and nodded.

''Al'right, then,'' Eldon said. He reached over to the end table beside the couch and picked up a small tape recorder. Placing it in his lap, he cleared his throat again and began, ''What I've here is an ordinary tape player. You got them two tapes I tole yah to bring, right?''

Elizabeth opened her purse and fished around inside until she produced them. She made as if to give them to Eldon, but he waved his hand in front of her and said, ''Nope. Don't wanna even touch 'em. Just so's you can't say I fudged with things.''

''What exactly do you plan to do?'' Elizabeth asked. Her curiosity was rising, even though she thought Eldon was failing miserably if he was trying at all to create any kind of atmosphere receptive to . . . whatever he was up to.

''Step by step is how we're gonna do it,'' Eldon said. ''Here yah go.'' As he handed the tape recorder to her, a smile curled one corner of his mouth. ''What I want yah t'do first is take the wrapper off one of them tapes and put it in'ta the machine.''

Elizabeth struggled to catch the opening tab on the cellophane covering, but after a moment got it, pulled it away, opened the plastic case, and shook out the blank tape. She pressed the button marked STOP/EJECT and, after opening the lid, dropped the tape into the slot and snapped the cover shut.

"Fine. Now press the play button," Eldon said.

"But the tape's—"

"Just press it."

Elizabeth did as she was told, and for the next few seconds, both she and Eldon listened to the faint hiss the blank tape made as it played.

"Nothin' on it, right?" Eldon said. His eyebrows rose into twin semicircles, and the smile on his face widened just a notch.

"I don't get this at all," Elizabeth said cautiously. "What did you expect to hear?"

"Why, nothin'a'tall, of course," Eldon answered. Pointing at the recorder, but being careful not to touch it, he went on, "Okay, you can stop that now, 'n' unwrap the other tape."

Again, Elizabeth did as she was told, even though she was now totally confused by what Eldon was doing. If this had anything to do with contacting her dead daughter, she sure as hell couldn't see how.

"This time press the play 'n' record buttons at the same time," Eldon said, "'n' then hit pause—what's it say there? Cue. Hit that cue button for a minute while I get set up."

Elizabeth did what she was told and saw the tiny red recording indicator light come on. Eldon hoisted himself off the couch and went over to the modern-looking component stereo system in the corner of the room. Elizabeth had noticed it when they had first entered the living room because it looked so out of place. He glanced back at her and said, "This here's somethin' my boys had when they was teenagers. Now they got them fancy things—what'd'yah call 'em? Laser disks or whatever! This'll work just fine for what we want."

Elizabeth sat and silently watched as Eldon switched on the radio. A burst of loud noise, sounding like the rush of falling water, filled the living room. She jumped involuntarily and almost dropped the tape recorder from her lap as she covered her ears with her hands. Eldon quickly spun the volume dial down, and the noise faded to a low but steady hiss, like the distantly heard surge of waves on a beach.

"That there's what's called *white noise*," he said, as he came back to the couch and sat down. He placed his hands on his knees and nodded with satisfaction.

"Uh-huh. Look, Mr. Cody, this is all very interesting, but I don't think you understand. The reason I'm—"

Eldon waved a gnarly finger at her and continued. "I've found from experimentin' that if I set the FM radio in this band area, up near 108, it works purty good. Most times, anyways. So, are'yah ready?"

"Ready for what?" Elizabeth asked, frowning as she shrugged.

"Ready to talk to your daughter, of course, or maybe someone who knows her," Eldon snapped. "What I want yah t'do is, when I signal yah, unpause the recorder. Then you can ask whatever questions you wanna ask. Just wait a little while between 'em so there'll be time enough for you t'get your answers."

"What—from you?" Elizabeth asked, completely confused by this operation. She *had* thought Claire DeBlaise was a nut case, but Eldon was easily taking the honor.

"*Course* not from me. From the spirit world," Eldon said, as casually as if he had been talking about a church social. "Yah'see, this white noise here on the radio acts like a . . . like kinda a beacon—a lighthouse. It draws the spirits in, attracts 'em like a magnet. I can never know who we're gonna get, but why don't you start askin' your questions with that blank tape runnin', 'n' we'll see what we get?"

"This is—" Elizabeth was about to say *crazy*, but she placed her forefinger on the cue button and watched Eldon expectantly. After a few seconds, he nodded and eased himself back on the couch.

Elizabeth's finger flicked the button. The tape began to roll behind the transparent plastic housing of the recorder. At first her mind drew a complete blank; the steady hiss of white noise on the radio was distracting; it drew *her* attention, never mind the spirits. Her eyes flicked back and forth between the radio and the red record light, and, after several seconds of silence, Eldon gave her a little "come-along" signal with his hand, and, clearing her throat, Elizabeth spoke.

"Is there . . . Is there anyone here?" Her voice was strained, and her eyes darted around the room, desperately seeking an anchor of some kind. The silvery flecks of dust were still spinning in the bar of sunlight, but she tensed when she imagined they were falling flakes of snow.

"I—uh, I'd like to speak with my daughter, Caroline," she continued haltingly. She cast a glance at Eldon, who held up his hands, indicating that she was to wait. After a moment, he again signaled for her to continue.

Baffled by what was going on and wondering what was supposed to happen, Elizabeth's awareness was filled by the static hiss coming from the radio. She wondered whether, if it kept drawing her attention, it might not do exactly what Eldon said it would—attract entities from the spirit world. But was that even possible? Or was she indulging in another foolish delusion?

"If my daughter is . . . is nearby," Elizabeth said, "I'd like to speak with her . . . I'd like to let her know that I—"

Her voice choked off, and she looked at Eldon with the sinking realization that he probably didn't know what had happened to Caroline or why she so desperately wanted to contact her. Elizabeth had to fight the impulse to switch off the recorder and explain everything to him before she went any further, but she hesitated, not wanting to do anything that might disrupt the mood of whatever the hell they were doing.

"I want to tell Caroline I . . . I'm sorry," Elizabeth said. Her throat constricted, and a warm rush filled her eyes. "I want to tell her that I . . . that I didn't mean for her to die."

She stopped, unable to continue as her mind filled with the remembered echoes of the three-syllable chant . . .

Car-o-line . . . Car-o-line . . . Car-o-line . . .

She glanced over at Eldon, who was just sitting there silently, watching her with an expression of . . .

Is that helpful concern in his eyes? . . . Or is he laughing at me? Does he think I'm a damned gullible fool?

Taking a deep breath that felt like fire in her lungs, Elizabeth mentally phrased another question. Each word arose in her mind as sharp and as clear as shiny metal . . .

Car-o-line, honey . . .

Elizabeth wondered if she would have the courage to say the thought aloud.

Can you forgive me for what happened?

Can you forgive me, Caroline?

Eldon caught her attention with a quick wave of his hand and asked by his expression if she wanted to continue. Making her mouth a straight, hard line, Elizabeth nodded and then said aloud, "Caroline—honey. Can you . . . can you forgive me for what . . . happened?"

For just an instant, the hiss of radio static varied, roaring louder for a split second, then rapidly fading. It sounded as if someone was over by the controls, wiggling them just a bit to cause a disturbance, but she could see that no one was there. Eldon was still sitting on the couch, watching her with either concern or amusement on his face.

"Can you, honey?" she repeated, her words followed by a silence that lengthened uncomfortably.

"I think that might do it for now," Eldon said. He shifted forward on the couch but was still careful not to touch the tape recorder in Elizabeth's lap. Pointing at the recorder, he added, "You can shut that thing off now, if yah'd like."

Unable to speak, Elizabeth pressed the stop button and, letting her breath out in a rush, slouched back onto the couch while Eldon went over to the radio and turned it off. Elizabeth was grateful for the time he allowed her to compose herself, even as dozens of questions filled her mind.

"So, are'yah ready to listen, or would'yah like to take a break?" Eldon asked, sitting back down on the couch. "I'll bet'cha Martha could find us something to drink."

"Water would be fine," Elizabeth said, surprised that she could even speak; her lips and throat felt desert-parched.

Eldon got up and walked into the kitchen, and again, Elizabeth was grateful for the time alone so she could try to absorb what had just happened. It was obvious to her that Eldon thought something would be on the tape that they hadn't heard while she was asking her questions. A wave of shivers shook her body when she wondered if anything like that was possible. How could radio static draw spirits who would then answer her questions? And how could their answers only be heard on a tape? She frowned as she looked around Eldon's living room, feeling uneasy about even the possibility that there really was an unseen world that could leak into the real world. That unseen eyes might be present, watching her, gave her a bone-deep chill.

From the kitchen, she could hear the sound of running water as Eldon filled a glass for her. The sound was so similar to the white noise on the radio that it sent another wave of chills dancing up her back.

There weren't any *spirits* around! There *couldn't* be! she thought—not here; not *anywhere*! And there wasn't any chance that running a blank tape in a tape recorder could pick up anything except the voice of the fool who thought there was going to be an answer from . . . *beyond*.

"Would'yah care for something t'eat?" Eldon called from the kitchen. "You must be hungry after working 's hard as yah did. Got some cookies here Martha made th'other day."

"Uh—no thanks," Elizabeth replied. "Just water will be fine."

A moment later, Eldon reentered the living room and handed her a tumbler filled with water and a few ice cubes. She smiled her thanks and took a sip, amazed at how damned good the cold water felt sliding down her throat.

That will put out the fire, she told herself, *and what I ought to do is put this whole crazy episode out of my mind*!

But that thought was soon cast aside when Eldon asked, "So do 'yah wanna hear what we got on the tape?"

After another sip of cold water, Elizabeth said, "Before we do, can you—like, could you explain some of this to me? I don't really know what's going on with all of this."

"I already tole'yah," Eldon said, sounding slightly impatient with her. "The radio noise brings the spirits here. I don't know who they are or what they're doin'. Sometimes they say so; sometimes they don't."

Elizabeth held the tape recorder on the flat of her hand and put it up in front of Eldon's face. A smile flickered at the corners of her mouth as she fought the impulse to ask him what kind of a fool he took her to be. Instead, she said, "What you're telling me is, when we replay this tape—"

"Which I made a point of not touchin' or tamperin' with in any way," Eldon interrupted. "I say that just so's you won't accuse me of pullin' a fast one."

"I haven't accused you of anything," Elizabeth said, "but you're telling me, when I rewind this tape and play it, I'll hear answers to my questions—right?"

Eldon smiled widely and said, "More'n likely."

Elizabeth chuckled aloud, took another sip of water, and then, shaking her head, said, "Okay then—let's see." She depressed the rewind button, waited until the tape was rewound all the way, and then hit the play button. The sound of blank tape hiss began, and she fiddled with the volume control to get it to a comfortable level.

"You'll need it up higher," Eldon said, indicating the machine with a wave of his hand, still careful not to touch it. "Lots o'times the voices ain't much."

Elizabeth complied by turning the volume up a notch and then sat back to listen. She couldn't deny the tight, wound-up feeling in her stomach as she waited to hear the recording made just a few minutes ago. It surprised her how sensitive the microphone was; it seemed to have picked up every sound of motion in the room. Maybe we'll even hear the sound of the dust falling, she thought. After a long pause, Elizabeth heard her recorded voice, echoing in what sounded like a vast, empty room.

"Is there anyone here?"

In the silence that followed, Elizabeth thought she heard something. Whatever the sound was, it was muffled and fleeting, and she passed it off as a sound either she or Eldon had made, shifting on the couch. She tried to remember exactly what each of them had done during her questioning, but she knew that she could never reconstruct it accurately.

And maybe that's how he tricks people, she thought. *By not telling you what's going on, he pulls . . . whatever sleight of hand he has planned, before you even know it.*

"I—uh, I'd like to speak with my daughter, Caroline," Elizabeth's recorded voice said. It sounded tinny, and she couldn't dispel the notion that it had been recorded in a vast room, not this cozy living room. The white noise of the radio continued unabated in the background.

There was nothing—no sound at all in the silence that followed that statement. Elizabeth looked questioningly at Eldon, but he simply nodded, sending her a silent signal to be patient.

After another long gap filled with white noise, Elizabeth's recorded voice spoke again. "If my daughter is . . . is nearby, I'd like to speak with her . . . I'd like to let her know that I—"

In the short pause that followed, Elizabeth clearly remembered the thoughts that had flashed through her mind. Again, she cringed with embarrassment as she wondered what Eldon knew of her situation. It bothered her that she would let herself be set up like this. Why was she so trusting and confident with a man she had just met?

"I want to tell Caroline I'm . . . I'm sorry," the recorded voice said.

Before all the words had been spoken, Elizabeth heard something on the tape—something that made gooseflesh rise instantly on her arms. From out of the speaker on the small tape recorder came a warbling rush of noise that rose to a peak and repeated several times before quickly cutting off. Her first thought was that it was the sound of a car passing by the house; but she had driven up Eldon's long driveway, and she knew that, even if a car had gone by the house, the recorder never could have caught the sound of its passing so clearly.

"Bingo! There yah are," Eldon said, as a satisfied grin spread across his face. He sat back and slapped his legs with the flats of his hands, making a double-loud cracking sound. Nailing Elizabeth with a sharp glance, he said, "Can'yah tell me what *that* was?"

Elizabeth's fingers felt as useless and senseless as balloons as she fumbled to stop the tape. Her hands were trembling as she pressed the rewind button, let the tape run backward for a little bit, then hit play again.

". . . to tell Caroline—

The sound—*what in the name of sweet Jesus is that sound*—began with the word Caroline, rose quickly and repeated, then cut off; but this time Elizabeth didn't get the impression that it was a car driving by the house. Her mind instantly caught what sure as hell sounded like foreign-sounding words being spoken, whispered like the harsh ripping of cloth.

"This is . . . weird," she said, but that was all. She clicked off the recorder and looked at Eldon, feeling suddenly empty and help-less.

"It's the spirit world," Eldon finished for her. "Someone from beyond is tryin' t'talk t'yah."

"It can't be," Elizabeth said, shaking her head in earnest denial. "This just can't be! It isn't *possible*!"

Eldon's smiled widened, exposing the stumps of his rotting teeth. The expression on his face was almost comical, and if she hadn't been so terrified just then, Elizabeth might have laughed aloud at his clownlike face.

"It ain't up to you or me to figger out what is and isn't possible," Eldon said simply. "Go on 'n' play the rest of the tape."

"I don't know if I . . . dare to," Elizabeth said. No matter what she thought about what was happening on an intellectual level, that sound, that *whooshing* noise sounding almost like another voice, reached deep down inside her and filled her with dread.

"Spirits generally ain't gonna harm yah," Eldon said calmly. "Usually they simply got some kinda message to pass on to the livin'. I ain't never encountered what I'd have t'say was an *evil* spirit, although I 'spoze there must be some."

It amazed Elizabeth how Eldon took what was happening so easily in stride. Possibly he could do that because somehow—she didn't know how, but somehow—he *had* manipulated the tape to get this sound onto it. His entire show about not touching the blank tapes or the recorder once she had picked it up were just that—a show designed to distract her from whatever it was he *did* do to screw around with things. It had to be that! It simply wasn't possible that static on a radio could attract spirits and make them speak!

Looking at Eldon, Elizabeth said, "Well, there are some folks"—she had to fight hard to keep her voice level and strong— "who think any amount of fooling around with stuff like this is . . . is downright evil. I don't know what we just heard. I have no idea! As far as I can remember, I didn't hear anything like that when we were recording, but I just can't—can't swallow this."

"Hold on a minute there," Eldon said. "Lemme see that tape."

Elizabeth pressed the stop button, ejected the tape, and handed it over to Eldon. He moved to take it from her but then didn't. Pointing over toward the stereo system, he said, "One of my boys rigged that tape machine there so it can play things backward." He chuckled and continued. "I 'spoze it was so's he could listen to them Satanic messages that are 'spozed to be in the rock 'n' roll music. You know—like the Beatles and such."

"Oh, sure—horrible Satan worshippers, every one of them," Elizabeth said, catching the gleam of humor in his eyes and smiling back at him.

"Why'nt you play the tape you just made past that sound, whatever the hell it is, then put it in'ta my tape player. Lot's'o times, the messages don't make sense till yah hear 'em backward. That little toggle switch there will make the machine run backward."

Elizabeth almost told him that this was getting completely ridiculous. Simply accepting that disembodied spirits even existed and could talk to you on a blank tape took quite a leap of faith. But then to propose that those messages from the spirit world could be recorded backward was just too damned much! There was something strange going on here. She didn't know what, but she sure felt like she was the sucker.

She went over and knelt in front of Eldon's tape deck, taking a moment to study the dials. After switching the amp from FM radio to tape player, she opened the cassette housing, popped in the tape, and pressed the reverse/play toggle. She adjusted the volume and then, sitting back on her heels, folded her hands in her lap as she and Eldon waited and listened.

At first they heard nothing but the same white noise, slightly distorted from being played backward. Then they heard the odd sound of Elizabeth's voice being played backward.

"That was the next question you asked, after that noise we heard," Eldon said in a hushed voice. Elizabeth glanced at him, about to say something, but he waved a silencing finger at her. "Shhush—now wait."

After the backward voice stopped, there was a split-second pause of intense white noise. Elizabeth expected the sound to be as indistinguishable backward as it had been when played forward. She wasn't ready for it when a whining voice hissed from the speakers, filling the room and sounding as clear as if it were right there beside her.

"I—saw—you—there," the high-pitched voice said.

It was obviously that of a young girl, but in the instant, blinding rush of fear, Elizabeth couldn't even begin to wonder whether or not it was Caroline's voice. Astounded and terrified beyond belief, she collapsed backward, away from the stereo. With frantic, fear-filled eyes, she turned and looked at Eldon, a scream building up inside her chest, seeking to escape.

The tape played on, and the voice continued, stuttering on the words, "Here I . . . here I . . ." It started to warble up the register, higher and higher until it faded away, leaving nothing but the reverse sound of white noise. With trembling hands, Elizabeth switched off the tape player.

"I tole'yah," Eldon said, smiling with satisfaction as he looked at Elizabeth and nodded. "We sure as hell got *someone*."

Elizabeth was trying desperately to compose herself as she got to her feet and, trembling violently, went back to sit on the couch. A slick sheen of sweat had broken out on her forehead. She didn't dare speak aloud for fear that nothing more than a terror-stricken whimper would come out of her mouth. She picked up her glass of water and took a sip.

"Why don't'cha play the rest of the tape forward, 'n' we can see if there's anythin' else," Eldon said calmly. "After that, we can play th'whole thing backward t'catch what we might've missed. I'd like to find out who we got here."

Elizabeth hesitated, then with a deep sigh went over to the stereo and released the reverse button. After pressing the play button again, she sat on the couch beside Eldon. Her knuckles were bone white, and she held her breath as she clenched her hands in her lap and waited to hear the recorded words repeated. The only relief she felt was knowing that, played forward, they wouldn't make sense . . . even though she now knew what they said.

When they came again, they were the same as the first time she had heard them—nothing more than a warbling rush that rose up high as it repeated itself several times and then abruptly cut off. Elizabeth let her breath out in a slow, deep whistle. Echoing in her mind, she could still hear that tiny, high voice.

"I saw you there! . . . Here I . . . Here I . . . Here I . . ."

For several seconds there was just a faint trace of recorded white noise from the radio; then Elizabeth's voice spoke out clearly, "I want to tell her that I . . . that I didn't want for her to die." As terrified and as disoriented as she had felt back when she recorded those words, she now found it reassuring to hear her own normal voice. But even as relief spread through her, she knew she would *never* be able to forget that other voice. Someday she might find the courage to listen to that tape backward again, in a calmer moment. She would like to determine, if she could, if that had been Caroline's voice. For now she wanted to dismiss it from her mind and continue listening to the tape.

"Caroline—honey," her recorded voice said. "Can you . . . can you forgive me for what . . . happened?"

Another white-noise pause was all they heard, but now it seemed to pulsate with possibilities.

"Can you, honey?" the tape recorder said.

As soon as the word *you* was spoken, another rush of noise filled the tape. It was different this time, thank God; certainly nothing that sounded like someone trying to talk! This new sound came in hard, steady pulses, and Elizabeth had the mental image of a searchlight spinning rapidly, sweeping a wide arc around and around, bright for just the instant it focused on her, then fading rapidly as it spun away. She suspected this mental image arose unbidden from Eldon's claim that white noise acted like the beacon of a lighthouse that drew attention from the spirit world. There was no denying there was *something* on the tape! The sound was dizzying as it warbled intensely, rising and fading and rising again.

"Oh, my God! Oh, my *God*!" Elizabeth muttered when she heard something that sounded like words flutter and fade in the rush of sound. "Oh, my sweet, loving *Jesus*!"

Elizabeth told herself *I can't be hearing this! It's got to be my imagination!*

Tension coiled inside her stomach like a poisonous snake preparing to strike. She was aware of a heavy-fisted pounding inside her head, and it took her a panicked instant to realize that it was her own heartbeat. A flush of cold gripped her body. She wanted to open her mouth, to say anything to Eldon that would break the tension that was spiraling up inside her, but she was filled with the fear that if she opened her mouth, all that would come out would be one long, never-ending scream. She had a vivid mental image of being hauled off to the psychiatric ward, still screaming until her throat and lungs began to bleed.

"D'yah hear that?" Eldon asked, his eyes twinkling with excitement. "D'yah *hear* that?"

Elizabeth nodded, even though her neck and shoulders felt like they were cast in iron. The rushing whoosh of words rose and faded, but each time they got clearer until, finally, there was no denying what was on the tape. Somehow—she didn't know how—Eldon's tape recorder, had captured the only two words that could cut into her soul like the blue-white flame of a blowtorch.

"*. . . Help! . . . Mommy! . . . Help! . . . Mommy! . . .*"

Elizabeth screamed. She wanted to get up off the couch and run from Eldon's house; run all the way back to Bristol Mills if she had to to get away from it; run until she collapsed on the roadside and simply died of exhaustion or fright.

"I think that might do it for now," Eldon's voice said.

The voice was so clear that, for an instant, Elizabeth wasn't sure if it had been on the tape or if Eldon had spoken those exact words again. "You can shut that thing off now, if yah'd like." She heard the recorded *click* from her shutting off the tape recorder. Then there was nothing in the room except the sound of the blank tape, with no white noise, thankfully, being played on Eldon's stereo. That sound and her own labored breathing filled the living room like the sound of a crashing tide.

Eldon got up off the couch and went over to the stereo system. He stopped the tape, then pressed the rewind button. Looking at Elizabeth, still sitting on the couch, he smiled grimly and said, "Well—*now* d'yah believe that somethin' like this is possible?"

Elizabeth's mouth made an odd gulping sound before she said, "I don't . . . know *what* to think."

"D'yah feel like listenin' to the whole thing in reverse now, or d'yah wanna take a little break from it?" Eldon asked.

"I could—" Elizabeth said, but then stopped and swallowed with difficulty. It felt as though a fist-sized rock was working its way down her gullet. "Another glass of water might be nice."

"I think I'll have a beer, m'self," Eldon said. He turned to go out to the kitchen, but just then a loud squeaking sound drew his attention to the tape recorder. Elizabeth gave a startled little yelp.

"Ahh, dammit!" Eldon shouted as he jabbed the off button. When he snapped open the cassette lid, Elizabeth saw the problem. The tape had wrapped around the pickup spool inside the machine. It stretched and broke as Eldon tried to pull the cassette out of the deck.

"Friggin' machine done et the tape," he snarled as he held up a long strand of wrinkled tape for her inspection.

"Is it ruined?" Elizabeth asked. She didn't voice it, but she felt a measure of relief, knowing she might never have to listen to that recorded voice again.

"'Fraid so," Eldon said as he pulled more destroyed tape from the innards of the machine. "Looks like I'm gonna have to cut it to get it all off the spindle. Damned shame, too! We had something purty interesting there, don't'cha think?" He glanced at Elizabeth and smiled. "'Least we got to hear it once. You can't deny there was something there."

"Umm," Elizabeth said, as Eldon started for the kitchen.

"I'll fetch yah that water, now," he said. "Don't'cha be goin' anywhere."

Elizabeth waited until he had left the living room before she collapsed back onto the couch. All the air in her lungs came out in one great, whooshing rush. She could hear the sounds Eldon made in the kitchen as he got their drinks ready, but deep inside her mind she could also hear something else—a faint, hissing white noise. Her eyes were sandpaper dry. She licked her lips nervously as she waited . . . trying like hell not to think that from now on, for the rest of her life, she was going to hear that warbling voice and those words, repeated eternally—

"I saw you there . . ."

"Help . . . Mommy . . . Help . . . Mommy!

FOURTEEN
Button

1.

The day after Elizabeth went out to Eldon Cody's farm was sunny and warm and by late morning, the temperature was heading up into the high seventies. Elizabeth knew she was being completely irresponsible, but she called Jake Hardy at the store and told him she was sick and wouldn't be in for work. She just didn't bother to notify Graydon that she would be missing her afternoon appointment.

After packing a picnic lunch, she threw a blanket and jacket into the back seat of her car and, with WXGL blasting a string of "oldies," headed out to the beach at Kettle Cove to spend the day—alone. After everything she had been through recently—especially listening to that eerie voice on Eldon's tape recorder—she needed time by herself to think.

She didn't understand how that recorded voice could have been real. It didn't seem even remotely possible that she could have heard someone sounding like a little girl say . . .

"I saw you there! . . . Here I . . ."

And did it sound like Caroline? she wondered.

Where could that distorted, backward message have come from? Eldon had made such a show of not touching the blank tape after she unwrapped it, so if it was trickery, it was damned slick trickery.

But she didn't think Eldon was a fraud, so she found it most comfortable to attribute that voice to some stray radio signals either the recorder or the FM had picked up. That *had* to be the logical explanation, but even so, it didn't explain everything, such as—why had she received the exact same message that had been haunting her all along? . . .

"*Help! . . . Mommy! . . .*"

Now that she had some distance from that afternoon at Eldon's, the whole thing was beginning to seem less real, and almost dreamlike. Elizabeth could almost convince herself that she *had* imagined hearing those words. The worst thing was something Eldon had pointed out to her just before she left his house. It was so simple, she was surprised that she had never considered the ambiguous meaning of the "*Help! Mommy!*" message. It could be read one of two ways, either as "*Help (me) Mommy!*" or *(I want to) Help Mommy*!

"Probably a damned good thing that the tape got ruined," Elizabeth muttered to herself as she pulled into the parking lot at Kettle Cove. Unpacking the car, she walked down to the beach. Any agitation she was feeling quickly dissolved in the shimmering blue waves of the ocean and the hammering heat of the sun. The light offshore breeze at her back was warm and soothing. It lifted her hair and blew if forward into her eyes as she looked seaward at the heavy swell of the waves. Taking a deep, even breath of the salt-tangy air, she kicked off her shoes, thoroughly enjoying the sensation of hot sand beneath her feet as she wandered over the dunes, looking for the perfect spot to sprawl out.

She felt like a schoolgirl playing hooky as she spread out her blanket and sat down. This, she told herself, was all the therapy she needed to drive away any thoughts about disembodied voices, nightmare visitors, dug-up graves, and severed hands.

For the number of cars she had counted in the parking lot, the beach was remarkably deserted. Elizabeth could see only nine other people, either lying on beach towels or propped up in beach chairs. The loudest sound was the tearing rush of waves as they folded over onto the sand and pulled back, making the glistening pebbles along the shoreline rumble like distant thunder. Below that, faint with distance, she could hear the cry of sea gulls wheeling high overhead.

The ocean was dotted with dozens of lobster buoys, and several boats moved with a faint putt-putting sound back and forth across the water. The beauty of the sights and sounds reminded her momentarily of the view from Graydon's office, but she didn't allow the twinge of guilt for missing her appointment to last for long.

The sun, sand, and salty air all worked their magic. Even before she ate her lunch, Elizabeth was feeling refreshed and revitalized. Several times she shook her head, surprised to catch herself sitting up and just staring out at the heaving ocean without any particular thought in mind as she watched the play of light and motion. After eating lunch and lying in the sun for another hour or so, she shook the sand from her blanket, picked up her things, got into the car, and headed back to Bristol Mills.

Just after she crossed the town line, though, her bubble of well-being broke and her heart skipped a beat. She saw in the rearview mirror a police car pull out from a side road behind her.

A quick burst of the siren told her she was the one he was after. She slowed and pulled over onto the shoulder of the road, her heart pounding and hands tightening on the steering wheel as she watched the police cruiser's door open and the cop get out. Her lap and arms were shaded by his shadow as he stepped up to the driver's window and leaned down.

"I'm sorry, officer, I didn't realize I was doing anything—" she said, turning to look up at the policeman. When she saw who it was, she finished with, "Why you lousy son of a bitch! You scared the hell out of me!"

Frank leaned down and smiled at her through the open window. In a low, menacing voice he said, "Just the facts, ma'm. I'd like to see your driver's license and registration please."

Only for an instant did Elizabeth think he was serious. Then his smile widened, and he burst out laughing.

"You bastard! For a minute, there, you had me wondering if I had done anything wrong," Elizabeth said. The flush of panic she had felt as soon as she saw the cruiser had made her buoyant sense of well-being instantly evaporate; and seeing Frank, smiling though he was, only reminded her of all the things she was trying so desperately to forget.

"Oh, make no mistake," Frank said, gripping the window's edge and looking in at her. "I wanted you . . . but for something other than a traffic violation."

"And what might that be?" Elizabeth asked, feeling herself tightening up.

"Well—" Frank said. He straightened up and crossed his arms over his chest and, looking up and down the stretch of road, took a deep breath. "I really haven't had a chance to talk to you since—"

"We don't have anything to talk about, do we?" Elizabeth snapped. "I'd like to go, if it's all right with you." The longer she sat there, the more she resented Frank for shattering her good mood.

If he tells me something else has happened, or that they found something else out at Caroline's grave, I'll scream, she thought. *I swear to God I will!*

Flustered, Frank shrugged and said, "I kinda thought—at least I *hoped*—we had something more to talk about. I mean, I don't want you to think that . . . you know, that night out at Bristol Pond was—was some kind of setup."

"Oh, really?"

"Yeah, really!"

Elizabeth sighed deeply, her hands tightening even more on the steering wheel. She watched her knuckles go white. The sound of her grinding teeth filled her ears.

"If you want to know what *I* truly felt," she said, "I'll tell you. You made me feel as though being with me was nothing more than part of your job. Part of your investigation! I felt like you were using me to get information about Doug—unless *I'm* still a suspect in what's been going on. Look, Frank, I don't have any delusions, all right? I mean, I didn't come back home thinking, ahh, now's my chance to pick up where I left off with Frank, that maybe we could start living the life we should have had together right after high school. Okay? That's bullshit! Whatever happened that night, happened; and now it's over with. The sooner we get on with our own lives, the better off we'll both be. Am I making myself clear?"

"Perfectly," Frank said. He swallowed with difficulty as he regarded her. He took a deep breath before continuing, surprised at how faint, how feeble his words sounded when they came out.

"But—I dunno. I was sort of hoping there'd be more to it than that," he said. Unable to look at her, he glanced down at the ground.

Elizabeth flashed him a questioning look. "What do you mean? I know damned well that you and those detectives think I might have been involved with what happened out at—uh—my uncle's grave!"

A dark curtain dropped over her mind, and she realized that she hadn't been able to say—*at Caroline's grave!*

"If you want the truth, that entire evening—even when we were out at the pond—I felt as though you were observing and testing and probing me to see if I said or did anything to give myself away."

"That's not true," Frank said, almost pleading. "It's not like that at all."

"Oh, sure—you say that now, but I don't feel it! If you had even the slightest interest in—"

"But I do," Frank said sharply. "That's what I'm trying to tell you, for Christ's sake! I *do* still feel . . . a lot for you." He took another deep breath and stared at her intently, his mouth set in a hard line. "Maybe you never felt it, but I sure did! As soon as I heard you'd come back home, I started hoping, as crazy as I knew it was, that you and I *could* pick up where we'd left off."

"We're adults now, Frank. Don't you think it's time to put aside these . . . these half-assed romantic notions?" Elizabeth asked. "Come on, Frank. We're just not the same people we were twenty years ago."

"Don't you think I know that?" he said. "But I didn't ask you out and *certainly* didn't want to make love to you simply because I was trying to get information out of you!"

"You sure as hell made me feel that way," she replied. That wasn't the truth, and she was instantly angry at herself when she felt her eyes beginning to tear up.

Frank knelt down beside the car window, his face level with hers. His eyes probed her, seeming to cut right through her defenses. She hated herself for even the tiniest impulse that made her want to reach out to him, grab him, hold him close, lose herself in him. Maybe all along she had been wrong about him, she thought. Maybe he was the one she could talk to, the one who could soothe her frayed nerves. Maybe he would be willing to listen to her and be there when she cried it all out.

No, Goddamn it! she told herself. *It can't be that easy! It's never that easy!*

Forcing her mouth into a hard line, she shook her head stiffly and said, "We're not the people we used to be, Frank. And no matter what or who you think I am . . . you just don't know me anymore."

"But I want to get to know you," Frank said, almost pleading. "I really do, and not how you *were*; how you *are*! For Christ's sake, Elizabeth, don't you understand what I'm trying to say? I love you!"

She looked at him and for several seconds was speechless. Then, her voice sounding low and gravelly, she said, "But Frank . . . I can't—love you." She hated herself the instant the words were out of her mouth, but she couldn't unsay them. "Don't *you* understand *that*? After everything that's happened, I don't know—" Her breath caught in her chest with a needle-sharp jab. "I don't know if I *can* love anyone anymore!"

Frank was about to say something, but just then the radio in his cruiser squawked, drawing his attention. He gave Elizabeth a lingering look and, waving his hands for her to wait, said, "Stay right here. I'll only be a second." With that he turned and ran back to his cruiser. Reaching in through the window, he picked up the microphone.

Elizabeth sat there watching him in her rearview mirror, letting his words repeat in her mind no matter how much she told herself she didn't want them to.

"Don't you understand what I'm trying to say? I love you!"

He leaned into the cruiser to replace the radio microphone, then came back to her car. Bracing both hands on the side of the window, he said, "Look, I've got to go. There's been an accident out on Burnham Road."

"Nothing serious, I hope," she said, nodding silently. She wanted just to sit where she was and not say anything else until he left. Her mind was a hissing blank of white noise and . . .

"Don't you understand what I'm trying to say? I love you!"

"Look, Elizabeth," Frank said. His voice was tight, and he

jabbed with his hands for emphasis. "I don't want you to feel any kind of pressure from me, all right? And I certainly don't want to force myself on you. But look—let's not cut anything off, either, okay? I mean, what's the harm in our just seeing each other?"

Elizabeth opened her mouth to reply, but he hushed her.

"Even thinking about, you know—what happened out at Bristol Pond that night," he went on. "I don't want you to think I'm just out to have sex with you. But that was . . . it was beautiful. Let's just—" He gasped with frustration and, cocking his head to one side, glanced angrily back at the waiting cruiser. "It sounds like something right out of high school, but can we at least be friends? We could go out to eat every now and then, maybe catch a movie or whatever. Just have a good time. Maybe we just have to give ourselves some space, some time to find out how we feel. Look, I've got to get out to Burnham Road, but how about tomorrow night? It's my day off. We could—I don't know, just go out for a drink and talk."

"Frank—"

"Just say yes," he said, beaming her a wide smile. "What's the Goddamned harm in that? I can pick you up at your house right after supper, say—eight o'clock?"

And I can tell you all about hearing the voice of my dead daughter on a tape recorder, she thought, fighting back a dark rush of fear. After considering for a moment and telling herself she could always cancel—over the phone, when she wouldn't have to look at the pleading pain on his face—she said, "Yeah—okay, I guess."

"Great," Frank said, clapping his hands together and rubbing them as he straightened up. "I'll see you then."

He ran back to the cruiser, got in, and turned around quickly, his lights strobing as he disappeared down the road. Sighing, Elizabeth shifted her car into drive and started back on the road to town, telling herself she had probably just made the worst mistake of her life by allowing Frank even the possibility of hoping.

2.

The phone in the living room rang late that night, about an hour after Elizabeth's parents had gone to bed. Elizabeth was sitting on the couch, flipping through old issues of *Reader's Digest*. Her first thought as she snatched up the receiver in the middle of its second ring was that it was Doug, calling to harass her with questions about where she planned to live and what she planned to do . . . or, worse, to talk about their getting a divorce. She couldn't disguise her surprise when she heard Dr. Graydon's voice on the other end of the line.

"Hello, Elizabeth," Graydon said. His voice sounded smooth and calm, but there was also a hard edge to it that she didn't like. "You missed your appointment today, and since I hadn't heard from you, I thought I'd call. Is everything all right?"

"Oh, yeah—sure," she stammered. "I'm fine. I'm sorry I didn't call to cancel, but I was—well—" She considered telling him she had to cover for a co-worker who had to go home sick, but she let that impulse pass. "The truth of it is, I skipped work today, too, and just spent the day out at the beach by myself."

"It was a nice day for doing that," Graydon said. "But you must realize that was a quite irresponsible thing to do."

"Well, I—"

"I can't very well fill my day with appointments and then not have people show up, now, can I?" He paused, but before Elizabeth could stammer her defense, he went on, "I don't mean to sound harsh, but, of course, you will pay for the missed session."

"Oh, yeah—sure," Elizabeth said. "I planned to. I'm sorry I didn't call, but I—"

"And in the future, I expect you to notify me if you're going to miss an appointment," Graydon said. "If you're serious about working with me, it's imperative that we proceed *my* way. Agreed?"

"I'm really sorry," Elizabeth said, even though she felt more anger at Graydon than any twinge of guilt. "It's just that, after everything that's been happening these past few days, I needed some time alone."

"Oh? What's been *happening* these past few days?"

"Actually, not much," Elizabeth said haltingly, even as a chill raced up her spine with the memory of hearing that voice on Eldon's tape recorder. "It's just that I—I've been busy."

"I hope you realize how important it is to keep things going now that you've begun this therapy," Graydon said. "It isn't something you should approach lightly. The point of therapy is not to do it when you feel comfortable, or when it's convenient. The point is to confront those things that are bothering you and deal with them head on, as painful as that may be at times."

"Oh, no, I realize that," Elizabeth said. She could feel her defenses going up, but right now she wanted to unburden herself to Graydon least of all. "But I—" An idea of what to say came to mind, and before she had fully considered it, she said it out loud. "You see, Dr. Graydon, I finally got up the nerve to go out to Caroline's grave." The lie tasted like thick phlegm in the back of her throat.

"What happened?"

Elizabeth swallowed and glanced nervously around the living room. She couldn't shake the feeling that, from somewhere in the dark corners of the living room, someone was watching her. Glancing over her shoulder, she half-expected to see two baleful, red eyes glowing in the darkness like angry coals.

"Well . . . although it wasn't easy, I'm glad I did it."

"And did you speak to her as we discussed?" Graydon asked. His voice had an eagerness to it that bothered Elizabeth. A tingle of chills raced up her back, and the feeling of being watched from behind intensified.

"Uh, no . . . not really. I didn't actually spend much time there—you know, at the grave," she said softly. "I just wanted to prove to myself that I could . . . go out there and not freak out or anything."

"Was this before or after your picnic out at the beach?" Graydon asked, with a measure of controlled anger in his voice again.

Elizabeth jumped at his question, as though his voice had given her an electrical shock. She knew she had mentioned taking the day off, and may have said something about going to the beach, but she was positive she hadn't said anything about having a picnic there. Was this just a perfectly natural assumption on Graydon's part, or had he found out somehow, from someone, what she had done? A cold, coiling tension tightened in her stomach, and she started wondering frantically why this conversation with Graydon—someone she was supposed to trust—was making her feel so uneasy.

"It was, ahh—before," she said. "Actually, a couple of days ago."

She was lying, but now that she had started talking about visiting Caroline's grave, she remembered the night she had driven out to the accident site. Shivers ran up her back when she recalled seeing that bony, white hand reaching, clawing up over the side of the road. She tried to push aside the frightening mental image, but it seemed only to get stronger, sharper.

"This is exactly why you should have kept our appointment," Graydon said sharply. "I would think you'd want to talk to me about it. Perhaps we should reschedule."

There was such a long pause that, finally, just to end the silence, Elizabeth said, "I don't really think that's necessary. Next Monday will be soon enough."

She was trying hard to fight back the rush of fear that was mounting up inside her. She didn't know if it was from talking to Graydon, from what they were talking about, or from other things that were stirring in her memory; right now it didn't matter. All she wanted was to hang up the phone and be alone with her thoughts. She didn't want to feel as though she had to spill her guts to Graydon or to Frank or to *anyone*!

"Actually, it might not be wise to wait that long," Graydon said.

"What—? What do you mean?" Elizabeth stammered, as the fear inside her intensified like the rush of an incoming tide.

"Exactly what I said," Graydon replied. "Next Monday might not be soon enough. We have to talk."

"About what?" Elizabeth said, keenly aware of the trembling in her voice. She could tell, just by the hard tone of his voice, that this could very easily lead to trouble.

"About a matter of great importance—to both you *and* me," Graydon replied. "I don't want to discuss it over the phone. I really think we should discuss this in person."

"Well . . . I don't know," Elizabeth replied. "I have to work tomorrow morning, and I—"

"The sooner the better—really! Look, Elizabeth, I mean it when I say I can't discuss it over the phone. Can we meet sometime tomorrow?"

The near-desperate tone in his voice bothered Elizabeth. She took a deep breath and said, "Like I said, I have to work tomorrow—"

"After work then. What time do you get off?"

For a moment, Elizabeth considered lying and telling him she had to work until closing, at nine o'clock, but instead she said "Five o'clock. But really, I have to—"

"Then could you meet me—say, at five-thirty somewhere? We can pick a place halfway between your house and mine. I promise I won't take any more than half an hour of your time."

What she wanted to say was, *No way! Not a snowball's chance in Hell*! She should hang up on him right now and, first thing tomorrow, start looking around for a new therapist. *She* was the patient, after all. No—make that *client*, and no matter what he had to tell her, he should be completely up front about it, if only so she would feel total confidence in him. This hinting and pleading was bullshit!

"Button," Graydon said, in the lengthening pause. He uttered the word so quickly, so quietly, Elizabeth had the fleeting impression he hadn't really said it. Like the message "*Help! Mommy!*" the word seemed to drift up from deep within her subconscious mind. She only *thought* she had heard him say it.

"Wha-what did you say?" she asked, a tremor shaking her voice.

"I said *Button*. I think you know what that means?"

Elizabeth looked down at her hand not holding the phone. She had squeezed it into such a hard, tight fist that the veins and tendons stood out in sharp definition. Her body shook as though she were sitting on a vibrating machine.

"Why did you . . . did you say that?" she stammered.

"I think you know why," Graydon said mildly, tauntingly.

"No, I . . . I don't," Elizabeth said, surprised that she could think, much less speak.

"You most certainly *do*," Graydon said. "And I think just the fact that I know what that word—that *name*—means to you should be enough to convince you to meet me tomorrow."

"Mother of Christ," Elizabeth muttered, blinking back tears as she stared up at the ceiling. She brought her fist up to her mouth and bit down hard on the knuckles. She had to do something to keep from screaming because, as far as she knew, there was no Goddamned way in Hell Graydon could have guessed that word—and what it meant to her! Not unless he could either read her mind or . . .

Doug! she thought in a flash. *That son of a bitch! What if all along Doug's been talking to Graydon? What if they're working together to drive me out of my mind?*

"How does five-thirty tomorrow sound? Where shall it be?" Graydon asked. His voice rose temptingly at the end of each question.

"There's—uh . . . I don't know. I haven't been back long enough to figure out where anything is."

"You know where the Maine Mall is, right?" Graydon said.

Elizabeth grunted.

"Okay, then—right across the street, heading to Portland, is a restaurant called the Ground Round. Maybe you've seen it. Meet me there, in the bar, tomorrow afternoon around five-thirty, all right?"

"Yeah—" Elizabeth gasped.

"I'll see you then," Graydon said.

He hung up the phone, leaving her sitting there with the steady buzz of the disconnected line drilling into her ear. For long seconds, she didn't move, didn't even blink! Her entire body felt as though it were being compressed, squeezed inward, by some immense, surrounding pressure. Her head was an overinflated balloon, ready to pop. Finally, though, shaking herself, she leaned over and replaced the phone. Still, she couldn't force herself to stand up. All she could do was sit there on the couch . . . sit and wonder . . .

How in the hell did Graydon know that long ago, in another lifetime, "button" had been the first word, other than "mama" and "dada," that Caroline had learned when she was about a year old? And how in the name of God did Graydon know that, for a short time, no more than a year or so, "Button" had also been Elizabeth's private nickname for her daughter, Caroline?

3.

Elizabeth was standing erect and stiff, looking down at Roland Graydon, who was kneeling in front of her, naked. He had his hands around her waist, and was pulling her to him with a strength that was irresistible. She could feel the pressure of his face, the stubble of his beard as he rubbed back and forth against her belly.

"I have you . . . now," he said, his voice deadened by the thick fabric of her skirt.

The effort to speak was too much for Elizabeth . . . just as difficult, just as *impossible* as resisting Graydon's rough embrace. Looking downward, though, she saw her hands, resting on the top of his head. She wasn't able to tell if she was trying to push him away or pull him closer. A dizzying, weightless sensation bubbled up inside her like a gush of warm water.

She heard Graydon say something else, but his voice was muffled; it sounded as if his mouth was filled with the cotton of her skirt. His clamplike hold on her hips tightened; his steely fingers kneaded the backs of her thighs. She could feel saliva flowing from his mouth, saturating the fabric of her dress.

"No . . . I—"

She could say no more as Graydon's hands slid up to the waistband of her skirt and started pulling it down.

How do I even know it's Graydon? she wondered. *I haven't seen his face.*

The grip tightened, drawing her hips forward. The nub of his nose moved in tight, lowering circles over her stomach. She looked down at his naked shoulders, at the thick bunches of muscles moving with supple strength beneath his smooth skin.

"Don't do this to me," she heard herself say distantly. "You shouldn't be doing . . ."

The circular motion of Graydon's head continued, increasing in its intensity. From down by her hips, she could hear the soft, animal-like chuffing sounds he was making. As much as she commanded herself not to, she clasped the back of his head and directed his face closer, tighter . . . and lower into her crotch.

"You really shouldn't . . ." she said. "You shouldn't be doing this to me."

He either didn't hear her or else chose to ignore her as his hands worked her skirt and underpants down her thighs and he pressed his face into her bare crotch. Elizabeth wanted to deny the warmth that radiated from her lower belly, but she couldn't. Looking down at him again, she caressed the top of his head, running her fingers through his hair. There was an intense tingling sensation in her lower belly, wet and warm, that spread through her belly and down her thighs. She knew—Oh, God! She knew!—what he was doing!

"No! . . . This isn't right!" she said. It shocked her that her own voice had a husky, sensual growl to it, as though what he was doing was making her revert into some kind of animal.

"Oh, yes, it *is*!" Graydon said. "This is *perfectly* right!"

The animal sounds he was making got louder. Suddenly, Elizabeth felt a sharp pain in her groin. She knew he was using his teeth, nibbling on her, trying to arouse her further. Now, in earnest, she tried to push his head away; but with a deep, angry growl, he snuggled tightly against her. More darting pain followed, and the hot rush Elizabeth felt got stronger, as if blood was running—streaming down her inner thighs.

"Stop it!" she shouted. The words echoed in her ears with a weird, cartoonish effect, like a sheet of metal being roughly shaken. When she looked down, she saw that Graydon's shoulders had sprouted thick clumps of black hair that rapidly spread down his back in a tangled mat.

"Stop it . . . right *now*!"

But Graydon held her fast, his hands clawing into the flesh of her butt. Sharp points of pressure, not at all like fingers, dug into her flesh . . . No! They didn't feel like fingers! They felt like *claws*!

Elizabeth wanted to scream. She wanted to lift her knee and drive it, full force, into the underside of Graydon's jaw. She wanted to splinter his teeth, to tear him apart with her bare hands if she could, but all she managed to do was stand there, struggling uselessly as his tongue and teeth and claws ripped into her flesh.

Finally, after terror-filled seconds, the scream that was inside her found its way out. Her mind and ears filled with a warbling, rising note of terror as she felt her abdomen torn to ribbons. Hot blood gushed from her stomach and crotch. Looking down, she saw the pink, rippled texture of her entrails as they uncoiled and draped like bloody ropes over Graydon's hairy shoulders.

Finally, as lances of pain, burning and bright, exploded through her, Graydon released the pressure. Her vision was swimming from panic and pain as she looked down and saw looking up at her—not Graydon, but a grinning wolf's face on a man's body. A thick coat of dark fur masked the knots of his arm muscles. The creature smiled up at her, its gory grin streaked with blood as its wicked tongue lapped its lipless mouth. Spiked teeth gleamed beneath the gouts of fresh blood.

The creature's mouth twisted, as if it was trying to form words, but blood was gushing so freely from between its teeth, any sound it tried to make turned into a thick, bubbly gurgle.

The weightless sensation Elizabeth had experienced before returned, but this time it felt . . . different, somehow. A steady roaring sound filled her ears. It sounded like the surge of water at the beach rolling inward, hissing like white noise on a radio, and then falling away from the beach with an irresistible pull . . .

—like Graydon's bloody grip on her.

—like the dizzy, black, floating feeling that threatened to carry her away.

She couldn't help but stare down at the grinning wolf's face and watch in silent fascination as the steaming, red blood flowed from its mouth, drenching its furry chest in tangled streaks. Distantly, she knew it was her own lifeblood she was watching flow freely down the monster's chin; those were her intestines, making wet slapping sounds as they uncoiled into the creature's mouth and onto the floor.

Again, the wolf's mouth moved, struggling as though it either was chewing her innards or trying to speak.

"What . . . ?" Elizabeth whispered, wondering why or how she could try to carry on a conversation even as she was dying.

". . . Button . . ." the wolf said, its face splitting into a wide, leering grin. Stained crimson by the hot flow of blood, its needle-sharp teeth made wicked clicking sounds as it spoke.

Elizabeth shook her head in denial even as a strong, dark pull yanked back on her shoulders. Her legs went rubbery, then lost all strength as the flood of blood drained from her groin.

". . . *Button*!" the wolf repeated, its voice a deep growl. It smacked its mouth, savoring the taste of warm, living flesh. "First *her* . . . and now *you*!"

4.

Elizabeth woke up screaming and discovered that her inner thighs were covered with blood. She had started her period.

FIFTEEN
Dark Meeting

1.

Frank and Norton were standing by the coffee pot in the squad room. Each of them had poured coffee, added milk and sugar, and were blowing over the tops of their cups to cool the coffee before chancing a sip. With his eyes narrowed, Frank was studying his partner.

"So," Frank said at last, "are you going to tell me where the fuck you've been?" His question sounded almost offhanded, but there was an undercurrent of intensity in his voice that Norton couldn't miss or ignore.

Norton's eyebrows shot up, and Frank was sure he was considering trying to run—just a little bit longer—with the lie that he had been sick at home. Finally, he shrugged and said simply, "I, uh—I had some things I had to attend to."

"Anything I should know about?" Frank asked, pressing the point. His concern was at least partly because Norton was his partner, but also, no matter what, he didn't want to see Suzie get hurt.

Norton considered Frank's question for a moment in silence, biting down lightly on his lower lip and sawing his teeth back and forth. His lip looked white, bloodless. At last, he shook his head stiffly.

"I don't think so," he said. His voice was much lower than usual. "It ain't anything important."

Frank nodded and looked away as if he had accepted the dismissal and that was the end of it; but, after taking a sip of coffee, he turned back to Norton and, jabbing his finger at him threateningly, snarled, "I'm gonna tell you this, and I'm only going to say it once!"

Genuinely taken aback, Norton looked at Frank with a crooked smile twisting the corners of his mouth. Frank could tell he wanted to laugh aloud but was afraid to.

"You're my fuckin' partner," Frank went on, "and I have to be able to count on you to back me up—all the fuckin' way! Now, for the past few weeks, I don't know why, there have been a few— let's just call them indiscretions. Anyone else on the force would've—"

"Oh, yeah?" Norton snapped, sounding like a juvenile wise guy. "Like *what*?" He twisted around so he could place his cup of coffee on the counter and tensed up, as though getting ready to throw a punch at Frank.

"Well, other than this bullshit of you not showing up for work and handing me the lame excuse that you've been sick, the most recent one I can think of was that night out at the cemetery when I told you to call for some backup and you didn't do it! You said you thought I was overreacting, remember?"

Tightening his flickering smile into a smirk, Norton nodded. "Yeah—I remember."

"It wasn't up to *you* to decide what to do, all right?" Frank shouted. His face flushed with anger, and just then all he wanted to do was deck his partner.

Norton shrugged and, shaking his shoulders, seemed to relax, but there was still a coiled-up tension in his stance that warned Frank to keep his guard up. Frank couldn't help but wonder what buttons he was pushing that would make Norton react so defensively. Could it be something as simple as that he was seeing another woman, and he was afraid Frank would find out and tell Suzie?

Or was there more?

"And over the past few weeks or months," Frank continued, "I don't think you've been acting like yourself. My bottom line is, I don't give a fiddley-fuck what you're up to! If you're screwing around or whatever, I don't give a shit! Not until it starts affecting *me* and *my* job! *Then* I start getting pissed. Can I make it any clearer?"

"For Christ's sake, man," Norton said. "Chill out, will yah?" He held his hands up, palms forward, and waved them as if he were surrendering.

"I'll chill out once you level with me and tell me where the Christ you've been for the past few days," Frank snapped.

Instantly, Norton tensed up again; then he shook his head tightly. "I just don't see where that's any of your business, all right? I mean, what I do on my own time is—"

"It *wasn't* your own time," Frank shouted, taking a menacing step closer to Norton. "I still had to go out there on patrol. I still had to hang my ass on the line."

"Christ, Frank. You're talking like this is fucking New York City or something," Norton said. "It's just a fucking hayseed jerk-water town. It's not like we've got the fucking Mafia running the town or something."

He was smiling, obviously trying to lighten the talk with a joke, but Frank read it as all superficial; just beneath the surface, he could feel Norton's nervousness twitching like raw, exposed nerves. And Norton's reaction definitely seemed more than was necessary if it was something like him seeing another woman. Was Norton stupid enough or greedy enough to get involved with something a little more serious—maybe a drug deal or something else a crooked cop thought might turn a quick profit? Maybe he was already in way over his head, and in trying to dig himself out was only digging his own grave deeper.

"You wanna know the situation?" Frank said, deciding that a more sympathetic approach might work. "I'm worried about you, and so's your wife. And I would think—whatever the hell it is you're involved with—you could at least tell me and her so we could stop worrying."

"There's n-nothing to tell," Norton said with a shrug. He was trying his damnedest to sound innocent, but the nervous sputter gave him away. "Honest to Christ. I just wanted a few days off to myself. I was saving up my vacation time for this summer, and I just needed a break."

Frank sighed and shook his head as though disgusted. "Fine—fine," he muttered. "Have it your way. But I'll tell you one thing! If you start fucking up—especially if you don't do what I tell you and *especially* if you get us into a situation where something you do or don't do puts *my* ass on the line—I won't hesitate to write you up or put you down! You hear me?"

Gnawing at his lower lip, Norton nodded wordlessly.

Frank looked at his nearly full coffee cup, wrinkled his nose, and then tossed it, cup and all, into the sink. "Worse than that," he added, scowling deeply, "I'll skin you and nail your fucking hide to the station door. Remember that!"

Norton regarded him with a frail, wise guy smirk. He looked like he was about to say something pithy—like *Ohh . . . can't you hear my knees knocking*?—but all he could bring himself to do was nod quickly and grunt. Frank turned and walked out of the squad room, leaving Norton standing there by the sink, looking and feeling stupid.

2.

Elizabeth was fifteen minutes late for her meeting with Graydon when she pulled into the parking lot beside the Ground Round. All day at work and then during the drive out to South Portland, she had considered simply not showing up. It wasn't as though she was afraid of Graydon or anything like that; she was plain sick and tired of feeling as though she had to explain herself to anyone and everyone.

The parking lot was crowded, which was surprising on a Tuesday afternoon, and she had to drive around back to find a vacant place. Glancing at her watch, she wondered if Graydon was the type who would wait around or if, even after only fifteen minutes, he would leave in a huff. Truthfully, Elizabeth didn't care whether she saw him or not. After all, he had been the one who sounded so desperate on the phone. The only thing that drove her on was her curiosity to find out how in the hell he had learned about "Button." She was positive she had never mentioned it during a session, so how the hell would he know the significance of that name?

Realizing she was just sitting there, her car idling as she stared blankly out at the traffic passing by on the Maine Turnpike, Elizabeth cut the engine, slipped the keys into her purse, and got out of the car. Walking around to the front, she entered the dimly lit restaurant.

For the number of cars in the parking lot, the place seemed remarkably uncrowded. Through the doorway to the right, she saw the bar and heard ripples of conversation and laughter, masked by the buzzing sounds of pinball machines and video games. Peeking up over the edge of the bar's double doors, she scanned the smoky room. She saw Graydon right away. He was sitting in the far corner booth, positioned so he could watch the doorway and would see her as soon as she arrived. He caught her eye and waved her over. Sucking in a deep breath, Elizabeth pushed through the doors and wended her way to him through the maze of tables.

"Sorry I'm late," she said, as she slung her purse onto the padded seat and plopped herself down. "I hope you haven't been waiting long. I didn't get out of work right on time." The lie felt transparent, but she told herself—again—that she didn't have to apologize to anyone for anything!

"Not long at all," Graydon said, although his nearly empty glass told her otherwise. Raising his hand up to signal the waitress, he asked, "Would you care for a drink?"

Elizabeth shrugged. "I dunno—white wine, I guess." She considered having something stronger, but she was determined to make this meeting short and sweet; she certainly didn't want to fuzz up her thinking with booze.

The waitress came over to the table, and Graydon said curtly, "A white wine for the lady, and I'll have another Manhattan, straight up."

After the waitress went off to get the drinks, Elizabeth smiled at Graydon and settled back into the padded seat. She told herself to relax, but she couldn't push aside the feeling that she shouldn't have shown up today; the feeling had grown all the stronger, now that she was with him. She noticed something about Graydon that she had noticed that night in the bookstore, as well; maybe it was as simple as seeing him outside of his office, in an element that wasn't his own, but she detected a darkness, a furtive sneakiness about him—especially in his eyes—that bothered her, putting her instantly on her guard.

"Well, then," Graydon said. He let his words hang in the air as he picked up his glass and drained what remained. After carefully placing the empty glass on the table, he folded his hands in front of him and leaned toward her. "As I told you over the phone, we have a lot to talk about. There are some things I . . . I can do to help you, and ways you can help me."

Elizabeth was a bit taken aback by the directness of his approach, and she decided to respond in kind. Clenching her hands into fists under the table, so that Graydon couldn't see, she said, "The first thing I want you to tell me is, how did you know about that name?"

Graydon blinked his eyes rapidly a few times, then smiled benignly. It wasn't a warm or gentle smile by any means; it had the same stealthiness she saw in his eyes. In a sudden rush of fear, the dream she'd had about him, where his face had slowly transformed into that of a wolf as he ate her intestines, rose unbidden in her mind. She looked at him now, fearing that in the shadowed corner of the barroom, his face was going to start shifting and he would transform all the way into a wolf that would lunge across the table and rip out her throat before she could scream.

"All in due time," Graydon said mildly. "I'll tell you everything—*everything*—you want to know, in its proper time. As I said over the phone, if we are to proceed, we will do it *my* way. Do you understand?"

Elizabeth nodded, but her reply was cut short when the waitress appeared with their drinks. She put down two fresh napkins and placed the drinks on them, then took Graydon's empty.

"Would you care to order anything to eat?" she asked pleasantly.

Graydon looked questioningly at Elizabeth who, in spite of the rumbling emptiness in her stomach, shook her head. "I'm fine for now," she said, and Graydon dismissed the waitress with a casual flick of his hand.

The waitress walked away, scowling and no doubt thinking she wasn't going to get much of a tip from this table.

Elizabeth wanted to press Graydon further on how he had known "Button" would get to her, but Graydon beat her to it by taking control of the conversation.

"Because you skipped our session yesterday," he said, "my most immediate concern is that you're having second thoughts about seeing me as a therapist. Of course, I understand that this is entirely normal—necessary, even." He paused to take a sip of his fresh drink. Elizabeth also raised her glass and drank. "A relationship with a therapist is as intense, I'd say sometimes it's even *more* intense, than a marital relationship. And it certainly requires care and consideration before you make a total commitment."

"Of course," Elizabeth said, just to say something. The wine felt warm and cloying as it trickled down her throat.

"And one thing I wish to make clear here is that, whether you continue with me or choose to find someone else, I think it's absolutely imperative that you continue to do therapy."

Elizabeth couldn't help but snicker softly and say, "Why? Are you convinced that I'm crazy? That I need help?"

Graydon shook his head in the negative. "On, no—no, I don't think you're *crazy*, not by any strict definition of the term."

Elizabeth let out a heavy sigh in mock relief and said, "Gee—thanks, doc."

"But I do see you as a woman who is nearly buried under an immense load of grief and guilt. Someone who is—"

"Well, Jesus Christ! Wouldn't you be?" Elizabeth said, fighting hard to control her outburst of anger. Professional or not, she didn't think it was at all appropriate for Graydon to sit in such pompous judgment of her mental state—especially out in public. It irritated her and only made her think all the more that—no matter *what* else—she was going to start looking for a new therapist.

A corner of Graydon's mouth twitched into a half-smile, and he replied, "Yes . . . yes, I suppose I would—" His eyes flickered for a moment as he glanced upward. "But I would be more inclined to *do* something about it, certainly not wallow in it!"

Elizabeth cringed at the hard, judgmental edge in his voice. That only made her anger flare all the more.

"I don't think I'm *wallowing* in it," she said, glancing nervously over her shoulder to see if their conversation was disturbing anyone else in the bar. Lowering her voice, she leaned closer to Graydon. "When you consider what I've been through over the last year and a half, I think I've done pretty damned well, all in all." She sipped her wine again, even though it did little to soothe her throat. "I've been through a lot of shit. I've experienced the death of a child—my *only* child, something *no* parent should ever have to deal with.

And yeah—all right, I was out there in the Twilight Zone for a while there. But I did hang tough. I kind of went off the deep end, but I came back. And sure, I may have . . . may have wanted to die, but I didn't! I *didn't* kill myself! I *didn't* give up!''

Graydon's half-smile didn't flinch as he cocked his eyebrows and nodded his agreement. "True . . . true," he muttered; then, after a slight pause, he added, "but you can't tell me it isn't crippling you emotionally."

Elizabeth took hold of her glass of wine, not entirely sure if she intended to take another sip or toss the contents into Graydon's face. She knew damned well she was being manipulated, and she wanted to rise to the occasion, to fight back at him if only to show just how Goddamned tough everything had made her.

"And for the record, I don't care *what* you say," she said, her voice lowering with contempt, "I'm not entirely sure I *do* need counseling. Whether you think I've 'made it' or not—I'm not sure it even *matters* what you think. What's important is what I think, and *I* think I'm doing pretty fucking good. I'm going to make it because I'm a survivor."

Leaning an elbow on the table, Graydon began massaging his forehead above his left eye. In the dim light of the bar, with noisy conversations going on all around them, Elizabeth thought he looked, not diminished and certainly not insecure, but—definitely —out of place . . . as though he needed to be in his office, on his own turf, in order to maintain complete control of the situation.

"Elizabeth . . . Elizabeth," Graydon said, shaking his head sadly. It surprised her when he reached across the table and grasped her hand tightly. His grip was warm, and the palm of his hand was clammy, slick with sweat. "Don't you understand that *I* can help you? More than you realize!" The tips of his fingernails were digging into her skin, and for a flickering instant, she imagined, not human fingernails, but claws—wolf's claws carving red furrows in her flesh. Unable to speak, and wanting to pull her hand away from him but not daring to, Elizabeth simply nodded, her face rigid with fear.

"I can prove to you just how much you need me," Graydon said in a low, menacing tone. "Not just anybody, but *me*! Just as much as *I* need *you*!"

"No . . . no, I . . ." Elizabeth stammered, shaking her head jerkily from side to side.

So this was it all along, she thought. *He's making a play. Everything until now has been nothing more than maneuvering to get me into the sack!*

"I can prove how much you need me by asking you one simple question," Graydon said, as his grip on her hand tightened even more, restricting the circulation in her hand so that pins and needles tingled through her fingers. "By asking one simple question and by answering one, I can convince you like *that*!" He snapped his fingers in front of her face like a hypnotist breaking the trance.

"Go ahead," Elizabeth said. Her voice was twisted and seemed to be coming from deep inside her chest.

Is that all I am to him, she wondered—*a puppet*?

"Okay," Graydon said, his eyes darkening as he frowned and, still holding onto her hand, leaned closer to her over the table. The pressure made Elizabeth's pulse slam in her ears. "Tell me this— have you spoken with your daughter?"

Elizabeth couldn't have been more stunned if a thousand volts of electricity had jolted her body. Her shoulders jerked backward, and every muscle in her body seemed to contract simultaneously. Cold, numbing fingers squeezed her brain as her mind filled with the deafening roar of . . .

White noise!

In the darkened recesses of her brain, she heard a high-pitched voice whisper—

"I saw you there . . ."

"Here I . . . Here I . . ."

"Help! . . . Mommy! . . . Help!"

"Well . . . have you?" Graydon asked. His eyes flashed with terrifying intensity.

Elizabeth's mouth gaped open, and her eyes felt as though they were bulging right out of her face as she stared at him. His lips moved, and she heard his words; but they seemed oddly disjointed, as though she were watching a movie whose soundtrack was a few seconds off.

"I . . . I tried," she stammered. Each word, each thought was a burning coal in the center of her brain. "I . . . really tried."

"How?" Graydon asked, as his grip painfully wrung her wrist. "*How* did you try?"

Wave after wave of confusion swept up over her, threatening to carry her away. The entire bar—the whole world—telescoped down into a tightly focused beam that was directed squarely at her. Her throat felt powder dry, and no matter how much she licked her lips, she knew she wouldn't be able to form words that wouldn't blow away to dust before she could say them.

"I have to know *how* you tried to talk to her," Graydon said. His dark eyes were wide and staring, twin pulsating pools of darkness that looked . . .

Like wolf's eyes! Elizabeth thought with panic, as her nightmare images rose more clearly in her mind. *And if he smiles now, will his mouth and teeth start gushing blood? . . .*

My blood?

Her free hand shook uncontrollably as she reached for her glass of wine and raised it to her lips. The sound of her swallowing was as loud as horses' hoofbeats in her ears. The liquid ran down her throat in a single, hot surge that threatened to gag her.

"I was . . . given the name of someone," she said, her voice no more than a gasp. "Someone who said he could communicate with the spirit world."

"Who?" Graydon demanded. "Tell me his name."

Against her will, feeling as if Graydon had hypnotized her and put her completely under his control, Elizabeth heard herself say, "His name's Eldon Cody. He lives up in Standish—a place called Black Hill Farm."

Graydon nodded, but Elizabeth didn't know if it was because he recognized the name or for some other reason.

"And what happened when you went to see this . . . this Mr. Cody?" Graydon asked.

Completely helpless, lost in the intensity of his gaze and the steady pressure of his grip on her hand, Elizabeth said, "We did something he said was . . . I think he called it E.V.P."

Graydon nodded his understanding. "Electronic voice phenomenon."

Elizabeth looked at him sharply, wondering how in the hell Graydon had known something like that.

"He used a blank tape and set his radio to what he called white noise," she continued. "I asked some questions aloud to Caroline, and she—or someone in the spirit world—was supposed to answer."

"And *did* she?" Graydon asked with sudden ferocity. "Did you hear any voices when you played the tape back?"

Biting her lower lip, Elizabeth nodded, but, suddenly mistrustful of Graydon, she said, "We heard something, but . . ."

"I saw you there! Here I . . . Here I . . ."

". . . But it was nothing we could make out very clearly."

"Help! . . . Mommy! . . ."

"You're sure of that?" Graydon asked, as he continued to apply pressure to Elizabeth's hand. His eyes swelled, seeming to pulsate with energy as he gazed at her.

Trembling, Elizabeth was unable to look away from his steady stare. Her voice sounded raw when she blurted out, "It sounded like Caroline!" Tears sprang from her eyes, but still she couldn't break the hold of his gaze. "I don't know for sure. I mean, I was just about scared out of my mind, but I could have sworn I heard Caroline say, 'I saw you there!' "

"And do you still have this tape?" Graydon asked.

"No," Elizabeth said, sighing deeply and shaking her head. "While we were rewinding it, it got tangled in the machine and ruined."

"Pity," Graydon said. He released her hand, shifted his gaze from her, and leaned back in the booth. "I would have been very interested to hear that tape."

Sobbing, Elizabeth mumbled, "I don't think I could listen to it again—*ever!*"

"And now that it's been a while," Graydon said, his voice rumbling deeply, "and you've had time to think things over—what do you think about it all?"

"I . . . I don't know . . . what you mean," Elizabeth stammered. Her eyes drifted over to her wine glass, and she picked it up and raised it to her mouth. This time, when she swallowed, the wine was soothing and cooling, as it should be. She emptied the glass in two quick gulps.

"I mean, quite simply, do you believe you did, in fact, hear your daughter's voice on that tape?"

Elizabeth could do nothing except sit there and stare at him, wondering exactly what this man was up to. Certainly the last few minutes went way beyond the normal bounds of therapy. And such a seemingly intense interest in the occult was way beyond the bounds of normal science. So what was his point? What was he getting at?

"I had asked you once before, during our last session, if you thought, in a general sense, that it was possible to communicate with the dead," Graydon said. The matter-of-fact tone of his voice completely belied what he was saying. "So now I'll stop beating around the bush and ask you directly: Would you like to talk with your dead daughter?"

Elizabeth's vision pulsated as she sat in stunned silence for several seconds. Then, slowly, her pulse slamming like a pile driver in her head, she nodded and said, "If it's at all possible—yes . . . I'd like to very much."

Graydon smiled solemnly. "And would you believe me if I told you I could arrange for you to do just that? Talk with Caroline?"

Stammering, Elizabeth replied, "I . . . I have no idea." She ran the flat of her hand over her face and did the best she could to control the tremors that shook her.

"Well, I don't usually like to be this blunt," Graydon said, "but not to put too fine a point to it, I can do just that. I can arrange for you not only to speak to your daughter, but to see her as well."

He reached down beside him and picked up a book he had hidden on the seat next to his leg. It was a rather large volume with a pebbly black-leather cover that looked almost like a Bible. Until now, Elizabeth hadn't noticed it there, but as he handed the book to her, he said, "Before we go any further, I have a proposition to make to you. Before you close your mind to any of this, perhaps because of your disappointment with the experiments you conducted with Mr. Cody or anyone else, I'd like you to read part of this book."

Still feeling stunned and drained, Elizabeth turned the book around in her hand so she could read the title stamped in gold on the spine. *Practicing the Black Arts*. She wasn't at all surprised by what she saw; it fit in perfectly, not just with their conversation, but with everything else that had happened to her in the past few weeks. Elizabeth knew her mind had reached and then gone well beyond the saturation point, to where she was numbed to just about everything . . .

Unless he can really—somehow—do what he says he can . . . Let me see and talk to Caroline!

"The book was originally published in 1884. This is a facsimile of the first edition. As I recall, rather ironically, I pointed out a paperback edition of this exact book to you the night we met in the bookstore. Do you remember?"

Elizabeth numbly shook her head as she stared at the book in her hands.

"No matter," Graydon said. "I'd particularly like you to take a look at Chapter Twelve, the chapter on necromancy. Now I realize this whole thing might be completely foreign to you, but I must admit, I felt right from the first time I met you that you were . . . well, I don't want to sound too mysterious about it, but I had a very strong gut feeling that you would be open to avenues such as these."

"I . . . I just don't know," Elizabeth stammered as she fumbled to slip the book into her purse. She realized the book was much too large to fit, so she held it in her lap. Her fingertips continually rubbed the textured leather cover as though seeking some kind of reassurance there.

"Read that chapter, and then we can get together again to discuss it," Graydon said. The dark intensity in his eyes shifted like passing storm clouds. He watched her a moment, then leaned back and smiled with satisfaction, knowing that Elizabeth would do *exactly* what he had asked.

Elizabeth made a move to get up to leave, but before she did, he froze her with a glance. Slowly, she eased herself back down into the seat.

"Before you go, there's one more thing," Graydon said, lowering his gaze.

"What's that—?" Elizabeth said, barely able to stop her voice from shaking.

"I told you I would answer one simple question for you," Graydon said.

"What question was that?" Elizabeth asked. "I mean, God!—after all of this . . . this talk—" She exhaled noisily and shook her head as though dazed as she stared at the book she was holding.

"After what you just hit me with, I've got a couple of hundred questions. I wouldn't know where to start."

Graydon smiled, but the smile was far from warm and friendly. A coiling, dark dread encircled her heart; Graydon's smile was much too much like the cold, hard grin of the wolf he had become in her nightmare.

"You wanted me to tell you how I knew the name *Button* would be significant to you, remember?"

Elizabeth nodded stiffly. "Right—" she rasped.

"The answer is quite simple," Graydon said with a shrug. "Caroline told me."

3.

"I've been calling all evening," Frank said. "Your folks must be getting sick and tired of me calling, but—uh, I thought we had a date."

Elizabeth sighed deeply and cradled the phone against her shoulder. It was almost eleven o'clock. She had just walked into the house and hadn't even had a chance to say hello to her parents, when the phone rang. She sat down heavily in the kitchen chair, feeling totally drained. As she listened to Frank's voice, barely hearing his words, her fingers brushed lightly along the edge of the book Graydon had given to her. She didn't at all like the uneasiness she felt just reading the title.

She had only now arrived home because, after meeting Graydon, she hadn't been able to face going straight home. With so much hitting her all at once and so much to think about, she had left the Ground Round, gotten onto the Maine Turnpike, and taken a long, aimless drive north. After making it to Waterville, she had stopped, tried to eat something at a Burger King, and then started back to Portland along Route 202, through Lewiston and Gray.

"I'm sorry," she said softly, "I had to meet with . . . with my therapist, and—"

"You mean *Dr.* Graydon?"

"Yeah," Elizabeth said, not liking the emphasis he put on the word doctor. "After that, I was pretty wiped. I had a lot to think about and just wanted to be alone for a while. I forgot that you were coming over.''

In truth, she had remembered her date with Frank and had thought about it but, just like when skipping her appointment with Graydon, she had decided to hell with it and simply not bothered to call.

"You *forgot*! You have no idea how good it is for my ego to hear you say that,'' Frank replied. He laughed softly into the phone, trying to inject a note of humor, but she could tell how deeply he was hurt.

Elizabeth's eyes felt red-rimmed and raw as she balanced Graydon's book on her leg and casually flipped through the pages as she talked with Frank. Listening to him reminded her of things she now felt were so far gone from her life that she would never experience them again; he made her remember how normal and safe everyday life used to feel, and how nice it was when people could meet and fall in love . . . or, even if they didn't fall in love, they could do things together just to have fun, like going to the movies or out for a few drinks, just to be together.

But that's not how real life is! She thought bitterly.

There was an aching chill in her heart, both for herself and for Frank. She knew how honest and sincere he was in his interest in her, but the kind of life he was looking for was already too far out of reach. In *real* life, people die, sometimes brutally and horribly, sometimes for no apparent reason. People end up hating the person they once loved; they end up verbally, sometimes physically abusing each other and getting divorced. And in the end, as much as they try or pretend, people don't—they *can't*—understand what's happening to them until, finally, life becomes nothing more than a bitter, agonizing experience. She could almost understand how, once you've lived long enough, you could actually look forward to dying, if only to stop the pain of living.

Until—finally—you can't wait for it to be over, Elizabeth thought bitterly.

Even as the words formed in her mind, she remembered the mind-numbing fear she had experienced when, less than a year ago, she had tried to end it all by cutting her own wrists. Until now, she had never seen any humor in what had happened, but she almost laughed aloud when she remembered that Doug—not the "friend" she had told Graydon—had been the one to find her spread-legged on the kitchen floor, bleeding from the slices in her wrists. Doug had called the ambulance and had gone with her to the hospital. She had changed the truth because she had never been able to accept that he could have—but didn't—turn her own words around on her from the night Caroline died . . .

"If it hadn't been for me, you'd be dead now!"

And she could just as easily have said to him exactly what he had said to her after that night . . .

"Don't you understand? She meant everything to me! I might just as well die!"

"Elizabeth . . . ?" Frank's voice said, breaking into her thoughts like a wrecking ball slamming into an abandoned building. "Did you hear what I said?"

"Uh—what was that?"

"I said it's too late for a movie, but maybe we could still go somewhere for a drink."

Elizabeth's eyes teared up as she looked idly down at Graydon's book. She had inadvertently opened it to Chapter Twelve and couldn't look away from the illustration on the facing page. It was an old-fashioned print of a man dressed like a medieval wizard. He was standing inside a five-pointed star drawn on the ground in front of an iron-gated mausoleum, and at each point of the star there burned a candle. In one hand the man held an open book; in the other he held a magic wand. All around him, swirling in a confusion of smoke and lichen-crusted tombstones, were demonic-looking figures—ghosts, demons, and devils . . . all reaching out toward the man whose face, in spite of the horrors surrounding him, displayed a remarkable calm.

As if he's in complete control, Elizabeth thought, *like Dr. Graydon wants to be*!

"Well . . . ?" Frank said.

"No, I, uh—" Elizabeth took a shuddering breath. "I just want to read for a while and then get some sleep. I haven't been sleeping very well lately."

"I don't have another day off until next Tuesday, but maybe we can do something then," Frank said.

Elizabeth grunted noncommittally.

"Maybe you should write it down on your calendar, or tie a string around your finger so you won't forget," he suggested, laughing.

"Yeah—sure," Elizabeth replied distractedly.

She couldn't take her eyes away from the drawing in the book. The longer she looked at the face of the man in the drawing, the more convinced she became that he looked exactly like Graydon. She realized she was just responding to the power of suggestion. Graydon had given her the book, and she was imagining these similarities; she was convincing herself it looked like him. Or, if in fact the man *did* resemble Graydon, it was nothing more than coincidence. Since she had returned home, stranger coincidences had happened, so something as simple as this wasn't entirely impossible.

"Are you feeling all right?" Frank asked. "You sound . . . I don't know—different. Kind of distracted."

"I'm fine—really, just beat," Elizabeth replied.

"Well, think about next week, okay? I'll give you a call in a day or two."

"Sure," Elizabeth said.

She listened as Frank hung up on his end of the line, then reached up and replaced the receiver on the wall phone near the table. She was expected at the store first thing in the morning, and she knew she should go to bed right now. After the last few nights—and the nightmares she'd been having—she needed at least a solid eight hours of sleep. More would be better. But rather than head straight upstairs, she started reading the chapter Graydon had suggested. For the next two hours, she sat at the kitchen table, leaning intently over the book as she read and reread Chapter Twelve, "The Ancient Science of Necromancy."

From Chapter Twelve, Elizabeth learned more than she ever thought she would want or need to know about raising the dead in order to communicate with them. There was a brief survey of the pervasiveness of such activity in many cultures, all of which, while interesting, struck Elizabeth simply as folklore and superstitious nonsense rather than real *science*, at least as she understood the term.

The last and longest section of the chapter, however, gave detailed descriptions of exactly how to go about summoning up the dead in order to speak with them. Elizabeth felt a deep chill when she read the description of the magical properties of the Hand of Glory. That someone—*who*?—had used her uncle's severed hand as just such a thing seemed obvious. The book reiterated exactly what Frank had told her when they'd met last Thursday; that the power of the hand was most potent if it was from a hanged man or a suicide. The book also detailed the protective properties of the pentagram, the incantations used to raise the dead, and what the summoner had to do before being allowed to speak with the dead, as well as which questions were appropriate and inappropriate to ask.

It was nearly one o'clock in the morning when Elizabeth finished reading the chapter a second time. She closed the book and sat back in her chair, feeling completely drained. Confusion and fear twisted in her mind like heavy storm clouds. She wanted to get up and get a drink of water, but she wasn't sure she even had the strength to stand. What she had read was bad enough taken as fiction, but it was staggering to consider that people long ago and, apparently, even now—people as seemingly sane as Roland Graydon—thought they could actually *do* this!

Everything she was learning about the ancient magic associated with necromancy put more and more pieces of her own situation together for her. Some of these realizations hit with all the energy of a bolt of lightning, while others came on more slowly and finally swept through her mind like the icy shock of an ocean wave.

One thing was that what she had *thought* were mere coincidences, were now starting to fit into place for her. Maybe there really *was* a pattern, some overriding master game plan to everyone's life. Christians, astrologers, and other so-called psychic people seemed to think so. What if they were right? What if we really are just pawns in some cosmic drama of which we can get only hints?

But even if life *is* all preordained, Elizabeth believed that it was up to her, as it was to each individual, to work out her own life pattern. It was up to her to judge whether she thought such perceived "coincidences" were either "good" or "bad." If she defined every connection in her life as negative, then, sure, someone like Dr. Graydon would have to classify her as paranoid. But if she saw and made the exact same connections and regarded them all in a positive light, it was no longer paranoia . . . it was what people throughout the ages have defined as a "religious" experience. Elizabeth actually wished she could embrace this perception that life truly is all connected, and that it is all for the good!

"And does Graydon honestly think he can do this?" she whispered aloud, as she closed the black book and stared blankly at its cover. It was obvious that this book was more than a history of magic; it was a practical manual. And just as obviously, Graydon believed he could use it . . . either that, or else he was dangerously deluded.

But if Graydon is deluded, how could he know what the name *Button* meant to her? Was *that* just another coincidence, or was it tenuous proof that he was in touch with some kind of occult power? Although he had denied having ever spoken with Doug, maybe he had. He might be lying simply to manipulate her.

But why manipulate her . . . to what purpose?

Elizabeth granted that Graydon had a commanding presence, an attractive charisma . . . no, something deeper, something darker than that. Was it possible that Graydon was a black magician of some sort, someone who exercised power by gaining hypnotic control over a person? If he could be connected with what had happened out at Uncle Jonathan's grave or—as horrible as it was—the murder of Barney Fraser, shouldn't she get in touch with the police and tell them her suspicions? If she didn't want to talk to Frank about it, she knew she could go directly to Detective Harris.

Oh, yeah—sure, that would sound just *great*! Call up the town cops and tell them her therapist, Dr. Roland Graydon, of South Portland, practices black magic and is using the severed hand of a suicide—her Uncle Jonathan!—to raise her daughter Caroline from the dead. That would no doubt earn her a first-class ticket to a rubber room in the state mental institution in Augusta.

But what about the nightmares she had been having?

—What was she to make of the recurring dream about all those doorways that led into the exact same room where the old crone, who Graydon suggested was nothing more than a guilt-projection of herself, waited to show her what she had in her shopping bag. Would Elizabeth see Caroline's head—or her own—centered in a roaring ring of fire?

—What about the nightmare she'd had of using the Ouija board to spell out messages that, in light of more recent events, all seemed to be connected with what had been happening around town lately? Was she crazy, or did it all truly make a paranoia-inducing kind of sense?

—And what was she to make of her blatantly sexual dream where Graydon, kneeling in front of her, had chewed out her stomach and intestines with a wolfish, ravaging hunger? Was this, too, simply some kind of projection on her part, or was she in imminent danger from him?

—And most important, perhaps, how could *anyone* explain away, either as coincidence or delusion, the voice she had undeniably heard on Eldon Cody's tape recorder? Even if it *wasn't* Caroline's voice, *someone* had said those words! What were the odds that she would actually *hear* that same message she had received before?

"*Help! . . . Mommy! . . . Help! . . .*"

If Eldon Cody hadn't known enough to set her up—and how could he?—then how could she write it off as simple coincidence? Something like that would defy the hugest possible odds. It made winning Tri-State Mega-Bucks look like a sure thing.

Or maybe *she* was responsible. Maybe she had some bizarre psychic power she wasn't even aware of and was able to project her thoughts—her fear and guilt—into reality, enough so she would actually be able to hear them in Claire DeBlaise's "sitting" room and on Eldon Cody's tape recorder.

There was most definitely something . . . something *weird* going on. It certainly wasn't natural or normal!

Elizabeth had no doubt that Graydon had been involved in the disinterment of Uncle Jonathan. He—or someone working with him—had cut off her uncle's hand and was using it for magical purposes. Frank had told her about that other occurrence out in the cemetery. If she was right about her therapist, it meant Graydon was responsible for Barney Fraser's murder and, possibly, the fire that had killed Henry Bishop. The right thing to do, the sensible thing to do, was to turn Graydon in or, at the very least, make an anonymous phone call to the authorities.

But what it all came down to, finally, was—what if Graydon was right? What if he really could do what he said he could do?

Maybe all along he had been doing these things to prepare her, mentally and emotionally, to accept his power, his control over her. It was obvious how miserable she was over the death of her daughter; perhaps he was *seducing* her, in the deepest sense of the word, into trusting him so she would accept his offer of help . . . to allow her to speak with Caroline one last time! Maybe he saw that that was what she needed to be finally and completely free of the guilt she had from that night a year and a half ago.

But what if there was something beyond all of this? What if it was the exact opposite of what Graydon was telling her? What if he had no power at all but—somehow—*Caroline* had an important message and was trying to contact *her*! Was that possible? Could spirits "on the higher planes," as Claire would put it, come back to talk to the living?

It made a twisted kind of sense that, if she accepted it was even remotely possible to speak with the dead, she should just as easily accept that the dead could speak to her. Just as there were numerous historical instances of necromancy, as Graydon's book proved, there were even more instances of divination through a variety of methods ranging from the Ouija board and seances and "channeling" in darkened rooms to dream visions of the dead contacting and advising the living. On the rare occasions she had thought about it until now, Elizabeth had always assumed such things were either delusions or simple parlor games. Maybe her acceptance of such things now came from an accumulation of pressure, lack of sleep, overwrought nerves, anxiety, and Graydon's wearing down of her resistance. Regardless—it was there! It was being offered to her, and it sure as hell *seemed* possible!

If her daughter had some message to get to her, Elizabeth wondered what it would be. What reasons did the dead have to come back?

She knew the most obvious superstitious reasons: ghosts return either to haunt the place where they met their sudden and unexpected death, or else they came back to complete some unfinished earthly business before "passing on" to the next spiritual level.

Warning or revenge? . . . warning or revenge? . . .

Which was it?

Elizabeth considered the ambiguity of the message she had received—*Help! . . . Mommy!* Was Caroline calling to her for help? . . . or was she saying she was trying to break through so she could help her mother?

A numbing chill gripped Elizabeth when she recalled the night she had gone back to the accident site and had seen—thought so, anyway—a skeletal hand—*possibly Caroline's?*—reaching up over the edge of the roadside. She couldn't deny that she had felt directed to go out there that night . . . as though she was being forced to go, pushed out there against her will by a power she didn't understand.

Did Caroline lure me out there that night? Was she trying to reach back from beyond the grave and contact me?

Why?

Such confusing thoughts filled Elizabeth's mind like black, icy, unseen hands, reaching for her from the surrounding darkness. The kitchen, where she sat, seemed as cold and as narrow as a coffin. The sound of her own labored breathing rasped loudly in her ears. Outside, the night smothered the house, filled with horrible potential.

Does Caroline know something? Does she have a warning to give me of some unseen danger? . . .

Or does she have some unfinished business? Is there something more sinister? . . .

Does she want to get back at me for letting her die? . . .

"*Help . . . Mommy . . .*"

"Help mommy do *what*?" Elizabeth whispered, as she gazed inwardly at the dark curtains folding over her mind. Help mommy get rid of her guilt by killing herself? Is *that* what Caroline wants?

"No . . ." Elizabeth whispered. Her breath hitched in her chest as tears poured from her eyes. "I can't believe it! Not Caroline! She loved me, and I loved her!"

But if Caroline wasn't trying to return for revenge, then she had to be trying to tell her something. She might know something only someone on the "other side" could know—and she was trying to get through to her mother, trying desperately to *help* her *mommy* . . . before it was too late!

SIXTEEN
Further Investigations

1.

Detective Harris was hunched over his typewriter, carefully plugging away at the keys. A cigarette dangled from his lower lip, and thin blue rafts of smoke hung in several layers in the room. Sunlight was pouring in the window behind him, shadowing his face. Frank thought he looked more like an earnest newspaper reporter than a detective.

"Hunt and peck, huh?" Frank said, poking his head into the room. He entered without an invitation and sat down in the chair beside the desk, waiting for Harris to acknowledge him.

"Yeah," Harris finally muttered, barely looking up, "and it's a Goddamned *long* hunt." Twin streams of blue smoke shot from his nostrils. "What the fuck can I do for you?"

Frank scratched the back of his head and took a deep breath, "I've got a few questions for you, if you have the time."

Scowling, Harris snapped, "I *never* have the fuckin' time. What'd you want to know?"

"What do you think the chances are for the Red Sox this year?"

"You're a Goddamned laugh-riot, you know that?" Harris said, eyeing Frank narrowly. "What the fuck—you think I've got all day to waste bullshitting with you?"

"Hey! Lighten up, for Christ's sake," Frank said, waving the smoke away from his face. "I was just trying to make conversation."

"Listen up, asshole; I've got an unsolved murder, an extremely suspicious case of arson, a disinterred corpse, and half-a-fuckin'-million other things to do, so if you don't mind . . ."

"Actually, that's what I wanted to talk to you about," Frank said. "I wanted to know how the Fraser investigation was going."

Harris's scowl deepened as he flicked the ash off his cigarette and shrugged. "I just fuckin' told you. Zip! Zero! Zilch!"

"No leads? Nothing at all?"

Groaning, Harris shifted forward in his chair, grabbed a pad of paper and a pencil from his desk, and said, "Here—lemme write that down for you." Sticking his tongue out between his teeth, he started forming letters with all the earnest effort of a preschooler, saying in a sing-song voice: "That's Z-E-R-O." Tearing off the sheet of paper, he stuffed it into Frank's shirt pocket. "I assume you can read. If not, take it home and have your mommy read it to you."

Frank snickered as he took the paper and glanced at it. "Hey—you're the guy who told me what *assume* makes," he said, before crumpling it into a tight ball and, with a quick hook shot, popping it into the wastebasket by the wall.

"Two points. Glad to see you're good at *something*," Harris snarled. "Look, if you don't have anything more urgent than a bleeding rectum, I'd just as soon get some fuckin' work done."

"Okay, okay—I just had a quick question for you. Has the name Roland Graydon come up in any of your leads?"

Harris looked at the ceiling for a moment, took a drag off his cigarette, then with a loud *whoosh* blew the smoke out the corner of his mouth. "Nope. Should it?"

Frank shrugged. "I'm not sure."

"What the fuck is this all about, Melrose. I mean, if you don't mind telling me . . ." He waved one hand at Frank in an encouraging, "come-on-'n'-tell-me" motion.

"It's just . . . I'm not sure," Frank said, scratching behind his ear.

"You've been hanging around Willis too much," Harris said. "Looks to me like you got his cooties. Look, if you think I should know something about this guy Graydon, I wouldn't mind you telling me why. You got something you're not telling me?"

Frank shook his head. "I don't think so, it's just that a . . . a friend of mine has been seeing this guy. He's a therapist of some kind, and I—"

"Lookee here, flatfoot," Harris said, taking up the pad of paper again and hastily printing a single word. Smoke rose into his face, making him squint as he held it up to Frank. "See anything funny about this?" he asked.

In block letters was the single word: THERAPIST.

Frank shook his head and watched, perplexed, as Harris wrote something else on the paper below the word.

"See it now?" he asked. Using the same word, Harris had simply added a space between two of the letters. When Frank looked at the paper again, he read the words: THE RAPIST.

"That's cute—real cute," Frank said coldly. He found little humor in Harris's word game because it related so directly to the threat to Elizabeth. "Why don't you tell me something useful."

"You want something useful?" Harris asked, arching his eyebrows. "Here's a little tip for you. They always go back to the scene of the crime . . . *always*"!

"Christ, you're full of wisdom today."

"Well, Melrose, if you've got anything I *need* to know about this Graydon character or about why *anyone* might be messing around out there in the cemetery, now's the time to spill your guts. Otherwise"—he made a causally dismissive gesture with his hand—"be careful the doorknob doesn't bump your ass on your way out."

Frank pushed back the chair and stood up.

"Thanks for the entertainment," he mumbled, as the steady *click-click* of Harris's typewriter resumed. Once he was out into the hallway, though, what Harris had said about criminals returning to the scene of the crime struck him as possibly profound. Maybe that's exactly what he should delve into—every possible reason someone might have for doing anything to Caroline's grave. It might go all the way back to the night of the accident. The place to start would be at the Portland Public Library, where he could check out the newspaper accounts of what had happened that night.

2.

Aunt Junia was washing dishes at the kitchen sink when Elizabeth knocked on the screen door and then cautiously entered. She tiptoed just in case Elspeth was napping in the living room.

"Elizabeth!" Junia exclaimed. "What on earth . . . ? We sure have been seeing a lot of you lately."

Shrugging, Elizabeth smiled weakly.

"Well, don't just stand there in the doorway like a stranger. Come on in. I'll put on the coffee pot."

Elizabeth walked over to the kitchen table, slid out a chair, and sat down. "That isn't necessary," she said. "I just—" She clapped her hands together and rubbed them nervously. "I don't know. I was just—feeling like I needed someone to . . . to talk to."

"What's the problem, Elizabeth?" Junia said. She dried her hands on the dish towel as she came over and stood behind her niece. Without a word, she began rubbing the back of Elizabeth's neck. "My goodness! Your neck muscles are all bunched up. What's got you so worked up?"

Elizabeth tried to turn to look up at her aunt, but the pressure Junia was applying to the back of her neck prevented that, so she just lowered her head, closed her eyes, and tried like hell to enjoy the massage.

"If there's something bothering you, you should talk it out with your mother," Junia said. "I always thought you and she got along just fine."

"We do . . . or did. I dunno," Elizabeth said. She let her head bob around loosely as Junia's surprisingly strong fingers kneaded the wire-tight muscles and tendons. She imagined feeling each individual vertebra pop back into place. "It's just that—" She finished with a long and deep sigh.

"Well you can talk to me about it, if you want," Junia said. "There, is that enough?" She stopped the neck rub and went to sit down opposite Elizabeth. The concerned, loving expression on her face cut through Elizabeth's blues—at least a little.

"Where did you ever learn to do that?" Elizabeth asked as she rotated her head, feeling an undeniable relaxation.

"I have to massage Elspeth's back several times a day," Junia id. "The doctor showed me where the nerve centers are and how work them. But you didn't come over to talk neck rubs."

"No—I didn't," Elizabeth said, shaking her head. Already, she uld feel the tightening begin again, as though someone were serting slender steel rods in between her shoulders and running em up her spine, right into her brain.

"So tell me," Junia said, leaning forward with an expression of ep worry on her face.

"I don't know where to begin," Elizabeth said, raising her hands a gesture of helplessness. "I mean, it's all so . . . confusing."

"Why don't you start by telling me what happened yesterday," nia said kindly. "We can work our way back from there."

"Even that's so—so confused," Elizabeth said. Tears were building up in her eyes, and she told herself—commanded herself—to ntrol them. *Don't break down now and get Junia all upset*, she ld herself.

"Well then . . . how about if we talk about what you want to do xt?"

Against her will, Elizabeth felt warm tracks of tears run down ver her cheeks. Her throat was constricted, and she was surprised at any words came out at all when she opened her mouth.

"I have no idea," she rasped. "I mean, my whole life's such a ess. First I lose Caroline—then my marriage falls apart. And now —I'm positive coming back home was a mistake."

"How can you say that?" Junia asked. "Elspeth and I have been verjoyed to see you, and I'm sure your parents—even your father, his own tight-lipped way—are happy as clams to have you ound."

"Oh, I know—I know," Elizabeth said. Her voice was low and usky from the emotions she was choking back. "But you know, eing Frank and this . . . this other man—"

"What other man?" Junia asked.

Elizabeth stiffened and looked at her aunt, suddenly fearful of w much or how little she should reveal. In the privacy of her own oughts, knowing everything she knew, she couldn't sort things t, so was it fair of her to expect Junia or anyone else to help her al with things if she didn't tell all?

"I didn't want to mention this to you, mostly because I didn't want you to be upset, but I've been seeing a therapist—a psychiatrist in South Portland—ever since I got home. Before that, even, I was seeing someone in Laconia."

Junia nodded silently, allowing Elizabeth to continue at her own pace.

"Actually, I've been seeing a therapist since right after the night of the accident. You know—to help me deal with . . ." Her voice trailed away, and she was unsure whether or not she should tell Junia about her attempted suicide. ". . . To help me deal with everything that's happened," she finished lamely.

"That's understandable," Junia replied mildly.

Elizabeth sniffed and wiped her nose with the back of her hand. Then, looking squarely at her aunt, watching her, trying to judge her true, unguarded reaction, she decided to tell her everything. "Especially after I . . . tried to kill myself last spring."

Junia's eyes widened with surprise, but only for an instant. "I can understand that you were distraught by what happened," she said. "But I hope—I pray—you don't feel that despondent ever again. After losing my brother that way—" She tried to say more, but her face paled and her voice shut off with a strangled gasp.

Elizabeth's lower lip began to tremble uncontrollably as she stared into the warm, comforting eyes of her aunt and saw fear and deep pain there.

"I don't think I really wanted to die—not really," she said. "But after I lost Caroline . . . I mean—Jesus! I sure felt like I wanted to! Ever since that night!"

"I hope you realize that the important thing for you to do is to keep on living," Junia said. "I think that's what Caroline would want, too, don't you?"

"Oh, I know that," Elizabeth replied, her voice no more than a gasp. Tears were streaming down her face, now, and she reached blindly for a napkin from the holder on the table and began wiping her eyes with quick, hard strokes.

"But that's all in the past," Junia said. "And no matter what we think or feel, it's gone. I've always thought the most important thing is the future. Let the past be. You can choose to remember it fondly r to get over the painful parts—whatever. But you can *never* let ruin your future. So let's talk about that."

Elizabeth took a shuddering breath and stared down at her hands, ghtly folded in her lap.

"What do you plan to do from here?" Junia asked.

All Elizabeth could do was shake her head. She wanted desperately to tell her aunt everything . . .

—Tell her about Frank Melrose and the incredibly confused and onflicting emotions she felt about him; that he, at least, seemed arnest and sincere about wanting to start up their relationship and ee where it would lead; that she wanted and needed to feel a man's ove but didn't know if she would even recognize it or ever fully ust it when or if she ever did find it.

—Tell her about Dr. Roland Graydon and the absolutely bizarre roposition he had made to her, that—through necromancy, black agic—he wanted to raise Caroline's spirit so that Elizabeth could lk to her daughter and tell her how sorry she was that she had to e; that reading about the "black arts" late at night and terrifying erself was one thing, but that in the clear light of day, such ings—even such seemingly silly and harmless things as the seance ith Claire and the more frightening voices she and Eldon had corded—seemed mere delusions, the products of unstable and ossibly dangerously unbalanced minds.

—Tell her about the nightmares and the twisting guilt, the dark oughts that still circled around in her brain like sleek, hungry arks, just waiting to snag her and pull her under; that, in actual, old, hard truth, she *was* tired of living; that she had absolutely no ith in herself and saw no hope for the future, and that she probably *ould* be better off dead!

But she couldn't tell Junia that; she couldn't say *any* of it!

Covering her face with her hands, she wailed, "I have no idea hat I'm going to do," then collapsed forward onto the table. Her obs were muffled by her hands, and she was only distantly aware at Junia had come over to her again and begun patting her reasuringly on the back. The warm tears flowed, filling her hands, hile Junia stood beside her, simply muttering, "There, there, dear . . there, there . . ."

3

Sitting in the darkened research room at the Portland Public Library, Frank carefully read through the *Press Herald* and *Evening Express* accounts of the accident that had killed Caroline Myer. After the third time through, he concluded that there was nothing new to glean from the articles. He was ready to pack it in and head back to Bristol Mills when Baker, the research librarian, asked him if he had thought to check the obituaries for both people who had died that night.

"Both people . . ." Frank muttered, feeling an uncomfortable twinge. All along, he had been focusing only on what had happened to Caroline that night. He had completely forgotten that someone else—Sam Healy, the man driving the Buxton town snowplow—had also died. Frank zipped ahead on the microfilm until he found the funeral announcement for Wednesday, February 15, 1988.

"Son of a bitch! Son of a *fucking* bitch!" he whispered, reading and then rereading the brief write-up on the death of Sam Healy of Bar Mills, Maine. He couldn't believe the immense implications of one sentence near the bottom of Sam's death notice.

SAMUEL R. HEALY

BAR MILLS—Samuel R. Healy, 42, of Hollis Rd., died Monday night while driving a Buxton town snowplow, as a result of injuries sustained in an accident involving a stalled car on Route 22 in South Buxton.

He was born in Portland, son of Paula and Jack Healy, and was a 1966 graduate of Bonny Eagle High School.

He worked for the highway department of the town of Buxton and, prior to that, served with distinction in Vietnam as a Marine. He was an avid hunter and a member of both the Sebago Gun Club and the NRA.

Surviving are his wife, Donna B. Healy, now living in Bristol, Rhode Island; one son, William K. of Sherman Oaks, California; and his uncle, Roland Graydon of South Portland, who raised him following the death of his parents in 1954.

A memorial service will be held at 10 A.M. at St. Luke's Church in Hollis Center. Burial will immediately follow at Evergreen Cemetery, Bar Mills.

Fighting a cold surge of panic, Frank read the funeral notice a third and then a fourth time, just to make absolutely certain his eyes weren't tricking him, before he got up from his chair and signaled to Baker, waving at him to come over.

"Yeah—?" Baker said, leaning down close to the microfilm machine. The green glow of the screen gave his face a ghastly hue.

"How can I get a paper copy of this—in a hurry?" Frank asked. He was surprised at how shaky his voice sounded.

A cop is never supposed to feel panic or be afraid, he told himself, but he was already imagining the obituary that would run for Elizabeth if he didn't warn her in time . . . if it wasn't already too late!

"Just this page?" Baker asked.

Frank nodded.

"Just get it on the screen and press this button on the side," Baker said. He did the operation as he was describing it. From inside the microfilm machine, gears started grinding. "Costs a quarter a page. Honor system. You can pay at the desk before you leave."

"Great. Is there a phone nearby I can use?" Frank asked. He glanced around the reference room, fighting back the urge to grab the photocopy, run out to his car, and speed back to Bristol Mills.

Baker considered for a moment, then asked, "Is this official business?"

Frank hesitated, then nodded. "Uh, yeah—I'd guess it is."

"Then use the one at the reference desk," the librarian said. "You have to dial nine to get an outside line, but I—" Whatever else he had to say trailed off as Frank dashed over to the desk, snatched up the handset, and hurriedly dialed a number from memory. On the third ring, a woman's voice on the other end of the line said, "Hello." He knew instantly that it wasn't Elizabeth.

"Hello, Mrs. Payne," he said, forcing calmness into his voice. "This is Frank—Frank Melrose. I'd like to speak with Elizabeth if she's around."

As Frank was speaking, Baker picked up the paper copy of the page from the machine and walked over to the reference desk to hand it to him. Frank glanced at it quickly and silently nodded his thanks. With his free hand, he dug into his pants pocket for a quarter, which he placed on the desk next to the phone.

"She's not home right now," Rebecca said. "I would think she's still at work. You might want to try her there. She's got a job dow to Hardy's, you know—''

"Yes, I do. Would you do me a favor and ask her to call me an make *sure* she does? She can either leave a message for me at th police station or on my answering machine at home. I really hav to get in touch with her this evening.''

"It sounds quite urgent,'' Rebecca said.

"Oh, no—not really. But I do have to talk with her about som thing,'' Frank said. He hoped he was successfully masking the pani he felt.

"You know something, though—'' Rebecca said. "When sh left for work today, she said something kind of funny to me . . .'

"What was that, Mrs. Payne,'' Frank said, his shoulders tensing

"Well, she said she didn't want to take any phone calls, and tha if anyone called while she was out, she didn't even want to kno about it. I thought that was kinda strange at the time. Don't you?'

"Yes I do,'' Frank replied. He knew that Elizabeth was inte on avoiding him, and was suddenly fearful that this could cost he her life. "I'd appreciate it if you'd make an exception in this case. Before Rebecca could comment that it indeed sounded urgent, Fran said, "Thank you very much,'' and pressed the button to disconne the call. Looking at Baker, he asked sharply, "Is there a phon book around here?''

Baker opened the bottom desk drawer and took out the directory and Frank practically grabbed it out of his hands and started flippin through the pages until he found the number for Hardy's Hardware His hand was shaking as he hurriedly dialed the number. As muc as he wanted to push aside the feeling that it might already be to late, he couldn't ignore the icy cold that had blossomed in the p of his stomach. When Jake answered, Frank wasted no time.

"Jake, this is Frank. I have to talk to Elizabeth. It's urgent.''

"Wish I could help you,'' Jake replied, "but she waltzed in he this morning and just up 'n' quit on me. I ain't seen her since— I'd say since 'round eight o'clock this mornin'.''

"Son of a bitch,'' Frank said. "Son of a motherfucking *bitch*!'

"Yeah, I know,'' Jake said. "I mean, I don't hold it against he or nothin', but I would've appreciated at least a few days notice I'm pretty shorthanded 'round here as it is, this time of year.''

"Wish I could help," Frank snapped. "Look, if by chance you see her, tell her to call me at the station, okay?"

"Sure," Jake replied. "What's this all ab—"

"Gotta go. Thanks, Jake." Frank said. He thumbed the hook, then dialed the police station.

"Good afternoon. Bristol Mills police," said a voice. Frank instantly recognized Mark Curtis, the day-shift dispatcher.

"Mark—this is Frank. Have there been any calls for me today?"

After a slight pause, Mark replied, "Nothin' on the incoming sheet. You expecting something important?"

"Look, I don't have time to explain it all, but I'm expecting a call from Elizabeth Myers—write that name down and tape it to the phone. I can't tell you how important this is. If she calls, I want you to find out where she is and tell her . . . tell her to get her fucking ass over to the station right away."

"Should I use those exact words?" Mark asked. A lilting chuckle colored his voice.

"I'm not shitting around, Mark. This could be serious!" Frank yelled. "If she calls, tell her I've found out something about Graydon that she has *got* to know right away."

"Okay, sir," Mark answered. "Anything else?"

For a second, Frank considered asking to have a squad car drive out to the Payne home just to have a look around, but he realized that might be jumping the gun, at least at this point. One small, rational voice in the back of his mind was whispering that, still, everything he had found out and everything he thought was circumstantial; it would never hold up in court.

Yeah, another—louder—voice in his mind said, *but circumstantial can still get you killed*!

"No, I—uh, I guess that's all for now," Frank said more mildly. "I'm heading into the station right away."

"Catch you later, then," Mark said, before hanging up.

Frank hung up the phone and, after thanking Baker for all of his help, left the library on the run. He pushed the speed limit all the way back to Bristol Mills. Unfortunately, he had plenty to occupy his thoughts. None of it was pleasant.

He granted that a direct connection between Graydon and the accident that had killed Elizabeth's daughter, while certainly unnerving, was by no means proof that Graydon was plotting some kind of revenge against Elizabeth. Hell, if Elizabeth hadn't mentioned the accident to him during a session, Graydon might not even have made the connection yet. But then again, she had sought therapy in the first place, Frank assumed, to help her deal with that tragic loss, so she must have said *something* about it to her therapist.

THERAPIST . . . THE RAPIST.

Harris's sick joke came to mind with a nauseating rush.

The bothersome thing was the sizable odds against it being just a coincidence that so many strange—downright weird and *deadly* —things had happened in town recently. He hadn't been the only one at the station to notice that they coincided with Elizabeth's return home. *Something* was most definitely happening—something that directly involved Elizabeth. Frank was certain that Harris suspected her of involvement, but he was even more convinced now that she was the target—the victim, not the victimizer. *Everything* that had happened seemed directed to undermine her sanity, not help it. And who better to do something like that, to know how and when to hit her right where she was most vulnerable, how to manipulate her mental weaknesses, than someone she thought was trying to help her? Graydon hadn't struck directly at Elizabeth yet because he was using the time to toy with her, get her off balance and keep her that way . . .

To do . . . what? Frank wondered.

What were the chances that, in looking for a therapist, Elizabeth would just happen upon the name of Roland Graydon? Or even more improbably: what were the odds that if Graydon did hold Elizabeth directly responsible for the death of his nephew, Sam Healy, he could manage events so that he would end up as her therapist? If this was some convoluted revenge plot on his part, things sure had played perfectly into his hands . . .

Possibly *too* perfectly to be left to mere chance, Frank thought. This was another circumstantial connection that would never hold up in court, he knew, but it sure was convincing . . . and scary as hell! He didn't have any answers; he didn't want to try to figure out *how* Graydon had made things work out his way, or even *what* he planned for his sick, twisted revenge. But Frank was damned well going to make sure Elizabeth knew about all of this before she spent another minute in Roland Graydon's presence!

4.

"Tonight! We *must* do it tonight!"

The intensity in Graydon's voice surprised and unnerved Elizabeth. She was sitting on the couch in his office, watching him as he paced the floor by the windows. Although not entirely sure this was a smart thing to do, she had driven out here straight from Junia's house. She had considered giving her mother a call, to tell her she wouldn't be home for supper, but had decided against it, telling herself she didn't have to check in with her parents on *everything* she did!

Through the office windows, Elizabeth could see the slanting yellow light of the setting sun. It cast long, dark shadows on the rocks that lined the coast, and colored the water a deep steel gray. The ocean heaved with rolling swells that made her think not of water, but of strong, supple muscles working beneath an animal's fur. Lost in the intensity of his thoughts, Graydon never once paused to look out at the view.

"I don't see why there's . . . there's any need to hurry," Elizabeth stammered. "I mean, I just read the chapter you wanted me to read last night. I haven't had time to absorb—"

"What did you think?" Graydon snapped, smacking his fist into his open hand for emphasis. "Did it make sense to you?"

The wild gleam in his eyes unnerved Elizabeth. Flustered, she shifted uneasily on the couch. Graydon walked over to her, standing so close to the couch that he towered above her. The memory of his face, transforming into that of a wolf as he feasted on her innards, rose in Elizabeth's mind with a razor-edged chill.

"I thought it was . . . interesting," she said, shifting in her seat to put as much distance as she could between them.

"Interesting? *Interesting*!" Graydon shouted. "That's all you can say? It was *interesting*!"

Helpless and confused, Elizabeth raised her hands in a gesture of pleading. "A lot of it was . . . scary."

Graydon snorted with disgust. "Scary to anyone who lives in ignorance and fear! To anyone who doesn't have the *courage* to take matters into their own hands!" He clenched both fists and punched the air between them. "Here I have offered you something—something wonderful! Something miraculous! To actually be able to see and talk to your dead daughter, and the best you can say is it's *interesting*?" He turned from her in disgust. "Perhaps we should forget the whole thing." He walked over to the windows again and stood with his back to her, his hands on his hips as he silently regarded the gunmetal gray ocean.

At a complete loss for words, Elizabeth sat staring blankly at Graydon's back, almost overwhelmed by the confused and irrational thoughts colliding in her mind. She imagined that she was swimming far out on that steel gray ocean, being pulled by death-cold, irresistible currents further and further from land.

A small voice in her head was whispering that this entire discussion was absolutely insane! It was simply impossible to raise the dead or to communicate with them—by *any* means! Claire DeBlaise, Eldon Cody, and Roland Graydon—all of them were deluded. At the very least they were harmlessly crazy; at the worst, dangerously insane! This man in particular, this *doctor*, this *psychiatrist* who was supposed to help her sort out and deal with the confusion in her life, was only compounding her problems by holding out to her even the slight possibility of such an absurd, fantastic thing. It was more than professionally irresponsible; it was criminal!

But another voice inside her was telling her that, while she might not believe in anything supernatural, there certainly were things in the world that defied explanation. Even the string of coincidences that had happened to her in the past few weeks *seemed* to be more than mere chance. It was uncanny how, when she thought about it, everything fell so neatly into place . . .

"Help! . . . Mommy! . . ."

She couldn't forget the desperately repeated message she had received in her dream about the Ouija board, and that she had heard so loudly she was convinced it was not just in her head, but audible, in the "sitting room" at Claire DeBlaise's, and that both she and Eldon Cody had heard—without *any* doubt—on the tape recorder.

She couldn't forget that someone—she had no doubt, now, that it had been Graydon—had dug up the corpse of her Uncle Jonathan—*a suicide*—and cut off his hand for use as a Hand of Glory. Frank had told her about the other incident at Caroline's grave. Had that been when Graydon had contacted Caroline's spirit and discovered the significance of "Button"?

"I'm scared," Elizabeth said, her voice no more than a trembling whisper. "*Really* scared!" She looked pleadingly at Graydon's back, wanting desperately for him to turn around and say something comforting to her, something reassuring. But Graydon didn't move; he stood there as motionless and as silent as a statue. For a panicked instant, Elizabeth thought he had died on his feet; she couldn't detect even the faintest motion of his breathing.

Her first impulse was to get up and leave. Get the Christ out of this madman's office! Leave him standing there by the window, thinking and believing whatever lunatic ideas he wanted to believe, and not let him bring her spiraling down into total insanity with false promises and vain, impossible hopes!

"I'm really scared," she repeated, "because I don't . . . I don't want to believe even for a minute that you honestly can do what you say you can."

She jumped, startled, when Graydon turned around very slowly and regarded her with a long, steady stare. Framed against the declining day outside the window, his face was an indistinct blur. She could see only his eyes, which seemed to glow with a light of their own.

"But you *must* believe," he said passionately. His voice resonated deeply, sounding like a distant explosion.

"But . . . why?" Elizabeth pleaded. "Why should I put *any* hope in what you say? It's just not . . . not possible!"

Graydon chuckled ominously. Elizabeth couldn't detect the slightest trace of humor in his laughter.

"I'd say, quite simply, don't knock it until you try it."

A flash of anger rose up inside Elizabeth, and she wondered if he had been stringing her along all this time for some therapeutic reason. Could that be all it was? Some incredibly crazy test of how suggestible she was?

"You sound pretty glib about it all," she said, not quite daring to voice her opinion that he might be leading her on.

Graydon suddenly pointed angrily at her, jabbing his finger like a saber in her direction. "You told me you *believed* what you heard on that tape! That the voice was your daughter's!"

"I—I'm not so sure, now," Elizabeth said, completely flustered. "I mean, the more I think about it, the more I start to doubt everything that's happened."

"You said you clearly heard a voice and that, as best as you could tell, it was the voice of your daughter."

Elizabeth shrugged. "Don't you think maybe I heard what I *wanted* to hear?"

Graydon shook his head as though thoroughly disgusted with her. "You sought out this man Eldon Cody. No one made you go see him. And you were the one who went with your aunt to see this— this charlatan spiritualist, Claire DeBlaise! It seems to me you wouldn't need much more convincing that such things are possible!"

Elizabeth slumped back on the couch, feeling completely powerless. Graydon's anger at her seemed genuine, not some kind of teasing, testing ploy. Beneath her terrifying confusion, somewhere deep within her mind, an alarm sounded. It had to do with something he had said—something that didn't seem quite right.

"So," he said emphatically, "if you want to see it, if you want *proof*—come with me. Tonight! Come to your daughter's grave and you can see for yourself what I can do!"

Elizabeth's throat made a soft gagging sound as she shook her head from side to side. "No, I—I wish I *could* believe you," she whispered. "I really do."

She stiffened suddenly when it finally came to her . . .

I never told him I went with Junia to see Claire! How does he know about that?

Chills raced up her back. All along, she had assumed Frank had followed her out there that night. Was it possible that it had been Graydon?

"So come with me . . . tonight," Graydon repeated. He moved swiftly over to her and knelt down in front of her. His hands came up and lightly but firmly grasped her shoulders. He started to pull her forward, close to him. Numb with terror, Elizabeth looked steadily into the swelling pools of his dark eyes. She could feel a power there that drew her in as inexorably as the surge of the ocean outside his office windows.

"Tonight," he whispered, rising to bring his mouth close to her ear.

His breath was warm on her skin. Against her will, a heated flush of passion swept through Elizabeth's body as Graydon brought his face closer to hers. Strong waves of desire melted her last shreds of physical and mental resistance. He shifted forward, bringing his body up close to hers as his arms moved slowly to embrace her. His arms were surprisingly strong as he held her tightly, crushing her in a powerful embrace. Her nostrils filled with his musky aroma.

"Tonight," he repeated softly. His lips brushed against the side of her face, fanning a hot line of breath along the edge of her jaw, then lower, to her outstretched neck. A tingle of fear raced up her spine when she imagined his face shifting, transforming into the salivating jaws of a hungry wolf. She tensed, waiting to feel the swift sting of his needle-sharp teeth as they sank into the flesh of her neck. Her vision got hazy and, looking down, she expected to see him grinning up at her, his mouth streaked with her flooding lifeblood.

No! . . . No, don't do this! a voice whispered in her mind. *This isn't right! Don't let him manipulate you!*

She couldn't deny the dizzying flush of emotion she felt as he held her tightly and kissed her lightly on the lips. She expected him to crush her to him, his hands rubbing violently over her as he tried to undress her. But that didn't happen. Breaking off the kiss, Graydon pulled away from her and stared at her unblinkingly. His voice was low and commanding when he whispered, again, *"Tonight!"*

But as Elizabeth gazed back at him, unable to turn away or resist, in her fevered imagination she heard him say something else . . .

"Button . . . First her . . . and now you!"

SEVENTEEN
Waiting for Midnight

1.

"Frank Melrose called this afternoon," Rebecca said as Elizabeth burst into the kitchen, interrupting her mother and father at their supper. "He said it wasn't important; but if you ask me, he sounded kinda worked up."

Elizabeth nodded stiffly as she closed the door, but she didn't move; she just stood there, not even able to decide whether she should sit down and have something to eat or go straight upstairs to her room. Even now, more than an hour after leaving Graydon's office, she felt threatened . . . unclean from his touch. A numbing, cold swept through her body.

She felt dirty, and couldn't stop wondering which had been smeared most by his touch—her body or her soul? All she knew right now was that she wanted—she *needed*—a long, hot shower.

As painful as it was, she knew Graydon was taking advantage of her; he was *using* her, like a toy, for his own, selfish purposes. She wanted to think that *if* he had tried to go any further, she would have stopped him . . . at least used having her period as an excuse not to have sex with him; but she had felt so helpless, so much under his control, as if she had no will of her own.

But I do, dammit! she thought angrily. *I'll show him how strong I am!*

That's all he's wanted all along, she told herself. He's a control freak who has to be in command. He's strongest when he's in a setting where he holds the reins, like his office. How many other patients—clients—does he use like this?

Elizabeth was nauseated by the vivid mental image of being a puppet for Graydon. With nightmare clarity, she imagined him reaching his hand up inside her head and, like a puppet master, making her do and say what he wanted her to do and say. He was using the abilities he had to manipulate his clients into doing what he wanted—especially into screwing him. That was what he'd wanted all along. The *last* thing she should do is go through with anything else Graydon wanted—especially this insane, impossible plan he had for tonight!

"I—umm, I don't feel like talking to Frank," she said, not daring to look directly at her parents for fear they would see everything reflected in her face. Her voice was trembling. "I just don't want to deal with him. If he calls again tonight, tell him I'm not home." She felt so drained, so used up, she was surprised she hadn't collapsed already; but she still stood there by the doorway, unable to take another step for fear of crumpling into a heap on the floor.

"Well, I suppose if it's that all-fire important, he'll get back to you," her mother said, turning back to her meal. "If you didn't eat while you were out, help yourself. Everything's still warm." She waved her hand at the array of food on the table. On the serving platter there was a nice chunk of broiled steak, and beside that a dish of peas, a bowl of mashed potatoes, and a bowl full of salad.

"No. I—I'm not hungry," Elizabeth said. The sight of the cooked meat made her stomach churn. A sickening, sour taste flooded her mouth. All she could think was . . .

He did it to me! Just like in my nightmare, that son of a bitch! He's nothing more than a wolf, waiting to rip me open!

If Graydon had tried to press on with his advances—if that's what they were—would having her period have stopped him? . . . Or would it have spurred on his passion?

And what did he mean by whispering "*Tonight*?" That they would do the necessary ceremony? Would she see and talk with Caroline tonight? . . . Or, now that she was under his control, would he have his way—completely—with her . . . tonight, in the cemetery?

With a massive effort of will, Elizabeth started across the kitchen to the doorway into the hall. The stairway upstairs looked like it was a hundred miles away. She was vaguely surprised that neither her mother nor her father commented on the unsteadiness of her walk. She felt as though she was lurching like a drunkard.

"I'm going to take a quick shower," she said with effort, "and then I think—I think I'll turn in early tonight. I'm beat."

Her mother raised her eyebrows in silent concern. All Elizabeth could think was, *Does she have any idea? All along, has she been talking to Junia, and does she know all about what I've been doing?*

She felt a slight measure of relief when she had left her mother's questioning gaze and her father's taciturn silence behind in the kitchen and started up the stairs. She was so weak-kneed she had to hang onto the handrail to keep from collapsing. The lie that she was going to go to bed after her shower tasted like thick phlegm in the back of her throat. Even though she knew it was well past the boundaries of sanity, she knew what she would do later . . . *tonight* . . .

No matter if it was against her will or not, she fully intended to meet Graydon at Caroline's grave in Oak Grove Cemetery just before midnight—just to see if he could *really* do what he said he could!

2.

The phone rang just as Elizabeth was stepping out of the shower. She quickly wrapped a towel around her head and put on her bathrobe as she dashed over to the nightstand beside her bed and picked up the phone. Covering the mouthpiece with one wet hand, she held the receiver tightly against her ear and listened.

"Hello," she heard her mother say on the downstairs phone.

"I'm sorry to bother you again, Mrs. Payne, but I was wondering if Elizabeth's home yet."

Elizabeth recognized Frank's voice and held her breath, waiting for what seemed like five minutes before her mother replied.

"I'm sorry, Frank," she said at last. "She still hasn't shown up."

Frank's exasperated sigh came over the line as clearly as though he were beside Elizabeth in her bedroom. Standing weak-kneed beside her bed, the gentle tug of blood flowing deep in her belly, Elizabeth felt vulnerable; she wondered if she was more threatened by Frank or by Graydon. A spark flickered in her mind, and thinking she might truly be able to trust him, she had a sudden urge to let Frank know she was listening on the line.

What she should do right now, she told herself, is ask her mother to hang up so she could talk to Frank—or better yet, ask Frank to come over to the house so she could talk to him face to face. Maybe that would help convince her that she wasn't losing her mind. She should be able to trust Frank with everything she had figured out about Graydon's involvement with what had been happening around town—the digging up of her uncle's grave, the ceremony done over Caroline's grave, and—possibly—the murders of Barney Fraser and Henry Bishop.

"Ohh, that's too bad," Frank said. "I really need to talk to her."

"Is there—do you want to leave her a message? I can tell her when she gets home," Elizabeth heard her mother say. The halting way she spoke seemed, at least to Elizabeth, to reveal the truth in spite of her words.

"No—I just wanted to talk to her," Frank replied.

There was most definitely an urgency in his tone of voice. After Graydon had taken advantage of her weakness this afternoon at his office, all Elizabeth could think was that it was Frank's need for sex. He—like Graydon—was nothing more than a hungry wolf, wanting to feast on her, to suck the lifeblood from her!

"I'll be sure to tell her you called, though," her mother said. "I—uh, expect she'll be home any minute now."

"She can reach me at the station," Frank said. "I should be here—oh, another hour, at least."

"Fine, then," her mother said. "Thanks for calling."

"Thank you," Frank said and then hung up. Elizabeth waited to hear the second click of her mother hanging up before she gently cradled the phone. Letting a deep sigh escape her, she sat down on the edge of her bed and started to towel-dry her hair. In spite of her cozy bathrobe, gooseflesh rippled over her arms and legs.

She tensed, waiting, and then, as expected, heard the tread of her mother's feet on the stairs. Then came a quick rapping on her door.

"Yeah?" she said shakily, dropping the towel into her lap. A cold band seemed to tighten over the ridge above her eyebrows, and blinding pressure built up behind her eyes. The goose bumps spread up over her shoulders, and her teeth chattered.

"That was Frank on the phone," her mother said through the closed door.

As if you didn't already know, Elizabeth thought, suspecting that her mother knew she had been listening on the extension.

"Yeah . . . ?" She said. The tension in her head increased along with a steady, pulsing beat in her temples.

"He sounded like he really wanted to talk to you."

You could have told him you were there, Elizabeth added for her.

"So?"

"So—I think it wouldn't hurt you to give him a call."

And you know damned well I heard him say he's down at the police station.

"I *really* don't want to talk . . . to him or anybody else right now," Elizabeth said. A headache was unfolding behind her eyebrows, mushrooming like a heavy, fast-moving storm cloud. She clenched her jaw to stop her teeth from chattering as the chills racing through her body intensified.

"Suit yourself," her mother said through the closed door. "But I'll tell you one thing . . ."

"What's that?" Elizabeth asked, feeling a wave of desperate exasperation. She was suddenly fearful that if she spoke or heard too many more words, her head would explode.

"I think that if the two of you are . . . are seeing each other, if you know what I mean, both you and he are fools. I'm not saying I don't like Frank, but until you straighten out a few . . . other things in your life, I think you're both jumping the gun."

"Don't worry," Elizabeth snapped. "Frank Melrose and I are not *seeing* each other. If he . . . if he—" For a moment, that was all she could say as her anger at Frank suddenly exploded like fireworks in her mind. "If he *ever* calls again, tell him to leave me alone! Do you understand?"

"If you have any message for him," her mother replied, "then I expect you'd better deliver it yourself. I'm not about to become your messenger girl."

There was a slight pause, and Elizabeth could imagine her mother leaning close to the closed bedroom door.

"Good night, Elizabeth."

"G'night," Elizabeth said, letting her body unwind as she listened to her mother's footsteps going back downstairs. They were barely audible above the steady pounding inside her head. As wave after wave of confused, black, and tangled emotions swept through her, she collapsed back onto her bed and closed her eyes so tightly they began to hurt. When she chanced to open them, the light in her bedroom was shattered into a dazzling display of yellow spikes and swirling patterns. From the corner of her eye, she caught a glimpse of her alarm clock and just barely made out the time.

"Six-thirty . . ." she whispered, with a voice as dry as sand. Five and a half hours to wait . . . five and a half hours that she *knew* would seem like forever!

She wished that she could slip into a nightie, climb in under her covers, fall asleep, and forget . . . forget *everything*! Let Graydon go out to the cemetery and wait long enough to realize she wasn't coming. Let him wait until dawn! Let him go straight to hell, for all she cared, and let him take his manipulative, scheming, bullshit male ego with him!

"I'm going crazy!" she rasped aloud as she thrashed about on the bed, pressing her fists against her throbbing head. "I'm going absolutely, stark raving out of my mind!"

Whimpering softly, she covered her face with her hands and, closing her eyes again, pressed as hard as she could against her forehead. That still didn't stop the heavy-fisted hammering in her skull. She hated what she knew, but just as surely as Caroline was dead, she was positive she would *never* get a wink of sleep . . . not now—not tonight—not *ever* unless she went out to Caroline's grave with Graydon.

And she knew, even if it meant her own death, she would do exactly what Graydon told her to do if only she could talk to Caroline one last time. Only then—maybe—would she find some peace and calm inside herself.

3.

"You're obsessed," Norton said, glancing over at his partner as he took the turn onto Brook Road. Even before the wrought-iron cemetery gate came into view, Frank slowed the car to less than ten miles per hour.

Leaning over the steering wheel, Frank scanned both sides of the road. It was well past nine o'clock. The bone white full moon rode high in the sky, casting a silvery light over the woods and fields. As they approached the cemetery, its moonlit tombstones spread over the hazy gray hillside looked like a distant city. The trees behind the cemetery were hard-edged black lace against the dusty night sky.

"I'm not obsessed," Frank said softly. "I'm just checking things out, like we've been told to."

Norton snorted with suppressed laughter. "Yeah—right. As if anything else is gonna happen out here." He, too, glanced over toward the cemetery but then looked quickly back at his partner.

"This makes—what? Four times you've been by here tonight. What the fuck do you think you're gonna see, anyway?"

Frank eased the patrol car to a stop in front of the closed cemetery gate. He snapped the switch on his side-mounted spotlight and swung it in a wide arc across the graveyard. Thick shadows weaved dizzyingly as the light swept back and forth. The names on a few of the closest tombstones jumped out in high relief, but everything else about the place looked peaceful and quiet.

"Come on, man," Norton said. "Kill the light! You're gonna wake up the neighbors." He laughed aloud at his own joke, then fell silent when he noticed that Frank wasn't sharing his humor.

"Too many things have happened around here for my own comfort," Frank said, still keeping his voice low as he squinted, following the trailing beam of the spotlight.

"Yeah, well, nothing else is gonna happen. D'you think anyone'd be stupid enough to come out here, just knowing how you're hovering around the place. Christ!" He sniffed with laughter again. "If anyone sees us out here, they'll probably call the cops on us!"

"I'm just doing my job, if that's all right with you," Frank said, snapping off the spotlight and shifting the cruiser into gear.

"Let's go find ourselves some real action," Norton said. "Like maybe we can catch a speeder out on Old County Road. It's probably too late to catch ourselves any dope pushers hanging around the schoolyard, wouldn't you say?''

As he eased the cruiser back onto the road, Frank glanced over at his partner and frowned. "Cut the shit, all right?" he said. "I'm just keeping an eye on things in case something happens."

"Nothing's gonna happen out here," Norton said. He twisted around and looked back at the cemetery fence as it receded into the darkness. "Not tonight, anyway."

4.

The hours plodded by slowly as Elizabeth lay on her bed, her mind a tumbling cascade of fear. Several times she had the unnerving sensation that someone was in the dark room with her. Every time she closed her eyes and tried to will herself to sleep, she would feel—literally *feel*—cold, eerily glowing eyes glaring at her from the inky shadows in the corners of her room. Someone . . .

Who? The old crone . . . or someone else?

. . . was staring at her with—what? Malevolent hatred . . . or something else?

She couldn't shake the feeling that someone was nearby, trying to contact her, wanting—but unable—to get through to her. She wasn't sure how she knew or sensed this, because, whenever she opened her eyes and looked around, she never caught even a fleeting glimpse of anything unusual.

Remembering the dreams she had had over the past few weeks only made things worse, and several times she bolted upright in her bed, convinced that she had been—or still was—dreaming. Fear choked her, and she expected to look down and see the Ouija board on her lap. She would watch helplessly as her hands—or skeletal hands blending out of the darkness—moved the pointer and spelled out a message.

And what would the message say? she wondered, fearing to the core of her soul that she would see the words spelled out, blazing in slashes of raging fire.

Help! . . . Mommy!

. . . Or she would look up and see the old crone, standing there in the dark room, holding out to her the well-worn shopping bag, asking her—begging her—to look inside where she would see . . . perhaps Caroline's face, perhaps her own, surrounded by spiked tongues of flame. The blast furnace intensity would peel the flesh from her face, sear her to the bone, and then dissolve even her bones to nothing but glowing red coals and gray ash.

. . . Or maybe she would see her husband standing beside her bed. What if all along Doug had been doing this to her? What if, by planting seeds of fear and doubt deep in her mind, he was driving her slowly crazy? Could he be working directly with Graydon? Could the two of them be controlling her, forcing her closer and closer to the brink of madness out of revenge, simply because she had stopped Doug from trying to save Caroline that night?

Sometime around ten o'clock, her parents came upstairs to bed. She heard her father's shoes scuff down the hallway past her door without a pause. She heard her mother pass by, too, but she hesitated at the door, obviously considering whether or not she should check in on her daughter. Then she, too, went to her own bedroom. Lying on her bed, her body rigid with tension, Elizabeth realized she had been holding her breath and let it out in a long, whooshing sigh.

She glanced at the clock beside her bed and saw that it was only ten-thirty, still too early to leave. No longer able to lie there on her bed, she swung her feet to the floor and stood up. From the bathroom down the hallway, she heard the sound of water running and the toilet flushing as her parents got ready for bed. She didn't want to chance turning on her light just yet, in case her mother walked by her room again and saw the light under the door. In darkness, she started pacing back and forth across her bedroom floor, still feeling as though every time her back was turned, glowing eyes materialized out of the pressing darkness and watched her.

She knew exactly how long she paced back and forth because she stared at the illuminated face of the clock every time she walked past the bed. At eleven fifteen, long after she had stopped hearing her parents moving around in their bedroom, she pulled on her socks and sneakers. Quietly approaching her bedroom door, she held her breath as she eased open the door and peeked out into the hallway.

Her parents bedroom door was closed tightly, and the house was deathly quiet. Only the low-wattage bulb at the foot of the stairs was on, casting a sickly yellow glow into the hallway. Elizabeth stepped out into the hallway, and eased her bedroom door shut, praying the old hinges wouldn't squeak, then tiptoed down the hallway, moving quickly down the stairs. She froze every time one of the steps creaked under her weight, but after listening tensely for any sounds from her parents' room, she continued down into the entryway. After grabbing her jacket from the front hallway coatrack, she patted her jeans pocket, making sure she had the house keys, then opened the back door and slipped out into the cool, moist night.

The full moon was high in the sky, casting thick, swirling shadows under the trees lining the driveway. A gentle breeze hissed in the leaves overhead, making the moonlight flicker. Elizabeth started down the driveway to the road, grateful—at least—that she no longer felt the presence of unseen eyes watching her. With barely a glance to the left or right, she walked briskly to the road and headed toward Oak Grove Cemetery.

As she walked along the road's edge, beneath the streetlights, Elizabeth watched her shadow swing around under her feet and then stretch out in front of her. It eased the burden on her mind to remember the dozens, probably hundreds of times she had watched her shadow move like this on those nights she had snuck out of the house at night when she was younger, either to meet her friends or one of her boyfriends—usually Frank.

As soon as she thought of Frank, she cringed, unable to stop from wondering what could possibly have been so urgent for him to keep calling the house as he had. There was no denying the urgency in his voice. She tried to force this, along with any other thoughts about Frank, out of her mind. Just then, she saw headlights come around the bend in the road, aiming straight at her.

"Oh, shit," she muttered, crouching for a moment on the roadside and wondering what to do. She was between streetlights, and the car was far enough away so that she knew she hadn't been seen yet, but she had to act fast.

Her first thought was to say to hell with it—it didn't matter *who* saw her walking down the road, even at this time of night. She had every right in the world to be out taking a walk. But even stronger was the impulse to duck off and hide in the woods before the headlights reached her and the driver—whoever it was—discovered her. It was more than a flashback to the caution she had used when she was a kid and had snuck out late at night. Considering the strange things that had been happening around town—especially in light of what she intended to do tonight with Graydon—it would be best if no one saw her out tonight. Some neighbors might consider even a late-night walk suspicious.

Turning quickly, Elizabeth scampered down the road embankment and into the brush. Unseen branches swished at her, snapping at her face and hands as she ran deep into the woods and then, turning, crouched low to the ground, held her breath, and waited. She heard the throaty rumble of the car's engine, but it seemed to take forever for the car to come down the road.

A strangled little cry escaped her when the car was about fifty feet away from where she was hiding. A brilliant light suddenly blasted from the passenger's window. At first, Elizabeth didn't know what it was, but then she realized it was a spotlight. The car crept slowly closer, the cone of light lancing out into the darkness and weaving back and forth as it skimmed through the roadside brush.

Elizabeth wanted to drop down and hug the ground, but she feared that any motion now would give her away. The light swung closer, pushing like a laser through the underbrush. A cold sheen of sweat broke out over her forehead as it weaved ever closer to where she hid.

Elizabeth could see that the car was a police cruiser. The siren and lights on the car roof looked like dark bull's horns. The car windows were open, and although she could hear the policemen talking, she couldn't quite make out what they were saying. The beam of the spotlight grew more intense, and Elizabeth fully expected to see the brush spontaneously burst into flames as it swung back and forth. Closer and closer it came, sweeping in a silent ripple through the trees, casting long shadows that weaved sickeningly. Elizabeth had to bite down on the tip of her tongue to keep from crying out.

"You realize this is fuckin' ridiculous, don't you?" the cop by the passenger's window said.

The policeman driving—it *has* to be Frank, Elizabeth thought—said something just barely audible over the muffling rumble of the car's engine; it sounded like: "I thought I saw someone walking alongside the road."

"Just your imagination, ole buddy," the policeman holding the spotlight said.

Finally, the cone of light swept over Elizabeth, blinding her for an instant. In her fear-induced state, she imagined it lingered on her for several seconds before moving on, tracing its way through the woods to her right. She was astounded when the light continued to sweep past her, plunging the surrounding woods into inky darkness.

As the cruiser moved slowly away from her, she heard the policeman by the open window say something else, but it was lost in the distance. With a slow, shuddering gasp, Elizabeth let out the breath she had been holding.

Are they looking for me? she wondered, watching fearfully as the taillights disappeared around the bend in the road. She couldn't help but wonder if Frank's wanting so desperately to talk with her had anything to do with him and his partner carefully searching the side of the road. Had they been alerted, somehow, about what she and Graydon planned to do? Had her mother come down to her bedroom to talk and, discovering her missing, notified the police? Maybe the best thing to do, the safest thing, was to go home and forget all about this foolhardy episode.

But as silence and darkness dropped back down over her, Elizabeth became only more firmly resolved to go through with this midnight meeting with Graydon. She knew now, though, that she would have to be careful and keep an eye out for the police.

Deciding it would be safer to stay in the woods than to walk boldly down the street, Elizabeth made her best guess at direction and, trusting in the brightness of the full moon to light her way, struck out through the woods toward the cemetery.

As she thrashed through the thick undergrowth, she couldn't stop the flood of scary thoughts and images that filled her mind. Not too far from here was where Henry Bishop's dog had uncovered the body of Barney Fraser. She knew she was letting her imagination run away with her, but several times she stopped in her tracks and looked around, convinced she had heard a low, hollow moaning beneath the gentle sigh of the wind. And what did she think she'd see—a gauzy white fluttering thing that could be just a beam of moonlight falling onto a tree trunk . . . or something else? Even in the warmth of her jacket, she felt goose bumps rise up on her arms.

Elizabeth plunged deeper into the woods, figuring she had to be nearing the cemetery. The sound of frogs in the lowland swamp grew steadily louder until they masked even the crunching sounds her sneakers made trampling the leaves on the forest floor. It seemed to be taking longer than it should have to get to the cemetery, but rather than assume she had missed her goal and was wandering far off the mark, she told herself it made sense that it would take longer to forge her way through the dark woods than it would to go along the road.

A tightness built in her chest when, after what seemed like more than half an hour, she still hadn't broken through to the clearing of the cemetery. She couldn't see the slightest break in the trees up ahead, and now she began to worry that she indeed might have wandered off course. She had no idea where the road was, whether it was beside or behind her, and before long she had to admit that she had gotten herself lost. Even telling herself that, no matter what, if she kept the full moon on her left, she would eventually have to hit on Old County Road, didn't make her feel any better. It was embarrassing and slightly scary to think that she could get herself so confused so easily.

"Oh, great . . . just great," she muttered as she beat her way angrily through the dense brush. The sound of the frogs was even louder as she approached the lowland—so loud, in fact, that she shivered with fear as she wondered what other sounds the frogs might be masking. Waves of steadily rising panic made her ribs ache and her eyes sting. She started swatting at the branches that blocked her path. Her soft, muttered curses filled the closing darkness, but once she realized how heavily she was panting, she stopped to rest, leaning back against a tree and forcing herself to take deep, even breaths.

It was ridiculous for her to be lost like this! She had played in these woods all her life. Why was she even out here in the first place? Was it simply because she wanted to avoid Frank or anyone else who might see her out walking at night? Why was she being so damned furtive? Was she embarrassed that she even entertained the notion that Graydon could—somehow, magically—let her communicate with Caroline?

The whole damned thing was absurd!

Any rational person knew that it was patently impossible to see or talk to the dead. Dead was dead, and that was the end of it! No matter what Graydon did tonight, just like the things Claire DeBlaise and Eldon Cody had done, there had to be some trickery involved or else some rational explanation. She was a damned fool for even starting out on something like this, much less for getting herself lost in the bargain!

As Elizabeth looked around at the moonlit woods, the gray, glowing tree trunks, the sprays of glittering leaves, and the hard, black shadows they cast, it was easy to convince herself that she had been lost for hours. She should at least have been able to hear the sounds of passing cars out on Old County Road—if indeed she was heading in the right direction—but the night song of the frogs still filled the woods. Anyway, at this hour, there probably weren't all that many cars going by . . . unless it was the police cruiser, looking for her.

Allowing for the movement of the moon as it reached its peak and began its westward decline, she figured she was still pretty much on track. Before long, with a rush of relief, she saw a clearing up ahead in the woods. She moved toward it, slashing with her arms through the undergrowth, and saw to her immense relief the southern edge of Oak Grove Cemetery.

The fence on this side of the cemetery rose high, towering in straight black lines against the glowing night sky. Elizabeth didn't even consider scaling the fence to get inside . . . not unless she found the front gates were locked. After everything that had happened out here, she wouldn't be surprised to see a police cruiser parked right out front. Crouching low and keeping to the shadows of the trees, she walked down to the road.

Just as she reached the corner of the cemetery fence, Elizabeth saw something and immediately dropped low to the ground. A car's headlights glowed far down the road, heading toward her. It might be Graydon, arriving for their meeting, she thought, but she knew it would be foolish of him to make so obvious an approach. She lay flat in the grass, watching. Her breath caught in her throat when the harsh beam of the spotlight shot out from the car. It was the police again—Frank and his partner—coming back up the road, obviously still interested in checking out the cemetery.

The fresh aroma of damp soil filled Elizabeth's nostrils as she hugged the ground while the yellow beam of light swept over and past her. She watched it ripple along the iron fence, pausing for only an instant at each gate before moving on. Elizabeth could see that both gates were closed. As soon as the police car disappeared down the road, she got up and walked as boldly as she dared to the front gate.

She pushed the iron gate open and cautiously entered the cemetery. As she eased the gate shut behind her, she toyed with the scary thought that, now that she was inside, the gate would slam shut and lock with a deafening clang!

The location of Caroline's grave was vividly etched into Elizabeth's memory. If she had felt fear while lost in the woods, it was nothing compared to the dizzying wave of panic that swept through her now as she turned slowly and looked up the gently sloping hill.

"Oh, Jesus," she whispered, shivering wildly as she took no more than three small steps up the road. She glanced up at the silent globe of the moon, now starting its decline in the sky. The reverse side of the letters spelling OAK GROVE CEMETERY stood out like spidery scars against the night sky.

Terror like hard, black ice filled her mind when she considered that just up there, over that moon-soaked ridge, was Caroline. Not her grave; not her tombstone; not her memory—*her!* Dressed in her beautiful white dress, her hands clasped over her cold, motionless chest, she was lying six feet below the sod, shut forever in impenetrable darkness beneath the polished pink marble marker.

I can't go through with this! she told herself as she stared above the silent rows of tombstones. *I just can't!*

Her eyes were stinging, and for a moment, she forgot all about Graydon, the police cruising by the cemetery, and everything and everyone else in the world. *Her* world, her entire reason for living was up at the top of that hill, as cold and as lifeless as the heavy earth that covered her.

A flicker of motion off to her left caught her attention. Elizabeth let out a shrill scream when she turned and saw a hazy gray figure materialize from behind one of the tombstones. Horrified, she watched, unable to move as the shape silently coalesced and, raising one arm into the air, started toward her.

Elizabeth backpedaled frantically until the iron fence halted her. She wanted to cry out, but after her first surprised screech, her throat had closed off and wouldn't make any further sound.

"Elizabeth," a deep voice said. In her overactive imagination, it sounded like a low, animal growl.

Speechless, Elizabeth didn't dare take her eyes away from the shape as it came slowly toward her.

"I was afraid you had changed your mind," the voice said. Now—for the first time—she recognized Graydon's voice.

"No—I, uh, I was delayed," she managed to say. To her fear-heightened senses, even her own voice sounded thick with resonance. The moon was behind Graydon, but she was finally able to discern the moon-shadowed outline of his face. She heaved a deep sigh of relief, but the coiling tension in her gut was only minimally lessened.

"I had to park out on Route 22," Graydon said, once he was beside her. "There's a place just off the road where I hid my car so . . . well, so no one would find it right off, anyway."

"I saw a police car go by twice while I was on my way out here," Elizabeth said. "It looked to me as though they were patrolling the cemetery here—" She cut herself off and cringed when, from off in the distance, she heard the whoosh of tires on the road.

Graydon heard and noted the sound of the passing car as well, but he dismissed it with a wave of his hand. "That's out on 22," he said. "As for the police . . ." He snickered with laughter. "Well, I don't think we have to worry about them tonight."

"We're not going to do . . . anything illegal, are we?" Elizabeth said. "I mean—I don't think I could take it if we have to . . . if I—" She cut herself off, unable to finish voicing her fear that Graydon and she were here to exhume her daughter. It was unnerving, with the full moon behind him, not to be able to see his face directly. Was this another one of his control tactics? she wondered. He could see her face in the moonlight, but she couldn't see his.

"No, no," he said, although she found little reassurance in his voice. "What we'll be doing has nothing to do with grave robbing or anything of the sort. Even if the police *did* arrive and find us up here, we wouldn't be doing anything illegal. The teenagers who come out here to drink and get high break more laws than we will tonight."

"I don't know," Elizabeth said, still struggling with a bad case of second thoughts. "I mean, this whole thing is . . . is—"

"A miracle," Graydon finished for her. "What you're about to see is the absolute apex of necromantic art." He waved his hands wildly over his head, his hooked fingers clawing upward as though summoning demons from the deep. "And I have complete and total faith in you, Elizabeth, that you'll be strong enough and brave enough to face what has to be done." Clenching his fists, he shook them at the sky.

"I—I'm not sure," Elizabeth stammered, completely taken aback by the near-maniacal intensity with which he was speaking. It was so obvious that this man was out of his mind and possibly dangerous; she was a total fool for believing *anything* he said.

"Oh, but I know you *are* sure," Graydon went on. "Because the rewards for you—and me—will be absolutely . . . incredible." He lowered his hands and, gazing up at the moon, its silver light lining his profile and making his eyes glimmer brightly, took a deep breath. "The hour draws near," he said, more softly. "I have all the materials we'll need over here." He turned and walked back to where he had first materialized, fully expecting Elizabeth to follow along.

The part of her brain telling her to get the hell out of here was getting louder, more insistent. She hesitated at the cemetery fence, still unsure if she even *could* walk any further into the cemetery. The thought that the chain would magically rise and wind itself through the bars of the gate, trapping her inside with this madman, still terrified her.

"Aren't you coming?" Graydon asked, turning to look back once he realized she wasn't behind him.

"I—" But that was all she managed to say as she looked down at her feet and saw them begin to shift forward across the moonlit grass. Her feet looked distant, foreign to her, and she couldn't ignore the overpowering sensation that someone else was controlling them, moving them for her.

"If we don't hurry, we'll miss the most opportune time," Graydon said. He picked up a rather large bundle from behind one of the gravestones and walked over to the grass strip in the center of the dirt road.

Wave after wave of chills darted like icy spears through Elizabeth's body as she shuffled forward into the cemetery. Her shoulders were hunched, and she tensed, waiting to hear the heavy *clang* as the gate locked itself behind her. When it didn't come, she felt a measure of relief, but that was quickly shattered when she heard Graydon's next words.

"Come on, Elizabeth," he said, sounding impatient and anxious. "We've got to begin soon. Your daughter is waiting to talk to you."

EIGHTEEN
The Summoning

1.

As much as she wanted to deny it, Elizabeth couldn't ignore the cold squeezing that constricted her chest as she walked beside Graydon up the hill toward Caroline's grave. In spite of her earlier attempts, this was the first time she had actually come up here since returning home; and even now, she couldn't believe she was doing it . . . especially under such bizarre circumstances.

"How—uh, what exactly are you going to do?" she asked Graydon, once they reached the crest. She didn't look at him; her eyes were fixed on the gravestone, illuminated by the blue wash of moonlight. The name and dates chiseled into the polished marble surface were etched in inky blackness.

CAROLINE JUNIA MYERS
OCT. 27, 1981–FEB. 15, 1988

The cold glint of moonlight reflecting off the polished stone sent a wracking shiver through her body.

"It's not what *I* intend to do that's important," Graydon said, as he placed the bag he was carrying onto the ground and stood back, thoughtfully regarding Caroline's grave. "It's what *you* do that'll be important."

"You'll have to—" Elizabeth's voice choked off as tears filled her eyes and her vision blurred. "You'll have to tell me what to do," she finally said.

"Oh, don't you worry about a thing," Graydon said. He looked at her, his thin smile widening. "You'll know *exactly* what to do when the time comes." He rubbed his hands together eagerly and then knelt down and opened the bag, which made a rustling sound like a crackling fire, which reminded Elizabeth of her nightmare as the old woman opened her shopping bag to show her . . .

Caroline's head, surrounded by flames!

Graydon extracted several objects and placed them on the ground beside him.

Elizabeth shivered and hugged her arms close to herself as she watched him go silently about his preparations. In the moonlight, she couldn't distinguish most of the items Graydon had brought, but her heart skipped a beat when she saw moonlight reflecting off the edge of a long, sharp-looking knife blade.

"Wh-what's that for?" she asked.

Graydon chuckled softly and said, "All part of the ceremony . . . all part of the ceremony."

"I don't see why—" she started to say, but then she let her voice drop off and just stood silently and watched.

The night closed in around her, encasing her and Graydon in a tight, dark shell. Overhead, the spanning sweep of the Milky Way was diffused by the light of the moon to no more than a hazy blue glow. From the woods behind the cemetery, the distant call of a whippoorwill echoed mournfully, and from deep in the swamp came a loud chorus of frogs. Overhead, she heard the high roaring of the wind in the trees, but where she and Graydon stood, the air was curiously quiet. Everything around her seemed strangely transformed, distant. Elizabeth couldn't shake the feeling that the small patch of ground where they stood—including Caroline's grave—had somehow been magically removed from the real world.

Graydon finished emptying his bag and then, after sitting back on his heels for a moment, looked up at Elizabeth and cleared his throat.

"What I'm going to do with this"—getting to his feet, he held up something to show Elizabeth, but she couldn't make out what it

was—"is inscribe a pentagram, a five-pointed star, on the groun
over your daughter's coffin."

There was a crinkling of paper as he opened the smaller bag h
was holding and then, bending down, began tracing a pattern o
the ground. Elizabeth wondered how he could work with just th
glow of moonlight to illuminate what he was doing, but he seeme
to have no problem as he sifted a fine white powder that looked lik
chalk dust onto the ground.

"Once we begin," he said, his breath puffing from the effort o
bending over and working, "both you and I have to make sure w
don't step outside this design."

"Why's that?" Elizabeth asked tightly.

"Suffice it to say that, once we've started, do not step over th
lines," Graydon said. His tone of voice was harsh, almost angr
sounding. "Don't even touch them. Even the tiniest break in th
line could be disastrous."

Elizabeth nodded slowly, unable to look away as she watche
Graydon outline the large five-pointed star on the swell of groun
over Caroline's grave. The star-shape had a diameter of ten feet o
more. Although she could see Graydon's darkened silhouette as h
worked, the pentagram seemed to appear from nowhere, like a
illusion on the dark grass.

The powder absorbed the light of the moon and gave it back with
a faintly pulsating greenish glow, like the illuminated hands of a
alarm clock. The finished design looked upside-down to Elizabeth
One point, what she would have called the "top," was aimed dow
toward the foot of Caroline's grave. A point stretched out on eithe
side of the mounded grave, and the last two points angled in th
direction of Caroline's tombstone. The total effect made the desig
look like a representation of a goat's horns, and Elizabeth wondere
if that was Graydon's intention.

Elizabeth could keep herself slightly detached by watching Gray
don work on the design; but when she let the actuality of what the
were doing sink in—that no more than six feet below them Carolin
reposed in eternal, cold darkness—her legs went rubbery. Sh
locked her knees to keep from falling, and fervently prayed that sh
wouldn't faint, even as the soft whooshing of her pulse in her ear
sounded louder, like muffled drums.

Why am I even doing this? And why am I allowing him to do this? she wondered, as fear coalesced inside her.

"Just about got it, now," Graydon said, huffing from the effort as he sifted one last handful of white powder onto the pattern. He straightened up and brushed his hands on his pants legs. "There— that part's all set."

Elizabeth couldn't stop dwelling on the thought that she was so close to Caroline's lifeless body. So close . . . so close to her baby. To stop the rushes of fear, she tried to focus on the flood of questions that arose, but she couldn't stop thinking that both she and Graydon were crazy to be out here doing this. It was insane for him to believe he could actually summon up her daughter's spirit; and she was just as insane to think he could. All of this preparation was just some . . . lunatic show.

Dead is dead! she repeatedly told herself, *and I'm not going to start living a normal life until I fully accept that Caroline is gone . . . lost forever*!

But what if death *isn't* the end of it all? she wondered. What if we *do* continue to exist on some other plane of existence? And what if people like Graydon *do* have special knowledge and skills that allow them to contact the dead?

Having rolled the bag of white powder tightly shut, Graydon was just stooping to place it back into the larger bag when he glanced down the hill and saw a car's headlights swing up into the cemetery entrance.

"Get down! Quick!" he whispered harshly.

Without thinking, Elizabeth dropped to the ground and stared down the sloping hill. Her breath was a hard, hot lump in her chest as she watched the car pull to a stop and then just sit there in the cemetery entrance, its motor idling.

"It's the police!" she whispered, when she saw the outlines of the flashers and siren. She glanced fearfully over at Graydon, who was crouching behind Uncle Jonathan's tombstone.

"Don't worry," he snapped. "We'll be all right."

From the corner of her eye, Elizabeth saw the white-lined design on Caroline's grave. She flushed with panic, thinking that if the police came up here and found them doing what they were doing, she and—especially—Graydon would positively get connected to the other incidents that had happened out here. She glanced over her shoulder at the woods behind them and considered making dash for safety. Better to be lost in the woods all night than to b implicated in grave robbing, arson, and murder!

For long, dragging minutes, the car stayed right where it was No one got out. No beam of a spotlight swept over the cemetery Nothing. Just the idling car. Elizabeth's impulse to bolt and ru grew stronger. She almost screamed when she heard a soft *clic* behind her and, turning, saw the shadowed outline of a gun i Graydon's hand, resting on Jonathan's tombstóne.

"What the hell is that for?" she hissed.

Graydon was silent as he stared down the hill at the waiting car He seemed as solid, as immobile, as a funerary statue, but then h said softly, "Just a little extra insurance that we won't be disturbed."

Elizabeth opened her mouth and was about to ask him if Barne Fraser was dead because he had been a disturbance to Graydon ou here on another night, but she thought better of it.

The car's engine rumbled like the distant growl of a beast; the it suddenly revved up. Elizabeth tensed and glanced again at wha looked like the quickest path into the woods if she had to run. Sh sensed Graydon's nervousness, too, masked though it was, and tha only compounded her rising fear.

The car's engine whined loudly, and then, with the red glow o its taillights brightening the road behind it, the cruiser backed u and swung around onto Brook Road.

"Jesus Christ," Elizabeth muttered as she collapsed onto th ground, feeling completely wrung out.

"I don't think they'll be back for a while," Graydon said mildly He lowered the gun and, after clicking on the safety, put it bac into the bag. "Certainly, we'll have enough time to do what w came here to do."

Saying that, he dug around inside the bag for a second and the produced what in the darkness looked like five sticks of dynamite.

"Hold these," he said, handing them to Elizabeth, who realized by their waxy feel that they were candles. She held one up to th moonlight and inspected it, guessing it was either dark blue or black

Walking around the outside of the pentagram, Graydon hurriedly scooped out a small depression in the ground at one of the five points. He beckoned to Elizabeth, who came over and handed him a candle, which he stuck upright into the hole he had made and then patted excess soil around to support it in place. She followed him around the outside of the star and watched as he did the same to the other four candles. When he was done, he stood back and looked at her, smiling widely, his teeth flashing in the moonlight.

"We're just about ready, now," he said, unable to mask the excitement in his voice.

"I know this probably isn't the time to mention it," Elizabeth said, "but I was just—you know, wondering if there is any . . . *danger* doing this." She knew her question sounded dumb, and she fully expected Graydon to say something like, *Helluva time to ask.* She was surprised when he answered her mildly.

"What's about to happen is something not many people have ever experienced. And I won't lie to you, Elizabeth. There most definitely are certain risks. But you have to trust me on this." He reached out from the darkness, gripped both of her arms, and gave her a bracing shake. Moonlight glinted, cold and hard, in his eyes. "Once we start, if you stay inside the pentagram, you'll be completely . . . *safe.*" In the short pause before he said the word *safe*, Elizabeth had the impression he had been about to say *within my power.*

"Just remember—I'm the one in control here," Graydon continued, his voice lowering with intensity. "You have to do *everything* I tell you to do—without hesitation and without question. If you let your fear get in the way of what we're going to see and do, then—yes! I'd say you *definitely* would be in danger."

"Of . . . what?" Elizabeth asked through dry lips.

Graydon's grip on her arms tightened. When he shook her again, she felt as though it was not so much to buoy her up as it was to control her, to intimidate her. She tried to pull back out of his hold, but he kept her arms locked in his grip.

"You *will* do what I tell you to do. *When* I tell you! That way, everything will work out . . . just as I've planned it," Graydon said.

"Can I—ask you one more thing before we start?" Elizabeth said. Her voice trembled horribly, but she was surprised she didn't just start screaming from the winding anticipation. The wind whistled, high and shrill above them, and the night closed down on her like a black satin-lined coffin lid. In her imagination, she saw Graydon's eyes flash with the sparkling gleam of an animal's eyes. His coiled nerves were braced, waiting for his face to transform into wolf's just before he leaped and ripped out her throat.

"I suppose, before we begin the ceremony, I can allow one more question," Graydon said, sounding entirely condescending. He glanced down the hill toward the cemetery gate, as though expecting to see the police cruiser there again, before adding, "But we really *must* hurry."

Elizabeth cleared her throat and swallowed before she spoke. "I was just wondering—you know, about my uncle's hand that you—"

"Ahh, the Hand of Glory," Graydon said. There was a strong note of awe in his voice when he said the words.

"That's what you call it?" Elizabeth asked, feeling a racing chill. She recalled the discussion she had had with Frank about the same thing.

Graydon nodded. "Through the centuries, the Hand of Glory has been a very powerful magical talisman," he said. "Of course, back in the Middle Ages in Europe, it was most potent if it was the hand of a hanged criminal."

"Or a suicide, right?"

"Yes," Graydon said. "But you see, that was, I'm ashamed to say, a slight mistake on my part—"

"My uncle committed suicide," Elizabeth said, almost as if she hadn't heard Graydon's comment.

"He what—?"

"He killed himself," Elizabeth said. "I never even knew until—"

"He killed himself! He was a suicide!" Graydon said, almost howling. "That explains why it was so . . . so effective." After another snicker, he calmed down and then added, more thoughtfully, "Isn't it odd how these things have a way of working themselves out?"

"But what . . . what was it used for?" Elizabeth asked, as a rush of chills danced up her back. "It was horrible that you did something like that."

"The Hand of Glory is potent in and of itself," Graydon replied. "It was used primarily as a means to gain access to a house in order to rob it. You see, the magician would either place a candle in the dead hand or else, using a flammable mixture, ignite the fingers and thumb. The power of the Hand was such that everyone who saw the flame would fall asleep, and the magician, who had control of the Hand and thus was immune to it, would be at liberty to steal whatever he wanted from the house."

"But then . . . why did you use it out here?" Elizabeth asked. Her voice threatened to choke off as tears filled her eyes. "Especially on my daughter's grave?"

Graydon's teeth flashed in the moonlight as he smiled at her. "Why, so I could gain *control* over her, of course. I used the Hand of Glory to summon her. And now you'll be able to do the same thing! See her and talk with her."

Elizabeth shook her head in vigorous denial, wondering how Graydon could discuss something so gruesome, so horrible, with such detachment. Was it further proof that he was crazy, or that she was really losing her mind—or both? She knew she should be upset, completely freaked out to be here in the cemetery at midnight with a man who was telling her he had spoken with her dead daughter! How could he have done such a thing? If he was capable of doing that, what other horrible acts—including murder—might he be able to do?

"But why did you choose my uncle to dig up?" she asked, forcing a steadiness into her voice that she didn't feel at all.

"*Control!*" Graydon said forcefully, slapping his palm with his clenched fist. "It gives me the *power!*"

Elizabeth shook her head, confused. "But I don't get it," she said. "I mean, how could you have known about what my Uncle Jonathan did?"

Again, Graydon snuffed with laughter. "I didn't," he said, "I had no idea. I never even intended to use him, but apparently, because of the way he died, it was enough for my magical purposes." Before Elizabeth could say anything else, Graydon snapped his fingers loudly and said, "We really must hurry if we're going to go through with this."

Elizabeth sucked in a deep breath and held it, then let it out with a slow whistle as she nodded her agreement. "Okay—what do we do next?"

2.

"Goddamn! You ain't going out there *again*, are you?" Norton asked. The cruiser was parked in front of the 7-Eleven, its nose aimed toward the road. Norton was sitting in the passenger's seat, sipping coffee and munching on a doughnut. He stretched his arm out and glanced at his wristwatch. "Why—Christ, it's almost midnight. There ain't anything going to happen out there."

Frank grunted and, leaning his head back, scratched his neck. He wasn't drinking coffee tonight, which was unusual for him, but he felt wound up and wire-tight enough without it. Now that he had some more details about Roland Graydon, he couldn't push aside the feeling that Elizabeth was in serious trouble. He also was bone-deep positive that whatever else was going to happen, was going to happen out at Oak Grove Cemetery, at Caroline Myers's grave . . . and *soon*!

"Chalk it up to intuition, then," Frank said, regarding Norton with a sidelong glance. "I just don't have a good feeling about it tonight. I've been doing a bit of investigating on this guy, this psychiatrist Roland Graydon. You ever hear of him?"

Norton took a slurp of coffee and shook his head tightly. "Not till just now."

That's a lie, Frank thought, recalling that he and Norton had discussed Roland Graydon a week or so ago.

"Well, he's a shrink who lives over in South Portland. He's been seeing . . . a friend of mine. And I don't like some of the shit I found out about him."

"Yeah? Like what? You mean to tell me you know something 'n' you're not gonna tell your ole pardner?" Norton asked. Frank didn't miss the hard stare Norton gave him in the darkened car.

"I'll tell you all about it when we get there," Frank said. "You about done?" Without waiting for a reply, he cranked the ignition. The cruiser jumped to life as Frank pumped the accelerator a few times.

"Yeah . . . yeah," Norton sputtered. He popped the last piece of doughnut into his mouth and wiped the crumbs on the back of his sleeve. "Just take it easy on the bumps in the road, all right?"

As Frank pulled out onto Main Street and headed north, Norton sat up straight in his seat. Frank noticed his partner's sudden alertness, and several times he glanced at Norton's face, glowing pasty white in the dim light of the dashboard. He wasn't sure, but he thought he could read—what?—agitation, maybe, or some kind of tension in Norton's eyes. Was Norton really upset about something, or was he just imagining it?

The radio squawked with static. Norton's hand shot for the microphone as he said, "Hey! Maybe we got something interesting." But the call wasn't for them, so he let his hand drop to his side and looked straight ahead as the cruiser came up to the turn onto Brook Road. As Frank signaled and slowed for the turn, he most definitely picked up a coiling tension in his partner that just plain-old shouldn't have been there. When Norton spoke, the tightness in his voice only confirmed Frank's suspicions.

"This is a real fuckin' waste of time, I hope you realize," Norton said. He finished the sentence with a rising squeak in his voice. Frank knew it was because the cemetery entrance gate had come into view. He tapped lightly on the brakes as he slowed to take the turn onto the dirt road.

"I just want to—" he started to say, but that was all he got out before he detected a quick motion from Norton. As he swung the car in under the cemetery gate, he heard a soft *snap* sound, then the *hiss* of leather and a gentle *click*. Looking to his right, Frank saw that Norton had eased his revolver out of his holster. He cocked it and brought it to bear on Frank.

"Brad, what the fuck are you—?"

"You're not going up there," Norton said tightly, indicating with a quick nod the road leading up over the hill. He shifted forward in his seat and pressed the revolver to the side of Frank's head. "Just stay right where you are, pardner, and don't try anything stupid." His voice was an octave higher than usual, but Frank didn't doubt he meant business.

"Don't talk to me about *stupid*," Frank said softly. He jammed the shift into park and sat with the engine idling.

"Look, Frank," Norton said. "I don't want to have to shoot you, all right? But I will if I have to."

"Why would you go and do a stupid thing like that?" Frank asked. He could feel Norton's hand shaking, making the muzzle of the revolver vibrate against the side of his head. He swallowed and, in the dark interior of the car, quickly tried to assess his chances of fighting back.

"I've got my reasons, all right?" Norton replied tightly.

"Just what the fuck do you think you're doing?" Frank asked. He tried to shift to look at Norton, but the pressure of the gun to his temple stopped him. "What the fuck's going on, anyway?" A sheen of sweat broke out on his forehead, and he wondered if Norton's trigger finger might be sweating, too . . . and if it just might slip by mistake.

Norton took a deep breath to control his voice before he spoke. "Something you weren't supposed to find out about," he said. He shifted away from Frank, fearful that he was coiling up, preparing to try to disarm him. Leaning back against the passenger's door, he pointed the revolver at a spot behind Frank's right eye. "You just keep your eyes straight ahead. We're gonna have to kill a little time before we can decide what to do with you, but you can start by telling me *exactly* what you found out about Roland Graydon."

Frank shrugged helplessly and eased back in his seat. He wanted to try to lull Norton into letting his guard down, but he jumped and gripped the steering wheel tightly when he saw Norton flinch. Shifting his gaze to the side, he stared in disbelief at the unblinking eye of Norton's .357.

"Well, I—uh, I found evidence to suggest a connection between Roland Graydon and that incident of grave robbing you and I stumbled onto a few weeks back."

Norton chuffed with laughter. "Stumbled . . . yeah, I guess that'd be a good word for it."

"What?" Frank said. "You know something more about it?"

Norton remained silent. His eyes gleamed coldly in the light from the dashboard. Frank sensed that, if he was going to try something, he would have to try it soon because with each passing second, Norton's confidence about his control over the situation was rising.

"You aren't so fucking stupid you think you can get away with this, are you?'' Frank asked, not really expecting Norton to reply. ''I mean, even if you kill me, whatever it is you're involved with is gonna come out sooner or later. Why don't you put the gun away, and we can talk about it?''

Norton burst out laughing, then quickly regained control of himself and said, ''Yeah, right . . . sure. I'll reholster my gun so you can haul my ass in. That's rich!''

Frank opened his mouth to say something else, but a sudden explosion of pain caught him in the side of the head. He yelped as a flash of light shot through his brain. For just an instant, he thought he'd been shot; then he realized Norton had nailed him with the butt end of his revolver. Dazed, he brought his hand up to his head. His fingers came away sticky and warm, and he felt a trickle of blood run down to his collar.

''Why don't you just back the fucking car on out of here,'' Norton commanded roughly. ''Head out on Mitchell Hill Road, so that if I do end up wasting you, I won't have to disturb any of the neighbors.''

''What—?'' Frank said, but that was all. Blinding pain still rippled through him. He shook his head in an attempt to clear it, then eased the cruiser into gear and backed out of the cemetery. He bit his lower lip, wishing to hell he could think more clearly as he gripped the steering wheel with both hands and drove slowly down Brook Road toward Mitchell Hill Road. As much as he was worried and concerned about how—or if—he was going to get out of this situation, he couldn't stop wondering what in the name of Christ was going on back there at Oak Grove Cemetery . . . and what the fuck Norton had to do with it.

3.

Moving quickly, Graydon went from point to point of the pentagram and, using a cigarette lighter, lit each black candle in turn. In spite of the wind blowing high in the trees, at Caroline's grave not even a slight breeze disturbed the flames. The candles burned with a cold, yellow light that illuminated the area, casting the surrounding area into deeper darkness. With the addition of each candle's light, Elizabeth saw with increasing clarity her daughter's name and birth and death dates carved into the stone. Waves of dizziness threatened to knock her over.

"Step into the center of the pentagram. Quickly!" Graydon said. He waved his hand anxiously at her as he knelt beside the bag and loaded his hands with an assortment of items. In the glow of the candlelight, Elizabeth again saw, along with various other implements, the long blade of a knife. Cold fear gripped her as she considered what use it could possibly have during the ceremony.

Elizabeth stepped into the center of the design, careful not to kick or smudge the white outline. Then she waited, her stomach tightening as her eyes flicked back and forth between Caroline's headstone and Graydon. She was burning to ask him what she should expect next, but fear held her tongue.

"Now remember," Graydon said, entering the design and standing behind Elizabeth, so close she could feel his warm breath on the back of her neck. It raised goose bumps on her arms. "You must not say *anything* until I indicate that it's all right. And you absolutely *must* do what I tell you to do—without hesitation. When you first see Caroline, you'll be—"

"I—I really will see her?" Elizabeth asked. She choked on the raw burning in her throat, surprised that she could speak at all.

"Oh, I assure you," Graydon said. "You'll see her, and soon. For now, just be patient."

With that, he slipped his hand into his left coat pocket and removed something; she couldn't quite see what it was. He approached the two candles pointing toward the headstone and, bending down, reached out with both hands and sprinkled onto each flame a fine powder that glittered in the moonlight. With a sudden, blinding flash, accompanied by a dull *whoosh*, two green flames shot at least six feet into the night sky. Startled, Elizabeth jumped back. Only after her pulse slowed was she aware that Graydon was muttering something softly under his breath. She caught herself before she spoke aloud to ask him what he was saying.

Time seemed to dilate, to stretch out like a looping strand of Silly Putty and lose all meaning, as Elizabeth stood in the center of the design, watching and listening as Graydon went on with his ceremony. Several times, he threw the fine white powder into the flames of the candles, making green fire flash into the air like bolts of hissing lightning. Heavy smoke wafted up into the sky, masking the stars and hanging like a rippling black curtain above the grave. The air was filled with a nauseating smell of sulfur that parched Elizabeth's lungs with its thick, cloying fumes.

Elizabeth never understood a word Graydon was saying; it sounded as though he was muttering snatches of Latin; several times she had the impression he was saying things backward, and her nervousness only intensified when she recalled the backward voice she had recorded with Eldon Cody's white noise.

"Watch," Graydon said suddenly, making Elizabeth jump. Knowing or sensing that he meant for her to look at Caroline's grave, Elizabeth let her gaze drop down to the ground. The yellow flames of the candles deepened to orange. Mixed with the brilliant green flashes, they made the white lines of the pentagram vibrate with a hallucinatory intensity. Elizabeth found it difficult to focus and had to blink her eyes rapidly to dispel the illusion that the pentagram was actually floating up off the ground. At first, it looked to be no more than an inch or two above the close-cropped grass; but even as she stared long and hard at it, it seemed to rise higher and higher, until it was hovering more than a foot in the air.

I'm imagining all of this! Elizabeth told herself, and the thought crossed her mind that the smoke she had inhaled from whatever was making the candles flash green was some kind of drug. Maybe that was how Graydon achieved his results—by drugging his clients and working with the power of suggestion and hallucination.

Either that or I'm asleep, dreaming, she thought.

Whatever the explanation, it sure as hell *looked* like the pentagram had magically levitated. And Elizabeth was positive it wasn't simply the power of suggestion that made the ground in front of Caroline's gravestone look like it was moving. At first there was nothing more than a subtle motion she could have easily dismissed as the result of the flickering candlelight; but the longer she stared at the ground, the more violent the movement of the grass and soil became. She had the impression of a large, tangled knot of black worms or snakes seething on the grass, growing larger with each passing second.

"Is that—" she started to say, but Graydon hushed her with a

sharp hiss that seemed oddly magnified in the darkness. Magnifie
by what? Elizabeth wondered, feeling wave after wave of franti
fear clawing at her mind. What the hell is happening?

She couldn't tear her gaze away from the ground over her daugh
ter's grave. The longer she looked, the wider and more active th
seething blackness became until she was convinced the dirt itsel
had magically come alive. She wasn't sure quite when it happened
but at some point she saw—and fully accepted—that the groun
over Caroline's grave was thinning out, becoming almost invisible
She had the sense that, if she bent down and reached out her hand
her fingers wouldn't be stopped by the hard-packed soil and soo
they would pass right through it and down . . . down into the eart
all the way to the smooth wooden surface of Caroline's coffin!

Oh, Jesus! she thought, resisting the truth of the illusion an
fighting her mounting terror that Graydon had drugged her and wa
playing with her mind, causing this hallucination to happen.

But she couldn't deny what she was seeing; there was no wa
she could be imagining this. The ground covering Caroline'
coffin—even under Elizabeth's own feet—was now nothing mor
than a heaving, churning black tangle, like storm clouds being rippe
apart by gale-force winds. Elizabeth resisted a dizzying wave o
vertigo as she looked down, imagining she was floating high in th
sky. Her awareness was drawn inexorably down, into the black voi
below her.

Through the darkness, she could see with nearly mind-numbin
clarity that something was struggling to emerge from the blac
maelstrom at her feet. Long, thin, and white, at first it looked lik
some kind of strange insect or creature, scrambling upward towar
her. Her eyes struggled to pierce the pitchy blackness, to focu
clearly on what she was seeing, but for long, drawn-out seconds
all she could perceive was a white smear of activity fluttering lik
helpless birds caught in a storm. And then, in a jolting instant, sh
saw what it was—two hands, reaching up toward her out of th
darkness beneath her feet.

"Oh, my Lord," she muttered. She clamped her hands over he
mouth to keep from screaming as her legs gave way, and she droppe
to the ground. She was dimly surprised when her knees hit soli
ground and she didn't just keep falling, tumbling headlong int

nothingness, but that sensation was lost in the complete horror of watching those two bony hands claw up toward her from the darkness of her daughter's grave.

Elizabeth groaned with the physical effort of looking away from the apparition as she glanced over her shoulder at Graydon. He had been standing close behind her, but her vision telescoped madly, and his figure receded to an impossible distance. She tried to open her mouth to speak, but when her lips moved, all she could hear was a slow, steady rumbling that sounded like huge boulders, tumbling down a mountainside in a landslide. A spark of recognition lit up in her mind when she saw something long and gleaming in Graydon's upraised hand, but she pushed that aside as she lurched to her feet and stared down at the ground.

The hands were coming closer, reaching up at her from the churning blackness. Fingernails, grown long and curling in upon themselves, a sickly ivory color beneath caked dirt, clicked viciously. And then, as Elizabeth watched with mind-numbing horror, a face materialized, leering up at her from the black earth. The pale face was framed by a twisting tangle of long, blonde hair; the dried flesh of the face was withered and rotten, crawling with worms and maggots. Although the features seemed somehow blurry and out of focus, as though seen through heavy layers of gauze, Elizabeth immediately recognized who it was.

"Oh, my *God*!" she gasped, as every ounce of strength snapped out of her body. "Oh, my sweet, loving Jesus! . . . *Caroline*!"

The face floated at her feet, suspended in the whirling blackness as it drifted closer, rising from the depths of the earth. Caroline's eyes were open, staring at her with a cold, hollow gaze, as though they were seeing nothing at all—or else piercing right through to her soul! A freezing draft of putrid air blew upward into Elizabeth's face, making her hair stream back over her shoulders. She hugged herself and rubbed vigorously on her upper arms, but that did nothing to stop the wave after wave of numbing cold or the lances of blinding panic that skewered her mind.

"This can't . . . can't be . . . happening!" she heard herself say.

"You have to hold her down," a hard, commanding voice said from behind her. "If you are to have control over her, you must hold her down just as the book described it."

Elizabeth shot a terrified glance back at Graydon, her eyes widening with confusion.

"Go on!" Graydon commanded. He had to shout to be heard above the roaring wind that raged up from the grave. "You have to grab her by the shoulders and wrestle her down. Hold her there! Otherwise, *she* will have control over *you*!"

Elizabeth's eyes flashed back down in front of her when she felt an icy chill encircle her ankles. Caroline's hands and face were more clearly resolved, and her thin, dead hands were wrapped around Elizabeth's legs, tugging violently as she tried to yank her off balance.

"Don't let her get control of you!" Graydon shouted.

Elizabeth kicked her feet back, breaking the hold; then she dropped to the ground and, not knowing what else to do, reached out into the blackness until she felt her hands connect with something that felt like decaying cloth.

The dress Caroline was buried in! she thought as an ache of sadness exploded in her heart. Beneath the cloth, she could feel her dead daughter's thin shoulders, like cold, unflinching marble.

"Do it! Pin her down! If she gets a hold on you, she'll drag you down with her!" Graydon shouted. His voice sounded far behind her; it had a curious echo effect to it. Elizabeth barely noticed it as Caroline struggled in her grasp, trying to break the hold she had on her.

Hot tears flooded Elizabeth's eyes, blurring her sight as she flexed her numbed arm muscles, forcing them to come to life. Blind panic filled her mind. She didn't see how she could resist the brutal force that was welling up at her from her daughter's grave. There was no shaking, no violent churning, as there had been in the soil when this madness had started; just an inexorable upward push that made Elizabeth feel as though she were helplessly riding a hydraulic lift. She winced when the hooked fingernails sank into her upper arms and squeezed tightly.

"You *have* to control her!" Graydon continued to yell. "She'll only yield if you can prove that you're stronger than she is!"

Sweat broke out on Elizabeth's forehead and mixed with the tears streaming from her eyes. A thick, salty taste filled her mouth. Elizbeth felt her heart stop and go ice cold in her chest as her dead daughter's face loomed closer and closer to her own, condensing like wispy clots of smoke into a twisted, tormented expression of pain and effort.

As the struggle continued, Elizabeth saw with stark horror that her blurred vision of Caroline's face hadn't been just the result of her own tears. There was a thick, creamy white fluid smeared all over Caroline's face. It reminded Elizabeth crazily of vernix, the thick mucouslike substance that, along with blood, covers a baby at birth. She saw worms crawling within that curdled white fluid. Breathless from her efforts, Elizabeth wished she had enough air left in her lungs to scream. Her brain was completely overloaded as she looked down at the horribly distorted vision of her daughter.

Vision? she thought. *No! This is too damned real to be a vision or hallucination!*

Caroline's jaw made a horrible clacking sound as it worked back and forth, gnashing her teeth. Elizabeth knew it was impossible for there to be any air in her daughter's dead lungs, but she could see the thick, milky fluid bubbling as Caroline's mouth opened and closed, like a fish gulping in water. The coiled tension in her daughter's corpse built steadily, ready to explode up at her. Elizabeth wasn't sure whether the explosion would be physical or mental.

Caroline's lips twisted and twitched as she tried to form words, but the fluid covering her face choked her, filling her mouth and throat, making it impossible for her to speak.

How can she speak? How can the dead speak? Elizabeth wondered crazily as she heaved forward, trying to pin her daughter's steel-hard shoulders to the ground. *What in the name of Heaven and Hell could this . . . this apparition possibly have to say?*

"You have to clean her mouth out before she can talk to you." Graydon's voice boomed from the darkness behind her. "Remember the description in the book?"

Frantic with fear, Elizabeth looked behind her and was stunned by what she saw. Graydon was still standing with her within the protection of the pentagram, but beyond the white lines of the star, the night was a riot of activity. Where there had been silent, moon-washed tombstones and a gently sloping hill before, now the night was swirling with strobing red and blue lights. At first, her eyes saw only confusion, but after a moment, the chaos resolved into dozens—hundreds—of twisted, humanlike figures.

"I . . . How?" Elizabeth said, no more than a strangled gasp.

"Pin her with your knees and scoop it out with your hands . . . either that, or else suck it out," Graydon said.

Behind him, the spinning madness of figures intensified. Elizabeth saw horribly deformed shapes, sick parodies of humanity with hooved feet and clawed hands, horns, and gaping, fang-filled mouths. Wicked, sparkling eyes watched the struggle unblinkingly. Elizabeth had the distinct impression they were all willing her to lose the struggle. Arms were upraised, and legs kicked high as the figures silently twisted and leaped in the flickering red glow of flames. Dimly, at the edge of awareness, Elizabeth heard the wild shrieks and doom-filled moans as the figures increased their frantic dance.

"I . . . can't!" she sputtered. The pain of Caroline's fingernails gouging into her arms was too intense; the upward thrust was unrelenting.

"You must!" Graydon shrilled. "If you don't, she'll have you under her power!"

Shifting her legs forward, Elizabeth tried to brace Caroline's shoulders, but her daughter wiggled and twisted, resisting all of her efforts. Slowly, like two heavy-laden ships on an inevitable collision course, their two faces came closer and closer together until, nose to nose, they touched. Caroline exhaled a bubbling expulsion of rotten breath. The icy wind from the grave streamed viciously around Elizabeth's face, pushing her back violently; but she strained her neck forward and brought her mouth closer to her dead daughter's mouth.

"*Go on! Do it now!*" Graydon shouted. His voice was almost lost in the rising cacophony of shrill wailing all around them.

With all the effort it takes to breathe in a strong gale, Elizabeth sucked in her breath and then pressed her lips hard against Caroline's cold mouth. There was a jolting shock as their lips met. Elizabeth exhaled noisily through her nose and then sucked hard, as though giving her dead daughter some perverted form of artificial respiration. The rancid taste of dead flesh and sour milk filled her mouth, making her stomach revolt.

"She can't speak until you get her mouth clear," Graydon hollered.

Elizabeth gagged down the rush of vomit that exploded into her throat as the worms wiggled inside her mouth, churning the sickly fluid. She spat the stuff out, took another deep breath through her nose, exhaled, and then sucked furiously on her dead daughter's mouth again. Thick chunks of horrible corruption filled her mouth. Twisting to one side, she again spat out the sickening fluid. When she looked down, she saw that Caroline's mouth was still bubbling with milky clots. Nausea compressed Elizabeth's stomach as though it were in a giant's steely grip.

Steady, rapid pulse beats hammered in Elizabeth's ears, almost —but not quite—drowning out the rising sound of demonic voices screeching at her from the surrounding red-lit night. Embracing her daughter's corpse as though cradling a baby, Elizabeth pressed her lips to Caroline's a third time and, with what she knew was her last effort before she collapsed, sucked more of the horrible-tasting liquid into her mouth. Involuntarily, she swallowed some before she could turn and spit it out. A coldness like death filled her seething stomach.

Shuddering with the effort to hold Caroline down and not vomit, Elizabeth looked down at her daughter's face. The hollow, glazed eyes had taken on a deep, throbbing semblance of life. The irises pulsated with a dull blue glow that steadily intensified, drawing her awareness like a magnet. Try as she might, Elizabeth couldn't look away. Then, finally, as the last few ounces of strength faded from her arms, a violent upward explosion sent her reeling backward. She collapsed onto the ground like a useless, wrung-out cloth.

Cringing in horror, Elizabeth watched as the figure of her daughter materialized more clearly and then, floating up out of the dark ground, rose into the air. For several paralyzing seconds, the pale, desiccated figure, dressed in the frilly white funeral dress, hovered high in the night sky; then it settled like a perching bird of prey onto the rounded top of her gravestone, just outside the protective pentagram. Luminous and shimmering, the eerie blue glow of Caroline's body filled the night around her, blending at its extreme edges with the chaotic red flickers that colored the space outside the pentagram.

Elizabeth couldn't look away from the vacant stare of her daughter's dead eyes. Caroline regarded her mother with the unnerving, unfocused gaze of a blind person. Her waxy white face was immobile, expressionless.

"Go ahead! Speak to her!" Graydon commanded. "Tell her what you have to tell her. *Go on!*"

The frantic, excited tone in his voice surprised Elizabeth, and she had the fleeting impression that he might have succeeded beyond even his own wildest dreams.

Elizabeth cleared her throat, but the rotten taste of the creamy fluid still clung to every taste bud, making it impossible to speak. Wave after wave of nausea crested within her, threatening to spew the contents of her stomach onto the ground, but at last, after taking in a breath of fetid night air—a breath that might possibly be her last, Elizabeth thought—she spoke.

"Caroline . . . honey . . . I can't . . . can't believe this is really you."

Squatting on the tombstone, the apparition of Caroline moved her mouth. Her face and jaw muscles contorted with effort; rotten tendons stood out like steel cables beneath the pale skin of her thin neck, but no sound came from her throat.

Elizabeth looked up at Caroline's lifeless face and cold, staring eyes. This certainly looked like her dead daughter, but she was so far removed from the loving, happy child Elizabeth remembered that she told herself this could be nothing more than an illusion, a projection.

"I don't . . . I don't know how to say what I've wanted to say to you for—for so long," Elizabeth stammered, tears coursing down her cheeks. She tasted salt in the corners of her mouth. "I just— since that night, I've been wanting to tell you how much . . . how sorry I am that you—that I never wanted for you to die. I hope you can believe that, honey! I just couldn't . . . couldn't—"

Her voice choked off with a gagging sound, and she watched in horror as the figure of her daughter subtly shifted. The pale, dead skin of her face stretched and started to flake off, dropping to the ground in paper-thin pieces and exposing the worm-eaten bone beneath. Flat, yellow teeth caked with dirt flashed into a widening smile that exuded evil.

This isn't an apparition, a ghost, Elizabeth told herself through the roaring maelstrom in her mind. *I struggled with it; it had weight, strength, substance. I'm staring at the actual animated body of my dead daughter!*

Caroline's decomposing face twisted as, with great effort, her mouth tried again to form words. Elizabeth waited, shivering with tension until, at last, her dead daughter raised her arms and reached up into the smoky night sky. With a rough, ripping sound, her body stretched up and up. The gauzy funeral dress disintegrated. Pieces fluttered to the ground like fog. Caroline's frail arms lengthened and thickened, and her thin chest expanded with a roaring intake of breath. When the thing that had been Caroline spoke, its voice echoed like a cannon shot.

"You . . . have . . . *failed!*" the visage bellowed, glaring down at Elizabeth. Dull echoes rolled in from the surrounding night, intensifying rather than fading as they reverberated.

Elizabeth crouched in a tight ball on the ground, her hands rising protectively to her face. Between slitted fingers, she looked up into the night sky as the shape that had been her daughter . . .

No! her mind wailed. *This isn't Caroline! This can't be Caroline!*

. . . towered above her. It kept expanding until, little by little, the face and figure of Caroline Myers dissolved into that of a grinning, leering demon. Cold power radiated from its green, cat-slit eyes. Filaments of blue flame danced and twined around its black-scaled body, casting dizzily wavering shadows as its cruel mouth stretched into a wide, evil grin. A thick, forked tongue flicked serpentlike from between its pointed teeth.

"You are now within my power!" the horror growled, beastlike, as it reached forward with both clawed hands and made a violent grasping motion. "And now your soul is *mine!*"

NINETEEN
The Sacrifice

1.

"I wish to Christ you'd stop telling me how fuckin' stupid I'm being," Norton said angrily.

With Norton's revolver pointed at the base of his skull, Frank was driving slowly down Mitchell Hill Road, just waiting for an opportunity to catch Norton's guard slipping, even just an inch. They left the few houses that lined the road far behind them. The headlights of the cruiser washed the tree-walled road as if they were passing down a long, narrow tunnel. Flashes of moonlight cut through the thick leaves overhead.

"I'm just trying to convince you that, whatever it is you're involved with, if you go any further with it, you're never going to get out."

"Do you honestly think I won't get nailed for what's happened already? You mean to tell me you didn't already think I had something to do with killing Barney Fraser?"

"What—you?" A chill tightened Frank's stomach.

"Yeah—I was there . . . and even if I didn't start the fire at Bishop's, you don't think I'll get connected with it? Shit, man!" He snorted with laughter, tight and high in his chest.

Frank smiled grimly as he bit down hard on his lower lip. "Why the Christ did you—"

"Because both Bishop and Fraser knew too much! 'Specially Fraser," Norton replied tightly. "Like you do now, unfortunately. So both of 'em had to be shut up, just like you're gonna be shut up." Pointing with his revolver, he indicated the deserted stretch of road ahead, glanced behind them, and said, "You can pull over right here."

Frank coasted to a stop, then slipped the shift into park.

"This is *real* fucking stupid," he said. He was repeating himself for about the tenth time because he knew how much it was getting on Norton's nerves.

"Well, pardner," Norton said with measured control, "if I'm so fuckin' stupid, you must be stupider, 'cause I got the better of you. Anyway, I can take some reassurance, knowing your miserable ass is buried and rotting out here in the middle of nowhere. Now cut the engine and get the fuck out of the car."

Frank obliged, leaving the keys in the ignition as he eased the driver's door open and stepped out onto the road. His shoes made a loud crunching noise on the asphalt. Norton hadn't told him to turn off the cruiser's headlights, so he'd left them on and now used the light to scan both sides of the road, looking for the best place to head if he decided to make a run for it. With Norton covering him so well, he doubted he'd make it very far, but he knew he was going to have to at least try.

Norton got out on the passenger's side and slammed the door shut hard. The sound echoed in the still night like a gunshot, making Frank shiver. He found little reassurance in the thought that if you can hear the shot, you're not dead yet because—so they say—you never hear the one that kills you.

"Come on, man," Frank said tightly, watching as Norton came around to the front of the car and directed him into the woods with a quick wave of his revolver. "We've been partners for too long to fuck things up like this! I'd never blow the whistle on you."

"Shut the fuck up and get moving," Norton snarled, seeming to gain confidence with each passing second.

"Then think about Suzie, for Christ's sake!" Frank pleaded, putting more nervousness and tension into his voice than he truly felt. He had to try anything—*everything*—to get Norton to lower his guard.

"I don't give a rat's ass about Suzie," Norton said tightly. "She good at sucking my cock, and that's about it. Are you gonna mov your ass, or do I have to waste you right here?"

Frank hesitated, then stepped out of the glare of the headligh and into the shadowed woods. From far off, he heard the whistlin of a whippoorwill. His father had always told him the whippoorwi was a bird of ill omen; for the first time in his life he began t believe it.

Norton stayed by the car, using his gun to track every step Fran took.

"The least you could do before you kill me, you know, is te me why," Frank said. He felt as helpless as an animal snared in trap. He knew that soon, within seconds, maybe, he might be dea on the forest floor, his senseless ears filled with the distant whistl of a whippoorwill as the rolling echo of Norton's gun faded.

"You're too fucking close to Graydon," Norton said. "You'r right fuckin' on top of him. And don't bullshit me. I don't believ for a second you won't turn me in. You and that Myers bitc are—" He raised the revolver and leveled it squarely at Frank head. "You're expendable." He took careful aim, braced his wris and said, "Sorry 'bout this, pardner."

Frank tensed as Norton slowly squeezed the trigger; then he fe a heady rush of relief when he heard only a faint *click*.

While Norton stood there, looking in amazement at the useles gun in his hand as he clicked it several more times, Frank charge up the slope at him. Lowering his shoulder, he hit Norton just belo the belt in a tackle that would have done him proud on the footba field. His speed carried them both across the street and out of th glow of headlights. Norton went down, and even before Frank full weight landed on top of him, Frank was cocking his fist up i the air. Norton struck the ground, flattened, the wind knocked ou of him, just as Frank's fist descended like thunder, catching Norto squarely on the bridge of the nose. Frank smiled wickedly when h heard another sharp *click*—this time the sound of breaking bon and cartilage in Norton's nose. Norton howled like an animal i pain.

"You're one lousy fucking son of a bitch," Frank snarled, as h shifted his weight onto Norton and pinned him down with both knees.

Norton thrashed wildly, but the pain flooding his body, radiating from his shattered nose, blinded him. It was already too late to resist, but he continued to struggle uselessly.

"You're also one *careless* son of a bitch," Frank said. For emphasis, he brought his fist down hard onto Norton's face a second time, fully enjoying the squishy feel of Norton's ruined nose. He was panting heavily, but more from excitement than effort as he brought his face up close to Norton's.

"I checked into Graydon, all right, you miserable motherfucker," he said heatedly. "I think your biggest mistake was assuming I was just as fucking stupid as you are. Didn't Harris ever tell you what *assume* makes?"

Frank shook his head and clicked his tongue as though scolding a schoolboy.

"When you missed those few days from work, I figured out you must be in on . . . whatever the hell Graydon's doing. He had to have help from inside because Harris and Lovejoy hadn't nailed him. They may be dumb, but they're not *that* dumb! Then, a couple of days ago, Elizabeth complained to me that she didn't want me tailing her. Now, I knew damned well I hadn't been tailing her, but *someone* had. Coincidentally, it was during those three days you took off from work. It didn't take much to put it all together. You were following her around and reporting back to Graydon. Am I right? . . . I said—am I *right*?" For emphasis, he gave Norton's chin a hard jab. Norton's teeth made a satisfying clicking noise.

"Yeah—" Norton grunted as Frank's weight crushed down on him. Thick streams of blood ran from his nose and the corners of his mouth and down the sides of his neck. In the moonlight, it looked like spilled ink.

"And I'd even bet good money you were the asshole who spray painted that black-magic symbol on the police station wall, too. I remember that day. You were the only one there who didn't seem all that surprised about it. Am I *right* again?"

Another punch got another affirmative nod from Norton and made the blood flow more freely.

"Cocky bastard! So once I found out about the connection between the accident that killed Elizabeth's daughter and Graydon, I was positive you were helping him out, keeping him informed on the investigation, such as it was . . . maybe even doing some of his shit work. So you were the one who set the fire at Bishop's house, huh?"

Norton shook his head in vigorous denial.

"Yeah, sure. But you *did* say you were there when Barney Fraser was killed, right? And I bet Graydon had you dig the grave and bury him."

Frank punched Norton's jaw again and smiled at the crunching sound his teeth made. Norton's eyes glazed with pain as he shook his head in vigorous denial. "I didn't kill no one," he sputtered. Bloody spit flew from his mouth and hit Frank in the face.

"Now I don't know what you and Graydon are up to, digging up corpses and all, but—" He paused to wipe the blood from his face with his sleeve; then, using the heel of his hand, he jammed upward on Norton's nose. Norton yelped with pain and shook as though he'd been electrocuted. "Well, *one* thing you sure as shit don't know is that a good cop always checks his revolver before starting his shift. Didn't you know that?"

Norton's pain-filled eyes glowed dimly with understanding as to why his revolver hadn't fired.

"That's right, fuck-face. Figuring the shit was going to hit the fan sooner or later, I took the liberty of going into your locker and unloading your gun, you stupid fuck!" Satisfied that the fight had gone out of Norton, Frank sat back, sighed, and wiped his forehead with the back of his hand. "I sure am glad you didn't think to check it."

Norton tried to say something, but the blood flowing back into his throat made him gag. Frank shifted his weight off him and rolled him onto his stomach, pinning him to the ground. With his face pressed into the forest floor, Norton made soft snuffing sounds as though he was choking on blood and saliva, but Frank truly didn't care if the man suffocated. After a moment, though, he realized that Norton was laughing.

"You mind telling me what you think is so fucking hilarious?" Frank shouted. He released the handcuffs from his utility belt and roughly pulled Norton's arms up behind his back. With one quick, practiced motion, he slapped the cuffs onto Norton's wrists. Not even caring if he dislocated both of Norton's shoulders, he grabbed him by the elbows and pulled him to his feet, making sure he yanked Norton's arms as far back as they would go. With a quick kick in the ass, he sent Norton staggering back onto the road. When they got to the cruiser, he slammed his face hard onto the hood.

Between gurgling chuckles, Norton was trying to speak, but all that came out of his mouth was a thick stream of frothy blood. The chuffing sound of his laughter made Frank's anger flare all the more.

"You didn't tell me what you think's so Goddamned funny!" Frank snarled. He pulled back on Norton's arms, making him wail in pain as he raised him, and then smashed his face down hard enough onto the hood of the cruiser to dent the metal. The sounds of Norton's agony rose shrilly, echoing in the woods.

"It . . . doesn't . . . fucking . . . matter . . . anymore," Norton sputtered. A pool of his blood filled the dent in the hood. He looked like a Hollywood vampire who had feasted to satisfaction.

"What? *What* doesn't matter anymore?" Frank shouted, leaning down close to the helpless man and giving him another sharp jerk on his cuffed arms.

"You . . . knowing . . . about . . . Graydon," Norton said. He twisted his head to one side, snorted loudly, and tried to spit at Frank. The glob landed with a plop on the hood of the car, beside his head. "'Cause . . . it's . . . already . . . too . . . late . . ." His throat made a loud gagging sound. "She's . . . probably . . . already . . . dead!"

2.

Strong arms encircled Elizabeth from behind and lifted her. For a flashing instant, as her feet drifted off the ground, she thought the demon . . .

Yes! It has to be a demon! An evil spirit of some kind! This can't be what Caroline has become!

. . . was doing this, levitating her somehow; but, glancing over her shoulder, she saw the side of Graydon's face as he pinioned her arms roughly to her side.

"What the—" she said.

He cut her off with a tight squeeze that forced all of the air from her lungs. Once he seemed assured she would remain silent, he lowered her gently to the ground. The pressure around her chest eased as he drew one arm back, but the other still held her tightly. Any restraint was unnecessary, however, because Elizabeth couldn't tear her gaze away from the horror that was crouching on top of Caroline's tombstone. All traces of Caroline's face were gone. The creature's cold, unblinking green eyes studied her as it licked the curled tips of its talons.

Elizabeth sensed that Graydon was doing something behind her, but her attention was riveted to the *thing* that had assumed her daughter's form. The demon raised its arms high over its head, breathing rapidly in and out, its lungs roaring as they bellowed, continuing to expand.

"That's not—it can't be . . . it never—was—" she whispered, but that was all she could say. Crashing waves of blackness swept up and over her. Even though she was *positive* her feet were rooted within the safety of the pentagram, she felt tossed and turned, buffeted about as though caught in the sickening whirl of a tornado. Would the pentagram truly protect her, as Graydon had said? she wondered. Why was he holding her? Did he want to prevent her from stepping outside the design . . . or did he have other plans?

Graydon whispered something behind her, close to her ear, but it was lost in the steadily rising roar as billows of blackness, keeping time with the monster's raging breath, tugged at her, threatening to throw her off balance and pull her under.

Elizabeth thrashed her head from side to side, trying to force her gaze away from the beast, but her eyes, like steadily tracking radar, couldn't pull away from the hypnotically glowing green eyes. In their center, she saw a brilliant red flickering, and Elizabeth knew she was staring into the core of the Inferno.

Again, Graydon said something behind her. She still couldn't make out his words; it was as if he was still speaking in Latin, mumbling something either to control or—she hoped—send the demon back to where it had come from. A glimmer of understanding rose in her mind when she sensed a quick motion at her side and then saw Graydon's free hand rise up level to her eyes. In his grip was the gleaming silver blade of the knife she had seen earlier.

"Here," he rasped. "Take this."

For a heartbeat, frozen in fear, Elizabeth's brain commanded her body to move but got no response. She had no idea what Graydon wanted her to do with the knife. Would it give her some kind of control over this demon? Would it give her the ability to command it? Then, with a soul-numbing coldness, she realized that he had lowered the blade and was pointing it toward her chest, directly at her heart.

"Take this!" he commanded, his voice ripping like the wind in her ears. "Use it!"

Looking up, Elizabeth saw that the demon on Caroline's tombstone had ceased its growth, and now, at its full power, it crouched, hunching like a predatory bird as it stared at her expectantly. Thin, cruel lips peeled back, exposing glittering, pointed teeth. The face was a horrible combination of human and reptile, scaly and glistening. The red glow in the beast's eyes flashed with steady pulses that matched the frozen pounding of Elizabeth's heart.

"I said, *take* this and *use* it!" Graydon shouted.

Elizabeth watched, helpless to resist as her hands rose up from her side and gripped the leather-bound hilt of the knife. Every knuckle joint felt welded into place as she tightened her grip on the knife handle. She had no sense of breathing as she stared, long and hard, at the glittering blade. The metal caught the red glow of the demon's eyes and shattered it into jagged tongues of lightning.

"*Use it!*" Graydon said. "He *demands* a *sacrifice.*"

The demon on the tombstone tilted its head back and stared up at the night sky. The wind high above the cemetery roared like a hurricane. Cold moonlight gave a harsh, blue outline to the beast's ghastly, underlit features. Drawing strength from the surrounding blackness, the creature opened its mouth wide. Its teeth gleamed with the cold, bone-white light of the stars as it opened its throat and roared . . . with laughter.

"A . . . sacrifice?" Elizabeth stammered, her voice no more than a grating whisper.

"He wants *you*," Graydon hissed, sounding almost desperate. "He *wants* you to *do* it!"

Elizabeth shook her head in short, sharp jerks of denial, but she couldn't resist the pull of the knife. She stared in numbed fascination at the gleaming razored edge of the blade and knew that with it she could end all of her pain and grief. It was as if the blade were made of pure iron, and as if she—her heart—were a magnet, drawing it inexorably forward.

"No, I—" she whimpered as she tried to fight against the steady pull. The pointed end came closer and closer to her chest. Elizabeth had the insane impression that the demon was somehow controlling the blade, directing it, pushing it into her chest. She caught the reflection of the beast's eyes in the shimmering blade and thought of the ring of fire she had dreamed surrounding Caroline's face.

"*Do it*!" Graydon shouted. "Do it *now*!"

Elizabeth struggled. Her arms trembled, and her muscles twisted like snakes as she fought desperately against the relentless force that was pushing the blade nearer to her heart. She felt a stinging jolt of pain as the thin point lanced through her jacket and blouse, driving straight toward her heart. As much as she tried not to, she imagined her heart, slimy with fresh blood, sliding from a gaping wound in her chest and, still pulsing, dropping to the ground at the demon's feet, where it would scoop it up and eat it in one quick swallow. She clearly imagined the fountain of blood—her own blood!—pumping out onto the ground to which she knew she would soon fall, lifeless.

And where will my soul go? she wondered frantically as the knife point pierced her skin. *After devouring my heart, will this thing—this creature that isn't Caroline—sweep up my soul and plummet with it down into the deepest reaches of Hell?*

Every pore of Elizabeth's body opened as sweat, hot and sticky, flooded out of her. Air burned inside her lungs as though she had inhaled the flames that blossomed in the core of the demon's red eyes. Her muscles were strained beyond their limit; her bones felt like they were crumbling to powder beneath her skin. She watched as her own hands pressed the blade deeper into her chest, feeling the clammy trickle of blood running down inside her shirt. She let out a strangled, helpless whimper, but it was lost in the explosion of raging wind overhead and the cruel, demonic laughter that swept around her.

3.

Frank's foot nailed the accelerator to the floor and never let up as the cruiser shot up Mitchell Hill Road to Brook Road and toward Oak Grove Cemetery. He didn't even think to put on his flashers, sound his siren, or radio the station. All he could think was that something—something horrible, something that involved Elizabeth—was being acted out at the cemetery right now, and he either had to stop it or die trying!

The cruiser sliced through the dark night, as if pulled inexorably forward by the steady cones of light from its headlights. Trees and houses whipped past the windows, and the road unscrolled with rapid twists and turns, but no matter how fast he went, Frank couldn't fight the impression that he was sitting still, getting nowhere. The only thought in his mind was, *I have to get there before it's too late!*

Norton, still unconscious and handcuffed, was sprawled in the backseat behind the protective wire grill. His face was resting in a puddle of blood. Before tossing him in there, Frank had disarmed him of anything, even his belt and shoes, that he could use as a weapon if he came to before this was all over. But there was little pleasure in the thought of what was going to happen to Norton after tonight. Certainly, by what he had said, he would be implicated in the deaths of Barney Fraser and Henry Bishop; but Frank realized he hadn't read Norton his rights, and no doubt a sleaze-bag lawyer would get him free on some half-assed technicality.

Frank's heart was hammering in his chest. He had the vague fear that he might be so worked up he would have a fatal heart attack before he could find out what was happening at the cemetery, much less do anything about it. His sweat-slick fingers gripped the steering wheel and jerked it roughly back and forth to keep the cruiser on the road. Finally, after what seemed like an hour or more, he saw the black bars of the cemetery fence up ahead on the left.

"Fuckin'-A," he muttered, as he pressed down hard on the brakes. "Fuckin'-A-straight!" The rear tires hissed loudly as they locked up and skidded over the sand at the side of the road. With a sickening, drifting feel, the cruiser fish-tailed as though sliding on ice. In an instant, Frank realized he was spinning out. He jerked the steering wheel in the direction of the slide but didn't release the

pressure on the brakes; he knew he was committed and would jus
have to pray for the best.

The headlights revealed the side of the road as the night-drenche
landscape swung past him in a slow, belly-flipping glide. The cem
etery fence flickered by like the rough frames of an old-time movie
Tombstones jiggled and jerked with the illusion of motion, and the
they spun out of sight. A loud crash filled Frank's ears as the driver'
door folded inward. Glass exploded into his face like a shower o
diamonds. There was a loud *thump*, but Frank wasn't sure if it wa
the sound of Norton's body hitting the backseat floor, or the un
derside of the cruiser as it dove into the gully. He was suddenl
spinning upward, vaguely realizing that the car had flipped in th
gully and was rolling over. His ears and mind filled with the shat
tering sounds of glass breaking and metal twisting out of shape
When his head slammed against the steering wheel, his vision fille
with bright streaks of light that expanded rapidly and then wer
sucked back down into darkness. He wasn't aware of it when th
car door flung open and spilled him onto the shoulder of the road
where he lay in a heap, not more than twenty feet from the totale
cruiser.

4.

. . . "Mommy! . . . No!"

The voice came to Elizabeth from the darkness, wavering in an
out like a distant radio signal gaining and losing strength. Elizabet
thought crazily of the voice she had heard coming from Eldon Cody'
tape recorder, only now it seemed to be coming from several di
rections at once.

"Help . . . Mommy . . ."

Every muscle and tendon in Elizabeth's neck felt as if they wer
ripping as she turned to look behind her. She could still feel th
presence of Graydon, standing close behind her like a solid wall
preventing her escape; but from the darkness beyond him, the whirl
ing red flaming figures had thinned out, leaving behind only pul
sating blackness as deep and quiet as starless space. But inside tha
blackness, Elizabeth saw something—a faint motion, a glistening

blue light that darted in and out of focus like the light of a lighthouse, pulsating in thick fog.

"*. . . Don't . . . do . . . it . . .*"

The voice swelled, gaining strength, but then just as quickly it faded, leaving behind the impression of having been . . . nothing more than the roaring wind overhead.

"Do it *now*, Elizabeth!" Graydon said. His voice was low and intense; it forced her to look back at her hands and the blade that was burrowing into her chest. "Do what *I* tell you! Do what *he* commands!"

The stinging pain centered above her heart radiated outward, spreading through her shoulders and down into her belly. A warm, gushing rush flowed over her stomach, and Elizabeth wondered with an unnerving detachment if this was her panic spreading through her, riding a cresting wave of adrenaline . . . or if it was her blood, flowing from the self-inflicted wound? The burning memory of the nightmare with Graydon, transformed into a beast, chewing open her stomach, spilling out her guts, rose unbidden in her mind.

From the top of Caroline's tombstone, the demon inhaled with a roar and swelled even larger into the night sky until it towered up against the stars like an ungodly statue brought to life. The beast's breath bellowed rapidly in and out, slamming swirling eddies of wind into Elizabeth's face. Everything in front of her was drenched with bright orange light, like a raging fire, as hammering blasts of heat washed over her.

"*. . . Mommy . . .*" wailed the glass-fragile voice from the darkness behind her. "*Don't . . . Don't do it!*"

The knife sank deeper, slicing cleanly, almost painlessly now, through veins and muscle until it met the hard resistance of bone. The blade twisted in her hand as though it had a will of its own and was seeking the space between her ribs. No matter how much she struggled to resist the inwardly pulling blade, it moved slowly, unrelentingly deeper.

"First *her*! . . . And now *you*!" the demon roared, filling the night with hollow, booming laughter. "Your miserable soul is *mine* now! *Forever!*"

Huge hands and hooked talons reached for her from the darkness, but they didn't cross the lines of the pentagram. Elizabeth knew now, that all along Graydon had planned for her to die this way as a sacrifice to the demon. But maybe, in spite of his plans, the pentagram actually was protecting her. This thought gave her the faintest hope to resist, even as the pain in her chest spiraled up the scale and drilled into her brain.

Elizabeth's throat made soft grunting sounds as she pushed back against the pull of her own arms directing the blade which sought her heart. In frozen moments of horror, she imagined how it was going to look when her lifeless body was discovered, slumped over her daughter's grave; Graydon would disappear, and the entire incident would be written off as a descent into black magic, madness, and suicide resulting from her despondency over her daughter's death. Above the flood of questions as to how all of this had come about, though, there was one commanding question . . .

Why? Why did Graydon do this to me?

Sweat and tears streamed down her face as she twisted her head to one side, trying to catch a glimpse of Graydon standing behind her. She could feel his cold, evil presence, but all she could see of him was a red-infused blur.

"*Mommy! . . . I want to help you, Mommy!*" the faint voice wailed from the darkness.

Elizabeth had the mind-numbing realization that this was not some other demon, calling to her from the darkness of Hell, luring her to destroy herself. No! This had to be, in fact, the soul of her dead daughter, struggling to manifest itself in the physical world to *warn* her . . . to *help* her.

"Car-o-line!" Elizabeth gasped, wincing with pain.

She felt Graydon tense when she called out her daughter's name. His dark presence urged her to plunge the knife deeper and deeper toward her heart even as the hope that Caroline was untouched by such supernatural evil as this demon or human evil such as Rolanic Graydon gave her hope to live and strength to resist. Rippling pain crashed through her, both from the knife point and from the effort she was making to resist it.

"*Mommy! . . .*" the voice called, sounding hopelessly feeble against the ear-shattering bellows of the beast. "*I can help you, Mommy! . . .*"

"You . . . lousy, rotten . . . son of a . . . *bitch*!" Elizabeth snarled as she glared over her shoulder at Graydon. "Why? Why are you doing this?"

Graydon leered over her shoulder at her, his face resolving in her vision. His mouth split into a wide grin even as his eyes reflected his own stark terror of the demon perched on the tombstone, clawing out of the darkness at them.

"Because of what you did to my life," Graydon said. His voice was low and raspy, fighting for control. "Because of what happened that night your daughter died! *You* and you *alone* killed my nephew, and with your suicide—your *sacrifice* now—I'll get what I've wanted for the past year and a half!"

"What—? You're crazy!" Elizabeth stammered. She barely understood his words. She thought he was still muttering nonsense, but then it hit her. "Do you mean—?"

"That's right," Graydon said. "The man driving the snowplow, the man who ran into your stranded car and died the same night your precious little Caroline died was my nephew, *my* nephew, Sam Healy! You never once spent a second of thought on the other person who died that night!"

"I . . . never knew," Elizabeth said, her voice breaking.

Graydon sneered. "For the past year and a half, I've been waiting for this! I've been carefully sowing the seeds of my revenge. When you moved back to Bristol Mills, I couldn't *believe* it! And then, what luck that your therapist in New Hampshire actually referred you to me. To *me*! But it wasn't just luck or chance. Oh, no! I *planned* it! I *worked* for it! I made vows and I performed certain rituals to make absolutely *certain* that it would all work out this way."

His laughter rose, a high, cruel note that pierced Elizabeth's ears.

"I used your uncle's hand—the Hand of Glory! With it, I got what I needed from Caroline—"

Elizabeth made a raw, tearing sound in the back of her throat.

"Oh, yes! Yes! I came out here to the cemetery one night and used the Hand of Glory to raise the spirit of your daughter. I spoke with her and got what information I needed to make sure I could control you. Unfortunately, I was interrupted by the police. But anyway, the Hand of Glory isn't powerful enough to bring the dead

back to life. Oh, no!'' Graydon trembled wildly with excitement
"No, for that, I need a *human* sacrifice! I need the *blood* and *life*
of someone who truly believes. So now you will die—by your own
hand! And with that, I'll get what I bargained my soul for. *I'll get
my nephew back from the dead!*''

"Mommy! . . . No!''

"You . . . can't . . . !'' Elizabeth muttered. She twisted to her
left, but even as she did, the knife sank deeper into her chest. Pain,
searing like fire, zinged along her nerves. From the darkness behind
her, she clearly saw the glowing blue figure shimmering, resolving
into focus and approaching her, drifting over the ground like a wisp
of smoke. In disbelief and horror, she saw her dead daughter reaching out toward her, her arms outstretched as though grasping for
someone who had fallen overboard, reaching . . . reaching with
hands as insubstantial as fog.

Graydon followed Elizabeth's gaze, and his eyes widened with
surprise when he saw Caroline's ghost drifting toward them. His
lips peeled back in a vicious snarl.

"No! She can't help you now!'' he shouted. "She's too late!
She's too weak to resist *us!*''

Even as he said that, the gauzy blue figure of the young girl
slipped out of the black night, drifting without a trace of resistance
within the pentagram design. Elizabeth recoiled as she felt chill
tendrils of fingers brush against her hands and arms and then, with
a strength that shocked her, grab her wrists and start to pull back.
The effort aided Elizabeth's own efforts to draw the knife away
from her chest, and relief flooded her when she looked down and
saw the blade pulling from the sheath of her chest.

"*No!*'' Graydon wailed. "I won't allow it!'' He swung around
in front of Elizabeth and leaned forward, trying to drive the blade
back into her chest. He swung out wildly in an attempt to push the
ghostly figure aside, but his hands passed through Caroline's shape
as easily as if she were made of shimmering light.

From the gravestone, the demon reared back its head and let loose
a shrill screech of rage. Flames flashed from its eyes, and searing
waves of heat withered the grass all around the tombstone, setting
it on fire. But the flames only licked up to the white line of the

pentagram design; there they stopped and winked out, as though they were nothing more than brightly burning candles being blown out on a birthday cake.

"I *will* have my revenge!" Graydon sputtered; but even as he did, the blue figure of Caroline, passing clear through him, pulled back hard on her mother's hands. The knife continued to withdraw but still wasn't clear of the wound it was making when, suddenly, the night crashed with three sharp, echoing roars. For a numbed instant, Elizabeth thought the demon's rage had intensified. Only dimly was she aware of the searing pain in her wrist. She looked in horror and saw that her hand just below her thumb was nothing more than a pulpy wreck. After a frozen moment, blood began to run freely from the wound and down her arm.

"Stop!" a voice shouted from the darkness.

Elizabeth cringed when the concussion of two more explosions filled the night. She heard a wet-sounding *thunk-thunk*, and watched in horror as Graydon's face exploded into a bright red splash. He spun around in a lazy half-circle and then crumpled in slow motion to the ground. Between Elizabeth and Graydon, the glowing blue figure of Caroline vanished with a slow, rippling fade. With a diminishing wail of anguish, the demon on Caroline's tombstone sucked back into the night and was gone, leaving behind a thick sulfurous odor.

The sudden release of pressure sent the blade spinning end over end into the darkness. A watery weakness swept through Elizabeth's body. She struggled to stay standing, even though she had no sensation of her legs supporting her. The whole world around her rocked and pitched violently back and forth.

Struggling to focus, she looked into the cold, smoky night. The face she saw moving rapidly toward her from the darkness was ashen white. Thick gouts of blood ran in tattered ribbons down over its eyes and cheeks. Its mouth was open, and as it came closer to her, the vision spoke, but Elizabeth could make no sense of its words. Thinking she was still falling forward into the open earth and onto her daughter's coffin, she imagined she was a diver, arching smoothly into still, black water. Distantly, she heard the soft *thump* of impact as her head hit the ground, but then she was lost in total darkness. Her last thought before she was sucked down into darkness was . . .

It's another demon from Hell, coming to take my soul!

5.

"Oh, my God! Elizabeth! *No!*" Frank shouted as he staggered up the slope of the cemetery hill. He didn't have the time to process, much less believe, what he was seeing. The night sky at the top of the hill flickered wildly with bright lights that made it difficult to see exactly what was going on, but it sure as hell looked as though Roland Graydon was struggling with Elizabeth, trying to stab her with a wicked-looking knife. On reflex, Frank drew his revolver, crouched, took careful aim, and cracked off five quick shots. He felt only mild satisfaction through his fear when he saw Graydon's body jerk violently and then drop to the ground.

Gritting his teeth against his pain, he dashed the rest of the way just in time to see Elizabeth crumple face-first onto the ground. An inky splotch of blood blossomed on the ground beneath her chest. Frank rolled her over onto her back and watched as the blood saturated the thin fabric of her jacket. He leaned over her, ripped open her blouse, and inspected her wounds. Her body spasmed violently as nerves fired and twisted her overstrained muscles into impossible contortions.

"Oh Jesus! Oh *Jesus!*" Frank muttered as he stared at the slice the knife had made. Blood pumped like thick oil out onto the ground. Frank hurriedly untucked his shirt, ripped off a piece of cloth, and pressed it tightly against the wound.

"Come on!" he murmured, rocking back and forth on his knees, cradling Elizabeth's body as if she were a baby. "Come on, Elizabeth! Don't lose this one!"

For a long time—Frank had no idea how long—he sat there on the grass, applying pressure to stop the steady flow of blood. Eventually he succeeded, and, not long after that, he saw Elizabeth's eyelids flicker. Her breathing, which had been rattling and faint, now seemed stronger.

"You wait right here, babe," he whispered, as he eased her fla on the ground and stood up. "I've just got to go back to the cruiser and put in a call for some help. Don't worry. I'll be right back."

With that, he raced down the hill and out of the cemetery to where his smashed cruiser lay on its roof in the ditch. Reaching in through the smashed windshield, he fished around blindly until his fingers grasped the radio microphone. Praying it would still work, he stood up shakily and pressed the call button. Relief flooded him when the dispatcher at the station answered him.

"Oh, Christ," he muttered as black waves of dizziness brought him to his knees in the shattered glass and metal. "Oh Jesus, God—thank you . . . thank you!"

"Is this some kind of joke?" the dispatcher said.

Rubbing his blood-smeared hands over his face to clear his mind, Frank took a deep breath and, just before passing out, mumbled, "Better get an ambulance out to Oak Grove . . . There's been some—" Before he could say the word *trouble*, he collapsed backward onto the ground.

6.

Pain was all she knew even before she became aware. Centered in her chest, it seared along her nerves, steadily intensifying rather than deadening.

—Pain!

. . . Like jagged, throbbing currents of electricity. Every inch of her body was bathed in intense pain. She was twisted and skinned and viciously jabbed by pain from every direction at once.

—Pain!

. . . Like a cold voice from the dark, calling her, luring her to come to it, to follow it down into a flaming red Pit that only promised more pain . . . sharper pain.

—Pain!

. . . Like flat sheets of honed razors slicing through her body, sectioning it into a multitude of parts that all writhed in agony; pain that reached into the very center of her soul.

—Pain as she had never known pain before . . .

. . . directionless and without end.

TWENTY
Healing

1.

The sunlight slanting through the open slats of the Levolor blinds turned everything fuzzy-edged and glistening. Objects in the room shifted and transformed with a rubbery, hallucinatory wobble. The edges of the window sill jiggled with points of white and yellow flame. The air in the room had a deep-water density to it, and sounds coming from somewhere—the clanging of metal on metal, the scuff of feet passing over the floor, the rustle of starched cloth—rippled the air with their passing wake. The entire room sparkled with energy.

With a stinging intake of breath that pierced her chest like the jab of a steel-tipped lance, Elizabeth tried to move but found even the slightest motion restricted. She opened her eyes to mere slits to allow in just a fraction of the hurtful yellow light and saw—and recognized—that she was in some type of institutional bed. Her view of the window was hazy, but through thick layers of shifting lights, she thought she saw metal bars on the windows. With an unvoiced groan, she released the useless muscle tension in her body and let her mind slip back down . . .

. . . down . . .

. . . down into a pain-filled blackness, and then deeper, where even the pain couldn't reach.

Oh, my God! she thought, struggling futilely against wave after wave of dizziness and panic. *They've locked me up after all! I'm in the mental ward!*

But at least there's no more pain down here, she thought, as sludgy, black bubbles popped in her mind and she sank even deeper into herself. From far away she heard voices, but she couldn't tell if they were outside or inside her head. She tried to understand what they were saying, but everything was incomprehensible, like the backward Latin Graydon had recited during the necromantic ceremony.

Had that been real? Had any of that been real? Or was I out of my mind all along, and I imagined every bit of it? she wondered. The deeper she went, the less frantic she became as she drifted through a detached calm, falling backward . . . down . . . and down . . .

Two—maybe three—different voices ping-ponged in conversation, but none of it made any sense until she heard a voice she definitely recognized: her mother's.

". . . her father and I have no idea what she was doing out there."

". . . Strange design they drew over her daughter's grave . . ."

". . . No idea that she even *thought* about such nonsense . . ."

Elizabeth stirred, but knowing her body was strapped to the bed, she didn't renew the struggle. Instead, she forced her awareness up to the surface, passing through the pain until she returned to the shimmering light in the hospital room.

". . . Not even sure she can hear us," one of the other voices said.

". . . How long this will go on . . ."

". . . Which way it's going to go . . ."

". . . No way of knowing at this point . . ."

Elizabeth's mind jumped with the sudden understanding that these people were discussing her. Her brain sent out a message to her hand to rise, even if it was only a small amount just to signal that she could not only hear, but also understand; but her hand was frozen in place, locked to her side as though paralyzed.

". . . The trauma she's suffered has been intense, and it's natural that her body would shut down like this . . ."

". . . If only to help process the shock . . ."

". . . But she will be all right . . . eventually? . . ."

Again, Elizabeth recognized her mother's voice and the desperation that colored it. Like tatters of fast-moving storm clouds, tangled emotions and thoughts flittered through her. She redoubled her efforts to move, to produce just a twitch of a finger or a flicker of an eyelid, but no part of her body would obey the commands of her brain. *Aren't my eyes open*? she screamed inside her mind. Not even the faintest ripple of sound would come from her throat. Her desperation rose higher until she could practically hear it—a high-pitched whine that bordered on the edge of awareness.

She watched, her heart wrung with sadness, as tears coursed down her mother's face. And then another realization hit her, hard, like an oncoming car. Her mother was dressed in black, and her father had on the suit and coat he only wore on two different occasions: weddings and funerals.

". . . pity she had to die," her mother was saying, her voice drifting to Elizabeth's awareness through her flood of sadness and panic.

". . . better not to see her this way, after all," her father said. Even he, with his stiff posture and firm-set mouth, seemed about to break down into tears. The sides of his face looked sallow and thin, as though he had been struggling with sadness for centuries.

Do they think I'm dead? Am I laid out in my coffin at the funeral home? Is that why I can't move? Elizabeth wondered. Her brain was spinning faster and faster into a whirlwind of terror. Every fiber of her being willed her throat to open and scream the words: *But I'm not dead! . . . See! I'm not!*

". . . she's at peace now . . ."

". . . with her loved ones . . ."

I'm not dead! Elizabeth's mind wailed, but as she looked from one saddened face to another, a warm, churning sensation of calm spread through her stomach. There was suddenly no fear in the idea that she might be dead—just an overwhelming sadness that she couldn't see or talk to her mother and father to say one last good-bye . . . *Look at me! I'm not dead*! she wanted to shout. *I'm still alive! Look at me!*

But no amount of frantic effort or concentrated calmness would produce even the slightest stirring of sound in her throat.

Where's Aunt Junia? Elizabeth thought. She could understand why Aunt Elspeth wasn't here, it being so difficult for her to get about, but why wasn't Junia here to see her off? Especially if she was dying . . . or already dead! Junia had gotten the whole thing started by encouraging her to see those people. She should be here!

Suddenly, Elizabeth felt a warm rush travel down her legs from her belly. It reminded her of when she had been pregnant with Caroline, the night her water broke as a prelude to delivery. She knew she wasn't pregnant, so her first thought was that it was the warm flow of blood rushing through her body and healing her. She experienced a tingle of fear when she recalled the nightmare of Graydon transforming into a wolf as he feasted on her innards. An arctic wind swept through her when she remembered . . .

Had it all been a dream?

. . . the demon perching on Caroline's tombstone and saying: "Your soul is *mine* now! *Forever*! . . . First *her*, and now *you*!"

Elizabeth's thoughts were suddenly interrupted by a loud *thump* sound. She was surprised to see that none of the other people in the room looked over to the door when it slammed open and a dark figure walked in and came over to the bed. At first, Elizabeth thought this must be a hospital orderly, coming in to take her physical remains away; but then she noticed how the "orderly" was dressed.

No one works in a hospital dressed like *that*! Elizabeth thought.

The person, an old woman, was wearing a tattered dress and a long woolen sweater. Moth holes peppered the sleeves. Her gray hair hung in loose snarls down to her shoulders. Her wrinkled face was shrouded and, even in the direct light, had a curious shadow cast across it. In her left hand she was carrying a large shopping bag.

"Hey, Elizabeth—I've come to see yah," the old woman crooned, leaning over the bed and looking for all the world like the wicked witch in *Snow White*.

Spears of terror shot through Elizabeth's mind, and she saw with horror that her left hand lying limply on the sheets, actually twitched. None of the people gathered around the bed seemed to notice the old woman, much less the motion Elizabeth had made. She looked up, wishing frantically that she could say something—*anything*—

to alert the people to this woman, who stood there unseen among them.

The old woman leaned closer to Elizabeth's face. In her fevered imagination, Elizabeth could feel the cold drafts of the woman's breath washing like clammy water over her face. The crone reeked of the putrid rot of the grave.

This can't be happening! Elizabeth thought. *I'm already dead!*

The sound of paper rustling crackled like fire as the old woman lifted up her shopping bag and rested it on the bed railing.

"I brought a little somethin' for yah," she said, smiling widely and exposing a mouth that was filled with rotting and blackened teeth. She hissed, "Wanna *see* what I've got here in my bag for yah?"

Elizabeth knew she had no control over herself, but she violently willed herself to shake her head back and forth in denial. She could feel each vertebra crunch as she tried to move her neck.

"*Wanna see?*" the old lady wheezed.

Elizabeth's mind roared with the echoing sound of the crone's ancient voice. With just a slight push, she could imagine the voice suddenly dropping down low and hollow, booming with evil laughter, like the voice of the demon she had seen—*imagined*!—crouching on Caroline's tombstone. At any instant, she expected to see the frail body of the old woman tremble and swell as the wrinkled, liver-spotted skin peeled away, exposing the black scaly body of the demon. It would expand to fill the entire hospital room. Muscular, black arms and hooked talons would reach for her, and a leering, fang-filled smile would open to devour her.

"*Your soul is mine, now! Forever!*"

Elizabeth willed every ounce of mental energy into moving her head, if only to deny, right up to the end, that this creature might steal her soul and carry it to the flames of Hell.

The old crone smiled and laughed softly as she opened the top of the bag. After peering down into it for an instant, she scowled deeply as she reclosed the top. Leaning close to Elizabeth's immobile face, she snarled wickedly, "I'll show yah if yah want to see!" Her voice rose up on a teasing, tempting note. "Are you *sure* you don't wanna see?"

If the scream that was building up inside her mind ever found its

cape, Elizabeth was positive it would shatter the hospital-room
indow. She watched in stark, mounting horror as the old woman
ened the bag again and tilted it down toward her fear-widened
es.

"Come on, Elizabeth . . . Have a little peek," the woman said
a thin, wheedling voice.

Elizabeth tried to look away, but the open mouth of the shopping
ag slid down to the side of the bed with a slick, easy glide. Her
es were drawn in horrid fascination to the dark opening.

"See what I have?" the old lady crooned. "Look . . . Look
side here."

Elizabeth felt a quick, jerking pulse and a burning pressure in her
est as she stared into the bag.

"See . . . ? I have *all* of your fears in here!"

Elizabeth looked . . . and saw. The woman suddenly pulled her
nds back, and the shopping bag disappeared with a faint *poof*. It
ft behind a squiggling trail of smoke which quickly disappeared.
The crone smiled and said, "All gone."

Elizabeth's eyes snapped open, and she found herself staring up
her mother, her father and two doctors.

"Well, what do you know—she's coming to," one of the doctors
id, his voice tinged with excitement.

Elizabeth's eyelids flickered as she tried to resist the hurtful bright-
ss of the room. Her lips twitched into a faint smile. Then, before
nyone could respond, she drifted back to a deeper, more restful
eep.

From far away, she heard her mother's voice say, "Oh, my God!
hank you, Lord!"

2.

The next time Elizabeth opened her eyes, it didn't hurt half as
uch to look around. The Levolor blinds were closed, and the
verhead light was dimmed way down. She shifted in an attempt
sit up, but still felt the straps that held both of her arms and her
hest down tightly to the mattress. A fresh wave of panic swelled
side her as she struggled to piece together the confused and ter-
fying fragments of memories and dreams that whirled in her brain.

Am I in a hospital or the mental ward? she wondered. *Why a I strapped down to the bed? Why can't I even feel my legs?*

What's happened to me? Where are my mother and father? Whe are the doctors? Where's the old woman who wants to show n that she has nothing—absolutely nothing in her shopping bag?

Jagged bolts of pain lanced through her neck and head, but Eli abeth struggled to raise her head from the pillow and look arour the room. She gasped when she saw a person, sprawled motionless in the chair by the window. In the dim light, she could make o none of the features, but she had the unnerving feeling it might her old friend, the crone . . . or maybe it was herself . . .

"Wanna see what I've got?"

"I have all your fears in here!"

The old lady's voice rang in Elizabeth's memory, sending wave of chills racing up her arms and shoulders.

Yes! she thought, sucking in a deep breath and feeling an excite tingle throughout her body! *I'm alive!*

Her throat made a deep, strangling sound as her legs twitche and rustled loudly on the crisp sheets. In the silence of the hospit room, the noise was like an avalanche crashing down a mountain side, but the silent shape in the chair by the window didn't stir.

Looking down the length of her bed at the person in her roon Elizabeth tried to detect any sign of life. The figure was covere by a sheet, which added to the motionless, amorphous image. Th head was turned to one side, looking away from her, so all sh could see were strands of gray hair and the smooth curve of th cheek. The figure's shoulders looked frail, almost girl-like, an Elizabeth had the momentarily scary thought that when the figur stirred, she would see Caroline, her daughter. Perhaps, after al she had come to lead her mother over to the "other side."

Again, Elizabeth tried to form words in her throat, but the dr burning made it all but impossible. When she licked her lips, he tongue felt as if it were coated with sand. The dry feeling only g worse. Finally, her head dropped back onto the pillow, and she l her breath out in a long, slow whistle. She tensed when she clearl heard the figure in the chair shift. There was a hissing sound as th sheet slid to the floor.

". . . Water," Elizabeth rasped, unable to raise her head a secon time. She sensed rather than saw the figure as it approached the side of the bed. Even though her chest was burning with pain, she sucked in a lungful of air and waited . . . waited to look up and see . . .

Who?

"Elizabeth . . . Dear, you're awake."

The soothing sound of Aunt Junia's voice caressed Elizabeth's ears. Her mounting panic instantly uncoiled as she stared up in disbelief at her aunt, who was leaning over the bed railing and smiling at her. Elizabeth's first thought was that this, too, was a dream, and that, before she could smile back, Aunt Junia's face would dissolve into the demon's leering grin, which would roar and blast her to nothingness.

"Did you say you wanted a drink of water?" Junia asked in a soft, kindly voice.

Elizabeth nodded, her eyes flicking back and forth, unable to focus as Junia turned away from the bed and disappeared from view for a moment. When she returned, her face still hadn't shifted into that of a demon or of an ancient woman; it was still Aunt Junia, and she was holding a glass with a flexible straw up to Elizabeth's mouth.

Elizabeth sipped, and her mind and body exploded with relief when she felt water—*real, honest-to-God, cold, fresh water!*—slide into her mouth and roll down the back of her parched throat. She sucked on the straw eagerly, but Junia pulled it away and said, "Ut-ut. The doctor said you shouldn't have too much at first."

The corners of Elizabeth's mouth twitched into what she thought was a smile—or at least something close to it.

"Thanks," she said, surprised at how twisted and strange her voice sounded to her own ears.

"That's why I'm here, dear," Junia said as she replaced the cup onto the stand beside the bed.

"Where . . . is here?" Elizabeth said. She couldn't push aside the rush of fear that she had been committed to the mental hospital, that she was strapped to the bed so she couldn't get away.

Junia looked at her with a warming smile and said softly, "Why, you're in the hospital, Maine Med., of course. You were quite badly injured."

"Am I . . . Is this P-6?" Elizabeth asked.

Junia's face clouded and she shook her head. "P-6? I don't know what P-6 is."

"The psycho ward," Elizabeth said. "Am I in the psycho ward?" Already her throat was closing up; it felt as though it were the bottom of an hour glass, and the hour was over.

Junia laughed softly and shook her head. "Why of course you aren't!"

"Why am I . . . strapped down, then?" Elizabeth said. She wanted to ask for another drink of water but was afraid she would start screaming as soon as she opened her mouth. Before anything else, she had to have answers to certain questions.

"Why, because of your injuries, of course," Junia said. "Even with medication, since you began to regain consciousness, you've been thrashing about quite a bit. When Frank Melrose found you in the cemetery, before he—well, before everything else happened, that doctor, Roland Graydon, had already stabbed you in the chest with that knife of his. It was a pretty serious wound on top of the gunshot wound."

"Gunshot . . . ? Who . . . shot me? I—I think I remember seeing Frank . . . Melrose. He was there, too?"

"He was," Junia said. "He shot you in the hand . . . by mistake, of course. But he was hurt as well. He had a quite serious accident. He was trying to stop Doctor Graydon from doing . . . what he was doing."

Trying to kill me! Elizabeth thought, with a cold dash of fear. *He wanted to kill me and make it look like a suicide!*

She shivered, recalling her discussion about her suicide attempt during one session with Graydon. She realized—now—that he had used everything . . . absolutely *everything* she had revealed to him against her—all of her grief and guilt and fears about Caroline's death. All of it! She remembered him saying something that night in the cemetery about how he had plotted and planned . . .

"I made vows and performed certain rituals to make certain!"

. . . his revenge because he blamed *her* for the death of his nephew that night! It stunned her that he would use his position as her doctor to turn it all against her.

"He . . . Graydon—?" Elizabeth said.

More vivid but disconnected fragments of that night filled her mind. The pentagram drawn with luminous white powder over Caroline's grave—the black shape with claws and fangs she had seen sitting on Caroline's tombstone—the insubstantial blue figure of her dead daughter that had appeared and struggled with her to force the knife away from her chest—the series of explosions that had blown Graydon's face into tangled, red meat.

How long ago was that? she wondered, as worries about her sanity intensified. *How long have I been here?*

"Is Graydon . . . ?"

Before she could finish her question, Junia nodded. "Yes. Roland Graydon is dead." She glanced ceilingward before continuing. "I don't know how much of this I should be telling you. I mean, I don't want to say anything that will work against your healing."

Elizabeth gritted her teeth as a flicker of pain blossomed in her chest. "The truth . . . is always . . . healing," she said, even as she thought about how many times over the past year and a half she had told little "untruths," thinking she could protect herself and the people she loved from painful realities.

"Well then," Junia said, shrugging, "the truth is, nobody's really sure what was going on there that night. Roland Graydon is dead. You've just come out of a coma. And Frank Melrose, the only other person nearby that night, wasn't exactly clear about *what* he saw happening. He had sustained a quite serious head injury."

"Is he . . . all right?" Elizabeth asked. Another memory from that night stirred, one of Frank Melrose, his face smeared by thick gouts of streaming blood, running toward her from the darkness. She recalled hearing the sound of his revolver punching the night.

"He's fine . . . he's just fine," Junia said. "As a matter of fact, he's been here to visit you several times since you were admitted."

"How long . . . How long has it been?"

Junia's eyes flicked up at the ceiling again; but before she said anything, she picked up the glass of water and held the straw to Elizabeth's lips. Elizabeth sucked some more water into her mouth, letting it sit there for a moment before swallowing it. The pain in her chest intensified, but she had to have an answer. Licking her lips, she rephrased her question, just in case Junia hadn't understood her.

"How long have I been unconscious?"

"It's been . . . almost two weeks," Junia replied softly.

Elizabeth heard the words like a rapid series of explosions inside her head. "Two weeks . . . ?"

Junia nodded as she trailed her fingers soothingly across Elizabeth's forehead. "Yes . . . that long."

"I—I've been having this really weird dream," Elizabeth said. Her voice was a gravelly growl as she allowed the memory to surface of the old woman, leaning over the bed railing with her bag . . .

"Wanna see what I have for yah?"

"It's been . . . quite a strain . . . for a lot of people," Junia replied, nodding. "Doug's driven out from New Hampshire several times to see you."

The mere mention of her ex-husband's name made the ripple of pain in Elizabeth's chest increase. She wanted to say something about not wanting—ever!—to see Doug again, and if she was ever asleep for Junia or the hospital staff to keep him out; but then she thought better of it and remained silent.

"So why are you here?" Elizabeth asked, craning her neck again to look at the window. "Who's staying with Aunt Elspeth?" She couldn't be sure, but through the slats, it looked as though the sky was brightening. Could it really be approaching dawn? She supposed so. Anything was possible if it had, in fact, been two weeks since that terrifying night in the cemetery.

Junia's eyes clouded over. Tears formed and ran down her cheeks. "I'm sorry to have to tell you this, but Aunt Elspeth . . . passed away. Her funeral was yesterday afternoon," she said softly.

"Oh, my God," Elizabeth said. "She . . . died?"

Junia nodded solemnly, and Elizabeth could feel her own eyes misting up.

It wasn't just Elspeth's death that shocked Elizabeth, though now—for the first time—she realized why in her nightmares the old crone looked so frighteningly familiar. In one of her sessions with Graydon, he had suggested that the woman might possibly be Elizabeth's projection of herself, representing things about herself she was trying to hide from herself. It hadn't been that at all, Elizabeth realized. It was her namesake, her Aunt Elspeth, whose face she had vaguely recognized beneath the shabby clothing, the grimy features, and the unkempt hair of the woman from her nightmares.

Had that really been Aunt Elspeth, standing unseen beside Elizabeth's hospital bed yesterday? The day of her funeral, had Elspeth come to visit Elizabeth one last time, to show her that all of her fears were in the shopping bag . . . and then reveal that there was nothing there? It *must* have been Elspeth! Elizabeth remembered hearing both her mother and father talking about what a pity it was that someone had died; she realized now that they had been speaking about her aunt, not her!

And she came here, to the hospital, to help me . . . to show me that, even after everything I saw or think I saw in the cemetery that night, that all of my fears are as real and as solid as what I saw in her shopping bag . . .

Nothing!

"All gone!"

"I'm . . . so sorry," Elizabeth said, her eyes glistening as she looked at her aunt and read the deep pain in Junia's eyes. "I'll miss her . . . too." She vowed, even then, that once she was out of the hospital—and she knew she would leave; oh, yes, she was going to live!—she would use everything she had learned about loss and suffering to help Junia accept and cope with her recent grief, which was just as real and deep as what Elizabeth felt for Caroline.

"Frank's been by to check in on you just about every day, too," Junia said.

"I remember seeing him . . . that night . . . at the cemetery, with his . . . his face all bloody," Elizabeth said. She tried to shift in bed to get more comfortable, but the straps restrained her.

Junia placed a reassuring hand on Elizabeth's shoulder and eased her back down, forcing her to relax. "He said he'd like to stop by and see you, once you were feeling up to it."

Elizabeth had to blink her eyes rapidly as they flooded with tears. "I—I think I'd like that," she said softly.

"I told you he was injured when his car rolled over," Junia said. "He had some quite serious cuts on his face, but he's just fine now." She paused a moment, then added. "He's not working for the police anymore, though."

Elizabeth raised her eyebrows in surprise.

"He resigned as soon as he was released from the hospital. You see, there was quite a bit more involved that night than you realize," Junia said, lowering her voice again. "Roland Graydon died, sure enough, but apparently he had help doing those horrible things he'd been doing. You must know Frank's partner, Brad Norton."

Elizabeth nodded numbly as bitter guilt rose up inside her. She realized that, even if she hadn't been committed to the psycho ward, she almost deserved it for going along with Graydon's suggestions right from the beginning. Why had she done that? Or, more seriously, how had she let herself be led along so willingly and so blindly? Even if she had *never* suspected his plot to revenge himself on her for his nephew's death, she had suspected he was involved in the disinterment of her Uncle Jonathan, the murder of Barney Fraser, and the fire that had killed Henry Bishop. Just the thought that she had actually believed Graydon could communicate with her dead daughter was more than unsettling. It was ludicrous!

So if I'm not in P-6 yet, I still have a better than average shot at making it there, she thought with sour humor.

But if what she had experienced was impossible, how could she account for what she *had* seen that night in Oak Grove Cemetery? No matter what else, she most definitely had seen . . . something out of the ordinary, something that couldn't be casually dismissed as illusion or hallucination. Graydon's ceremony had raised something that night! Maybe Graydon had planned all along to raise the demon to push her—finally—over the brink. Or maybe he had succeeded in conjuring up far more than he had ever thought or believed possible. The demon she had seen—Yes! It had been as real, as solid as the stone that marked Caroline's grave! While at first it had assumed the shape of Caroline, it had been—truly—a dark and evil creature from Hell, just as surely as there had been something else—something airy and blue, emanating a purity and goodness that had helped Elizabeth in her struggle to avoid the killing blade of the knife.

"Well, apparently Brad Norton was helping Roland Graydon all along," Junia continued. "He's been charged with attempted murder, conspiracy to commit murder, and a whole host of other crimes. They think Graydon set the fire that killed Henry Bishop, so I don't think he's being tried for that. At least, not yet." Junia's expression faltered before she added, "They figure he and Graydon were the ones who disturbed Jonathan's and Caroline's graves, but Frank also mentioned that Norton said something about Graydon blackmailing Barney Fraser to do the job. Whatever! Hey—you're looking a little peaked, and here I am, gabbing your ear off."

"No—I'm all right," Elizabeth said, although the weakening quaver in her voice revealed the truth. "But—can I tell you one thing, Aunt Junia?"

Junia's mouth set into a firm, unsmiling line. "Of course you can, Elizabeth. You can tell me *anything*."

"That night, out there in the cemetery," Elizabeth said, swallowing with difficulty. "I don't know for sure what happened and what didn't. I'll probably never know; but one thing—I'm honest-to-God positive I *did* see Caroline! When . . . I don't know, whatever the hell was going on, I heard her calling to me." She shivered with the memory, her eyes widening with fright. "I kept hearing a voice crying *Help Mommy!* All along, I thought *she* needed help . . . you know, from the accident and the fire. Now—I'm not so sure. I think she might have been trying to tell me she could help *me*! But, whatever—I *know* this much! I saw her there! She came to me out of the darkness and she . . . She *did* help me!"

Junia's expression widened into a broad smile. She patted the back of Elizabeth's hand and said mildly, "You know, I'm not in the least bit surprised. Ever since you came back home, I've had this . . . this feeling that Caroline was with you, if you know what I mean."

An oily wave of fear crested inside Elizabeth. She felt it rise, break, and then begin to pull back in a rush as it dissolved into nothingness.

"I have all your fears in here!"

"I think I *do* know what you mean," Elizabeth said softly. "I mean, I always felt her here in my heart, but—" She tried to tap herself on the chest but couldn't, so instead she simply shook her head, even though it sent a crackling pulse of pain up the back of her head. "I don't know. I couldn't get rid of this feeling that she was always somewhere nearby, always just out of sight, but trying her damnedest to reach out to me."

"Look, dear," Junia said cheerfully. "The sun's coming up. You need to rest instead of listening to me gab all morning."

"No," Elizabeth said. She raised her head as best she could and craned her neck to look at the brightening bars between the Levolor blinds. Her body trembled with the effort of trying to sit up. "I like to see the dawn. Open up the shades, would you please?"

Junia nodded and walked over to the window, brushing away with her foot the sheet that had covered her while she slept in the chair. Her hand shook with the palsy of age as she pulled the rope to raise the blinds. Elizabeth saw the bright orange disk of the sun just creeping up over the fire-trimmed edge of the cityscape. Thin bands of purple clouds stretched like fingers across the pale blue sky over Portland. High overhead, several small dots that might have been sea gulls circled over the ocean.

"I don't think I'll need to be strapped down any more," she said, sighing deeply as an immense feeling of pleasure swelled through her. She felt buoyant, as light as a dandelion fluff, almost giddy when she considered that, in spite of the horror and grief and fear she had been through, she had made it! She was alive! She had survived!

A trickle of laughter bubbled out of her, but when she looked away from the early morning cityscape and looked at her aunt's reflection in the dust-glazed window, her heart skipped a beat. The morning sun was beaming in on Junia's face, but instead of seeing that aged, wrinkled face she loved so dearly, Elizabeth saw another face reflected in the glass. Bright, youthful eyes stared back at her, and gleaming white teeth flashed in a broad smile.

"Oh, Jesus—" Elizabeth muttered. Her body twitched involuntarily, pulling hard against the restraints. It took a moment for her numbed brain to recognize the face; but, as their eyes locked, she found herself staring directly at her daughter, Caroline.

Taking a deep breath to calm herself, she smiled widely and, addressing her daughter's reflection, said, "You know, Aunt Junia—I think you're absolutely right. I think Caroline's been here with me all along, trying to help me."